Bu

Ple
To
Or
Bo

—

Plea
by

To
cal
or
or

REVERSE NEGATIVE

Also by Shaun Clarke

The Exit Club
Dragon Light
Underworld
Red Hand
The Opium Road
Operation Millennium
Green Light

REVERSE NEGATIVE

SHAUN CLARKE

SIMON & SCHUSTER
A VIACOM COMPANY

First published in Great Britain by Simon & Schuster UK Ltd, 2000
Published simultaneously in paperback by Pocket Books, 2000
An imprint of Simon & Schuster Ltd
A Viacom Company

1 3 5 7 9 10 8 6 4 2

Simon & Schuster UK Ltd
Africa House
64–78 Kingsway
London
WC2B 6AH

Simon & Schuster Australia
Sydney

A CIP catalogue record for this book is available from the British Library.

Hardback ISBN 0–684–86060–0
Paperback ISBN 0–671–02947–9

Typeset by Palimpsest Book Production Limited,
Polmont, Stirlingshire
Printed and bound in Great Britain by
Omnia Books Ltd, Glasgow

With thanks to Jean-Paul Aubert

PART ONE

PARIS

CHAPTER ONE

The assassin, twenty years of age, bright as a pin, his blond hair hidden under his crash helmet, waited patiently on his motorcycle. Clive Sinclair-Lewis, the present Foreign Secretary, emerged from his home on the opposite side of the road, a good way down from where the assassin was parked, and slipped into the back of his chauffeur-driven Rolls-Royce.

This was a quiet side road in St John's Wood, London, lined with trees and filled with a mixture of elegant, neo-Georgian houses and broad-eaved villas. All the dwellings were hidden behind high walls, ornate, wrought-iron gates and spacious, well-tended gardens, and most of them were protected by high-tech surveillance systems. Because it was a road where only the wealthy lived, motorcycle messengers were often to be seen in it, delivering packages and documents too important to be entrusted to the badly run-down government mail service. This particular 'messenger', the assassin, waited until the Foreign Secretary's car had moved off. Then he kick-started his machine and followed the other vehicle from a safe distance.

As the Rolls-Royce drove into St John's Wood Road and continued parallel to the high wall of Lord's Cricket Ground, the assassin weaved his way through the steady stream of early-morning traffic until he was just behind the target vehicle. He stuck close to the Rolls as it made a turn, went along a short, narrow street and then turned again, heading into the Outer Circle of Regent's Park. The assassin kept a reasonable distance behind the Rolls-Royce until it had come to a halt in the traffic jam usual for the time of day around the Baker Street exit of the park.

Seeing the stationary Rolls, the assassin accelerated, raced up to the offside of the vehicle and braked to a halt beside the rear passenger seat.

Swiftly withdrawing a Browning High Power Mark 3 double-action handgun from the side pocket of his black leather jacket, he fired a continuous stream of thirteen bullets into the rear of the vehicle, creating a shocking din, blowing the side window to pieces and making the politician convulse violently, repeatedly, as the shells struck his head, neck and torso, passed straight through his body and tore the seat around him to shreds, filling the car's interior with swirling dust and exploding foam rubber.

Some bystanders screamed.

The Foreign Secretary did not scream. He had died without a sound. Even as he was falling sideways over the bloody seats and his driver, still behind the steering wheel, was frantically scrambling out of the vehicle to land on the tarmac on his hands and knees, the assassin was letting the handgun fall to the ground, grabbing the handlebars of his motorcycle and roaring away from the killing zone.

He continued on around the Outer Circle of the park, weaving expertly in and out of the heavy traffic along the terraces, to make his escape farther around the ring road, across Marylebone Road and down Park Crescent into Portland Place, where he soon managed to lose himself in the dense, fume-spewing traffic.

Knowing that his assassination mission had been accomplished so quickly, so efficiently, that the few people who had witnessed it would have actually *seen* very little – only his motorcycle racing away from the Rolls-Royce after the shots had been fired – he slowed down and threaded his way through a maze of back streets and across Tottenham Court Road and Gower Street before heading back east along Euston Road, keeping well within the speed limit, just another motorcyclist among many, making his way expertly between the slow-moving lines of double-decker buses, delivery trucks, commuter cars, taxis and other motorcycles. Feeling calm, in control, pleased with a job well done, he went past King's Cross Station, turned down Gray's Inn Road, continued along Holborn and Kingsway and around Aldwych, then crossed the windswept Waterloo Bridge.

Glancing left and right, he saw the vast sweep of the Thames glittering in summer sunlight, the great Victorian and Georgian buildings along its banks mixed with towers of glass and steel. His gaze took in Big Ben, the Houses of Parliament, the boats ferrying tourists in both directions along the river, and he felt a touch of pride that he lived here and could afford to do so at a time when the gap between rich and poor had so dramatically widened. He was earning his living as best he could and that was all a young man could do in these bad days.

Coming off the bridge, imagining the scene of chaos where the politician had been assassinated – the wailing sirens of police cars, medics spilling out of an ambulance, a growing number of media vans, shocked or excited onlookers – he smiled with quiet pride, thrilled to be living dangerously, then continued along Waterloo Road, weaved through the jammed traffic on the approach to St George's Circus and turned along Southwark Bridge Road.

He did not go as far as the bridge. Instead, he turned off again, heading into the web of back streets between Southwark and Bermondsey, and arrived eventually at a recently built underground car park. He drove down the ramp, inserted a plastic card into the box beside the closed steel door, waited for the door to tilt upwards on thick, squealing hinges, then drove all the way down into the basement.

The roaring of his motorcycle reverberated around the vast, gloomy space. The silence that followed, when he turned off the engine, seemed unreal and eerie.

He saw Bannerman instantly, standing well back in the shadows at the far end of the car park against the concrete wall, bulging out of his pinstriped suit, wearing a striped shirt and tie, his polished black shoes gleaming – a Neanderthal pretending to be civilized. Bannerman was the present Commissioner for the Metropolitan Police and as bent as any copper could be, which was saying a lot these days when the police force was more feared by the people than the underworld was. Now, standing against the far wall, between two rows of empty squad cars – this was, indeed, a high-security police car park – Bannerman's elongated shadow made him look even more fearsome than he really was.

Grinning, amused at Bannerman's pretensions, the assassin swung his leg off the motorcycle and propped the machine up on its stand. Then he removed his helmet to pat down his mussed-up blond hair.

'Hi, boss,' he said cockily.

'How did it go?' Bannerman asked, his voice gravelly and echoing eerily through the car park.

'Perfect,' the assassin said, starting towards Bannerman, keen to get his hands on an envelope that would, so he assumed, contain £20,000 in clean notes. 'Caught him on the Baker Street exit of Regent's Park. Emptied the pistol and dropped it on the ground, just like you told me. Lit out of there while those nearby were still trying to get to grips with what had happened. He was as dead as a dodo.'

'You're sure of that?' Bannerman asked.

'*Of course* I'm sure,' the assassin said, still walking towards Bannerman. 'The guy had thirteen fucking bullets in him and the car was a mess. He's dead, boss. Forget him. So, do I get paid or not?'

He was by now about halfway across the car park, close enough to be able to discern Bannerman's coarse features: that square block of a face, the slightly thinning dark brown hair, the rough skin flushed with good living at the taxpayer's expense. He saw Bannerman's cold smile.

'Well, *of course* you get paid,' Bannerman said. Then he looked left and right. 'OK, gentlemen, pay him.'

The lights abruptly winked out, plunging the car park into darkness and obscuring Bannerman. Then other lights came on, a wide ring of torches. The assassin, though dazzled, managed to see that the torches were attached to helmets: the helmets of the new breed of paramilitary police, even more Neanderthal-looking than Bannerman in their riot-control outfits hung about with clubs, grenades and pistols. Pistols that were now aimed right at him as the ambushers moved in for the kill.

Realizing what was happening, turning ice-cold with dread, the assassin glanced left and right but saw no escape route. He was about to throw himself to the floor when the roaring of all those pistols resounded like a cosmic explosion inside his head.

His brain was blown apart. Bullets punched him this way and that. He spun around, caught a glimpse of eternal darkness – and after that there was nothing.

He did not hear his own body hitting the ground, though it made a sickening thud.

'Right,' Bannerman said as the main lights came on again, illuminating the bloody remains of the assassin stretched out on the concrete floor. 'Get this lump of shit out of here and then clean up the mess. That damned motorbike, too.'

His men were quick and efficient. Even as some of them were picking up the body and sliding it into the back of an unmarked transit van, to be followed by the motorcycle, others, wearing dark blue overalls and carrying buckets and mops, were emerging from the darkness at the far end of the basement to wipe the floor clean.

Only when Bannerman and his hit squad had melted back into the shadows, when Bannerman's limousine and a lot of the squad cars had roared into life and left the basement car park, one after the other, did the unmarked transit van leave as well, taking away the dead assassin and his motorcycle. The van was driven straight to a police-controlled wrecking yard in Southwark. There, on Bannerman's instructions, it was crushed as an unlicensed vehicle. It was crushed with the assassin and his motorcycle still in the rear, though the engineers who completed the job had not been informed of that fact.

When the job was finished, the transit van, the motorcycle and the assassin had all been reduced to a square block of tightly compressed metal.

The anonymous assassin might never have been. There was no way to trace him. He was just another of the many nameless people who disappeared every week in this, the troubled Year of Our Lord 2005.

CHAPTER TWO

Brolin was having a great time, so the evening was slipping away fast. He had been in the pub for five hours, enjoying a lengthy get-together with some of his former SAS mates, engrossed in nostalgic conversation about the Good Old Days, chain-smoking and drinking one pint after another, so now he was feeling pretty good, despite his concern for what Joyce would think. He was, he knew, already too late for the dinner that she had doubtless prepared to celebrate their first year together. But he and his friends had not seen each other for more than eight months and he felt, perhaps because he was drunk, that this justified staying on a bit longer.

Darkness had fallen outside, over the rain-sodden pavements of Parkway in Camden Town, north London, and the sudden roaring of massed motorcycles made him look around, glancing over the shoulders of Don Clayton and Pat Dogherty, to see a gang of leather-clad teenage bikers outside, bunched up at the traffic lights, baying insults and making obscene gestures at the passers-by, practically begging for trouble. There were a lot of them these days, the disenfranchised young, and they formed a subculture of their own, breaking every law in the book and playing games with the cops. No wonder the police looked and acted more like soldiers these days: they were engaged in a war.

'Look at them,' Brolin said. 'Another bunch of teenage crazies. Not many of them'll see their old age. They just don't give a damn, those kids.'

'Why should they?' Don Clayton said, shrugging indifferently, looking at Brolin with crimson-streaked brown eyes peering out from behind locks of curly jet-black hair. 'Those kids have never had a job, they're not going to get one, they're despised by the rest of society and hounded by the police. So why *should* they give a damn?'

'They're not hounded *by* the police,' Pat Dogherty put in, his face bright pink beneath his thatch of red hair and pimpled like a teenager's, even though he was thirty-two years old. 'Those biker gangs *hound* the police. They harass squad cars with their bikes, throw petrol bombs at police stations, and deliberately try to draw their fire before racing away. They take pride in playing dangerous games and *that's* why the police hate them.'

'Fuck the police,' Brolin said. 'They deserve all they get. They're all fucking bent, if you ask me, and we know who's in charge of them.'

'Yeah, right,' Clayton said. 'That fat bastard who got the Regiment disbanded. I hope some biker throws a petrol bomb at *him* and turns him into a bonfire. It's all he deserves.'

They were referring to William Clive Bannerman, the present Commissioner for the Metropolitan Police. He had indeed been instrumental in getting 22 SAS disbanded the previous year on the grounds that its increasing use as an internal paramilitary outfit was undermining his own police force. Once the Regiment was disbanded, Bannerman had adroitly stepped into the hole created by its absence to expand his police force, increase its armaments and authority and gradually corrupt it, thus turning himself into one of the most powerful and feared men in the country. It was no accident, therefore, that Bannerman was reviled by just about every former member of 22 SAS.

'Anyway,' Dogherty said, mellowing slightly, 'we can't really complain about the bikers when we were once pretty much the same as they are now. I mean, anyone who joined the Regiment had to have a taste for danger. The enemy might have been different, but we played the odds as well. We were in it for the thrills, boys.'

'Damned right,' Clayton said. 'And I haven't had any thrills like that since I left the Regiment.'

'Since the Regiment left *you*,' Brolin corrected him. 'Since that bastard of a Police Commissioner got it disbanded.'

'Right,' Clayton said. 'Now all any of us have got to look forward to is having a drink and getting a bit of nookie. So how *are* your love lives going, lads?'

Brolin, Clayton and Dogherty were alike in that they had all been married, all had children – and all been divorced because of the tensions caused by their former SAS careers. While in the Regiment, Brolin had been something of a student of its history, reading every factual book – and, indeed, a great many novels – about it and learning that the strain placed on the marriages of its soldiers by the dangerous nature of its work had been the cause of numerous problems, in too many cases leading to divorce. Interestingly, the worst period had been during the twenty-odd years of the Troubles in Northern Ireland, when SAS men were sent regularly to the province under conditions of secrecy so severe that they could not even communicate with their wives. The strain of that was only compounded when the UDA or IRA threatened to assassinate SAS soldiers on the mainland and, as a consequence, many SAS homes had to be fitted out with high-tech surveillance systems and UCBT (Under-Car Booby Trap) detectors, a form of protection that actually led many wives to take to drink or Valium and other sedatives.

That had been before Brolin's time, but he understood what the damage could be when, in 1991, at twenty-one years of age, he took part in the Gulf War and was out of touch for a couple of months. By the time he returned, his wife, Jacquie, a year younger than him, not knowing where he was in Iraq or just what he was doing, and further tormented by various rumours about unnamed SAS soldiers being killed there, had taken to various pharmaceutical stress-relievers. She recovered from that particular bout but over the years, as the gap between rich and poor in Britain widened, as the Regiment turned increasingly to fighting urban terrorists and murderous criminals, the stress returned and gradually made her hysterical. This in turn caused desperate, ugly friction between husband and wife and during one of Brolin's many absences – when, again, he was not able to tell her where he was or what he was doing – Jacquie took a lover, which act made her even more hysterical. The final stage in the breakdown came when Brolin was placed on the 'hit' list of a British cyberterrorist who was threatening to break into his house and murder his family. When the house was placed under surveillance, filled with safety devices and, finally, when the family car was fitted with a UCBT detector, Jacquie could take no more of it and moved out with the two children, Ben and Sonja, then six and seven respectively, to set up house with her lover.

Virtually the same had happened to Clayton and Dogherty, so the three of them – the 'Three Musketeers' as they sometimes jokingly called themselves – ended up living bachelor lives. This turned out to be all the more ironic in that, a year after the break-up of Brolin's marriage, the Regiment was disbanded for good. They had all suffered for nothing.

'Love life?' Brolin asked rhetorically. He exhaled a cloud of cigarette smoke, sipped some of his bitter, then put the mug back on the counter and turned to Pat Dogherty. 'What's that he just said?'

'Something about a love life.'

'What's that?' Brolin asked of Clayton. 'Is it something I should know about or have I just forgotten it?'

'Don't come it with me,' Clayton said. 'Pat here told me that you're shacked up with someone. Blonde hair and bright green eyes with a strong personality.'

'He means a temper,' Pat explained.

Brolin grinned. 'A man has no secrets here. Talking of which . . .' He checked his wristwatch and saw that it was nine in the evening. He'd told Joyce that he'd be back for dinner at seven and that was well in the past. By now she'd be sending up smoke signals, all set to go on the warpath. 'Shit,' he said, 'look at the time. I'm gonna get crucified.'

'Under the thumb, are you?' Clayton asked.

'She squeezes my eyeballs occasionally.'

'You've always been drawn to temperamental women,' Dogherty said. 'It's your sadomasochism coming out. You probably like to be whipped.'

'Not as much as you might imagine,' Brolin responded. 'So I'm really going to have to leave you guys. It's drink-up-and-go time, folks.'

While Brolin was hastily swallowing down the last of his pint of bitter, Clayton glanced around the crowded, smoky bar, hoping to see a lone woman. Failing to find one, he sighed and said, 'Well, *I* wouldn't mind having a fight right now. I'd like a fight with *anyone*. I never thought I'd see the day when I'd end up acting as a security guard for a Marks and Spencer's in Oxford Street. Not quite what I'm cut out for.'

'Well, they need you,' Dogherty told him. 'Going into any big store these days is like entering a war zone. Security checks at the main doors, spy cameras all over the fucking place, and the constant dread that you're either going to buy food poisoned at source by some terrorist or be there when a home-made bomb, hidden somewhere by the same breed, explodes and blows you to Kingdom Come. You can see the tension in the faces of the customers. I mean, they're in and out, right? No more leisurely shopping with a girlfriend. They go in and they grab what they want and then rush out again. So they need you, believe me.'

'Hear, hear,' Brolin said.

'Look at me,' Dogherty continued, growing drunkenly agitated. 'I'm a guard with that fucking security company, keeping watch by the side of the armoured van while my mates take the cash in and out of banks, safety vaults, or whatever. I'm so bored I spend half of my working day wishing that someone *would* rob a bank and give me some action.'

'These days that shouldn't be the case,' Clayton said. 'I mean, *everyone's* getting robbed, *everywhere*, so why not your security company? Your reputation must have preceded you, keeping the wolves from the door.'

'No chance,' Dogherty said. 'It's just that it never happens. At least, not to this company 'cause they're paying protection to the cops and the cops, Bannerman's cops, have the fucking bank robbers in their pockets and are bleeding them dry. You want to rob our company, you need permission – and for that you go straight to Bannerman. Our company hasn't been robbed of a single Euro and it's all thanks to Bannerman. Just give him his regular commission and you won't have a problem.'

'That fat bastard,' Clayton said. 'He gets the Regiment disbanded, then he stitches up half the City and grows wealthier every day. I'd like to get that bastard up a dark alleyway and give him what for.' He turned to Brolin. 'So what about you? What are *you* up to these days?'

Brolin finished off his pint and wiped his lips with the back of his hand. 'Not much,' he said. 'Farting about at the moment. I've tried half a dozen different things, but they've never worked out.'

'What things?' Clayton asked.

Brolin shrugged. 'Oh . . . various things. A couple of months digging trenches just to keep myself fit. Lost the job when the foreman gave me a mouthful of abuse and I gave him a mouthful of loose teeth.'

'Good one,' Dogherty said.

'Then six months or so as a security guard for a fat cat from Kuwait, ensconced in a huge house out near Hampstead. Got sacked when I wandered away from his garden one day to have a couple of pints in The Spaniards.'

'Even better,' Dogherty said.

'Worked as a security officer out at Heathrow Airport, but left because I couldn't stand travelling out there. Hired myself out as a taxi driver for some time, but got fed up with drunks throwing up in the back of my car. Never paid tax on any of that income, so when they caught me, when I'd spent all the dosh, I signed on the dole to protect myself. I'm still legally unemployed but they're trying to push me into some kind of menial work, so I guess I'll soon have to look elsewhere. Not easy to settle down, is it, once you've been with the Regiment?'

'It sure isn't,' Clayton said.

Brolin looked at his wristwatch again and saw that it was nearly nine-thirty. 'Christ,' he said, 'I'm going to be slaughtered. I'd better get out of here. Are you guys coming or not?'

Clayton glanced at Dogherty. 'Another pint?'

'Why not? I don't have a lively lady to get back to, so I might as well go for broke.'

'Me, too,' Clayton said. Then he turned back, grinning, to Brolin. 'Are you *sure* you don't want another quick one? To fortify you for the wrath that's to come?'

'No, thanks,' Brolin said. He stared forlornly at his glass, but then glanced again at his wristwatch, not believing the time. 'I'm off,' he said. 'You guys keep in touch. If ever anything worth doing comes up, please give me a call.'

'You should be so lucky,' Clayton said.

'I live in hope,' Brolin replied. 'Have a good evening, fellas.'

'We'll try,' Dogherty said.

Brolin hurried out of the pub, into the bright lights and noise of Parkway, then turned right and headed along the rain-damp pavement. There were lots of drunks along the road, more so down by the Underground station, and kids on motorcycles were roaring past in both directions, out for a few evening thrills. As he turned down Camden High Street, where the traffic was more dense, the lights more numerous, he felt even drunker than he had in the pub and sensed that his patience might be limited if Joyce gave him a hard time.

In truth, he and Joyce had a turbulent relationship, fighting day in, day out, and while some of the blame, he knew, could be laid at his own doorstep, a lot also stemmed from Joyce's highly volatile nature. Brolin's wife, Jacquie, had been essentially passive, domesticated, wanting a quiet life, and the break-up of their marriage had been caused solely by her inability to deal with the stress engendered by his dangerous work. Joyce, on the other hand, had little to fear from his present work – or, more accurately, his unemployed situation – but, like many a mature woman living with a formerly married man, she was constantly insecure about their relationship and it had made her neurotic about trivial matters, causing her to pick on anything that would give her an excuse to explode and release her inner tensions. Her explosions were fierce and destructive, with insults hurled and objects smashed, but Brolin endured it because he liked her, was sexually attracted to her, and because he knew that he had to take the blame for a lot of the nastiness. He drank too much these days and was visibly restless, drifting from one job to another because he just couldn't settle. This would not have helped Joyce – it would only have increased her deep feelings of insecurity – but this knowledge wasn't enough to keep Brolin from exploding as well. Right now, as he turned into their street, just off the High Street, he experienced a deep, probably drink-induced frustration, that made him feel out of control. He would not take her shit tonight.

His apartment (and it *was* his apartment; Joyce had moved in with him) was on the second floor of a converted Victorian terraced house. Reaching his front door, Brolin rang the bell but received no response. He slipped the key in the lock and tried turning it, but the door had been bolted from inside. Feeling the anger well up in him, he bawled out Joyce's name, but again he got no response.

'Damn it, Joyce!' he bawled. 'I know you're in there! So open the door or I'll kick it in!'

'You bastard!' she responded. 'You drunken cunt! Get the fuck away from here. I'm not letting you in!'

'Open the fucking door!' Brolin bawled again, hammering his fist on it. 'Or I'll kick it open!'

'Bastard!' she screamed. 'You thoughtless shit! Get away or I'll call the police!'

Brolin stepped back from the door, raised his right leg and kicked as hard as he could. The lock was torn from its mounting with a dreadful screeching sound, splinters of wood flying everywhere. Joyce added a high-pitched scream to the bedlam as the door swung open so hard that it slammed against the side wall, creating a billowing cloud of dust from the smashed plaster. Brolin raced inside, turning right into the hallway, and saw Joyce backing towards the living room, waving her hands protectively in front of her face, her green eyes wide and bright under short-cropped blonde hair.

'Don't you hit me!' she screamed hysterically. 'Don't you dare lay a fucking hand on me!'

'I've never hit you in my life, you dumb bitch,' Brolin replied, actually stating the truth. Then, on an irresistible impulse, he launched himself at her.

With an even higher, still more hysterical shriek, as if she was being stabbed, Joyce turned away from him and ran into the living room, trying to slam the door shut behind her. Brolin kicked it open and raced into the room just as Joyce picked his cold dinner off the table – a roast in gravy, with mashed potatoes and vegetables – to hurl it at him. He ducked and the plate flew over his head to smash against the wall behind, pieces of porcelain and greasy food flying everywhere.

'Eat *that!*' Joyce screamed. 'It's been sitting there since seven o'clock, you bastard, while you were out getting drunk with your mates. Go fuck yourself, you mean cunt.'

'It's only dinner, for Christ's sake, you bitch! It's not the end of the fucking world!'

'A *special* dinner!' Joyce screamed. 'To celebrate our first year together! You thoughtless bastard! *You fucker!*'

With a surprising display of strength, she picked up a wooden chair and swung it at him. Brolin ducked again, though a chair leg caught him on the side of the head and warm blood splashed his face. Cursing, he wrested the chair from her, flung it across the room and then reached out to grab her, though she eluded him and raced into the bedroom, again attempting to slam the door behind her. Once more, Brolin kicked the door open. Joyce screamed again. Brolin saw a suitcase opened on the bed, piled high with her clothes.

'What's this?' he said quietly.

'Fuck you,' Joyce said, also speaking more quietly but with finely controlled venom, as she threw more clothes into the suitcase with sharp, violent motions. 'Fuck yourself until your arse drops off and your insides spill out. I'm leaving, you bastard. I'm taking no more of this. I cooked that dinner specially for you and now it's all ruined.'

'Because it's splashed all over the wall,' Brolin said sarcastically. 'Not because it went cold.'

She turned towards him, eyes blazing. 'Oh, very funny! Very smart! Always quick with the fucking sarcasm when you can't talk things out. Well, vomit it elsewhere. Don't vomit all over me. I don't need your sarcasm and I don't need your cock and I don't need to live with a fucking man who can't even hold a job down. I don't need all this fucking insecurity and your bachelor habits. I clean the fucking dishes, I scrub the fucking toilets, I mop the fucking floor, I do the fucking shopping, I let you fucking fuck me – and all I ever get in return is your fucking sarcasm.'

'Only when you're angry,' Brolin said. 'It's a natural response.'

Joyce's eyes grew even wider and she stared around the bedroom as if she was trying to find something else to throw at him.

'Don't even think about it,' Brolin said. 'If you hit me, I'll strike back.'

Joyce slammed the suitcase shut and viciously twisted the locks. 'Well, *of course* you would,' she snapped. 'Big brave soldier that you are. Hitting a woman would come naturally to you and make you feel even bigger. Go on! Why not hit me?'

She turned to face him, melodramatically turning her flushed cheek slightly sideways and pointing at it. 'Go on!' she repeated, jabbing at her face with her index finger. 'Hit me and see where it gets you.'

'Where will it get me?'

'I'll have the fucking police here in squad cars and you'll be in deep shit. Go on, cunt-face, *hit me!*'

Brolin certainly wanted to hit her, but he'd never done it before and he wasn't about to start now. He still felt pretty wild, though.

'Where are you going?' he asked, trying to keep his voice steady.

'None of your fucking business. Now get out of my fucking way.'

Brolin dutifully stepped aside. 'You're not the kind to just walk out into the streets. You must have somewhere to go.'

'That's right, you shit, you selfish cunt, I do have somewhere to go, so don't worry about me.'

'Another man, is it?'

'That's hardly your concern.' Joyce wrenched her overcoat from the wardrobe and put it on, then lifted the suitcase off the bed and turned back to face him, looking flushed and haughty. 'Now, are you going to let me go or not?'

'I'm not in your way,' Brolin said. He was, indeed, standing to one side of the doorway. 'The sooner you get the fuck out the better. I'll get my sanity back then.'

'You never had that to begin with,' Joyce said. 'Now goodbye and good riddance.'

She flounced out of the room, taking care not to brush against him as she passed, and hurried across the living room to the door that led into the hallway. She slammed that door behind her. Brolin determined not to follow her. He lost his cool, however, when he heard the sound of glass smashing in the hallway and realized that Joyce was smashing the two mirrors out there. Suddenly enraged again, he cursed aloud and raced across the living room, to tug the door open and grab her and beat the shite out of her. Luckily for her, he was too late. She was slamming the front door closed behind her as he rushed into the hallway, whose floor was now a glittering sea of broken glass. Even worse, his clothes, which had been hanging from hooks on the wall, were strewn all over the shards of glass and drenched in the discoloured water from a broken vase of flowers – ironically, Joyce's favourite vase.

Brolin stopped where he was. There was no point in pursuing her. Studying the mess in the hallway, he let his breath out in a loud, weary sigh that was, perhaps, a sigh of relief as well. Realizing that another chapter in his erratic life had ended, he went back into the messed-up living room to fix himself a stiff drink.

The telephone rang.

CHAPTER THREE

Sir Archibald Wainwright, the Minister for Foreign Affairs, an erstwhile colleague of the Foreign Secretary who had recently been assassinated, was waiting for Brolin in the Outer Circle of Regent's Park, equidistant between Hanover Lodge and the London Central Mosque. With his silvery-white hair, still surprisingly abundant, being ruffled by the breeze, Wainwright seemed a lot older than he did in his newspaper pictures, but he certainly looked distinguished in his black overcoat, black shoes, pinstriped suit with Old School tie, and a spotlessly clean white silk scarf. Towering over him, the 140-foot minaret of the Mosque was a dazzling vision of white and gold in the bright sun of this chilly autumn day.

As Brolin advanced towards Wainwright, whose secretary had made this appointment during that surprise telephone call the previous night, he glanced along the Outer Circle and saw, as he had expected, that a Rolls-Royce with tinted windows was parked a reasonable distance away, in the direction of Winfield House, and he knew that it would follow them at that distance as they walked along the pavement like two old friends out for a stroll. Should anything untoward happen, that car would accelerate dramatically.

'Good day to you, sir,' Brolin said, not sure how he should address such an important person, let alone one with a knighthood.

'Hello, Mr Brolin. I'm glad you could come.' They shook hands. Wainwright nodded in the direction of Hanover Terrace. 'Shall we go for a walk?'

'Fine,' Brolin said.

They started walking. Brolin glanced over his shoulder and saw the Rolls-Royce starting up and cruising slowly behind them, practically crawling, maintaining its distance. He smiled, glanced over the green sweep of the gardens across the road and then faced back to the front again.

'I have to say, I was really surprised to receive your call,' he said. 'I mean, coming from . . .'

Wainwright nodded. 'I know. Coming from so very high up and you a mere unemployed civilian. I'm sure it *was* a surprise.'

Brolin was just as surprised to hear that Wainwright knew about his unemployment.

That means they've been watching me, he thought. *They must watch everyone these days.*

This was, however, a subject he dared not raise, so he just said, 'What is it, sir?'

'We have a job for you,' Wainwright said. 'We can't even bring COBR into this, so I have to do it myself. I'm not speaking on behalf of COBR. This is straight from the PM.'

'The . . . *Prime Minister?*'

'Yes.'

Already surprised, Brolin now found it hard to believe his own ears. Even when serving with the SAS, neither he nor any other lowly member of the Regiment had had direct contact with COBR – an acronym for the Cabinet Office Briefing Room, which was in fact a committee of high-ranking politicians and military personnel that was convened only for discussions on operations of the most delicate kind. To have received a call from a member of COBR would have been surprise enough for Brolin; now he was walking along Regent's Park with the Minister for Foreign Affairs, being told that this meeting was at the specific request of the Prime Minister. It hardly seemed possible.

'Sir, to be told that makes me feel nervous. What kind of job is this?'

They were reaching the end of Hanover Terrace and Wainwright glanced, with what seemed like deep appreciation, at the bright blue pediments and statuary silhouetted against the bright sky. He probably lived in a house of similar grandeur; certainly not in a seedy apartment in Camden Town, now short of one resident.

'As you doubtless know,' Wainwright said, 'the gap between rich and poor in our society has led to ever-increasing levels of crime, with this city collapsing into a morass of violence wrought not only by local so-called *tribes* of working-class youth and habitual older criminals, but also by the very police force that, given ever-growing authority, has used it for massive abuses.'

'Yes, sir, I know that. I mean, it isn't exactly classified knowledge – it's on TV all the time – though information concerning the police is, of course, much less tangible.'

'Neatly put, Mr Brolin.'

'Just how *bad* is the police involvement, sir? Is this meeting to do with that?'

'Yes, it's something to do with that. The police abuses I just mentioned include blackmail, kidnapping, gang rape and contract assassinations. Those assassinated include major criminals, leading businessmen and important politicians. I'm sure you know, with regard to the last-mentioned category, that an extraordinary number of politicians of all persuasions have been killed in the past four or five years.'

'Yes, sir, I do.'

'Well, whilst some of those assassinations were paid for by criminals who wanted rivals removed, others were politically motivated and were carried out by a police force that's given up all pretence at moral responsibility. That police force, as both of us know, is headed by Commissioner William Clive Bannerman.'

'No, sir,' Brolin replied, now wondering – and growing more fearful – about what he was going to be asked to do, 'I didn't actually know that. I've heard that Bannerman's corrupt, but I certainly didn't suspect that he was into anything as bad as you're suggesting.'

'Unfortunately, he is.' They were now at Clarence Terrace and here Wainwright stopped for a moment to point to the centre of the road, at the traffic turn-off to Baker Street. 'That's where the Foreign Secretary, Clive Sinclair-Lewis, was assassinated only last week,' he said.

'Yes, sir, I know. I saw it on TV.'

'We see everything on TV these days. Come on, let's keep walking.'

Together they crossed the road, dodging through the

traffic to reach Cornwall Terrace and continue on around the Outer Circle. Brolin glanced back over his shoulder and saw that the Rolls-Royce was still following them, keeping its distance. He had no doubt that there were armed guards in that vehicle, ready to kill him or anyone else who threatened their boss. He turned back to the front again.

'Bannerman's police force,' Wainwright continued, taking his time to get to the point, 'is a tightly knit, highly secretive, heavily armed paramilitary force – more frightening to the general populace than are the urban tribes or even the organized criminals. Bannerman himself has become so powerful and so ruthless that even the most highly placed politicians, including the Prime Minister, fear him. This fear has been caused in part by the inside knowledge that Bannerman has been heading a paramilitary-style hit team that's responsible for the assassinations of the politicians who've been killed, often at the behest of corrupt businessmen or foreign despots who have their own interests and pay Bannerman highly for his services.'

Brolin was so shocked that he almost stopped walking, but Wainwright kept strolling on and he had to stick with him. He glanced across the Outer Circle, at Regent's College and the circular Queen Mary's Gardens, then he looked straight ahead again. He didn't really see what he was looking at; he was too stunned to concentrate.

'Regarding this,' Wainwright continued, speaking quietly and carefully, 'we have strong reason to believe that Bannerman was responsible for the recent assassination of the Foreign Secretary. He arranged it, we believe, because the Foreign Secretary had learnt that Bannerman was secretly setting up a deal with one of the world's most notorious gun-runners, the wealthy Algerian Arab, Feydal Hussein, who, like most of his kind, presently brings his weapons into Europe through Paris. Already known to spend much of his so-called *leisure* time in Paris, where he surrounds himself with armed body-guards and otherwise lives like a prince in the Ritz Hotel, Bannerman is due to return there to have a meeting with Hussein and arrange the largest illegal arms deal on record.'

Brolin gave a low whistle. Wainwright glanced at him, raised his eyebrows, then continued exactly where he had left off.

'Those arms will be sold on by Bannerman to the increasingly lawless urban tribes of London, as well as to the Russian *Mafiya* and Chinese Triads who, between them, as they battle for territory, are turning inner London into a war zone. Even worse, Bannerman's purchase and subsequent sale of those weapons will cement his relationship with both groups and make him the most powerful criminal figure in this country – a criminal who resides at the very peak of our law-and-order system. The Foreign Secretary learnt about this, confronted Bannerman with it, promising to expose him – and was assassinated in Regent's Park a few days later. As Bannerman had a very strong motive, we're sure that he did it.'

The sun was shining but the day was still chilly and Brolin found himself shivering slightly. He wasn't sure if he was doing so because of the cold or because of what he was hearing; nevertheless, he zipped up the windcheater jacket in which, as he walked beside the elegantly dressed Minister for Foreign Affairs, he was feeling pretty damned shabby. He hadn't thought to wear something better and now he felt like a fool.

'So why this meeting with me?' he asked. 'I mean, I'm not even with—'

'Particularly upset by that last assassination,' Wainwright interjected, obviously knowing what Brolin was about to say and not caring to hear it, 'and increasingly fearful of Bannerman's growing influence over both organized crime and politics, the Prime Minister has decided that Bannerman has to go.'

'Surely the Prime Minister can have him removed from his position?'

'No, he can't. Bannerman is now too powerful and the Prime Minister – I am loath to confess this – is now frightened even for his own life. He believes that if he tries to remove Bannerman from his position, Bannerman will have *him* assassinated. Right now, the Prime Minister's a frightened man – frightened not only for himself but also for his family. Bannerman's reach could now extend to Ten Downing Street because he has so many people in his pocket: ordinary policemen, security guards, even tradesmen coming and going every day – that man's into *everyone*. So whether by bombing or by other means, he could get to the Prime Minister. So we have to get rid of him first. We need you for that task.'

'Exactly what kind of task are we talking about?'

'Neutralization,' Wainwright said. 'Of a terminal nature. Naturally, as the government can't be seen to be involved in its own kind of assassination, the operation has to be clandestine.'

Thinking of how Bannerman had destroyed 22 SAS, working relentlessly for its disbandment and eventually succeeding, Brolin only had contempt for the man and was not averse to bringing him down. On the other hand, he was disturbed by the implications of such an order coming down directly from the Prime Minister. If it should be found out that the Prime Minister was involved, all hell would break loose – and Brolin would be responsible for it. In such a case, he would be instantly disowned and have no protection. Indeed, he might even be neutralized himself to keep his mouth shut. No one was safe these days.

'Why me?' he asked, then added what he had wanted to say before. 'I mean, I'm not even in the army any more. I'm not with the SAS. I'm not with anyone. So why me, of all people?'

Wainwright smiled. 'You've just said it, Mr Brolin. You're not with anyone any more. You're not with us or anyone else. You are, in fact, wonderfully anonymous – but you're also well trained. You were, so we're informed, one of the finest soldiers that the best fighting team in the world – the SAS QRF – ever had and that makes you exceptional. You also specialized, with the QRF, in the covert neutralization of a great many public nuisances. Last but not least, you'll be strongly motivated, since Bannerman is the man who destroyed 22 SAS and you, along with most of your former comrades, will surely loathe him for doing that.'

'Yes, I do,' Brolin said.

'Good,' Wainwright said. 'We're halfway there already. Can I take it, therefore, that you'll do the job?'

'Well, I . . .'

'What have you got to lose? We've been following you, Mr Brolin, and we know how you live and that things haven't been going too well for you. You've been through a succession of jobs, you're in debt to the Inland

Revenue, you're presently unemployed and bored out of your mind. We have it on the record from various sources that you've been drinking too much. With a man like you, that says all we need to know. You need a challenge. Now take it.'

Thinking back on his fight last night with Joyce, of her abrupt, violent departure, which was certainly for good, Brolin realized that he'd be in for a bleak time if his life didn't change. He had no woman and, right now, he had no future, so what *did* he have to lose? Anything was better than nothing and this was more than just something. This was a challenge indeed.

'What's your basic plan for me?' he asked.

'As an overt government-backed assassination of Bannerman could have serious political and social repercussions, it's been decided that his death must be made to look like an accident and that the so-called accident must occur outside Great Britain. Since Bannerman will be meeting Feydal Hussein next week, in the Ritz Hotel in Paris, we suggest that you do the job in that city.'

'Weapons?'

'It's supposed to look like an *accident*,' Wainwright reminded him with a touch of sarcasm.

'OK, no weapons. What about expenses?'

'As much as you require. Please don't stay in the same hotel—'

'That wasn't my intention.'

'—But apart from that restriction, you can check in anywhere you want and you'll be well provided for.'

'How?'

'Electronic transfer of funds every month from a well-protected Swiss bank account that can't be traced back to this government. The funds will go into an equally well-protected bank account in Paris, details of which you will, of course, be given. There should be more than enough but, in case you *do* need more, you'll be given a code-protected number that can only be called from a public phone box – no cellular phones, please.'

'Why not?'

'They're easily hacked into by phone-phreakers.'

'Right,' Brolin said. 'Who arranges my travel to Paris?'

'You do,' Wainwright said. 'You take your next fortnight's unemployment money, write to the benefits people the next day, saying you've found a job and are signing off, then buy the kind of transport to Paris that the money will cover, which may not be much – maybe you'll even have to travel by bus. Once in Paris, you go straight to the bank we've designated and pick up what you need. After that, you're on your own.'

'Who can I use if I need help? Are there any restrictions there?'

'You can use no one in any kind of official position, either here or in Paris. No one connected to this government. No one still serving in our armed forces. No one remotely involved with the police, no matter how much you trust them.'

'What about some old SAS buddies?'

'Are they out completely or are they still in the regular army?'

'They're out completely, like me.'

'You can use them on the understanding that this is absolutely covert, that if anything goes wrong we'll deny any involvement, and that there'll be no compensation of any kind should any harm – in the event that they actually survive – befall them. I'm sorry to be so pragmatic about this, but I'm sure you understand.'

'Yes, I do,' Brolin said. 'Anything else?'

'Yes.' Wainwright stopped walking and coughed into his fist. Brolin stopped as well and turned to face him. They were standing in front of a row of elegant Nash houses, directly opposite Cambridge Terrace and Cambridge Gate, and the wind here seemed colder. Dark clouds were starting to drift in from the east, promising rain. 'We can't afford to have you talk if you're caught and tortured,' Wainwright said, 'and Bannerman *is* reported to use torture. So . . .'

'You're going to give me something to take if that happens.'

'Yes,' Wainwright said.

'I join the Exit Club.'

'Pardon?' Wainwright asked.

Brolin grinned. 'That's an SAS expression for taking your own life. We took similar tablets with us into Iraq and even when we were fighting the urban terrorists right here in London. It's nothing new to me, sir.'

Wainwright sighed with relief. 'Good,' he said. 'Are you living alone right now?'

Now it was Brolin's turn to sigh. 'Just about,' he said.

'What does that mean?'

'My woman stormed out on me last night and she's not coming back.'

'Perfect,' Wainwright said without sympathy. 'Make sure you don't take anyone else in before you leave for Paris. We'll deliver what you need through your letter box – but it won't come by mail.'

'One of your couriers?'

'Yes.'

'When will that be?'

'In a couple of days. Three days at the most.'

'Then I sign off the dole and head for Paris?'

'That sounds right,' Wainwright said.

'Anything else?' Brolin repeated.

'I don't think so,' Wainwright replied. 'I think that about covers it. You'd better leave now.'

Brolin glanced along the road and saw that the Rolls-Royce had stopped, waiting for him and Wainwright to move on. Smiling, he turned back to Wainwright and held out his hand. Wainwright shook it. Brolin turned away and continued walking north, heading for Gloucester Gate. When he had walked a good distance, he glanced back over his shoulder and saw Wainwright clambering into the Rolls-Royce. When Wainwright had closed the door behind him, the Rolls moved off again, making a U-turn and heading south.

Brolin walked back into Camden Town and entered the first pub he saw. He knew that in a couple of days he would have to stop his heavy drinking, so he drank his way deep into the evening and slept soundly that night.

CHAPTER FOUR

Brolin spent the next couple of days sorting out private matters that would need to be looked after should he not return from Paris. These included such mundane matters as filling in and mailing a private health form to cover him if he became ill in that city; forwarding a revised will to his solicitor, leaving everything to his former wife, Jacquie; dipping deeply into his secret savings and paying six months' rent on his apartment in advance; getting a long-overdue service for his still excellent ten-year-old sky-blue Honda Accord; then collecting his last two weeks' dole money and finally signing off. He was employed again.

Close to midnight, two days after he had seen Sir Archibald Wainwright, a plain manila envelope was dropped through his letter box, indicating that no ordinary postman had delivered it. The envelope contained details of his protected bank account in Switzerland; details of how much money would be going into that account each month (it was a lot); the address of the Paris bank that would not only transfer in any money he required but also supply him with a French Eurocard in his own name; the phone number he was to use only from a public phone booth in the event that he needed more cash; and, most important, newspaper cuttings and intelligence reports on Bannerman's friend Feydal Hussein.

Brolin read the report. There had been much written on the subject of Feydal Hussein, but a lot of it was tabloid sensationalism and real facts were hard to come by, though there were enough to conjure up what the man was like. Born in 1960 to wealthy Muslim parents in the Beaucheray area of Algiers, Hussein had attended the University of Algiers and had been an outstanding pupil. He was, however, in trouble from an early age, seemingly rebelling against his respectable background, and was known to have spent a lot of time in the various *quais* of the Bassin de Vieux Port, reportedly as head of a gang of juvenile delinquents who mugged sailors and traded in drugs. In 1979, when Feydal was nineteen, he moved out of his home. – or, according to some reports, was thrown out by his parents – and moved into the Kasbah from where he ran a bigger, more mature criminal organization, mainly based on the control of the port's many exporters of wine, vegetables, oranges, iron ore and phosphates. When the local police were said to be closing in on him, Feydal had abruptly disappeared.

In 1985, when Feydal was twenty-five, he turned up in Marseille as the head of a gang of Vieux Port criminals rounded up by the police for their involvement in various forms of smuggling, pilferage, commercial vice, drug dealing and the taking of protection money from the numerous bars located along the waterfront district. The only member of the gang not given a prison sentence was Feydal, who was believed to have bribed the authorities in order to make his 'escape' and disappear from the country altogether. Certainly he disappeared.

Two years later, in 1987, Feydal resurfaced in Alexandria, Egypt, as a licensed importer-exporter living in Khalid Pasha Street in Victoria, one of the most exclusive residential areas of the city. He was by then superficially respectable, supposedly dealing in Egyptian furniture, which he exported to Europe, and office supplies, which he imported from the same place. But police intelligence reports indicated that he had been placed under constant surveillance because of his suspected involvement in the import and export of illegal weapons that were shipped in and out of the country as furniture and/or office supplies. Whatever the reasons, the Egyptian police must have been moving in on him because Feydal soon disappeared again.

Six months later he surfaced in Libya where he was reported to be making strong connections with dealers purchasing arms from, and selling arms to, various terrorist groups. A few months later he was in Tunisia, reportedly selling the arms he had purchased in Libya. A year later he was living in Paris, in the exclusive Bois de Boulogne area, but commuting regularly to London, where he stayed in an apartment in Park Lane and moved in wealthy, politically well-connected circles. Accepted because he too was wealthy, he enjoyed the high life but eventually shocked many of his upper-class conservative friends with his extreme hedonism, including holding orgiastic parties in the city's most renowned nightclubs and giving lavish dinners where hookers served the food before serving the guests in more intimate ways. Those particular social activities soon brought him to the attention of the tabloid press and they quickly turned him into a celebrity of the most scandalous kind. Thus, when attempting to set up some so-called 'legitimate' businesses in London, he was blocked by the Conservative government, which believed him to be responsible for the recent flood of illegal weapons into the country. Defeated in his 'legitimate' business endeavours, deserted by most of his former upper-class English friends, he moved back to Paris, where arms dealers, despite their shady backgrounds, could operate with relative freedom, moving north and south, east and west, from Europe to the Middle East, via Algiers and Marseille, with relative ease.

Nevertheless, by the year 2003, even the tolerant French were growing nervous about Feydal's staggering wealth, increasing power and blatant ruthlessness, particularly in view of the many prominent persons, some ethical, some not, who had reputedly died at his hands. Thus, when Feydal was forty-three years of age, he moved back to Marseille where he built his own Moorish-style villa high in the hills above the Corniche John Kennedy, overlooking the Mediterranean and surrounded by the palatial homes of the other *nouveaux riches*. Since then, Feydal had spent most of his time in Marseille where, it was reported, he was growing even wealthier from a wide variety of criminal activities, including high-class prostitution and drugs, though mainly from his worldwide arms dealing. Though no longer living in Paris, he still visited that city frequently, always staying in the Hôtel Ritz in the elegant Place Vendôme.

While most of the basic facts of Feydal's life came

from French and British intelligence reports, the tabloid press had covered his life in their own colourful way. Judging from the mass of press cuttings, Feydal was a champagne-guzzling, cocaine-snorting playboy who had left his Muslim teachings far behind him in order to indulge himself in the hedonistic pleasures of the sinful West, including private jets, luxury boats, fast cars and aristocratic, white-skinned beauties, many of whom provided their services on a strictly professional basis. The British press appeared to have dwelt little on Feydal's criminal history. However, though the French authorities were notably tight-lipped about the same subject, the French press was filled with stories, mostly unsubstantiated, about the individual murders he was believed to have committed and, more pertinently, about bloody, all-out firefights between large numbers of Feydal's heavily armed henchmen, holed up in some building or other in Marseille, and assault forces from France's Groupement d'Intervention de la Gendarmerie Nationale. As the GIGN was France's equivalent to the SAS, Brolin found this last possibility intriguing.

Finally, concerning the possibility of major gun battles between Feydal's men and the Gendarmerie, there were a couple of articles suggesting that Feydal's luxury villa in Marseille, set in many acres of ground, was patrolled by armed guards, secured with high-tech surveillance systems, and had landmines buried all over the grounds. While this last seemed like a James Bond fantasy, it could, given that Feydal dealt in armaments, be absolutely true.

Intrigued, realizing that he was dealing with no ordinary criminal, Brolin burnt the information on Feydal, had a good night's sleep, then packed his bags and booked his trip to Paris. Since his two weeks' dole money amounted to precious little, he had planned to go to Paris by bus, but recalling that the buses, which these days were only used by the ethnic minorities, were invariably stopped and searched at Customs, whereas cars and trains were not, he booked himself onto an early-morning Eurostar train. With a twenty-minute check-in time, he left at 0800 hours and arrived in Paris at 1223 hours local time, giving him most of the day to look around for suitable accommodation.

He had already decided where he wanted to live – not too close to, yet not too far from the Hôtel Ritz in the Place Vendôme – so, after lunch in a surprisingly elegant brasserie just outside the Gare du Nord, he took an RER train to Chatelet-les Halles, then changed onto the M1 Metro line and disembarked at Saint-Paul. Once out of the station, he made his way through the colourful Marais district, located north of the two river islands, and wandered around the area on the south side of the Rue de Rivoli until he found a small though far from cheap hotel, located not far from the Pont Louis-Philippe.

Though Brolin had a Visa card, he had no money in his English bank. Still, to get into the hotel he had only to present the card and his passport to the desk clerk and let him transcribe the required details from both items. In fact, Brolin had no intention of using his worthless Visa card to pay for anything. Once booked in, he showered, changed his clothes, then took himself off to the bank whose address he had been given in the manila envelope delivered by Sir Archibald Wainwright's courier. The bank was located in the Champs-Elysées, a virtual palace of steel and glass, and there Brolin was given instantly all the hard cash he required, plus a gleaming new plastic Eurocard in his own name. As the alarming rise in computer theft had made banks like this one (*and* the one in Switzerland) more secretive than ever, there was little likelihood that Brolin's electronic transfers – or, indeed, his Eurocard spending – would ever be traced by the Brits.

Back in the Champs-Elysées, with darkness gradually descending and the lights along the boulevard making it look like something out of a fairy tale, Brolin made his way back towards the Place de la Concorde, wandered along the elegant arches of the Tuileries, turned into the Rue de Castiglioni, then walked along to the lamplit splendour of the Place Vendôme. The vast octagon was dominated by a soaring column decorated with a spiral of bronze bas-reliefs depicting scenes from the Great Battles and surmounted by a statue of Napoleon, who had, with no great display of modesty, replaced the Sun King with his own sculptured likeness. Around the octagon were nineteen banks and the shops of the world's most famous jewellers.

The Hôtel Ritz was in the north-east corner, its façade surprisingly small beside the much more imposing Ministry of Justice; though luxury cars were parked along its front, the dark-suited chauffeurs leaning against their vehicles, talking to each other and smoking countless cigarettes. There were no paparazzi gathered outside the hotel – a sure indication that no one of great importance was due either to arrive or leave – so Brolin, who had no real reason to be here yet but simply wanted to soak up the atmosphere, wandered across to the main entrance, taking note of what he saw on either side – the Ministry of Justice, more jewellery shops, the useful escape routes north and south of the vast octagon – then turned away and returned the way he had come. As Bannerman and Feydal would not be arriving for another few days, he had time on his hands.

Well, not quite . . .

Knowing that he could not remain in his small hotel, since privacy was all-important, he spent the next couple of days engaged in the tedious task of finding himself an apartment in the fashionable Marais district, which would give him a direct line, either by foot or by Metro, to the Rue de Castiglioni and the Place Vendôme. Concentrating on the Jewish quarter located just behind the northern side of the Rue Saint-Antoine, he visited one estate agent after another, using his passable French, and viewed a great number of apartments until he found one to his liking. Located above a row of fashionable boutiques and art galleries in the Rue des Rosiers, it overlooked the colourful thoroughfare, directly faced a block of similar apartments, and had one small living room filled with antique French furniture, one tiny bedroom immaculately turned out, one bathroom with an inefficient shower and toilet, and a kitchen with too many pipes, a thunderous boiler and cracked tiles of a putrescent yellow. In the living room there was a telephone that worked and a TV that displayed a lot of white snow. Brolin was satisfied.

Checking out of the hotel to move into his apartment, he explained to the desk clerk that he had changed his mind about paying by Visa and wished to pay by Eurocard instead. Not concerned so long as the customer had a viable card, the desk clerk erased the old details and put in the new, then returned both cards to Brolin. Thanking him, Brolin picked up his suitcase and wandered back through the colourful maze of this side of the Marais, crossed the Rue Saint-Antoine and made his way to his new apartment in the Jewish quarter. Once settled in, he went for a meal and, though taking care not to drink too much, had a *pichet* of Sancerre. Over the wine he thought of what he should do next and decided, given what he knew of Police Commissioner Bannerman and Feydal Hussein, to break one of Sir Archibald Wainwright's restrictions.

Not that he was likely to use it, but he wanted a handgun. You just never knew.

Reminded by his reading about Feydal and his conflicts with the GIGN that he, Brolin, had a friend who had once been in that force, he gave that old friend, Jean-Pierre Duval, a call. Jean-Pierre, who moved around a lot, had a cellular phone that automatically picked up messages from his home in Nation and relayed them directly to him. He could read the messages and either answer them or not, but he responded to Brolin, with whom he'd had a great relationship when Brolin, as part of his counter-terrorist (CT) training, had spent a few months in a GIGN training camp in Bordeaux.

'Tony?' Jean-Pierre asked rhetorically. 'Is that *the* Tony Brolin?'

'*Oui,*' Brolin replied.

'Where are you calling from?' Jean-Pierre asked in perfect, if French-accented, English.

'Right here in Paris. I'm here for a couple of weeks and I'd love to get together somewhere.'

'*Parfait,*' Jean-Pierre replied, sounding enthusiastic. 'So where are you staying?'

'In the Marais. On the Rue des Rosiers. Are you free this evening?'

'For you I cancel the most beautiful woman in Paris. Do you know the Café Louis-Philippe? We got drunk there a few times. Enormous dog under the spiral staircase, more alive than we were. On the quai de l'Hôtel de Ville. Just down from the Pont Louis-Philippe.'

'*Oui*,' Brolin said. 'I remember it well. What time?'

'Eight o'clock, which is a good time to eat.'

'You're still a Frenchman,' Brolin replied. 'OK, I'll see you at eight.'

They had their drinks upstairs in the Café Louis-Philippe, overlooking the broad sweep of the Seine and the Ile Saint-Louis, with the Left Bank curving away on the far side. It was an unpretentious café, much favoured by the locals, and the place, ever popular, was busy when Brolin walked in. Jean-Pierre was already seated at a table by the window, looking about ten years older than he actually was, his face formed by broad experience, but this was offset by his shock of unruly thick brown hair and his obvious good humour. They shook hands and embraced in the French style, then Brolin took the seat facing him. Jean-Pierre already had a bottle of Merlot on the table and he poured Brolin a drink. They touched glasses and drank.

'So, Tony,' Jean-Pierre said when he had lowered his glass back to the table, 'what are you doing in Paris? Is this just a vacation? If so, we can have fun.'

'We had a lot of fun in the past,' Brolin replied, 'but no, it's not just a vacation. I'm here on some business.'

'What kind of business?'

'I can't tell you that.'

Jean-Pierre grinned knowingly. 'Ah, I see.' He tapped his nose with his forefinger. 'Say no more, my friend.'

'So what are you up to?'

Jean-Pierre shrugged. 'A little bit here, a little bit there.' Like Brolin, he was something of an adventurer, wandering restlessly from one project to the other, never finally settling. 'Right now I'm importing and exporting. Mostly furniture purchased cheaply in the Rue du Faubourg Saint-Antoine and sold expensively in Lyon and Bordeaux. It's not the most exciting life in the world, but it keeps me travelling and gets me away from home a lot.'

'Still married, then,' Brolin said.

Jean-Pierre spread his hands in the air like a supplicant and rolled his big brown eyes. 'Some things never change,' he said. 'Here in France it is accepted that a married man may have his mistresses and our divorce rate is lower than yours for that very reason. Pragmatism wins hands down.'

Brolin grinned, had a sip of his wine, then put the glass down again.

'So what about you?' Jean-Pierre asked. 'The last time you e-mailed me – a long time ago – you said that you'd just been divorced. What's happened since then?'

Brolin felt that he was wincing, though he wasn't; it was just that odd feeling. 'I'm not with anyone at the moment,' he confessed. 'I was until a couple of days ago, then the whole thing blew up. She locked me out of my flat, I kicked the door down and that was the end of it. She left, not me. This time I still have somewhere to live.'

Jean-Pierre chuckled at the thought of it, doubtless recalling Brolin's always volatile love life. 'Look on the bright side,' he said. 'Here you are, a bachelor in gay Paris. Things could be a lot worse.'

'They certainly could,' Brolin said.

They both drank in silence for a moment, then Brolin placed his glass back on the table and said, 'Do you still have any connection with the GIGN?'

Jean-Pierre shook his head from side to side. 'No. I still see some old friends now and then, but I'm not remotely connected. When I resigned, I did so for good and never looked back. I'd had one killing too many.'

Brolin knew what he meant. With the gap between rich and poor widening dramatically throughout Europe in the past decade, violent crime had risen dramatically and what had happened in Great Britain had also happened here. Paris and other cities had gradually broken up into urban ghettoes controlled by local 'tribes' of bikers, hot-rodders and so-called 'fast-runners' – the 'immigrant trash' gangs that didn't have their own vehicles and went just about everywhere by foot, except for when they used the Metro and terrorized the passengers. Most of the gangs, however, given easy access to the ever-growing Internet, with its overload of all kinds of information, including details of the purchase of explosives and the making of home-made bombs, were armed to the teeth and often created armed fortresses out of ruined buildings in run-down urban areas. They often abducted unfortunate victims, male and female, and took them into their redoubts in order to ransom them, torture them, repeatedly rape them and, just as often, kill them. The only way to get the gangs out of such fortresses was to launch major assaults against them, even if it meant bloody firefights. Invariably, the GIGN was used for this purpose, just as the SAS had been used in Great Britain. Thus Jean-Pierre, like Brolin, had seen more than his fair share of violence and been sickened by it. He had resigned for that reason.

'So you're connected in no way whatsoever?' Brolin asked.

'No.'

'Are you still connected in any way whatsoever with any other government department or organization?'

'No,' Jean-Pierre repeated. 'Why do you ask?'

'I need help,' Brolin said, 'but I can't take it from anyone in that category.'

Jean-Pierre stared steadily at him for a considerable period of time, then gradually offered a slow, intrigued grin. 'What kind of help, Tony?'

'I need a handgun. With luck, I won't actually have to use it, but I'd feel unprotected without it. I'm not supposed to carry one, but I'm damned if I won't. Does your importing and exporting run to that kind of item?'

Again, Jean-Pierre stared thoughtfully at him for a moment. Then he smiled and nodded. 'Yes.'

'A Browning nine-millimetre High Power handgun, preferably with double action, would be fine.'

Jean-Pierre nodded. 'I think I can manage that.'

'Good. What's the cost?'

'That depends on what I have to pay for it, but I'll charge you a fair price.'

Brolin knew that he would. 'Charge more than you normally would, Jean-Pierre, because it isn't coming out of my own pocket and the boss man is generous. When can you get it?'

'The day after tomorrow,' Jean-Pierre said.

'Can it be traced?'

'No. It'll be a weapon reconstructed from two or three different handguns, all sold off by disillusioned SAS men shortly after the regiment was disbanded. Those weapons would have been shipped out of Britain into somewhere like Marseille, then, in some backstreet workshop, taken apart piece by piece. The new weapon would have been made from some of those separate parts. In other words, the weapon will be unmarked and impossible to trace. A very *safe* weapon. What will you do with it once the job's over?'

'Dump it in the Seine,' Brolin said.

'*Parfait*,' Jean-Pierre responded with a broad grin. 'Sounds like an interesting business, Tony. I'd love to know more about it.'

'I repeat: I can't talk about it.'

'Any chance that you might need back-up at some point? I mean, I'm bored and I'd make myself available.'

'I'll keep it in mind. I'm hoping that won't be the case, but if I need you I'll call you.'

'Make sure you do,' Jean-Pierre said. 'Now, why don't we have dinner?'

'Why not, indeed?' Brolin said.

They had a leisurely French meal, economical and superb, then went their separate ways. Two days later they met on one of the broad boulevards that curved around the Ile Saint-Louis, just outside the reach of the lights on the Pont Neuf. There, in moonlit darkness, Jean-Pierre passed over the reconstructed handgun, wrapped in sackcloth and carried in the plastic bag of a well-known supermarket chain. No money changed hands. Jean-Pierre simply told Brolin what it would cost him and they arranged to meet a couple of evenings later for drinks. Brolin would then hand over the cash demanded. They were old friends who trusted each other because they had no reason not to. Two days later, they met for drinks as agreed and Brolin handed Jean-Pierre his cash in a plain brown envelope. Three hours and a lot of wine later, they went their separate ways again, both well laced and satisfied.

Brolin had thought about hiring a car but finally

decided against it because in Paris there was nowhere to park for any length of time. He would hire a car when and if he needed one; meanwhile, as Paris was easy to traverse by foot, he would either do that or use the Metro. That just about tied it up.

Now all he could do was wait and think.

Brolin waited and thought.

CHAPTER FIVE

Brolin waited and thought and . . . watched. In particular, he spent days scouting around the Place Vendôme, checking every shop, every arcade, every exit, and everyone who entered or left the Hôtel Ritz. He even memorized the faces of the paparazzi who hung around the square-shaped marble access to the Rue Madeleine, directly in front of the main entrance to the hotel, with their high-powered motorcycles and cameras that looked more threatening than sub-machine guns. The people entering and leaving the hotel had wealth stamped all over them and were treated with obsequious respect by the blue-uniformed caped doormen as they emerged from or entered their luxury vehicles. The men had the look of power brokers; invariably the women, whether old or young, were sophisticated, wearing the expensive clothes and jewellery that were sold right there in the Place Vendôme.

Brolin never entered the hotel. He didn't want to be

recorded by the hotel's videotape camera nor be noted and memorized by security people or other members of staff. He did, however, check the back of the building, making his way along the Rue des Capucines and into the narrow Rue Cambon to find that the rear entrance, located beside the Bar Hemingway, was always locked and could only be accessed by the ringing of a bell fixed to the side of the double doors. It was clear, then, that the rear entrance was only used on rare occasions; most likely when someone particularly famous was trying to avoid the ravenous paparazzi. Certainly, given the narrowness of the street and the lack of parking spaces, only someone desperate to escape the paparazzi would wish to use that exit. Assuming this, Brolin concentrated his focus on the front of the building in the Place Vendôme.

Eventually, when he knew the area off by heart, he prepared to observe the movements of both Commissioner Bannerman and Feydal Hussein. Though he had decided not to hire a car because of the parking problems, he realized, belatedly, that he would have to follow both men in order to build up a picture of their movements. For this reason, he decided to purchase a motorcycle. He didn't want a new one because he wanted no record of the transaction; instead, he checked through the 'For Sale' columns of *Fusac*, a free English-language magazine, and found an advertisement for a second-hand Honda NTV 650, supposedly almost new and being sold only because its owner was returning to the United States. Brolin placed a call and arranged to meet the owner of the motorcycle at 1900 hours that evening outside the American Library on the Rue du Général-Camou in the seventh *arrondissement*. He turned out to be a young American in his early twenties, fresh-faced, blond-haired, wearing blue denims and a black leather jacket. He confirmed that he had come to Paris for a year to learn the language, had purchased the Honda brand new shortly after his arrival, and was going to return to the United States as soon as he had managed to sell the unwanted vehicle. Brolin bought the motorcycle, paying in cash and writing a false name and address on the document of transfer. Leaving the well-pleased young man on the pavement in front of the library, he drove back to the Marais and parked the motorcycle in the courtyard of his apartment block. The door to the courtyard could only be opened with a code number, so the motorcycle was safe. Brolin went for a lonely meal in the Jewish quarter and slept soundly that night.

The following afternoon, about an hour before Feydal Hussein was due to arrive at the Hôtel Ritz, Brolin drove to the Place Vendôme and parked at the far side of the traffic lanes that curved around the soaring column of bas-reliefs. The location gave him a clear view of the hotel while not making him noticeable either to the police outside the Ministry of Justice or to any watchful hotel security men or chauffeurs doubling as bodyguards for their wealthy masters. After propping the motorcycle on its support leg, he withdrew a Paris guidebook from his pocket and opened it at random. Every time someone passed by, he raised the book as if he was boning up on the area, just like a regular tourist.

Feydal turned up exactly when he was supposed to, which was at 1400 hours on this Wednesday: eight days after Brolin himself had arrived in Paris. Confirming the image that Brolin had formed of him, Feydal arrived in an immaculately polished silvery-grey Mercedes-Benz with tinted windows. When the vehicle stopped in front of the hotel, a dark-suited chauffeur emerged from the front to open the rear door, Feydal stepped out and the flashbulbs of the paparazzi's cameras started frantically blazing away. Brolin was standing well away from the paparazzi, at the far end of the Ministry of Justice building, giving him an oblique view of Feydal who was tall and broad, with a healthy head of brown hair turning grey. He was wearing a long black overcoat over a grey suit, with a white silk scarf draped over both shoulders, framing his striped shirt and tie. He was accompanied by two bulky men, both wearing dark suits and turning their heads this way and that, scanning the area, keeping their eyes on the paparazzi and *badauds*: the passers-by and curiosity-seekers. The two men were obviously bodyguards and almost certainly armed. They waited until Feydal had entered the hotel and then they followed him in.

This was the beginning of an extremely tedious business. Brolin didn't know if Feydal would come out again that day, but he had no choice other than to hang around the Place Vendôme, keeping his eye on the main entrance to the hotel. In fact, he was not only waiting for Feydal to come out but also studying and memorizing, with the aid of a pair of small binoculars, the faces of every man and woman who entered the hotel from that point on, in case one of them came out later with Feydal.

One hour dragged into the next, each hour longer than the one before, with Brolin's only moments of light relief being his close-up study of the many beautiful women who entered and left the building, some of them literally breathtaking. He was, however, starting to feel immensely bored, frustrated and cold when, at 1950 hours, when darkness had fallen and the lanterns around the great octagon had come on, the familiar silvery-grey Mercedes-Benz drove up to the entrance and the chauffeur got out to hold the rear door open.

A minute or so later, one of Feydal's bodyguards emerged from the hotel, followed by Feydal himself, who had his arm around the slim waist of a striking raven-haired young beauty who, Brolin recalled, had entered the hotel about two hours ago. This suggested to Brolin that the young lady had spent most of those two hours in Feydal's room, perhaps in his bed. She and Feydal were followed out by the second bodyguard. The young lady, whose features could clearly be seen through Brolin's binoculars, was classically beautiful, though her face was oddly inexpressive. She was dressed in a deceptively simple figure-hugging black silk dress, low-cut at the front and falling to just below the knees, revealing fine legs and high-heeled shoes. She had an expensive shawl around her shoulders and her raven hair fell halfway down her spine. As the chauffeur opened the rear door a little wider to let Feydal and his woman get into the vehicle, the bodyguards spread out unobtrusively to cover both sides of approach and, obviously, to take action against anyone coming too close. When Feydal and the girl had slipped into the rear of the car, the first bodyguard followed them in, the chauffeur closed the door, and the second guard hurried around the front of the vehicle to take the seat beside the chauffeur.

Brolin was on his motorcycle before the Mercedes-Benz had moved away from the main entrance. It moved slowly past the Ministry of Justice, turned left and then right into the Rue de Castiglioni, and headed for the Rue Saint-Honoré. Brolin started his motorcycle and followed it. Keeping a good distance behind, ensuring that other vehicles were always between him and the Mercedes, he followed it along the Rue de Rivoli, across the Seine and along the Boulevard Saint-Germain to the bright lights and busy streets of Montparnasse. The Mercedes stopped in the bus and bicycle lane almost directly in front of the legendary La Coupole Brasseric, deposited its passengers there, then moved off again, obviously looking for a parking place. Brolin parked his motorcycle at the far side of the road. Feydal and his lady entered the brasserie. The two bodyguards remained outside, standing unobtrusively on the sidewalk within sight of the entrance. Knowing that he was in for a long wait, Brolin took a table in the glassed-in front section of the Le Select brassiere, located almost directly opposite La Coupole. He had a couple of beers while he waited.

Two hours later, the Mercedes reappeared and parked briefly again in the bus and bicycle lane in front of La Coupole. Then Feydal and his lady emerged, allowing Brolin, with the aid of his small binoculars, to see both of them up close. With his chocolate-coloured eyes, slightly hooked nose, full, lascivious lips and thick, slightly greying brown hair, Feydal looked like an ageing matinée idol. His lady friend was a good deal younger than he was, somewhere short of thirty, about five feet, six inches tall, with full breasts, a slim waist, long legs, lips and nose of fashion-model perfection, eyes a brilliant green under a fringe of black hair, skin smooth and marble-white. Her face, however, remained expressionless. Brolin noted this fact for the second time. Whatever lay beneath that beautiful mask, she was keeping it well hidden.

As Feydal, his woman and the two bodyguards were clambering back into the Mercedes, Brolin paid his bill and unchained his motorcycle. When the Mercedes moved off, he followed it all the way to the Rue du Faubourg-du-Temple in the tenth *arrondissement*. Again, as if by magic, a parking space had been made for the Mercedes-Benz, this time outside La Java, a stylish venue that had once hosted Edith Piaf but now specialized in Latino live acts. (Brolin knew most of the clubs because of his own forays into Parisian nightlife a couple of years back with his old friend John-Pierre Duval.) Once more, when Feydal and his woman entered the club, the bodyguards remained outside and the chauffeur drove off to find a parking space. Brolin watched and waited. Less than two hours later, the Mercedes reappeared. Feydal and his woman emerged from La Java, clambered back into the gleaming vehicle and were driven off again, with Brolin once more following a good distance behind on his motorcycle.

The next stop was Le Queen on the avenue des Champs-Elysées, a gay club noted for its full-on erotic dancing, abundance of drag queens and uninhibited homosexual interactions. Brolin and Jean-Pierre had never gone there because heteros were only allowed in when with gays, but Feydal and the girl seemed to have no problems in gaining entrance and were in there for another couple of hours. When they emerged, the Mercedes-Benz took them to the Rue aux Ours in the third *arrondissement*, where it stopped outside an even more notorious gay club, Le Dépôt, an immense black-painted former warehouse with rainbow flags fluttering outside. Feydal and his girlfriend emerged from the Mercedes, the former clasping the rump of the latter in his large hand, and entered the club.

Brolin had never been in that particular gay club either, but he had read about it in his Paris guidebook while keeping watch on the Hôtel Ritz and knew that it was large and multi-levelled, with condoms handed out for free at the entrance, jungle netting and exposed air ducts covering the ceiling, homoerotic videos projected on the walls, a pounding sound system, flashing strobe lights and, most important, an immense basement with pitch-black rooms and make-shift cubicles with holes in their walls for voyeurs who could look on while other homos got on with their business.

By this time, Brolin, waiting on his motorcycle at the other side of the avenue, was cold, tired and intrigued. He had already assumed that the inexpressive beauty with Feydal was his Parisian mistress, but now he was wondering just how broad Feydal's sexual proclivities were and if the young lady with him shared those proclivities or not. One thing, however, was certain: everything that he had read about Feydal's hedonism was undoubtedly true.

In fact, Brolin was compelled to stay awake throughout the night and the early morning, following Feydal's Mercedes-Benz from one club to another, some of them heterosexual, others homosexual, until the car returned to the Hôtel Ritz just after six a.m. When Feydal and the girl entered the hotel, his arm around her waist, she resting her head on his shoulder and clearly exhausted,

Brolin went back to his own, more modest place in the Marais and had a well-deserved sleep. He also had an erotic dream about Feydal's woman and awoke between drenched sheets.

CHAPTER SIX

Brolin was up bright and early the next day to keep his eye on Feydal. Again, he went to the Place Vendôme on his motorcycle, parked it at the far side of the soaring column, and watched the main entrance to the Hôtel Ritz from a point just in front of the expensive jewellery shops that would have hidden him from any particularly alert member of the security staff. As before, he alternated between pretending to be deeply engrossed in his travel book and studying with his small binoculars those entering and leaving the hotel. It was a deeply boring morning: he had made sure that he was there by 0800 hours and by 1100 hours he was beginning to think that either Feydal had left before his arrival or he was not going to come out at all.

In the event, Feydal emerged just before noon, again escorting the raven-haired beauty who today was wearing a belted fawn jacket and trousers of exquisite cut. She was also wearing a long scarf of red silk and carrying a black leather shoulder bag. This being a warm day, Feydal was dressed in a light grey suit with shirt and tie and immaculately polished black shoes. When he and the woman entered the waiting Mercedes, the bodyguards piled in as well and then the car took off, again driving along the Rue Castiglioni.

Brolin followed on his motorcycle. The Mercedes turned along the Rue de Rivoli, followed the flood of traffic around the vast open space of the Place de la Concorde, then swept along the Avenue des Champs-Elysées. It turned left at the Rond Pont, went down the Avenue Montaigne, then headed along the Cours Albert-1, part of the dual carriageway that ran alongside the Seine. When the Mercedes made another right turn at the Place de l'Alma and headed up the Avenue Marceau, towards the Arc de Triomphe, Brolin, still following it, assumed that the driver was either taking a deliberately circuitous route to shake off anyone who might be on his tail or simply avoiding the heavy traffic in the upper part of the Champs-Elysées. Certainly, he turned left at the Place Charles de Gaulle where the traffic was chaotic, entered the Avenue Foch and stopped, almost immediately after joining the right-hand one-way system, at an elegant apartment block soaring up from behind a high black steel fence. The door to a private underground garage swung open almost immediately, the Mercedes entered and the door closed behind it.

Brolin parked his motorcycle at the other side of the narrow street, chaining it to the black-painted railings around the entrance to an underground public car park, and crossed the road to check the names of those living in the apartment block. But he found he could not do this since the solid steel gates were locked and the apartments were set well back from the high fence. Frustrated, he returned to his parked motorcycle and waited for the Mercedes to emerge again.

About forty-five minutes later, the doors to the underground garage swung open again and the Mercedes emerged to turn right, heading back to the Place Charles de Gaulle.

Brolin followed on his motorcycle. This time the Mercedes dropped its passengers off at Chez Benoît, a trendy restaurant located near the Georges Pompidou Centre. There was now one extra passenger, however – a black-haired, brown-skinned man, most likely an Arab, wearing a dark suit with shirt and tie. Brolin managed to get a quick shot of his face with his compact camera just before the man entered the restaurant with Feydal and the blank-faced beauty whose hair, hanging down her back, was ink-black against the fawn of her finely cut figure-hugging jacket.

That's one hell of a woman, Brolin thought.

The Mercedes moved off to park and the two bodyguards took up unobtrusive positions on the sidewalk. Aware that he was in for another long wait, Brolin took a seat at one of the sidewalk tables of a café on the opposite side of the street, a good way down from the restaurant, ordered lunch and a *pichet* of Sancerre (having decided that this wasn't really drinking on the job) and kept his eyes peeled as he ate and drank. A little under two hours later, the Mercedes reappeared. Less than a minute after that, Feydal, the woman and the Arab emerged from Chez Benoît and Brolin took a couple more long-distance shots of the whole group before they clambered back into the Mercedes, along with their bodyguards, to be driven away again.

Brolin followed them on his motorcycle. The Mercedes ended up in the Champs-Elysées, where it deposited Feydal, the woman and the Arab at the Aviation Club de France, which had a restaurant, bar and casino. The bodyguards, admirably unobtrusive as always, accompanied them all the way to the entrance and then took up positions on both sides of the door as their master and his mistress and friend entered the building. This time the chauffeur was able to park the Mercedes on a *payant* at the sidewalk right in front of the club. Then he got out to lean on the bonnet, chain-smoke cigarettes and study the many attractive women passing by in the usual flood of tourists and locals.

Brolin sighed. He was in for another long wait. It was a long wait indeed, nearly all of three hours, but eventually Feydal and the other two emerged from the casino just as the chauffeur opened the rear door of the Mercedes. The whole group, including the two bodyguards, piled back into the car and Brolin followed them the short distance back to the same apartment block in the Avenue Foch. The Mercedes went down into the underground car park. It emerged an hour later. Brolin followed it back, through the dense evening commuter traffic, to the Hôtel Ritz where it deposited Feydal, his woman and the two bodyguards. When the four of them had entered the hotel, the Mercedes moved off again.

Brolin waited. He didn't want to, but he did. He wasn't after Feydal – it was Bannerman he had to get – but he knew that the key to neutralizing Bannerman could be in knowing what Feydal's routine was. Obviously, it included business as well as pleasure – and as the business possibly involved the Arab, it strongly suggested arms dealing. If Bannerman was coming here to make a deal for arms, he too would be meeting the Arab. So Brolin had to complete this task.

Night had fallen when Feydal emerged again. The time was 1930 hours. A cold wind had been blowing relentlessly across the Place Vendôme, now sublime in a combination of lamplight and moonlight, and Brolin was practically freezing. Feydal emerged, as usual, with his woman and the two bodyguards. They were all dressed in formal evening clothes and the woman looked ravishing. Though already yearning for food and sleep, Brolin followed them through another lengthy evening and early morning that began with a two-hour meal in Lucas Carton on the Place de la Madeleine, directly facing the church and flower market (more posh you could not get, Brolin thought) then continued with another round of nightclubs, this time including Les Bains Douches, where the beautiful people gathered, the Folies Pigalle, which specialized in striptease, but ending up, as it had before, in the notorious Le Dépôt, where the basement was a saturnalian hell.

Brolin couldn't help wondering, as he waited, what that ravishing, sophisticated beauty could be doing down there with Feydal. The possibilities loomed in his thoughts as a kind of torment.

They went back to the Ritz eventually. Brolin heaved a sigh of relief. It was just before dawn as he crawled back to his bed and found, to his despair, that he was too *tired* to sleep. He did sleep, of course, fitfully, and had another erotic dream about Feydal's woman. Later, when he awoke in his soaked sheets, he felt like a guilty teenager.

On the other hand, he had something to look forward to.

Bannerman was due to arrive soon and that was what Brolin was here for.

He was here to get Bannerman.

CHAPTER SEVEN

William Clive Bannerman, Commissioner for the Metropolitan Police, arrived at 1600 hours the following day. Not well known to the paparazzi, being a mere English police officer without a high media profile here in Paris, he emerged from a rented chauffeur-driven BMW without the customary explosion of camera flashbulbs and entered the Ritz without ceremony. That brief glimpse of him was, however, enough to give Brolin the impression of a physically huge man with a heavily-jowled, almost monolithic face that bespoke authority and cold-blooded self-interest. Though his arrival was unobtrusive, he was closely followed by a couple of bulky men, almost certainly corrupt Scotland Yard detectives acting as bodyguards.

Brolin waited, repeatedly checking his wristwatch, convinced that Bannerman, if he came out again today, would not do so until the evening. In the event, Feydal's silvery-grey Mercedes pulled up in front of the hotel at

1930 hours which was, Brolin knew, the time when the gourmet restaurants of Paris would be starting to serve evening meals. As soon as the Mercedes stopped by the sidewalk, Feydal's two bodyguards hurried outside to take up watch positions near the parked vehicle. Then Bannerman and Feydal emerged with the raven-haired beauty between them. They were all wearing evening clothes.

To Brolin's surprise, it was Bannerman who had his arm around the woman.

Bannerman's personal bodyguards did not put in an appearance, which suggested that they had been left in Bannerman's room or suite. Feydal's bodyguards, however, joined their boss and his friends in the Mercedes, one up front, the other in the rear, then the Mercedes pulled away from the kerb and turned as usual into the Rue Castiglioni. Brolin followed on his motorcycle, all set for another long evening.

Which he got. Clearly, Feydal was intent on giving his guest and potential business partner a good evening as they went from one place to another for the next six hours: first, a lengthy meal at Les Elysées du Vernet, located near the Charles de Gaulle Etoile and noted for its haute cuisine; a couple of hours gambling in the Aviation Club de France on the Champs-Elysées; a brief visit to the Lido de Paris, within walking distance of the former; then an interminable early-morning tour of the club scene, from the merely frolicsome to the notoriously decadent.

Brolin's sole interest in all of this was to note that Bannerman was obviously as hedonistic as Feydal, that he seemed inexhaustible, and that he always had his arm protectively around the waist of the dark-haired woman whom Brolin had previously assumed was Feydal's mistress. Now Bannerman was acting as if the woman belonged to him and Feydal seemed to accept the situation cheerfully. The woman, who was clearly tiring as the early morning wore on, remained otherwise as inscrutable as ever.

Money buys anything and anyone, Brolin thought. *Nothing else can explain that fat pig Bannerman with that particular beauty. There's just no fucking justice.*

Brolin went to bed exhausted just after dawn and slept until eleven in the morning. Consoling himself with the thought that it was unlikely that Bannerman would leave the hotel before lunchtime since he too had not gone to bed until dawn, Brolin got up, attended to his ablutions, then left the apartment and rode the motorcycle back to the Place Vendôme, where he took up his customary boring vigil. He felt better, however, in the knowledge that this was his last day of preliminary observation and that he would be seeing his friend Jean-Pierre tomorrow for dinner and, with luck, a helpful talk.

Bannerman emerged from the hotel, as Brolin had expected, at 1330 hours, again escorted by Feydal and the woman. Today it was Bannerman's two bodyguards who were on duty, slipping like Feydal's goons into the silvery-grey Mercedes-Benz after the others. Brolin followed the vehicle and this time found himself being led all the way along the Rue de Rivoli and the Rue Saint-Antoine to the Bastille, then along the Seine and up to the Gare de Lyon. Surprised to see the Mercedes pulling into the car park of the Belle Epoque-style railway station, the main artery to the south, including Marseille, Brolin wondered, with a touch of panic, if Bannerman and the others were planning to go on a journey. He settled down again, however, when he observed that they were carrying no travelling bags as they were escorted into the station by the bodyguards. Obviously, then, if not travelling, they were meeting someone who was either getting off a train or already waiting for them in the station.

Needing to know who that person was, Brolin left his motorcycle and followed the group into the station, noticing as he did so how stylish the woman looked in her expensive fawn overcoat and high-heeled black boots.

Keep your mind on your work, he silently reprimanded himself. *This is no time for day dreams.*

Once inside the station, Feydal, slightly ahead of Bannerman and the woman, with Bannerman's body-guards on either side, took them not to the platforms under the great glassed roof but up the broad stone steps that led into the Le Train Bleu buffet. Brolin watched the group entering the restaurant, passing under an enormous painting of a bridge (he didn't know which one it was) and two buildings that looked like the Grand and Petit Palais, both of which he had visited when last in Paris. Determined to learn if they were meeting someone in there, he went up the stairs and entered the restaurant.

He found himself in an immense, stunningly beautiful bar-buffet with enormous paintings from the early 1900s on the domed ceilings and on every wall. Initially over-whelmed, Brolin almost forgot to keep his eye on his quarry as his surprised gaze took in this dazzling wash of colour, composed of the many paintings that showed the different sites along the old railway network and the famous events of 1900, which was when the restaurant had been opened. After absorbing all this, he glanced to his left and saw that Feydal, Bannerman, the woman and the two bodyguards were entering a narrow corridor on that side of the restaurant, at the far end of the bar area which was furnished with an abundance of leather sofas and tables.

Not wishing to follow them immediately, Brolin sank luxuriously into one of the sofas, called for a waiter and ordered a glass of Leffe beer. Glancing around him, he saw that only a couple of people were in the bar area with him, either tourists simply checking out the place or travellers waiting for their train. Surprisingly, given the opulence of the building, one of those in the bar was a lone teenager wearing blue jeans, an open-necked shirt under a leather jacket and travelling boots, with a stuffed shoulder bag resting beside him on the sofa. He was drinking a beer and staring around him with wide-eyed curiosity, but the bow-tied waiters didn't seem to mind. The people seated at the tables in the restaurant area were for the most part properly dressed and exuded the kind of self-confidence that suggested wealth.

Pleased to find himself relaxing in such a place, Brolin enjoyed his beer while studying the attractive women dining at the tables (he hadn't gone that long without sex, but it seemed a lot longer) and, at the same time, keeping his eye on the corridor to his left. About thirty minutes later, the teenager finished off his beer, studied his Michelin Guide, then picked up his shoulder bag and left the bar. With his own beer finished and his curiosity getting the better of him, Brolin called the waiter, paid his bill, then wandered into the corridor located at the far end of the bar area.

It was a long, narrow passageway with booths and tables arranged along both sides – obviously designed to resemble a turn-of-the-century train carriage – and with an open area at the far end where, according to a sign on the right-hand wall, the *toilettes* were located. Brolin saw that Bannerman, Feydal and the woman were seated in a booth about halfway along the corridor. They had acquired a companion. There was a fourth person in their booth: the same black-haired, brown-skinned gentleman, probably Arab, possibly Lebanese, whom they had picked up the day before from his residence in the Avenue Foch. The two bodyguards were seated in the booth directly facing them. The Bannerman group were drinking what looked like *kirs* and the bodyguards, not so lucky, had been given beers.

Realizing that he might bring attention to himself if he abruptly turned away and left the corridor, Brolin fell in behind a man and woman who had just brushed around him and were heading for the far end of the corridor, presumably looking for the *toilettes*. With his face shielded by the couple, Brolin followed them along the corridor, not glancing left or right when he passed Bannerman and his friends. At the far end of the corridor, the man and woman entered their separate toilets. Following the man in, Brolin found him already unzipping himself at one of the urinals. Brolin did the same. They urinated side by side, the man whistling softly, Brolin staring in silence at the wall directly facing him. Brolin waited until the other man had washed and dried his hands before doing the same. Leaving the toilet shortly after the man had done so, he returned to the corridor ... and saw that Bannerman and his friends had disappeared.

Cursing silently, Brolin hurried back along the corridor and emerged into the bar area. To his immense relief, he saw that Bannerman and the others, including the

Arab, were now seated around one of the tables in the restaurant, clearly preparing to have lunch. The two bodyguards were seated at a smaller table nearby, obviously about to be fed as well.

Knowing that he was in for another long wait and realizing that he too was hungry, Brolin went to the snack bar downstairs, which resembled an American diner (all chrome and swivel chairs), where he had a quick *Croque Monsieur*, washing it down with a bottle of mineral water. When his meal was completed, he left the snack bar and crossed the concourse to the platform gates, where people were entering and leaving sleek silver trains. Standing with his back to one of the gates, he had a clear view of the steps leading up to the Le Train Bleu buffet. Brolin stood there for another two hours, smoking too many cigarettes, before Bannerman and his friends emerged.

The two bodyguards came out first, carefully scanned the busy station, then nodded to indicate that the others could follow them. Feydal and the Arab came out first, followed by Bannerman and the woman. All four followed the bodyguards down the steps to the concourse, then walked around the snack bar and out of the station. Brolin followed them. He was in time to see the Arab shake hands with Feydal and Bannerman, ignoring the inscrutable beauty, before walking to the taxi stand and taking the first vehicle in line.

Brolin was mesmerized by the woman, wondering what was going on behind that lovely pale face, wondering what she was thinking. The very thought of her in Bannerman's bed filled him with revulsion.

As the taxi containing the Arab was moving off, the others returned to the silvery-grey Mercedes-Benz and

Brolin went straight to his motorcycle. He followed the Mercedes back to the Place Vendôme and watched the group enter the Hôtel Ritz. As it was now nearly four in the afternoon, he was confident that they would not be coming out again until the early evening and that he had no reason for hanging around. Besides, he had seen enough by now and had a pretty good idea of what they would be doing tonight: out for a gourmet meal and then another long night on the town. He didn't need to see that again, had no need to follow them, since from tomorrow he would be taking more positive action, starting with his old friend Jean-Pierre when they met for lunch. Right now, Brolin had better things to do.

First, he drove back to his apartment in the Marais and parked his motorcycle. Next, he removed the film from his camera and took it to an instant-print shop in the Rue de Rivoli, located mere minutes from where he was staying. While waiting for the film to be developed – he had asked for good-sized prints – he went for a beer, contenting himself with a couple of *demis* because he was now approaching the stage where he would definitely have to keep his wits about him. Two hours later, when evening had fallen, Brolin returned to the shop and picked up the prints, which he studied at great length in his apartment, drinking only mineral water but smoking more than he normally did.

Though taken with a miniature camera and zoom lens, the photos, thanks to the advances of modern technology, were pretty damned good, showing the features of their subjects with great clarity. Brolin had caught them all: Bannerman, Feydal Hussein, the unknown Arab gentleman and, of course, the woman, whose face, even frozen by photography, drew Brolin like a moth to a flame. He tried to forget this, to stay strictly professional, but he didn't find it easy because her face mesmerized him.

What the fuck's got into you? he thought. *Concentrate on the job. Let's just see what we have here.*

To study William Clive Bannerman and Feydal Hussein together was to find nothing in common between them. Bannerman had a face to match his Neanderthal bulk: heavy-jowled, Protestant rectitude in the thin lips, his eyes, even in close-up, as dead as stones. It was a face to tell a story, in his case one of corruption: there was little that showed a softer side, let alone a glimpse of normal humanity. Bannerman had a face that illuminated his reputation; you saw it and you thought of the heavy breathing of a beast in its dark lair. The thought of Bannerman in bed with the woman made Brolin's skin crawl.

Feydal Hussein, on the other hand, was a different breed altogether, his features revealing nothing of his criminal background and reputation for ruthlessness. In fact, he looked quite the opposite, his face almost refined, his ageing handsomeness touched with Mediterranean good humour, albeit cynical and with shrewdness writ large. He was smiling in every photo, though his gaze was always watchful, and Brolin, to his disgust, could imagine him in bed with the woman, could imagine him charming her.

In not one photograph of Bannerman was he smiling: that was the difference between him and Feydal Hussein.

The so far nameless Arab lacked Feydal's humour, though he seemed just as sophisticated and had the lean and hungry look of a man who has spent most of his life struggling desperately to survive. In some photos he was smiling; in others he was not; but in all of them he showed an intensity that had probably been with him since youth. Brolin could not yet confirm whether the unknown man was actually Arab or not, but certainly he was from the Middle East and that was a deeply troubled area where every citizen was forced to take his life seriously. This one was serious. And there was something else about him that Brolin now noticed: in three of the photographs the Arab was gazing sideways at the woman and in every instance it was a gaze of thinly veiled disapproval. He might have had lustful thoughts about her himself, but he didn't approve of her. Beautiful and sophisticated though she looked, to the Arab she was Bannerman's French whore. That was what the look in his eyes said.

If the woman was aware of this, the photographs certainly did not show it. In every photograph she was, as she had been ever since Brolin had first seen her, hypnotically beautiful and inscrutable. There might have been a hint of weariness in her gaze, but nothing else was revealed. This was a woman who did what she had to do and kept her thoughts to herself, perhaps because she had no choice. This made her, for Brolin, more mysterious . . . and even more desirable.

It's just sexual deprivation, he thought, resolutely putting the photos aside and taking a deep breath. *It's only been a couple of weeks, not months, so get a grip on yourself. Either do that or do something about it before you go crazy. What the hell, let's get out of here.*

Brolin did something that he thought he would never have to do again. He took himself out, went to Le Halle, had a drink or two, then wandered along the notorious Rue Saint-Denis where he picked up a decent-looking whore. She took him to a seedy room, which was appropriate since he *felt* seedy, though thankfully he was anaesthe-tized with the drink that he had sworn not to take. In the event, he was careful enough to use a contraceptive but that only made the experience even less edifying. Worse still, the only way he could complete what he had started was by closing his eyes and conjuring up the image of that other, unknown French woman – Bannerman's woman. He returned to his own bed later that evening, feeling sick to his soul, but the raven-haired inexpressive beauty still haunted his dreams.

CHAPTER EIGHT

'The last time we were here,' Jean-Pierre said, 'it was the start of an exceptionally long evening that ended, in fact, about dawn. Those were good days, *oui*?'

'We were both younger then,' Brolin replied, 'and what made us feel good at that time could possibly kill us now.'

'That's exactly why we enjoy it,' Jean-Pierre replied with that grin that laid all the ladies low. 'It's the risks we take that excite us.'

Brolin sighed. 'Yes, I guess so.'

They had just finished eating in a small, cosy bar in the Rue Saint-André des Arts in the heart of the Latin Quarter and were now on their second *pichet* of *vin rouge*. Just like old times, indeed. The evening that Jean-Pierre was talking about had only been one of many grasped hungrily between rigorous bouts of training with the GIGN that had included real assaults, conducted as bloody experiments, against the growing number of violent teenage gangs who had turned the suburbs, or *banlieues*, of Paris into ethnic ghettoes. Given the toughness of the training and the danger of the assaults, which invariably ended in vicious firefights, it was little wonder that Brolin and Jean-Pierre had thrown themselves into the business of living with uncommon zest. In fact, on just about every occasion that they had been given time off Jean-Pierre had insisted upon showing Brolin, then a newcomer to France, the 'real' Paris that was, in his view, a city of countless hedonistic pleasures. Jean-Pierre had been a particularly good guide: he was, pretty much, irresistible to women and, though being married, rarely spent a free evening without a girlfriend. Having insisted, therefore, on taking Brolin under his wing, he had always also insisted that any woman he invited out for the evening should bring another one along for his 'handsome and gallant English friend'. So for a few months, while training with the GIGN, Brolin had led the kind of off-duty life that most bachelors could only dream of, including good food and wine, a wide variety of bars and nightclubs, and the kind of women that he might never have met had he been on his own. That Jean-Pierre could live that kind of life and still be happily married was, as Jean-Pierre himself had put it, 'a simple fact of French life'. Brolin didn't know if that statement was true or if Jean-Pierre was just winding him up. But his friend certainly knew how to live and Brolin envied him for it.

'Anyway,' Jean-Pierre now said, lighting a cigarette, blowing a cloud of smoke and eyeing the manila envelope that was resting on the table by Brolin's right hand, 'as you refused to let me bring some lady friends to this dinner, I take it that you've something confidential to discuss.'

'Correct,' Brolin said.

'You can discuss it now?'

'I don't have a choice,' Brolin said. 'I'm going to need your help, Jean-Pierre.'

The Frenchman smiled and nodded. 'Good,' he said. 'I was hoping you'd say that eventually. I'm so bored right now.'

'I don't know that I can ease your boredom, Jean-Pierre. It isn't that kind of help. Right now, I just need information.'

'Even that's better than nothing and it could lead to more.' Jean-Pierre nodded, indicating the manila envelope. 'Have you brought that for me?'

'Yes.' Brolin automatically pulled the envelope closer to his chest, but he didn't open it yet. Instead, he glanced around him. He and Jean-Pierre were in a darkly varnished mahogany booth at the rear of the bar and none of the other diners were close to them. The booth would protect them from prying eyes, though Brolin doubted that anyone in this café would take the slightest interest in them. It was a café frequented by an odd mixture of Sorbonne students and older men and women who popped in from the fruit stalls of the nearby market. The air was dense with cigarette smoke and the conversation was voluble. Returning his gaze to Jean-Pierre, Brolin said, 'I still can't tell you exactly what I'm here for, but I *can* tell you this much: I'm observing an Englishman who's staying in the Ritz Hôtel for a couple of weeks.'

'You can't tell me why you're observing him?'

'I'll only tell you if I have to.'

'Can you tell me who he is?'

'I'm interested in seeing if you recognize him.'

Jean-Pierre smiled and glanced at the manila envelope. 'Those are photographs, *oui*?'

'Yes – but not just of the Englishman.' Brolin continued talking as he pushed the envelope to Jean-Pierre's side of the table. 'I want you to tell me if you can identify *any* of these people. One of them is the Englishman I'm after, but I need to know as much as I can find out about the others before I do any more.'

'Any more of what?' Jean-Pierre asked astutely as he opened the envelope and withdrew the photographs. 'That comment suggests that once you've completed your observation you'll be taking some specific course of action.'

Brolin grinned. 'Well, you caught me there, Jean-Pierre. Yes, I'll be taking some specific course of action, as you so diplomatically put it, and I might need your help for that as well. Right now, however, I just need to know if you recognize any of those people.'

Jean-Pierre held the batch of photographs in his left hand and, with his right hand, flipped them over one by one, always moving the one on the top to the bottom. No one at any of the other tables could have seen the photographs, but it was instantly clear to Brolin, from the wrinkling of Jean-Pierre's brow, that he had recognized *someone*. When he had finished studying all of the photographs, he held the whole pile close to his chest, showing only the backs of them.

'Well?' Brolin asked him impatiently.

'I see a French man, a French woman, an Arab and a big, bulky man who is almost certainly English.'

'Do you recognize the Englishman?'

'No. Should I?'

'He's pretty famous – or notorious – in our country.'

'Not in ours,' Jean-Pierre said.

Brolin nodded. 'But you recognized someone,' he said.

'I could tell that by the expression on your face. So who did you recognize?'

Jean-Pierre passed the top photograph to Brolin. It was a photo of Feydal and the woman leaving the hotel, taken the day before Bannerman had arrived in Paris. 'Surely, my friend,' Jean-Pierre said, 'you must have known I would recognise *him* of all people.'

'Why should you?' Brolin said.

'Feydal Hussein. The biggest arms dealer in Europe at the moment. Nothing secret about that, though a lot of what he does behind the scenes *is* certainly secret. In fact, Hussein is a tabloid celebrity; the paparazzi love him. But why are you observing Feydal? Is he involved with your Englishman?'

'We think they're going to be involved,' Brolin said, 'in a way that isn't acceptable.'

'Not acceptable to whom?'

'The British government.'

'If the British government is involved – and if they're worried about your Englishman's involvement with Feydal – you must be talking about the arms trade. I mean, that's what Feydal's all about. What else could it be?'

'OK, it's the arms trade,' Brolin said. 'Did you recognize anyone else in those photographs?'

Jean-Pierre nodded. '*Oui.*' He leaned across the table to tap the photograph that Brolin was now holding. 'The woman.'

'Who is she?' Brolin asked.

Jean-Pierre leaned back in his chair. 'Very beautiful, *oui*?'

'No question about that,' Brolin said, 'but who the hell *is* she?'

'Marie-Francoise Lebon. Widely touted as Feydal's

Parisian secretary, though she's something a lot more
or less than that, depending upon your point of view.'

'You mean she's his mistress?'

Jean-Pierre nodded. 'But perhaps a little more than that
– at least, according to gossip.'

Brolin was inclined to trust the kind of gossip that
Jean-Pierre picked up. Though his friend had left the
GIGN and was, as he had stated, in no way officially
connected to it or any other government organization, he'd
always had a keen nose for intelligence and still sniffed
around for it. Jean-Pierre, for his own reasons, including
back-door deals to do with his various businesses, kept
in close contact with a lot of well-placed people, including
hard-nosed journalists, police officers and politicians. So
when he used the word 'gossip' he did not use it lightly.

'Can you clarify that?' Brolin asked.

'Well, as you doubtless know, Feydal spends most of
his time in Marseille.'

'Yes, I know that,' Brolin said.

'He only sees Marie-Francoise when he's in Paris; she
doesn't live with him in Marseille. In other words, she's
not his *full-time* mistress.'

'So?'

'So she only sees Feydal when he actually comes to
Paris and then, according to gossip, she's likely to be used
in more ways than one.'

'Such as?'

'Marie-Francoise was originally a high-class whore
who trawled the lobbies and bars of the best hotels in
the city – the Ritz, the Crillon and so forth – picking up
only the wealthiest and most powerful of men: politicians
and businessmen. That was *before* she got to know
Feydal. A couple of years back, she became involved

with Feydal and since then, according to gossip, more than one of her high-flying clients has been blackmailed into doing Feydal's bidding after spending a clandestine night with her.'

'Oh, boy!' Brolin exclaimed softly, trying to be glib about it but inwardly writhing with disappointment and an odd feeling of loss. Having spent yet another restless night dreaming about Marie-Francoise, soaking the sheets as he was dreaming, he had awakened that morning feeling ashamed of himself and almost hating her for having made him feel that way. Now, forced to listen to Jean-Pierre's revelations about her, he felt crushed with disillusionment and a burning resentment. He didn't know this woman at all, but he felt that he did. Even worse, he resented those who truly knew her and that feeling was, in his view, both inane and dangerous. If Jean-Pierre knew what he was thinking right now, he would laugh him out of this café.

'I mean, look!' Jean-Pierre continued, pulling out another photograph – one of Bannerman leaving the hotel with his arm around the woman. 'Judging by this photograph, your Englishman, Bannerman, is claiming Marie-Francoise as his own – at least for the length of his stay here. Clearly, since Feydal looks happy enough, the Englishman is taking the woman with Feydal's permission. What do *you* think this means?'

Brolin sighed, aware that he was obsessed with the woman for reasons that were not strictly professional; aware, even more, that the very thought of her in bed with Bannerman disturbed him unduly. In truth, he was jealous of Bannerman and hated the woman, this Marie-Francoise Lebon, for making him feel that way. At the very least, he felt stupid. 'I don't think it's blackmail,' he said. 'I think she's Feydal's gift to the Englishman. Either that, or Bannerman doesn't know that Feydal's fucking her in his absence. It's either one or the other.' He shook his head from side to side. 'But, no, it's not blackmail – at least, not in this instance.'

'What makes you so sure of that?'

'Because they're here, in Paris, to do business together and blackmail wouldn't even come into it. I mean, that man can't be blackmailed.'

'He can't?'

'No.'

'Why not?'

'Because he's the most powerful – and the most openly corrupt – law enforcement officer in Great Britain. He's William Clive Bannerman, Commissioner for the Metropolitan Police.'

Jean-Pierre raised his eyebrows in surprise. 'Really?'

'Yes, really.'

'Well, be that as it may, all men can be blackmailed, Tony. Even a police commissioner.'

'Not this one,' Brolin insisted. 'He's already notorious for being corrupt, but he's too powerful and ruthless to worry about what people think of him. In other words, a mere sexual scandal wouldn't damage him – not socially, not politically. His wife died a few years back and his reputation is such that his relationship with a whore wouldn't make anyone in England blink an eye. I mean, that man is putrescence and he knows it and takes his pride from it. I repeat, blackmail just wouldn't work on him.'

Jean-Pierre gave a low whistle of appreciation. 'And he's the one you're observing?'

'Yes.'

'Because he's here to do business with Feydal?'

'Correct.'

'Then that business can only be armaments.'

'It is,' Brolin confessed. He briefly summarized what Sir Archibald Wainwright had told him about Bannerman's plan to arrange with Feydal what could turn out to be the biggest illegal arms deal on record. 'Those arms,' he concluded, 'would then be used to turn London into a battleground, while making Bannerman even more power-ful and dangerous than he is right now. And believe me, Jean-Pierre, right now he's the most dangerous man in Britain, so he has to be stopped.'

'And you've been sent here to do that?'

'Yes,' Brolin admitted. 'But I don't want to make a move until I know just who I'm going up against.'

'Well, now you know,' Jean-Pierre said.

'Not quite. I'd really like confirmation that Bannerman is meeting Feydal to arrange an arms deal. I don't want to be set up.'

'Why would the British government set you up?'

'They wouldn't hesitate to set me up if they had other reasons entirely for getting rid of Bannerman and those reasons could themselves be corrupt. The whole system is now rotten from top to bottom and I could be just a cog in the machine. So I'd like to know if I'm really here to stop an arms deal – which for me would be justification enough for getting rid of Bannerman, whom I despise for personal reasons – and, if so, just who I'm going up against.'

'If Feydal's involved,' Jean-Pierre repeated, 'it has to be an arms deal – and it has to be big. Feydal would never involve himself in a deal that wasn't worth a fortune. So it's arms and it's big.'

Brolin took the photos back from Jean-Pierre, flipped

through them, then handed over the ones that included the Arab. 'What about him? Do you know who he is?'

Jean-Pierre studied the various photos carefully, then passed them back to Brolin, shaking his head from side to side. 'No,' he said. 'I don't know him.'

'I think he's Lebanese. Certainly from somewhere in the Middle East.'

'That's fairly obvious, Tony. Is he staying in the Hôtel Ritz as well?'

'No. He was picked up by Feydal and Bannerman from an apartment in the Avenue Foch.'

Jean-Pierre gave another low whistle of appreciation. 'That means money, my friend.'

'Middle East money. Which in turn could mean arms. I need to know just who that man is. Do you think you could find out?'

'Yes,' Jean-Pierre said.

'How soon?'

'By midnight,' Jean-Pierre replied with confidence, checking his wristwatch. 'If we don't make this a long night.'

'Then let's leave right now,' Brolin said. 'This one's on me.' He called the waiter, paid the bill, then picked up the manila envelope and left the cafe with Jean-Pierre. Together they stepped into the Rue Saint-André des Arts that was, at this time of the evening, packed and lively, with lights blazing out of Turkish pastry shops, smoky Greek restaurants, small, independent cinemas and book-shops that were still open, this being a quarter favoured by the Sorbonne students. It was also a quarter favoured by tourists and there were many about, swarming along this narrow street and into the equally busy side streets of Saint-Séverin like bees in a honeycomb. 'Do you need these photographs?' Brolin asked, waving the envelope in front of Jean-Pierre.

'*Oui*,' Jean-Pierre responded, reaching out for it.

Brolin, however, jerked it away from him. 'Who's going to see the photos?' he asked. 'Anyone official?'

'No,' Jean-Pierre said. 'No one official. A *journalist*. He's an old, trusted friend, I've used him for years and he won't ask any questions at all. If this Middle East gentleman lives in the Avenue Foch, my friend will know who he is – he'll have him on his computer. If my friend is home – and he rarely goes out at night, being a computer freak – I'll have the information by midnight. So make sure *you're* home.'

'I'm going straight back,' Brolin said. He handed Jean-Pierre the manila envelope as they approached the Place Saint-Michel. 'When do I get them back?' he asked.

'Shortly after I see my friend,' Jean-Pierre said. 'I'll slip the envelope under your door and the information you want will be in it with the photographs. Don't open your door when you receive the envelope, but call me if you have anything to talk about . . . say, half an hour later. I should be home by then.'

'OK,' Brolin said.

'What's your front-door code?' Brolin told him what it was and Jean-Pierre nodded, indicating that he would memorize it, then said, 'How will you get back to the Marais?'

'I'll walk across the Ile Saint-Louis,' Brolin replied, 'and be back in my apartment in twenty minutes or half an hour at the most. I'm making no detours.'

'*Parfait*,' Jean-Pierre said, checking his wristwatch again. 'That means you'll be back by eleven, so I'll drop by between then and midnight.'

'*Superbe*,' Brolin said.

They parted at Davioud's fountain, the most popular meeting place in the Latin Quarter, with Jean-Pierre hurrying down into the Saint-Michel Metro, carrying the manila envelope, while Michael turned into the Quai Saint-Michel, then crossed the Seine to Notre-Dame. Leaving the floodlit medieval splendour of the great cathedral behind him, he traversed the small island where Paris was born, walking along the poplar-lined streets of the Quai d'Orléans to eventually cross the river at the Pont Louis-Philippe and make his way from there into the south side of the Marais. Ten minutes later, he was back in his apartment in the Jewish quarter. The time was 2250 hours.

Brolin poured himself a drink and sat back to keep his eye on his own front door. Forty minutes later he heard a noise outside, then the familiar brown envelope was pushed under the door. As instructed, Brolin did not open the front door to identify either Jean-Pierre or his friend, but simply picked the envelope off the floor and emptied its contents onto the table. A note fell out with the photographs. Brolin checked that all of the photos were still there, then he read the note, written in Jean-Pierre's unmistakable florid hand.

The Arab in the photos is Idris Khadduri. Born in Benghazi but lives in a luxurious villa in the garden suburb of Giorginpopoli to the west of Tripoli. Educated at the University of Libya and in Cambridge, England. Speaks Arabic, English and French. Passionately pan-Arab and puritanically Muslim. Devoted to Colonel Gaddafi, supporting a strong interventionist position on the Palestine issue and other guerrilla and revolutionary organizations in Africa and the Middle East. As a professional arms dealer, he purchases weapons for those groups and also finances them in the long term with the sale of weapons to similar groups in Europe. Though ostensibly a government salesman for the crude oil sold by Libya to Italy, West Germany, France, the Netherlands, the United Kingdom and the United States, in fact he deals mostly in weapons, transporting them in and out of the port of Tripoli, often hidden in barrels listed as containing crude oil, to Algiers and Marseille. He also moves them, in crates listed as containing industrial machinery parts, via the Sabhā road south-west to Ghāt near the Algerian border and then, by local transport, into Algiers itself. His apartment in the Avenue Foch is financed by the Libyan government and is also used by members of Khadduri's so-called export company. So if Bannerman is talking to Feydal and Khadduri, he's certainly intent on purchasing weapons. Lose no sleep tonight.

Brolin lost sleep. Instead of going to bed, he gave Jean-Pierre just enough time to get back to his place in Nation, then called him up.

'How can I get to Bannerman?' he asked of Jean-Pierre.

'That should be obvious,' Jean-Pierre said.

'It's not obvious to me.'

'You get to him through the woman,' Jean-Pierre said.

'And how do I get to the woman?' Brolin asked.

'Through me,' Jean-Pierre said.

CHAPTER NINE

'I confess,' Jean-Pierre said, 'that I was being disingenuous when discussing her, but I felt that I had to talk to her first before getting back to you. I think she'll have good reason to want to help you, but if she does it will be extremely dangerous for her. So I thought that I'd better, as a friend to both of you, sound her out before confessing to you that I actually knew her. Do you understand, Tony?'

'Yes,' Brolin said. 'Naturally.'

'Good.' Jean-Pierre glanced around the hotel lounge, which was practically empty, with more potted plants and climbing vines than customers at this time of the afternoon, the lull between lunch and dinner. There was a spacious café between this lounge and the street, which led into the Place l'Opéra, and the café was where all the action was right now, with the customers, locals and tourists alike, dawdling over coffee and beer while watching the passers-by. Clearly pleased that they would have a lot of privacy when the woman arrived, the tables in the lounge being well spaced and, for the most part, now unused, Jean-Pierre turned back to Brolin. 'She'll be here in half an hour, so let's talk it through before she gets here. After that, it's all up to you.'

'Right,' Brolin said. He was, in fact, short of words and still trying to recover from the shock of the phone call he had received from Jean-Pierre that morning, telling him that he had fixed up an appointment with the raven-haired beauty whom he now knew to be Marie-Francoise Lebon: perhaps an occasional mistress to Feydal Hussein, certainly Bannerman's woman of the moment. That thought still made Brolin's stomach churn. 'So let me get this straight,' he added. 'You're an old friend of the woman's, you suggested to me that she could help me, but you didn't want to say you were a personal friend until you'd talked to her. This makes me nervous, Jean-Pierre.'

'Please don't be nervous,' Jean-Pierre said, smiling and shaking his head from side to side to deny any wrongdoing. 'Just let me explain.'

'Please do,' Brolin said.

Jean-Pierre picked up his cup of *café noir*, had a sip, then put the cup back down on the table. 'As you know, I was a member of the regular Gendarmerie before I joined the army and was transferred to the GIGN.'

'Yes, I knew that.'

'Well, when I was in the Gendarmerie, one of my jobs was to liaise with the security officers of the major hotels in Paris and check out anyone who used them on a regular basis for anything other than strictly residential purposes. We were concerned mostly with urban terrorists, burglars and muggers – you'd be surprised at how many people get mugged in their own hotels just after leaving their rooms – but we also checked out any prostitutes who were trawling the lobbies and bars of the hotels hoping to net well-heeled tricks. Marie-Francoise was such a lady. The managers of a couple of the bigger hotels told me about her, saying that she was a class act, that she was exceptionally beautiful, obviously sophisticated, and that they didn't really care about her being there so long as they knew that whoring was *all* she was up to. So they asked me to check her out and I did.'

'And?' Brolin asked, realizing that his good friend Jean-Pierre was teasing him with what could only be termed a histrionic pause.

'Interesting lady,' Jean-Pierre said. 'Now twenty-nine years old. Born and bred in Paris, in one of the very worst suburbs, a *banlieue* of much poverty and ethnic divisions, known for its high crime rate and frequent riots in which bombings and lootings were commonplace. Like many a whore, she was abused as a child – or so it seemed from her school records, though no charges were actually brought against her father, who was the obvious suspect. It would seem that her mother and friends had their suspicions, but each time Marie-Francoise was asked about it, she went into denial. Nevertheless, the evidence indicated that she *had* been abused, almost certainly by her father, and that the abuse had become even more regular when her mother fled home and did not return.'

'What does that mean?' Brolin asked.

'She was fished out of the Seine a few months later, her system shot to hell with too many drugs, with alcohol and cigarettes. The findings of the post-mortem suggested that she had been practically dead before she actually drowned.'

'You mean suicide?'

'Yes. Which only convinced the authorities even more that the mother had known about her husband's sexual abuse of their daughter.'

'Marie-Francoise.'

'Exactly.'

'OK. Please continue.'

Jean-Pierre exhaled in a loud, lengthy sigh, then continued his sorry tale.

'Marie-Francoise was then fifteen. She became a juvenile delinquent, picked up frequently by the *flics* for a variety of petty crimes, including shoplifting, mugging – she was in an all-girl gang that mugged old people – and even selling crack and ecstasy. Eventually, as usually happens in such cases, she moved on to a kind of informal prostitution – back-alley sex for money – that became progressively more frequent and more professional. When she had just turned eighteen – an eighteen-year-old beauty – a local pimp moved in on her, making demands under threat, and Marie-Francoise, already an independent spirit, abruptly took off.'

'Sounds like a determined, ambitious girl,' Brolin said.

'Oh, yes, she was – and remains so. However, in that particular instance she didn't travel far. By now routinely professional about selling her body, she used the money she had made from her whoring in the *banlieue* to rent an apartment near the Bastille. With that as her base, she started trawling the better parts of the city, notably around the Tuileries area, for customers with more class – and more money – than those in the *banlieues*. Because of her looks, she quickly became popular. She used the money to buy the very best in fashionable clothing, learnt etiquette from her upmarket clients, and graduated from the streets to the hotels where, with her fashionable clothes and new sophistication, she fitted in perfectly. Indeed, most of the managers actually liked to have her around because she added a bit of glamour to their hotels and certainly pleased their male residents. In short, they turned a blind eye.'

Brolin glanced around the large, almost empty lounge, a virtual jungle of potted plants, and let his gaze come to rest on the entrance, half expecting to see the woman walk in. Suddenly, he felt nervous about meeting her, though he still wanted to see her. Sighing, feeling like an awkward adolescent, he turned back to Jean-Pierre.

'She was still on her own by then?' he asked. 'Still working independently, I mean.'

Jean-Pierre nodded. '*Oui*. When I first met her, she was still independent, with no pimp or anyone else involved. I checked her background first, then I had a talk with her. She was in the bar of an hotel, just waiting to be picked up, so I sat beside her, showed her my ID and said we had to talk. She was surprisingly cool about it. No embarrassment or fear at all. I invited her for a drink in a booth where we could have some privacy. She accepted, smiling slightly, mockingly, looking into my eyes.'

'Jesus!' Brolin exclaimed in exasperation. 'What does *that* mean?'

Jean-Pierre grinned and continued. 'Later, when I asked her about that smile, she said she was expecting a little harmless sexual blackmail: the occasional session in return for my protection, a few quick, unpaid fucks in my police car. She didn't think for one second that

I was going to arrest her; she assumed I wanted to make her.'

'You *could* have done that,' Brolin said, 'and who the hell would have blamed you? But you didn't, I take it.'

'No, I didn't,' Jean-Pierre said. 'I prefer my women to volunteer. I just talked to her and told her that I knew what she was doing, that I didn't care about it, that my only concern was that she kept her game clean, did not use a pimp or do drugs, and did not, in any way, shape or form, try to blackmail her clients. She understood what I was saying. She could work if we had no trouble. Any trouble and she would lose all that she'd gained and end up in jail. She agreed: we parted outside the hotel and she walked away smiling. After that, we became friends. At least, friends of a sort. I mean, I'd see her in an hotel bar, waiting for clients, and I'd buy her a drink and just talk for the pleasure of her conversation. She'd tell me funny stories about her clients, teasing me, smiling slightly, cynically. She enjoyed telling tales.'

'I've never seen her smile,' Brolin said, recalling that cruelly beautiful, inscrutable pale face framed by ink-black hair. 'I haven't seen her smile once.'

'She never smiled a lot,' Jean-Pierre explained, 'but she did at least *smile* sometimes then. She stopped when she met Feydal Hussein and lost her independence. Not at once, but when he started sharing her around. *That's* when she stopped smiling. That was after my time, of course.'

'When you'd left the Gendarmerie.'

'Correct. That was six years ago. I lost touch with her during that period when I left the Gendarmerie, joined the army, transferred to the GIGN and, of course, met you. Now isn't that romantic?'

'Cut the bullshit,' Brolin said.

Jean-Pierre's grin was mischievous, but then he shrugged and turned more serious. 'Anyway,' he said, 'I didn't see her for a few years, more or less forgot her. And then, a couple of years back, when I had been transferred temporarily to the Service de Protection des Hautes Personalités—'

'*What?*' Brolin asked.

'The SPHP – a special branch of France's Interior Ministry that guards visiting dignitaries.'

'Sorry,' Brolin said. 'My pig ignorance. Please continue, my patient friend.'

'I will,' Jean-Pierre said. 'So there I was in the Hôtel Ritz, wearing civilian clothing, but actually a temporary, armed member of the SPHP, surreptitiously guarding a visiting dignitary who shall remained unnamed, when who do I see but my old friend, Marie-Francoise Lebon? Even more beautiful than ever, but this time accompanied by the notorious arms dealer Feydal Hussein, and not looking too happy about it.'

'What about you?' Brolin asked.

'Naturally, I wasn't too happy myself, having to guard a visiting VIP when a notorious arms dealer, well known to be trading with terrorists of every persuasion – therefore always a potential candidate for assassination by bomb or bullet, right there in the hotel – was resident in the same building at the same time. But what could I do?'

'What you had to do,' Brolin said.

'Correct,' Jean-Pierre responded. 'I guarded my VIP for two weeks, spending most of the time in the hotel, and I saw Marie-Francoise almost every evening, nearly always with Feydal Hussein and certainly never with any other man. However, I also saw her on her own, sometimes in the bar, other times in the restaurant, L'Espadon, and on one such occasion I approached her to have a talk with her. We became friends again – platonic friends as before – and she told me that she was still on the game, but that she kept herself free solely for Feydal when he visited Paris, always staying in the Hôtel Ritz. At least, that's what she told me when she was in the hotel – either at the bar or in L'Espadon, when Feydal was up in his suite conducting business, buying or selling arms. But later, when I had transferred back to the GIGN and was still seeing her occasionally, in my free time, she confessed enough to let me know why it was that she no longer smiled at all.'

'Why?' Brolin asked, now desperate to know, though not for strictly professional reasons. He despised himself for this weakness.

Jean-Pierre checked his wristwatch, then glanced around the almost empty lounge, obviously looking for Marie-Francoise. Failing to see her, he turned back to Brolin.

'I kept seeing Marie-Francoise off and on for the next couple of years, even after I had left the GIGN. In fact, I'm still seeing her, on average about two or three times a year, usually in some small *quartier* bar or, occasionally, in a more luxurious place like this, though always one that Feydal has never used and is unlikely to use. During these meetings, I have come to respect her a great deal and have learnt why it is that she's become a woman virtually encased in ice, hiding every emotion.'

'*Why?*' Brolin asked again, convinced that he was going to go mad if he didn't find out.

'You'd better ask her yourself,' Jean-Pierre said, 'because

it relates, much more than you can imagine, to what you want her to do for you.'

'Damn it,' Brolin insisted, 'tell me *now*.'

'I can't,' Jean-Pierre replied.

'Why not?'

'Because she's just this instant walked through the door and is coming to join us.'

Brolin jerked his head around to look at the lounge entrance and he saw that what Jean-Pierre had said was true.

Marie-Francoise Lebon, Bannerman's whore, was walking towards him.

CHAPTER TEN

Marie-Francoise came straight up to the table and stopped to stare down at Brolin and Jean-Pierre. She was wearing a finely cut black jacket, low-cut black top, skin-tight white pants that emphasized her long, shapely legs, gold earrings and black Versace high heels. She looked like a million dollars in more ways than one.

'*Bonjour*,' she said, addressing Jean-Pierre, not smiling, though her voice was as sensual as a feather on skin warmed by the summer sun. Brolin felt that voice as if it was palpable, seeping into his every pore.

'*Bonjour*, Marie-Francoise,' Jean-Pierre replied, smiling and languidly waving his right hand in Brolin's direction. 'This is my friend, Tony Brolin, about whom we have spoken.'

Marie-Francoise turned her head slightly to stare at Brolin for the first time. She had bright green eyes, the watchful, unreadable eyes of a big cat, under a fringe of black hair. Her face was slightly gaunt, though very beautiful, with pale, almost alabaster skin and high cheekbones. She nodded at Brolin, not offering her hand, then took the chair facing him, beside Jean-Pierre, and crossed her long legs. Brolin tried to keep his gaze off those legs, but it wasn't easy to do. He felt consumed by her presence.

'So,' Marie-Francoise said, fixing Brolin with her bright green gaze and speaking directly, fearlessly, to him in almost flawless, albeit French-accented, English 'Here I am. Jean-Pierre said you wanted to talk to me, so why don't you begin?'

'I hardly know where to start,' Brolin said.

'Why not start with Bannerman? Isn't he the one you want?'

'Yes,' Brolin said. 'He is.'

'Jean-Pierre said you needed my help with Bannerman but that's *all* he said. He said you'd tell me the rest. So, here I am. I'm all ears, *monsieur*.'

'Jean-Pierre didn't tell you why I need your help?'

'No,' Jean-Pierre put in, 'I didn't. I said that you had Bannerman under observation and that the kind of help you needed, if Marie-Francoise gave it, could put her in danger. I said she'd have to learn the details from you, which is why she's here now.'

Brolin nodded at Jean-Pierre, then turned back to meet the disconcertingly steady gaze of the woman. 'Are you willing to place yourself in danger in order to help me?'

'Not necessarily. Maybe. It would depend on what you tell me, *monsieur*.'

'Tony. Please call me "Tony".'

'We're not that intimate yet.'

Feeling that he'd just had his face slapped, Brolin actually blushed and gazed guiltily around the room.

'I like that,' Marie-Francoise said, addressing Jean-Pierre. 'The Englishman is blushing. A man who's still capable of blushing can't be all that bad.' She turned back to Brolin, forcing him to meet her steady gaze, not letting him off the hook. 'So,' she said, 'you must be as decent as Jean-Pierre said you are, though that doesn't mean you're trustworthy. The best of men can't always stick to their principles and that's my major concern here. Tell me what it is you want to tell me. Jean-Pierre here is my witness.'

'What does that mean?'

'If you lie – or if you tell the truth and then later go back on it – I have a witness to prove it.'

'Fair enough,' Brolin said, realizing that he was in the presence of a woman who would not be easily deceived and respecting her for it. 'So where do we start?'

'We start with you telling me what you're after. What I *could* get into trouble for.'

Fuck you, Brolin thought, determined not to be crushed by the feeling of having been put down. *You want to play tough, then let's play tough. Let's lay it all on the line here . . . Christ, you're so beautiful.*

'What I tell you depends on what *you* tell *me* about Bannerman – your relationship with him. I mean, I thought you were Feydal's girl.'

'I'm no one's girl. I'm a woman plying her trade. It starts and ends there. Do you mind if I smoke?'

'No, of course not.'

Marie-Francoise crossed her legs as she lit a cigarette and exhaled a cloud of smoke from moist, pouting lips that were neither too full nor too thin. Brolin felt his heart racing.

'I have reason to believe that's not true,' he said, determined to remain strictly professional.

'What's not true?'

'That you're no one's girl. I mean, you used to operate independently, then you got tied up with Feydal and now you're on Bannerman's heavy arm. That's an unusual arrangement, so I want to know how it came about and just what it means.'

She stared steadily at him for a moment, her green gaze unrevealing, then said, '*Oui*, what you say is true enough. You have to understand that Feydal's an extremely charming man when you first get to know him, a man who understands women, a man who also knows how to seduce them and then cleverly exploit them. So, despite all of my previous experience with men, despite the fact that I first knew Feydal as just another trick, a *rich* trick, he deceived me into thinking that our relationship could be more than that and, once having fooled me, made me dependent upon him.'

'You mean emotionally dependent?' Brolin asked.

'*Oui*. I mean that I made the mistake of taking him too seriously, imagining that he respected me more than the others had, even convincing myself that I loved him. And, of course, when Feydal grasped the situation, he was quick to exploit it.'

'In what way?'

'Do you really need to know this?'

'Yes. I have to know where you're coming from. I have to know why you're willing to turn against Feydal and help me with Bannerman. I have to know that you *mean* it.'

'You mean you have to know if I hate them enough to do what you want.'

Brolin shrugged. 'I guess so.' He saw the hint of a smile – the first he'd ever seen her give – on her lips and suspected that it might be contemptuous. That smile made him feel like a voyeur, another kind of exploiter, and he sensed that she knew this. It was not a good feeling. 'So you fell under Feydal's spell,' he continued doggedly, though in truth he could hardly think straight, 'and then he exploited you. Just how did he do that?'

'Like I said, he made me sexually and emotionally dependent upon him, then he exploited my feelings for him in order to take over my professional life – he certainly took it over each time that he personally came to Paris. In other words, he insisted that I devote myself to him when he came to this city; that whenever he was in Paris, I had to give up my other clients and stay with him in his hotel suite, just like his regular mistress.'

'And you agreed.'

'*Oui*. I *wanted* to stay with him, I wanted *him* – and that, of course, was my big mistake.'

'In what way?'

'Once he saw that I was willing to do that for him, he started asking for more.'

Looking into that beautiful, alabaster face, that steady, unfathomable green gaze, Brolin tried to imagine the distance that this woman had travelled, psychologically, emotionally, in order to end up where she was right now . . . as what she *was* right now. For, indeed, he found it impossible to make a connection between this cool, sophisticated beauty and the impoverished, ignorant, sexually fearful child that she must have been before making her escape from the *banlieues*. Escape from her father's sexual abuse, from her mother's alcoholic misery, from the crushing poverty and escalating ethnic violence of the post-Millennium years. To escape was one thing, but to have come so far was another, and that distance, which appeared to Brolin to be cosmic, suggested a fiercely determined, possibly ruthless soul behind that cool, self-protective exterior. Yes, she had come from the *banlieues* and now seemed entirely at ease in the Hôtel Ritz, with its rich and powerful clientele, so Brolin was sure that if she had her own reasons, she would do what had to be done. He deduced this even as he started floundering in his own desire for her.

'What do you mean, he started asking for more?' he said, again determined to remain strictly professional and referring to Feydal. 'In what way did he ask for more?'

Marie-Francoise smiled again. It was a slight smile, not hinting at contempt this time, but certainly mocking. Brolin's cheeks burned afresh.

'Other men,' Marie-Francoise explained. 'He had his reasons, he told me. He said he dealt with a lot of people, mostly men of great wealth, and that a woman who looked like I did could be helpful in his transactions. He wanted me to service these guys – to be *good* to them, as he put it, to keep them happy while they were here in Paris conducting their lengthy negotiations – to soften them up and make them easier to deal with. "Just be nice to them," he said. "Give them a good time. Stroke their cocks and their egos. You know how to do that." In other words, he reminded me that I was still a professional whore – it was as though he slapped my face with that reminder – then he told me that what he was asking me to do was nothing more than I'd already done in the past. In short, having seduced me and gained my trust, he put me back where I'd been: on a bed with a price tag on my ankle. A clever man, *oui*?'

'And you accepted it,' Brolin said, ignoring the girl's rhetorical question because he didn't trust the rage that he was feeling for Feydal Hussein. It was the rage of self-interest.

'*Please*, Brolin,' Jean-Pierre interjected, 'I don't think . . .'

But Marie-Francoise, obviously not as offended as Jean-Pierre, waved her hand to silence him. The cigarette was still smouldering between her fingers, the smoke briefly obscuring her face, but Brolin glimpsed that slight smile in the purple haze and was riveted by it. This time it *was* a smile of amused contempt, though Brolin hoped it signified contempt for all men, not just for him. He took comfort from that thought.

'Yes,' she said, 'I accepted it. I rationalized it to myself. I told myself that I couldn't deny what he'd said and that it made no difference to me. He was still paying me, after all, compensating me for my lost clients, paying more than I'd ever had before, and he would pay me for every man that I serviced at his request. I was shocked – because I'd convinced myself that I loved him – but then, of course, being a whore at heart, I felt obliged to accept it. I mean, what was the difference between his friends and the clients I would have had otherwise? To refuse would have been a ripe hypocrisy, so I went along with it. Also, so long as I agreed, I'd still be seeing him and I still, God help me, wanted that. So, *oui*, I agreed. I started to service those he sent me to and that trapped me completely.'

Brolin glanced at Jean-Pierre and saw him staring down at his own clasped hands, as if trying to hide his handsome, thoroughly civilized face. Brolin thought he knew why. Jean-Pierre, a womanizer, but a decent man and this woman's platonic friend, had also seen the contempt in her slight smile and heard it in her superficially calm, desperately controlled voice. He was staring down at his own clasped hands because, like Brolin, he felt ashamed of the things that men did. Now he and Brolin were conspiring to exploit this woman as other men had done, albeit in a slightly different way. They were going to ask her to continue to be Bannerman's whore and to relay back to them anything he told her. They might as well have been pimps.

'How did it trap you?' Brolin asked because he really had no choice in the matter; despite his shame, this was make-or-break time and he couldn't afford to break.

'Because once I agreed to it, I was letting Feydal be my pimp, letting him choose my clients, letting him dictate my life. And once I started, because of my feelings for him, my emotional dependence upon him, I just couldn't break away – at least, not for a long time. I only tried to resist when he decided to use me as a means of blackmailing certain of those men. When he did that, I reached the end of my tether and tried to get out.'

'*Tried?*'

Marie-Francoise gazed steadily at Brolin for a moment, then glanced at Jean-Pierre, as if seeking his support. But eventually, receiving only the Frenchman's veiled glance, she returned her unblinking gaze to the front . . . to Brolin's shamed face. 'Yes,' she said, 'I tried. Of course, I didn't succeed. I'd always known that Feydal was crooked, that he had a criminal record, that he'd grown rich by selling arms to all comers, irrespective of their politics, and that he had a reputation for being ruthless. I'd always known that, but it was something I rarely dwelt on, forever putting it to the back of my head in order to fool myself. Then, when I learnt that he was blackmailing some of the men he sent me to—'

'How did he do that?' Brolin interjected, still acting strictly professional.

'I always took them to an apartment that Feydal had rented for me. It was on the Champs Elysées. There were video and still cameras hidden in every room, including the kitchen and especially – naturally – the bedroom, to record us wherever we had sex. If Feydal couldn't get what he wanted from certain men, he would threaten to send photos or video films to where they would do the most damage – wives, newspapers, politicians, the police. More than once, when some tricks actually refused to be blackmailed, he sent the photos and films off and destroyed the men shown in them. I was in all those photos and video films, too, doing things you wouldn't believe, things that shamed even me, so when Feydal made the mistake of telling me what he was doing – he was boasting drunkenly – I was outraged and told him I was leaving.'

'You tried to leave, but you failed?'

'Yes. As I said, I'd always known that Feydal had a reputation for being ruthless. He certainly proved it by informing me, when I told him I wanted out, that I couldn't go because I'd become too valuable to him as his tool of blackmail. Then, when I insisted that I *was* going, he told me that if I didn't do what he said he would either kill me or, even worse, have me scarred for life, probably with acid thrown in my face.'

'You believed him?'

'Not at first. I told him to go to hell, then I walked out and returned to my apartment in the Marais – my own apartment; not the one that Feydal had rented for me in the Champs Elysées and filled with spy cameras.' Marie-Francoise shrugged; Brolin's heart went out to her. 'Anyway, in the early hours of that morning, I was awakened from sleep when someone slapped a strip of masking tape over my mouth, then wrapped it tightly around my head. Once silenced, I was tied by my hands and feet to the bed. Lying there, terrified, thinking of that threat about being scarred by acid, I was forced to look on as two men, neither saying a word, methodically, almost silently, destroyed most of my possessions – slashing curtains, paintings, walls, settees and cushions with flick knives; quietly breaking expensive vases and antiques; cutting up my passport, credit cards and other valuable documents with scissors, then using those same scissors to cut all my clothing to shreds. The wires to my phone, fax, computer and everything else electrical were cut. The carpets were cut to ribbons. They did all of this with cold, silent efficiency, then, when they were finished, they came and stood over my bed. One of them removed a small glass phial from his jacket pocket, uncapped it, held it right over my face, then slowly tilted it. Naturally, I couldn't scream because my mouth was taped. But I remember *trying* to scream and straining insanely to get off the bed before the acid splashed on my face. In the event, nothing happened. I heard the two men chuckling. I opened my eyes to see the one with the phial waving it to and fro, mere centimetres above my face, smiling sadistically while letting me see that it was empty. Then the other one bent over, touched the blade of his flick knife to my forehead and drew it lightly down over my nose to my lips and chin while saying, "Make one sound and I'll cut your throat, *chérie*." Then he slashed through the masking tape wrapped around my head, freeing my mouth, and also slashed through the cords binding me to the bed. "You have three days to buy yourself some more clothes," he said, "and report back to *Monsieur* Hussein in his suite in the Ritz. Make sure that you do it." Then both men walked out and left me there on the bed, naked and close to hysterical. Naturally, three days later, I was back with Feydal in his suite in the Hôtel Ritz. Naturally, he was as charming and as demanding as ever. Naturally, I then did everything he demanded . . . and that got me to Bannerman.'

For the first time, she turned away from Brolin and Jean-Pierre, looking less cool, even distracted, as if something in the armour of her psyche had been cracked by the very thought of the monstrous Bannerman. She inhaled deeply on her Gauloise, exhaled a cloud of smoke, then stubbed the cigarette out in the ashtray and immediately lit another one. The smoke streamed out on a sigh.

'Feydal *gave* me to Bannerman,' she said. 'I was his little *gift* to Bannerman. I can do what I like when Feydal or Bannerman aren't in Paris, but when either of them is here, I'm theirs and I don't have a choice in it. When they're both in Paris at the same time – when they're meeting, as they are right now – then I'm solely Bannerman's whore. Bannerman wanted me from the day he laid eyes on me, so Feydal just gave me to him. He's doing a lot of business with Bannerman and my task is to keep Bannerman sweet, no matter the cost . . . You want to know what the cost is, *Monsieur* Brolin?'

'I don't think so,' Brolin said.

'That's why you still blush, *Monsieur* Brolin, but please let me say this, perhaps just to make you blush even more. Being Bannerman's whore is the worst job I've ever had in my life – because that man is a pig.'

'In what way?' Brolin asked.

Once more the green eyes came to rest steadily upon him – the eyes of a big cat – and Brolin sensed that this woman, just like a big cat in this respect too, could be extremely dangerous if pushed too far. Indeed, though she now offered another slight, tight smile, there was no humour in it. Brolin wanted her, nonetheless.

'You want to know what we do together?' she asked with soft sarcasm. 'You want the full, stomach-churning details?'

'No,' Brolin said quickly. 'I didn't mean that. I just wondered . . . you know . . . what you meant by describing him as a pig.'

'What I meant is that the man is an animal and degrades me in ways you can't imagine. To degrade me is part of his thrill, but I won't be specific. Just take it as fact. I hate him – and now Feydal – with a passion and I want to escape. If what you're planning will help me break free, I'll risk anything for it.'

'*Parfait*,' Brolin said.

'So what, exactly, did Jean-Pierre mean when he said you want Bannerman?'

Wondering how much he could tell this woman without fear of betrayal, Brolin glanced at Jean-Pierre and saw his friend give him a nod that clearly meant he could tell her everything. Sighing, he turned back to Marie-Francoise and said, 'Neutralization.'

'Pardon?'

Jean-Pierre smiled at her and spread his hands in the air. 'Neutralization,' he said. 'A polite British euphemism for assassination.'

'Commissioner Bannerman has to be eliminated in what will seem like an accident,' Brolin explained. 'Are you still willing to help us?'

Marie-Francoise stared at them for a considerable time, her unfathomable big-cat's eyes moving left and right, from one of them to the other. She was doubtless wondering, as she studied each of them in turn, just how far she could trust them. Eventually, after what seemed like an eternity, she nodded and said, 'Yes.'

'You'll help me?' Brolin asked, because despite what he had heard he could no longer trust his own senses – the woman's presence was over-powering. 'You're really willing to help?'

'Yes,' Marie-Francoise repeated. 'I speak English, *oui*?'

'*Oui*,' Brolin replied.

Marie-Francoise sighed like a grown woman speaking to an adolescent and trying to be patient. That adolescent was Brolin. 'What kind of help do you need?'

'First off,' Brolin said, trying to keep his wits together, aware, at the very least, that he was not being strictly professional, 'can you tell me why Bannerman is in Paris right now and why he and Feydal are socializing so assiduously with Idris Khadduri?'

'Yes,' Marie-Francoise said. 'Bannerman is here to buy a lot of arms and arrange for their transportation into England. Feydal is the go-between. He introduced Bannerman to Khadduri, will act as a middleman for the purchase, and will then arrange to receive the shipment from Khadduri. As far as I can tell, the weapons will be shipped out from Tripoli and delivered to Marseille, where Feydal will receive them. Feydal will then arrange for the weapons to be sent on to Bannerman in England. All illegal, of course.'

'Where in England?' Brolin asked.

'I don't know,' Marie-Francoise said.

'And what's Feydal's interest in this?' Brolin asked.

'A vast sum of money,' Marie-Francoise told him. 'From Khadduri he receives a fat percentage of the money paid by Bannerman for the weapons. From Bannerman he receives a fat fee for finding Khadduri and then delivering the weapons. Those two sums of money are of great interest to Feydal. His greater interest, however, is Bannerman's promise that if he, Feydal, delivers the goods, Bannerman will ensure that he gets back into Britain and that a blind eye will be turned to his criminal activities in that country. Indeed, even as we speak, Feydal and Bannerman are discussing joint operations in your country. They're planning to join forces and then link up with the London-based Russian *Mafiya* and Chinese Triads to form the biggest criminal conglomerate in the world. So that's Feydal's main interest.'

'Jesus!' Brolin exclaimed without thinking. Then, reluctantly dragging his eyes from Marie-Francoise, he turned to Jean-Pierre. 'This is a hell of a lot bigger than I thought,' he said.

'*Oui,*' Jean-Pierre replied. 'No wonder the British government doesn't want to be seen to be involved in this case. You're in up to your neck, my friend.'

'Getting rid of them both at the same time might be our other option here,' Brolin said, now more determined than ever, despite his quickening heartbeat, to be strictly professional. 'I don't think we'd get any complaints.'

'Not if it's a so-called accident,' Jean-Pierre replied.

'It will be,' Brolin said. He turned back to Marie-Francoise, saw her crossed legs, long and shapely, sucked his breath in, let it out in a sigh that was too loud and then said, 'Are you still in?'

Marie-Francoise nodded. 'Yes. If it means getting rid of those two *bâtards*, then I'll take my chances. Just tell me what you want me to do, *Monsieur* Brolin.'

'Tony,' Brolin insisted. 'Please call me "Tony".'

'I told you, we're not that intimate yet,' she replied, crushing him once more. 'Just tell me what I have to do, *Monsieur* Brolin.'

'Not much,' Brolin said, trying to hide his bruised feelings. 'Just keep me informed. I need to know their daily movements in advance. I need to know when they plan to go on a drive. I need to know when and where they plan to go. Most importantly, I need to know when you're *not* going to be travelling with them. To be blunt, I need to know the best time and place to arrange an accident – and I don't want you there when it occurs.'

'How considerate you are, *Monsieur* Brolin. Perhaps that's why, at your mature age, you still blush.'

'Marie-Francoise!' Jean-Pierre admonished her, well aware of the fact that she was toying with Brolin.

'Never mind,' Brolin said, determined not to be made a fool of. 'So where did you learn your perfect English, Marie-Francoise, given that you came from a poor *banlieue?*'

'A poor girl who wants to make her way in the world and has no choice but to lie on her back has to learn a few languages. When I do something, I do it well, *Monsieur*, and, in the context of all the things I've had to learn, speaking English is no major achievement. I am yours to command, *Monsieur*.'

'*Merci*,' Brolin said. 'I'm truly grateful, *Madame*.'

'*Très bien*,' Marie-Francoise said flatly. 'I'll keep you

informed.' She checked her wristwatch, stubbed her cigarette out and uncrossed her shapely legs, preparing to stand up. 'I have to go now,' she said. 'They'll be expecting me back. When and where do I meet you?'

'Do they keep a tight watch on your movements?' Brolin asked, still trying to keep this strictly professional.

'No. They don't think of me as being a threat to them. As long as I keep Bannerman happy when he's in Paris, I'm free to do as I wish and I often return to my own apartment in the Marais, where I try to relax.'

'That's where I'm located,' Brolin said. 'In the Jewish quarter.'

'I'm on the other side of the Rue du Rivoli,' Marie-Francoise said, 'in an apartment just off the Rue Saint-Paul, almost down by the Seine.' She removed a calling card from her shoulder bag and gave it to Brolin. 'Call me at least once a day and leave a message on my answerphone. When I know that I'm free to go to my apartment, I'll call you and we'll arrange to meet somewhere. Now I have to be off.' She stood up, slung her bag over her shoulder, then glanced down at Jean-Pierre. 'The trouble that old friends can get a simple girl into,' she said laconically, in a perfect, albeit stagy English accent and with a slight, though genuine smile. '*Au revoir*, Jean-Pierre.' She turned away and walked out.

Brolin couldn't tear his gaze away from her until she had disappeared from view.

'Do you think you can protect her?' Jean-Pierre asked after a lengthy, uneasy silence.

'No,' Brolin confessed.

'That's what I feared,' Jean-Pierre said.

CHAPTER ELEVEN

Brolin spent the next week torn between his determination to remain strictly professional and his helpless, dangerous obsession with Marie-Francoise Lebon, whom he met on four afternoons and one evening during the next five days. All of the afternoon meetings took place in different locations around the Seine, some on the Left Bank, others on the Right, either in the lobbies of hotels that Feydal would never have cause to visit or in bars with a noticeable lack of other customers. Sometimes Marie-Francoise came to the meetings direct from a lunch with Feydal, with Bannerman or with both, in which case she was always dressed in exquisite, formal clothes. At other times she came straight from a free period in her own apartment and then she was dressed much more informally, usually in jeans, jumper and casual jacket, her hair pinned up on her head. Always, when she appeared in this mode, Brolin was taken aback by how youthful, fresh and innocent she looked.

For the first few days she had little to report, other than to confirm that Feydal and Bannerman were still negotiating with Idris Khadduri and that they had not yet reached an agreement about the number of weapons that could feasibly be supplied and how much those weapons should cost. In fact, as Marie-Francoise explained to Brolin, the negotiations were more of a ritual than a real requirement – a ritual based on Khadduri's Middle East background, where bartering was an integral part of any transaction and the wearing-down of the customer (in this case, Feydal and Bannerman) was part of an honourable tradition. Feydal knew this, of course, having a similar background himself, and was therefore relaxed about it, even amused. But Bannerman, according to Marie-Francoise, could scarcely bear the haggling and delays and often lost his temper with Khadduri. Because of this, the relationship between him and the Libyan was strained, with each man deeply resentful and suspicious of the other. Feydal, who had dealt with Khadduri many times in the past, was the glue that kept the whole thing together.

'He understands the game,' Marie-Francoise told Brolin as they sat face to face in an almost empty bar in a side street off the Boulevard Saint-Germain. 'Coming from Marseille, he's spent his own life in bartering and so he doesn't resent Khadduri's procrastination. He knows that he'll get an agreement sooner or later and he's willing to wait. Bannerman, on the other hand, is an impatient man, a man with a short fuse, and he keeps exploding at Khadduri, who treats the outbursts as an insult to his honour. Then Feydal has to act as a peacekeeper. Bannerman is, of course, also a racist and Khadduri knows it, which hasn't helped matters.'

'But there's no question of them not coming to an understanding,' Brolin said. 'I mean, is Bannerman's behaviour likely to blow an agreement out of the water?'

'No, I don't think so. Khadduri, like Feydal, is strictly professional and, like Feydal, he's had to deal many times with men whom he secretly despised – the bottom line was always the money. So I don't believe that Bannerman's attitude will stop Khadduri from making a deal. Besides, he's really negotiating with Feydal and those two understand each other. I think they both view Bannerman as a kind of nuisance who has to be tolerated. They're both going to make good money off him, so they'll tolerate him until they come to an agreement that suits all three of them.'

'How much longer do you think they'll take?' Brolin asked.

Marie-Francoise shrugged. 'Only a few more days, I think. It won't be long now.'

'I hope not,' Brolin said.

With no need to continue following Bannerman and Feydal around the city, Brolin now had a lot of time on his hands – and altogether too much time to think about Marie-Francoise. It had now been a long time since he'd had a proper woman – he didn't count that single sordid evening with the whore – and his sexual itch was becoming more distracting with each passing day. Nevertheless, he was convinced that his obsession with Marie-Francoise was something more than sexual hunger, something deeper than mere lust, and if that was the case he could find himself in a serious quandary.

If Bannerman or Feydal found out that Marie-Francoise was spying on them and reporting their movements back to Brolin, they would severely punish her, possibly even kill her, and that possibility had to be considered. In considering it, Brolin had to accept the fact that he could not protect Marie-Francoise and that if anything bad happened to her he was likely to blame himself. His guilt could then impair his normally pragmatic judgement concerning the job at hand, not to mention the personal pain that any harm done to her was likely to cause him. Knowing this, he found himself wishing for the job to be over quickly. But Khadduri kept stringing out the negotiations, eventually making Brolin feel as thwarted as, according to Marie-Francoise, Bannerman himself was.

'The fat pig is growing more frustrated every day,' Marie-Francoise informed Brolin as they sat side by side in the Jardin du Luxembourg, the woman smoking a cigarette, the man drinking beer from a plastic beaker, both facing the ornamental pond that reflected the afternoon sunlight. 'He keeps threatening to call off the negotiations and go back to London, but of course he won't do it. My only fear is that if he gets angry enough, eventually he'll take it out on me.'

'Has he done that before?' Brolin asked, distracting himself from Marie-Francoise's long, shapely legs, now exposed by a hip-hugging black miniskirt, by studying the many people eating, drinking, reading, conversing and kissing in that uninhibited French manner, either around the pond or in the shade of the horse chestnuts, beeches and plane trees. It was a fine, sunny afternoon and the Parisians and tourists alike were taking advantage of it.

'*Oui*,' Marie-Francoise replied. 'He often takes his frustrations out on me, though not with his fists, thank God. *Sexual* humiliation is his game. You want to know what he does?'

'No,' Brolin said quickly, for, indeed, he could hardly bear to think of Bannerman and Marie-Francoise together in *any* context, let alone engaged in sex of a possibly perverse, cruel kind. The very thought made his stomach churn. 'I only want to know what his movements are. I want this job over quickly.'

'Are you starting to feel frustrated, *Monsieur* Brolin?'

'Yes,' Brolin confessed.

'You're just like Bannerman,' Marie-Francoise said, then formed an 'O' with sensual, moisturized lips to exhale a thin stream of cigarette smoke. 'You're as impatient as he is.'

'I'm not remotely like Bannerman, *Madame*, so don't even suggest it.'

Marie-Francoise was unperturbed and continued to slyly mock him. 'I only meant it in regard to that one particular area – the little matter of patience. I certainly didn't mean it in any other way. You're so sensitive, *Monsieur*.'

'Am I?'

'I think so. A woman has to be careful what she says to you. Or is it just me, *Monsieur*?'

'Why should it be only you?'

'Because maybe, in your eyes, I'm a special case.'

'You're so vain,' Brolin said.

'Vanity doesn't come into it, *Monsieur*. Please remember that I'm *professional*. It's my job to make myself attractive to men and to sense when they're attracted to me. When it comes to men's feelings towards me, I've rarely been wrong – and I don't think I'm wrong about you.'

'In what sense?'

'You take your pride from being strictly professional about your work and you're trying to be that way with us, but you're not quite succeeding. You're attracted to me, despite your reservations, and these meetings between us make you uncomfortable for that very reason. Is this not true, *Monsieur?*'

'Yes,' Brolin confessed.

'You want me. Is that it?'

'Yes,' Brolin confessed again.

'You can have me if you pay me, *Monsieur.*'

'I don't pay for it,' Brolin lied, recalling with shame the whore he had picked up a few evenings ago in the Rue Saint-Denis. 'And even if I did, I don't want to mix business with pleasure in this particular instance. It's too important a job to be endangered by personal involvement. I'm sure you understand that.'

She smiled slightly, mockingly. '*Oui,*' she said. 'Naturally. Business always comes first. For Feydal, for Bannerman, for Khadduri, for me and for you, the bottom line is the work. Now let me get *back* to work. I'll call you tomorrow for another meeting. *Au revoir*, Monsieur Brolin.'

'*Au revoir,*' Brolin said.

They met late in the afternoon of the following day in a large, almost empty brasserie in the Rue Saint-Louise-en-l'Ile, not far from the cathedral of Notre-Dame. Marie-Francoise was wearing a finely cut, figure-hugging, off-white trouser suit with a low-cut black jersey, a long, brightly coloured scarf and stiletto heels. Her black hair had been pinned up on her head, thus emphasizing her high cheekbones and green eyes. She smoked one cigarette after another as Brolin, mesmerized by her beauty, drank a *pichet* of Sancerre and tried, with varying degrees of success, to keep his mind on the job. He had good reason to do so.

'Khadduri has finally come to some sort of an agreement with Feydal and Bannerman,' Marie-Francoise informed him, 'about the purchase of those weapons. Starting some time this week, they'll be having a series of meetings to finalize the details, all at Khadduri's apartment in the avenue Foch. The meetings will all take place at the same time: approximately nine in the evening, which gives them time to have dinner beforehand and then meet solely for drinks and the last stages of their negotiations.'

'All the meetings will take place in Khadduri's place?'

'*Oui.*'

'But *after* they've dined separately?'

'*Oui.*'

'So Feydal and Bannerman could be eating in a different place every evening and we don't know which route they'll be taking to Khadduri's place.'

'Wrong,' Marie-Francoise said, smiling broadly for the first time. 'That's the beauty of it. Because the meetings are so important and, I believe, because Feydal is concerned about Bannerman's growing impatience, Feydal suggested that he and Bannerman should eat together every evening in the Ritz, either in Feydal's suite or in the L'Espadon restaurant, to discuss their strategy before each meeting. So they'll be driving straight from the hotel to the Avenue Foch at approximately the same time every evening.'

'Will they take the same route every evening?'

'Yes, almost certainly. They'll take the long way round to the Avenue Foch – along the Seine – to avoid the traffic on the Avenue Champs Elyseés.'

'You mean that instead of going all the way along the Avenue Champs Elyseés, the driver will turn left at

the Avenue Franklin D. Roosevelt, head along the Cours
de la Reine, turn right again at the Place de l'Alma, go
up the Avenue Marceau to the Arc de Triomphe, then
turn left at the Place Charles de Gaulle and enter the
Avenue Foch?'

Marie-Francoise raised her fine eyebrows in surprise.
'*Oui*,' she said. '*Exactement*. How did you know that?'

'I followed them the first time they drove there,' Brolin
confessed, 'and I made the same trip a few times after
that in order to memorize the route.'

In fact, after having made that first trip, following
Feydal's silvery-grey Mercedes on the Honda motorcycle,
Brolin had realized that it was the same route taken by
the chauffeur driving Diana, Princess of Wales, and her
boyfriend Dodi Fayed on the evening they were both
killed in a so-called 'accident' that to this day, years
later, some were still convinced had been an assassination arranged by the British intelligence service. While
not necessarily subscribing to that theory, Brolin had
decided that, since Feydal and Bannerman would be
taking virtually the same route, he would try to stage
a similar kind of 'accident' before the Mercedes turned
away from the tunnel entrance and went instead up the
Avenue Marceau. Naturally, this could mean the death
of Feydal as well, which was not included in Brolin's
brief. But, given what Feydal was up to, Brolin doubted
that anyone back in Britain would criticize him for it. He
could not attempt to stage such an accident, however, if
Marie-Francoise was going to be in the Mercedes at the
same time as his two intended victims.

'Will you be going to the meetings?' he asked her,
bearing this thought in mind.

She shook her head. 'No. The meetings are strictly

confidential, so I've been excluded. Besides, Khadduri, a strict Muslim, doesn't approve of Western whores, particularly *this* one, even though he can't keep his eyes off me.'

'Maybe *because* he can't keep his eyes off you,' Brolin corrected her.

'Yes, maybe that.' Marie-Francoise smiled again. 'Either way, I won't be in the car, so you can do what you want.'

'You're sure these meetings are going to start some time this week?'

'Yes, I'm sure. Bannerman's actually given Feydal and Khadduri an ultimatum, saying that his time is running out and that he has to be back at work, in Scotland Yard, by next Monday. In other words, his so-called vacation ends this weekend and the business has to be resolved by then.'

'Today's Monday,' Brolin said. 'That only leaves four more evenings to the weekend. Surely they have to start the meetings soon.'

'*Exactement*,' Marie-Francoise said. 'Either tomorrow night or Wednesday. They can't wait any longer than that.'

'Then you should know by tomorrow,' Brolin said.

'I will. Feydal's going to ring Khadduri in the morning and my bet is that the first meeting will take place tomorrow evening. My suggestion, therefore, is that you stay in your apartment tomorrow afternoon and wait for my call.'

'I'll do that,' Brolin said.

Leaving Marie-Francoise, he returned to the Marais district, dropped into a brasserie for a quick evening meal, then went back to his apartment, hoping for a good night's rest. In the event, Brolin did not sleep well. Instead, he tossed and turned all night, drifting in and out of unconsciousness, having a disturbing mixture of erotic dreams and half-awake musings about Marie-Francoise, whom he could not shake out of his thoughts despite his repeated, silent avowals to keep his mind on the job.

The following morning, after breakfast, bearing in mind that Marie-Francoise had told him to remain in his apartment all afternoon and wait for her call, he decided to make a final check of the route from the Hôtel Ritz to the Avenue Foch. This time he did it walking, trying to memorize every significant detail along the route and taking notes on anything that could help him or that might give him problems.

Eventually, based on what he had seen during the long walk, he decided to arrange for the 'accident' to occur just before the entrance to the tunnel that went under the Pont de l'Alma. He would strike Feydal's Mercedes broadside with another car – an unmarked one – forcing the driver to swerve to the left just before the tunnel entrance. This would give Feydal's driver no choice but to enter the notoriously dangerous tunnel at a speed and angle guaranteed to make the vehicle crash. As Brolin already knew from his research, the curve-and-dip configuration of the Alma tunnel made it next to impossible to negotiate at high speeds. Thus, if he, Brolin, pressed Feydal's driver to accelerate as he was nearing the tunnel entrance, then struck the Mercedes broadside *before* it could turn off into the Avenue Marceau, the driver would be forced down into the tunnel even as he was swerving into the left lane. In doing that, he would almost certainly crash into the left-hand wall.

Before that happened, however, Brolin would have

turned to the right, away from the tunnel, and would be making his way up the Avenue Marceau to the Charles de Gaulle Etoile. By the time Feydal's car had crashed, therefore, Brolin would already be heading out of central Paris to dump his own car in some forlorn *banlieue* where it would probably be stripped down by the financially impoverished locals and its separate parts sold off to a wide variety of backstreet garages. To Brolin, now desperate to get moving, this seemed like a good scheme.

He was, of course, also desperate to see Marie-Francoise. So, once he had reconnoitred the route from the Hôtel Ritz to the Avenue Foch, he returned to his apartment in the Marais and waited for her call. It came at three that afternoon.

'You have my address?' she asked.

'Yes,' Brolin replied.

'Come over right now,' she said.

Brolin put the phone down, put on his jacket and left the apartment. In order to get to Marie-Francoise's place, he had only to cross the Rue de Rivoli, mere minutes away, then walk down to the far end of the Rue Saint-Paul and enter a picturesque cobblestoned courtyard. The apartment was on the second floor of a modernized eighteenth-century building and Marie Francoise opened her door the instant he rang the bell. She was wearing an open-necked check shirt, tight blue jeans and flat shoes. Her black hair had been pinned up on her head, making her green eyes look even bigger and brighter than they normally were. The mere sight of her moved him.

'Come in,' she said, stepping aside to let him enter. He did so, automatically glancing about him to see a small, elegant living room with contemporary furniture, modern paintings, a white-carpeted floor and a window that gave a stunning view of the Ile Saint-Louis and the broad sweep of the Seine. When he heard the door closing behind him, he turned back to face her. She looked thoughtfully at him, then nodded in the direction of a two-seater black leather settee. 'Take a seat,' she said. Brolin sat on the settee. 'Would you like a drink?' she asked him.

'Are you having one?'

'I had lunch with Feydal and Bannerman in the Ritz, including red wine, so now that I've kicked off my high heels and put on my casual clothes, I'm going to relax with an Armagnac. It's so nice to be wicked.'

'That'll do for me,' Brolin said.

He couldn't keep his eyes off her as she went to a glass-fronted cabinet located beside a large TV set and withdrew a bottle of Armagnac and two glasses. She placed them on the glass-topped table in front of him, then took the black leather armchair at the other side of it, directly facing him. He watched her pale, stem-like fingers as she poured the golden liquid into the two glasses, put the cap back on the bottle, then passed one of the glasses to him and picked up the other. He imagined those fingers working their magic on him and almost blushed – as he had blushed before in her presence – when he realized, with despair, what he was thinking. She leaned across the table, her eyes shining, and held her glass out to him.

'*Santé!*' she said softly, with a sly, perhaps slightly mocking smile.

'Cheers,' Brolin said. They touched glasses and took a sip of their respective drinks. Then Marie-Francoise sank back into her chair and crossed her legs which, in the skintight blue denims, looked long and curvaceous. 'So,' Brolin continued, discomfited by that slight, ambiguous smile and those gleaming green eyes, 'you had lunch with them and now you've something to tell me. What's going on?'

'The first meeting with Khadduri takes place this evening,' she told him.

'At nine o'clock?'

'*Oui.*'

'Do you think they'll come to an agreement right away?'

'I doubt it. My belief is that Khadduri, knowing that Bannerman has to return home at the weekend, will wait until the very last moment before striking a deal.'

'Which means I've got a bit of time left,' Brolin said.

'Correct,' Marie-Francoise said. 'A bit of time, but not too much. My suggestion is that you do what you have to do as quickly as possible.'

'Can you confirm the route they'll be taking?'

'No. But my bet is that they're going to take their usual route – the one we've already discussed – and if they take it this evening, it's the route they'll take *every* evening until they've reached a final agreement.'

'So I follow them this evening and assume, whatever route they take, that it's the same route they're going to take every evening this week.'

'Yes,' Marie-Francoise said. 'It's not guaranteed, but it's as good as you're going to get.'

'Thanks to you,' Brolin said.

Marie-Francoise smiled. It was a genuine, warm smile. Brolin could see no mockery in it this time and that made him feel good. '*Merci,*' Marie-Francoise said. She picked up her glass, had another sip of Armagnac, then put the glass down and lit a cigarette, blowing a thin stream of smoke from those pouting lips that mesmerized him all over again.

'Yes?' she said.

'Pardon?'

'You look like you're in some kind of a trance.'

'Sorry,' he said, hoping to hell that he wasn't blushing. 'I was just thinking about what I have to do. You've given me something to think about.'

'Have I?'

'Yes.'

'This job you're doing?'

'Yes.'

'And that's all you're thinking about?'

'Yes. Why do you ask?'

She shrugged. 'I just wondered, that's all. I mean, you're English and pale-skinned, but now, though you're not actually blushing, you seem a little bit flushed. I'm wondering why, I suppose.'

'Why do you think?' he asked.

Her smile was slight and disingenuous. She raised her left hand in the air and opened her fingers, drawing Brolin's gaze to them, almost as if she knew what he had been thinking and had decided to tease him. 'Oh,' she said, shrugging, 'I don't know. Flushed cheeks because of a racing heart, perhaps due to tension. You've good reason for that, *oui*?'

'*Oui*,' Brolin said.

'Because of the job, *oui*? Because of the danger. Even a man as professional as you must think of the danger.'

'Absolutely,' Brolin said.

'So,' Marie-Francoise said. She was smiling slightly, teasingly, drawing him to her like a mesmerist. 'You think of danger and you get a racing heart and it brings a flush to your cheeks. This is what it is, *oui*?'

'*Oui*,' Brolin said, wanting to reach out and grab her, to push her back into that armchair and lie on top of her, to bury himself in her, lose himself, and to hell with tomorrow. He really wanted her that much. 'If you say so. *Oui*.'

'No,' she said. 'I *don't* say so. Those flushed cheeks mean something else. I don't believe that a man like you has a racing heart because he thinks he's in danger.'

'No?' Brolin said.

'No,' Marie-Francoise said. Her smile was beautiful and cruel . . . or beautifully cruel. 'Danger is your profession, what you've lived with all your life, and almost certainly the only fear you've ever felt is the fear of boredom. Would that bring a flush to your cheeks? No, I don't think so. I think the flush in your cheeks – the flush caused by a racing heart – is due to something other than mere danger. I think it's something more personal.'

'Do you really?'

'*Oui*.'

'So what is it?' Brolin asked.

'It's me,' Marie-Francoise said.

Brolin knew that it was true, but it still came as a shock. That she had seen it and was willing to say it left him feeling defenceless. At the same time he was relieved, wanting her to know how he felt. And so, in a quiet delirium of relief and desire, though his racing heart accelerated, he stood up and walked around the glass-topped table to look down upon her. He felt unreal at that moment, divorced from himself. He did not seem to be the professional that he had taken pride in being. He only knew that, despite what he had come here for, what he wanted more than anything in the world was simply to *have* her. Knowing this – and knowing that she knew her men – he just stood there, gazing down upon her, waiting for her to make the first move and relieve him of guilt.

'Don't even think about it,' she said flatly, brutally. 'That's what I'm trying to tell you. What I'm doing, what I'm risking, is for my own freedom – freedom from Feydal and Bannerman – so I don't need you for anything other than what I hope you'll be doing. You now have all the information you need, so go out there and use it. *Au revoir et à bientôt.*'

Shocked and hurt so much that he shook with anguish, Brolin left the apartment.

CHAPTER TWELVE

Despite being shaken by Marie-Francoise's rejection of him, Brolin did not waste his time. First, he phoned Jean-Pierre at his home in Nation, asking if they could have an urgent meeting, any time, any place, so long as it took place that day. Clearly intrigued, Jean-Pierre said, 'Yes,' and they arranged to meet at ten that evening on the steps of the Opéra-Bastille.

Brolin had agreed to that because it gave him enough time to get to the Place Vendôme on his motorcycle, wait for Bannerman and Feydal to emerge and enter their chauffeur-driven Mercedes, accompanied by their body-guards, and then follow them all the way to Khadduri's apartment block in the Avenue Foch. They took exactly the same route that they had taken before – the route discussed by Brolin and Marie-Francoise – so Brolin had to assume, rightly or wrongly, that they would also take it the following night and stick to it every evening they had to meet.

He did not turn back immediately. Instead, after watching the silvery-grey Mercedes drive down into the private underground car park beneath the apartment block, he leaned his motorcycle against the black-painted iron railings of the public car park opposite the building and stood there for some time, studying the various windows and wondering just which apartment was Khadduri's. Even when he realized that he was wasting his time – that he had no way of deducing which apartment Khadduri lived in – he stood on, having time to kill and feeling slightly insane. Occasionally he glanced over his right shoulder to see the lights of the city illuminating the Arc de Triomphe, the flood of traffic around it, but mostly he kept his gaze focused on the apartment block directly in front of him, imagining Feydal and Bannerman behind one of those shaded windows, discussing their huge arms deal with Khadduri.

This was what he was here for – this was the task that he had been set – but instead, when he tried thinking of Feydal and Bannerman, he was haunted by visions of them fucking Marie-Francoise, first one, then the other, then both of them together, taking turns, playing games, as Marie-Francoise, not smiling, inscrutable, bent to their every whim. He imagined this, perhaps, because he kept thinking of all the places that the two men had visited together, particularly the late-night places – the discos and striptease clubs and gay bars and orgy warehouses – and couldn't stop himself from wondering just what, precisely, they had done in those places and, more importantly, why they had taken Marie-Francoise with them. He kept thinking, in short, about Feydal's hedonism and, even more, about the extent to which Bannerman, notoriously corrupt, was casting his evil shadow over Marie-Francoise.

Brolin pondered on all this as he looked up at the apartment block where Idris Khadduri lived, even though he knew that Marie-Francoise was not there at this time. He knew, too, that even if she had been she would not, because of Khadduri's strict Muslim view of her, have been doing any of the things that he, Brolin, was so vividly imagining.

It was the very *thought* of Feydal and Bannerman, he realized eventually, that made him imagine such things. Nevertheless, despite what she did or did not do with those bastards, he now wanted to help her escape from them. That need, which had become an obsession, was not what he had come here for.

You're here to kill that bastard Bannerman, he thought, *and that's* all *you're here for. If you kill the other one, Feydal, in the process, too bad. But stop thinking of the woman – she's not in this – and get on with the job. Stop being so fucking dumb.*

Thus resolved, getting a grip on himself, he got onto his motorcycle and drove back to the Bastille to meet Jean-Pierre. By the time he reached his destination, Jean-Pierre was waiting, as they had arranged, on the steps of the Bastille-Opéra, not looking remotely out of place in the hordes of young people, students and tourists, who were scattered around him. When he saw Brolin, he stood up, waved his right hand and grinned, then pointed to the restaurants facing the river.

'Let's take a table at one of those cafés,' he said. 'We can talk freely there.'

They did just that, taking a table in a crowded brasserie facing the Bastille-Opéra and feeling secure in their conversation because of the noise generated by the pop music wafting out of the loudspeakers. They felt safe in the noisy throng.

'So what will you have to drink?' Jean-Pierre asked, as his gaze took in the many attractive young ladies passing by.

'A beer would be fine,' Brolin said, also eyeing up the girls.

Jean-Pierre nodded, called for the waiter, ordered the beers, then caught Brolin's wandering eye and grinned. 'You like what you see, *oui?*'

'Yep,' Brolin said. 'I'm trying to keep my eyes off the jailbait, but it isn't that easy.'

'Too young for you by far,' Jean-Pierre said, his gaze roaming from the two big-breasted, long-legged and suntanned teenagers that Brolin had been looking at, both carrying backpacks and dressed in skintight T-shirts and shorts, to a couple of more mature ladies who were sitting at a table farther down, both wearing sensible, sophisticated clothes and sipping what looked like *kirs*. 'Those are more your own age group and style – and I'm sure you could charm them.'

'Not right now, I couldn't. Besides, I'm not looking for a permanent relationship; I just want some quick fun. In and out and away. It's been so long since I've been with a woman that I'm beginning to forget what it's like.'

Jean-Pierre chuckled. 'That bad?'

'Take my word for it,' Brolin said. 'I mean, you get more women in a week than I get in a lifetime, but right now I'm *famished.*'

'It's either work or pleasure,' Jean-Pierre said, 'and right now you're working.'

'Too true, Jean-Pierre. Right now I'm working and I'm glad because it's better than boredom.'

'You were bored in England?'

'It was getting that way. I could never find a job that

held my interest and I saw my life slipping away, day by boring day. In truth, I was drifting, just coasting along, trying to kill my boredom with drink and a succession of women, none of whom were taken too seriously. Trouble came to me easily.'

'Cigarettes and whisky and wild, wild women.'

'Exactly.'

'It was the break-up of your marriage that did it. That kicked the rocks out from under you.'

'It was the disbanding of the SAS that did it. That hurt more than the break-up.'

'The break-up came first and shook you up more than you knew. You missed the stability, having something to work for, something to come home to, and when it went, when you lost your wife and kids, you simply went adrift. Then, when the Regiment was disbanded, you lost your bearings completely. That's why I'm pleased to know you're working again, irrespective of what kind of work it is. You're a man who has to keep busy.'

'Damned right,' Brolin said.

He looked up as the white-jacketed waiter returned to their table, placed a *pression* in front of each of them, slipped the bill under the ashtray, said, '*Voila!*' and then departed, weaving expertly between the other tables with the empty tray balanced on his right hand. Brolin held his beer up in the air and he and Jean-Pierre touched glasses.

'*Santé,*' Jean-Pierre said.

'Cheers.'

'So, my friend,' Jean-Pierre said when they had both sipped some beer, 'why the urgency? My wife hardly ever sees me and the one day I promise to be home is the day you call and say that I absolutely *must* meet you. This is serious, *oui?*'

'*Oui*,' Brolin said.

'So what can I do for you?'

'I need a car,' Brolin said.

'Cars are easy to obtain,' Jean-Pierre said, 'so you must need a special car. What kind do you want?'

'A heap,' Brolin said. 'Untraceable. Preferably out of a wrecking yard. A car that I don't have to buy legally and that can't be traced beyond its wrecking-yard documentation. You have access to Gendarmerie wrecking yards. Find me one of those vehicles.'

'Where will it be used?'

'Right here in Paris.'

'And once it's used, where will it be dumped?'

'In a street in some ghettoized *banlieue*.'

'Am I allowed to ask what it will be used for?'

'I'd rather not say.'

'I have to know what it's going to be used for. Otherwise I can't be involved.'

'An accident,' Brolin said.

'A traffic accident?'

'*Oui*.'

'No weapons involved?'

'No,' Brolin said.

Jean-Pierre nodded. 'OK. I could get you a car. But whatever you're involved in, my friend – and you don't have to tell me – a car accident strikes me as the least precise way to go about it. Car accidents are not that easy to pull off and you, having been in the SAS, know that as well as I do.'

'Yes, I do,' Brolin admitted. 'I'm not keen on the idea myself. But my brief doesn't allow for anything else.'

'Why not?' Jean-Pierre asked.

'I can't use a weapon. It can't seem like an assassin-ation. For reasons I can't explain, it *has* to look like an accident. Now, will you help me or not?'

'No,' Jean-Pierre said. He glanced around the Bastille, at the swarms of people, the lights of the backed-up traffic and of the funfair near the river, then said, holding up his index finger: 'One: any accident you arrange could lead to other accidents and cause mayhem on the road, with an awful lot of innocent people hurt.' He added his middle finger to his raised index finger. 'Two: even if you decide to ignore the possibility of a bloody pile-up, with lots of innocent victims involved, your accident will not necessarily neutralize your chosen victim and could, indeed, leave him alive and in one piece while his driver, say, might be the one to die. So, no, my friend, despite what your orders are, you cannot attempt to arrange a traffic accident within any acceptable parameters – or, at least, within the kind of parameters that you, when you were in the SAS, would yourself have insisted upon.'

'Damn it,' Brolin said. '*Shit!*'

He felt frustrated and foolish because what Jean-Pierre had said was correct and he, Brolin, had, deep inside, known it all along. But he had suppressed that knowledge because of his awe for the people commissioning the job – the British Prime Minister, no less, through the Minister for Foreign Affairs – and also because of his personal hatred for William Clive Bannerman, the corrupt Commissioner for the Metropolitan Police who had led the fight to have the SAS disbanded. So Brolin now had to admit to himself that, despite his pride in his professionalism, he had let personal motives – in this case vanity and animosity – cloud his normally clear judgement.

Of course he couldn't arrange a traffic accident without endangering innocent people. *Of course* he couldn't guarantee that, even if he did so, his intended victim would be the one to die. In other circumstances – say, back with the SAS – his common sense would have told him all this. But these were not normal circumstances. Nevertheless, because of what Jean-Pierre had said Brolin felt like a fool.

'You're right,' he said eventually, with a sigh that escaped his lips before he could stop it. 'But, damn it, what else can I do? This hit can't be seen as an assassination. They were adamant about that.'

'You're talking about the British government, aren't you?' Jean-Pierre said.

'Yes,' Brolin confessed.

'And the target is Feydal Hussein?'

'No. The target is William Clive Bannerman, the Commissioner for the Metropolitan Police in London. Bannerman's become a threat to the British government and they want him out of the way. He's arranging a big arms deal with Feydal and they want to stop that as well. So Bannerman has to go.'

Jean-Pierre nodded, calmly taking this in. As a member of the GIGN, he had occasionally been called upon to perform the same kind of task, so Brolin's task neither shocked nor surprised him.

'So,' he said. 'It's not so much that the hit can't be seen as an assassination as that it mustn't be traced back to the British government.'

'Right,' Brolin said.

Jean-Pierre grinned and raised his hands in the air, fingers outspread. 'Why worry?' he said.

'Pardon?'

Jean-Pierre lowered his hands again and leaned towards Brolin. 'This is France,' he said. 'It's well known here in France that Feydal deals in arms often purchased and transported illegally, usually through Marseille or Algiers. He's widely hated, in particular – and this too is certainly well known here – by the French-Algerian underworld, which views him as a renegade, and there are many who would like to assassinate him.'

'Meaning?' Brolin asked.

'Very simple,' Jean-Pierre said. 'We neutralize Feydal and Bannerman at the same time, then anonymously contact the media to claim responsibility for the assassination, saying we're members of the Algerian underworld and that Feydal was invading our territory. It will then seem like a straight-forward gangster assassination of Feydal with Bannerman just being an English VIP in the wrong place at the wrong time. Almost certainly, in such a case, no one will think that Bannerman was the primary target. He'll seem like a mere . . .' Jean-Pierre shrugged. '*Accident*?'

Excited, realizing the wisdom of what Jean-Pierre was saying and annoyed with himself for not having thought of it first, Brolin said, 'So what you're suggesting is that I don't have to even *try* to make it look like an accident. I just *shoot* the fuckers.'

'*Exactement*,' Jean-Pierre said. 'Shooting is the way the French-Algerian underworld would do it, so you can use a weapon without fear. Also, if you shoot only your chosen targets, those in the rear of the car, the driver will remain in control of his vehicle and not cause an accident. This is a clean way to do it.'

'Right,' Brolin said, putting it all together in his head and feeling more relieved with each word spoken. 'I still hit them while they're on their way by car to the Avenue Foch, but instead of causing a crash, I just shoot them.'

'*Oui*,' Jean-Pierre said. 'The only question is, how do you do it?'

'Are you willing to help me?'

'My boredom is presently being stretched to the limit of endurance so, yes, I'm more than willing – I'm keen. But how can I help, apart from locating a car for you?'

'Are you still a good driver?'

'Of course. The kind of training I got in the GIGN is never forgotten.'

'Will you drive the car for me while I sit in the rear with my handgun?'

'*Oui*,' Jean-Pierre said. 'But where do we do this?'

Brolin removed a notebook and ballpoint from his inside jacket pocket, then drew a rough diagram of the Place de l'Alma and the entrance to the tunnel that bypassed it. 'They'll be coming along here,' he said, tapping the drawing with the tip of his ballpoint, 'and slowing down to make a right turn into the Avenue Marceau. When they slow down, you'll pull up beside them, parallel to them, real close, thus preventing them from turning off, and stay there until I've emptied my weapon. Once I stop firing, you accelerate and head up the Avenue Marceau to the Place Charles de Gaulle. From there you make your way out of Paris and go to the worst, most ghettoized *banlieue* you can think of. We dump the car there and make our way back to Paris by train. How does that sound?'

'*Parfait*,' Jean-Pierre said. 'I'll get you an unmarked car as soon as you need it. So when *do* you need it?'

'Not later than the day after tomorrow. Can that be arranged?'

'*Oui*,' Jean-Pierre said. 'I'll look for your car tomorrow morning and can guarantee to have one by the afternoon.'

'Terrific. Do that and we can strike tomorrow evening. The sooner, the better.'

'Right,' Jean-Pierre said. 'I'll call you as soon as I have the car, so make sure you're in your apartment when I call.'

'I'll stay in all afternoon.'

'Where shall I pick you up?'

'I don't want that car even to be seen in the Marais, so I suggest that you park it on a *payant* somewhere well away from our area of operations and just leave it there until we actually need it. Call me after you've parked it. You can give me the car's details over the phone and tell me where it's parked. We'll meet at the car at seven tomorrow evening and drive from wherever it's parked to the Place Vendôme. The rest starts from there.'

'Excellent,' Jean-Pierre said. 'Another *pression*?'

'Why not?'

When two more beers had been served, they touched glasses and drank, then Jean-Pierre said, perhaps to ease the tension, 'So what about Marie-Francoise? Have you been seeing her every day since I introduced you?'

'*Yes*,' Brolin said.

'And?'

'And what?'

'What do you think?'

'I think she's attractive, determined, highly intelligent and pretty sharp with her tongue.'

Jean-Pierre grinned. 'I thought you'd notice the sharp tongue. But do you *trust* her, my friend?'

'Yes. I think she fears and loathes Bannerman enough to want to get rid of him. She isn't well disposed to Feydal either, so she has no guilt there. She desperately wants her independence back and this is her way of getting it.'

'Do you like her?'

'What does that mean?'

'Do you find her attractive?'

'Yes.'

'Do you like her as a person?'

'I'm not sure. I can't think too clearly about that. I can't forget what she does for a living. I can't bear to think of her in bed with that fat pig Bannerman. She makes fun of me and that doesn't help me either. So, no, though I certainly find her attractive, I'm not sure that I like her.'

'She's been through a lot,' Jean-Pierre said. 'She's been shaped by experience, most of it bad. Given her background, given what she's been through, I'm amazed she's still civilized.'

'So am I,' Brolin said. 'She's civilized and she's dangerous.'

'To whom?' Jean-Pierre asked.

'To me,' Brolin said.

Jean-Pierre grinned again. 'You find her attractive *because* she's dangerous,' he said, 'and, as we both know, you like danger.'

'That's true enough,' Brolin said, 'though I don't think I'm attracted to Marie-Francoise just because she's dangerous. She's a hell of a good-looking woman and *most* men would find her attractive. Don't *you* find her attractive?'

'*Oui*,' Jean-Pierre confessed. 'Though I've never been romantically involved with her and now I don't want to be.'

'Why?'

Jean-Pierre shrugged. 'Maybe because we're friends and I want it to stay that way. Maybe because of my suspicion that under that hard veneer she's still hurting from what happened to her in the past. Maybe because of my belief that a woman like that, who sells her body for a living, could only let herself love the one man that she'd be willing to die for. Maybe because she's too *serious*.'

'You think she's too serious?'

'Yes. I couldn't be careless with that woman and then walk away. Maybe that's why I *stay* away.' Jean-Pierre shrugged again and raised his hands in the air in a gesture of defeat. 'But who knows, my friend?'

Brolin grinned. 'Not me, that's for sure.'

'Ah, well,' Jean-Pierre said with a broad grin, 'this job may be finished tomorrow night and then you'll go back to London and not see her again. That may be for the best.'

Brolin nodded. 'I reckon.' He took a sip of his beer, then checked his wristwatch. 'It's getting late,' he said. 'I think you should go back to your wife and make good that promise to spend at least this evening with her.'

Jean-Pierre grinned. 'A good idea, my friend. It's always best to keep the home fires burning, even if only now and then. A little warmth goes a long way.'

They both finished off their beers, stood up, shook hands, then went their separate ways. Jean-Pierre immediately went down into the Metro, obviously intending to take the train to Nation, where he lived, while Brolin, who had no wife to return to, walked at a leisurely pace all the way back to his empty apartment in the Marais. Once there, he went straight to bed.

CHAPTER THIRTEEN

Jean-Pierre called just before 1600 hours the following day to say that he had obtained a car for the job. It was a badly battered four-door Honda Accord, but its 1600cc engine was in perfect condition. Jean-Pierre gave Brolin the registration number and told him that the car was parked on a *payant* in the Rue de Paris, just off the Porte de Montreuil. They agreed to meet by the car at 1900 hours.

Brolin was there on time, but Jean-Pierre had beaten him to it and was already seated behind the steering wheel of the vehicle. He nodded to indicate that the rear doors were unlocked, so Brolin slipped in, taking up his position on the offside. Checking his wristwatch, he saw that it had just turned seven. It was dark outside.

'Everything OK?' Jean-Pierre asked.

'No problems,' Brolin replied. 'What about you?'

'No problems at all.'

'This heap runs OK?'

'It runs a lot better than it looks. The engine is sound.'

'Are the licence plates genuine?'

'No. I took them off another car bound for the pulping machine.'

'Good. You still want to do this?'

'Absolutely,' Jean-Pierre said. 'I haven't had as much fun in ages. This is better than sex.'

'Not quite,' Brolin said. 'All right, get going.'

Jean-Pierre switched on the ignition, put the car into gear, then pulled away from the kerb and headed for the Porte de Montreuil. Once there, he turned into the Boulevard Davout and from there made his way to the Bastille via Nation. The Bastille was packed with back-packers, general tourists and people going in and out of the brasseries and cafés. The traffic here was horrendous and Jean-Pierre had to shift down to second gear until he had made his way across to the other side of the Place and was travelling along the Rue Saint-Antoine.

Looking out through the rear window, Brolin saw the lights of the bars and restaurants and the street lights. The pavements were packed with pedestrians, including girls in tight short skirts that showed off their shapely legs. Brolin didn't know quite what it was with Parisian ladies that made them seem so attractive, but certainly they seemed so to him. It was not that they were prettier than they were elsewhere, in London, say, but they somehow managed, with a combination of sheer self-confidence and a flair for dressing individually (an artfully angled beret here, a beautifully knotted scarf there) to *seem* more good-looking than women else-where. Naturally, when he studied those good-looking, vibrant Parisian women, he thought immediately of

Marie-Francoise and had to forcibly put her out of his mind. He did so by leaning forward in his seat to speak to the back of Jean-Pierre's head.

'Don't go all the way along the Rue de Rivoli,' he said. 'Turn off instead at the Palais Royal and go along the Avenue de l'Opera. We can't park this heap in the Place Vendôme in full view of the Ritz security or even the Gendarmerie outside the Ministry of Justice, so turn into the Rue de la Paix and park in front of one of the shops just before reaching the Place itself. We'll wait for them there.'

'You won't be able to see the front of the hotel from there,' Jean-Pierre reminded him. 'We'll be on the right-hand side of the road, so your view will be obstructed by the shops.'

'No sweat,' Brolin said. 'You just park there, stay in the car, and I'll get out and mix with the tourists around the exit steps to the Rue Madeleine. The minute Feydal's Mercedes appears in front of the hotel, I'll return to the car and inform you. The Mercedes will depart by going along the front of the Ministry of Justice and then making a turn into the Rue Castiglioni. When the Mercedes comes into view, you can head straight across the Place and slip right in behind it. OK?'

'OK,' Jean-Pierre said.

He did as he was told and was soon driving along the Avenue de l'Opera which, with its abundance of airline companies and travel agents, looked not much different from certain parts of central London.

Gazing out at the surprising number of familiar names made Brolin imagine briefly that he was back in England. He automatically reached across his midriff to press his hand against the Browning 9mm High Power handgun that was holstered in the cross-draw position on his left hip. The weapon was already loaded with the safety catch on and he touched it just to reassure himself that it was still there. He withdrew his hand as the car turned into the Rue de la Paix.

Jean-Pierre pulled up to the kerb in front of a row of jewellers' shops, just before the short, elegant street opened out into the dramatically spacious Place Vendôme, dominated by the soaring memorial column of the Grande Armée. Darkness had fallen and the lanterns around the vast octagon were turned on, bathing the Place in a yellow light. As Jean-Pierre had stated, Brolin's view of the façade of the Hôtel Ritz was blocked by the far end of the row of shops.

'OK,' Brolin said, speaking to the back of Jean-Pierre's head. 'I'll get out and mingle with those gathered outside the hotel. When you see me heading back to the car, you'll know that the Mercedes has arrived and you can turn on the ignition.'

'Will do,' Jean-Pierre said.

Brolin clambered out of the Honda, closed the door behind him, checked that his holstered handgun was well hidden under his jacket, then made his way along to the Place Vendôme. As usual, a few paparazzi and a lot of tourists were milling about the exit to the Rue Madeleine, directly in front of the Ritz. Also as usual, a mixture of chauffeur-driven limousines and taxis were lined up along the north side of the octagon, preparing to pick up customers from the hotel. Brolin had deliberately brought his pocket-sized guide to Paris with him and he sat on the marble wall of the Rue Madeleine exit. Others were also seated there, hoping for someone famous to emerge from the hotel. Brolin pretended to be deeply engrossed in his reading while looking up frequently, like those around him, to survey the entrance to the hotel. Well-dressed people came and went with great frequency. Limousines and taxis pulled up and drove away repeatedly. The lamplit Place Vendôme looked as romantic as a vast movie set.

Checking his wristwatch, Brolin saw that it was nearly eight-thirty, which meant that Feydal and Bannerman, if they were coming out at all, would be emerging soon. And, indeed, about ten minutes later Feydal's silvery-grey Mercedes entered the Place Vendôme from the Rue Castiglioni and drove around to the front of the hotel via the narrow approach road.

Almost immediately, Feydal and Bannerman emerged, flanked by their two bodyguards. All the men were wearing suits and ties, though the massive Bannerman looked as if he was about to burst out of his. The chauffeur was already out of his seat and holding the rear door open for them as the four men approached the Mercedes. Feydal and Bannerman clambered into the back, followed by one of the bodyguards, as the fourth bodyguard went around the front of the vehicle to take the seat beside the chauffeur.

As the chauffeur was closing the door behind his passengers, Brolin eased himself off the marble wall of the Rue Madeleine exit and hurried back to the parked Honda. Jean-Pierre saw him coming and instantly turned on the ignition. Brolin had barely managed to clamber into the back seat when Jean-Pierre slipped the car into gear and moved off, heading straight across the Place Vendôme and catching up with the Mercedes just as it made a turn into the Rue Castiglioni.

As the Mercedes drove into the Rue de Rivoli with

Jean-Pierre right behind it, though keeping a reason-able distance, Brolin withdrew his Browning 9mm High Power handgun from its holster and placed it on his lap. The safety catch was still on.

The Mercedes moved in slow traffic past the Jeu de Paume museum and into the Place de la Concorde, magnificent in lamplight, its fountains floodlit, the pink syenite-granite obelisk of Luxor soaring seventy-five feet above the traffic swirling chaotically, noisily around it. Recalling that the Place de la Concorde was known as a test of nerve for any driver not used to it, Brolin was happy to let Jean-Pierre be the one to make his way around it while sticking close to the Mercedes up ahead. In fact, the pursuit of the Mercedes only made the circuit more dangerous, but Jean-Pierre managed it with the aplomb of a born Parisian and was soon following Feydal's car along the Cours de la Reine, the dual carriageway that ran parallel to the Seine, with Les Invalides floodlit and spectacular on the far side, the *Bateaux Mouches* going in both directions along the river covered with ribbons of sparkling lights, and the Eiffel Tower, a virtual pyramid of spotlights, soaring high in the distance.

The traffic along the dual carriageway was dense and moving fast, so the journey to the Place de l'Alma took no time at all. Indeed, within minutes of escaping the chaos of the Place de la Concorde, Brolin saw that they were racing along the Cours Albert-1, still right behind the Mercedes, on the approach to the notorious Alma tunnel.

'Get ready!' Jean-Pierre exclaimed.

At that very moment, as the Mercedes ahead was slowing down in preparation for its right-hand turn and as Jean-Pierre was pulling out into the offside lane to block it, and at the instant when Brolin was starting to roll the rear window down, another car, a Saab 9-5 Estate, suddenly pulled in right in front of the Honda, to be sandwiched between it and Feydal's Mercedes.

'*Merde!*' Jean-Pierre exclaimed.

'Shit!' Brolin added as he finished rolling the window down and felt the wind on his face, hearing it and the traffic as a sudden explosion of noise. He raised the handgun from his lap and released the safety catch. 'Damn it, go around him!' he told Jean-Pierre. 'Get in front of that bastard!'

'*Oui!*' Jean-Pierre responded. Then he wrenched on the steering wheel, using his horn and keeping it wailing as he swept back into the offside lane, squeezing danger-ously in between the cars already there, forcing one to accelerate and another to slow down, both angrily tooting their horns at him. Then he swept even farther out, going around the car in front, passing mere inches from it before burning into the turn-off lane just as Feydal's Mercedes was about to pull over to make its right-hand turn at the Place de l'Alma.

Jean-Pierre accelerated, gaining ground on Feydal's Mercedes. Then he pumped his foot brake, slowing down as he pulled up beside the Mercedes, blocking its entrance to the turn-off lane. He slowed down even more as the driver of the Mercedes looked out, his eyes wide and startled, before he started pulling back into the middle lane to avoid being struck by the advancing Honda.

Jean-Pierre moved up beside the slightly swerving Mercedes and then decelerated enough to keep parallel with it as it moved back into the middle lane, missing the turn-off to the Avenue Marceau.

The two cars stayed parallel and Brolin looked out of

the rear window to see Feydal and one of the bodyguards, both in the rear of the Mercedes, staring straight at him.

Bannerman was at the other side of Feydal, half shielded by him.

Brolin raised the Browning 9mm High Power handgun, holding it in the classic two-handed grip, one hand steadying the other, his wrists resting on the window frame, just as the Mercedes pulled violently away to the inside lane, forced down into the tunnel.

He saw the bodyguard aiming a pistol at him.

Realizing that Jean-Pierre had also missed their escape route, the right-hand turn into the Avenue Marceau, Brolin opened fire, using the Browning's double action to cock and release the hammer repeatedly with continuous pressure on the trigger, sending six of his thirteen bullets into the rear of the Mercedes. The side window exploded, shards of glass flying everywhere – but only after Feydal had disappeared from view, obviously dropping to the floor and taking Bannerman down with him, even as the Mercedes accelerated dramatically and raced away from the Honda.

At that moment, the siren of a police car wailed.

Cursing, Jean-Pierre floored his accelerator and also raced down into the tunnel, keeping to the middle lane and catching up with the Mercedes, still in the inside lane. The Gendarmerie squad car, which seemed to have appeared out of nowhere, came up behind the Honda, its siren still wailing dementedly and its rotating light flashing.

With nothing to lose, Brolin waited until the Honda was once more parallel to the Mercedes, its rear side windows now a mess of broken, jagged-edged glass, and fired another seven shots, aiming low even though he could actually see neither Feydal nor Bannerman, both of whom were obviously still on the floor of the vehicle or stretched out on the seat. Brolin, however, *did* see the bodyguard materializing above the lower frame of the window to aim his pistol at him again.

'*Go!*' Brolin bawled, throwing himself back on the seat, below the level of the window frame, as the bodyguard's shot shattered the window, showering him with pieces of broken glass. He covered his face with his arms, protecting himself from the flying shards, then felt the Honda surging forward as Jean-Pierre put his foot to the floor again, getting out of the line of fire and also trying to lose the Gendarmerie car that was coming up from behind.

'Fuck it!' Brolin exclaimed, talking only to himself, realizing that he had made a mess of it – or, rather, that one ignorant French driver, the owner of the Saab, had made a mess of it for him. Then he straightened up again, glancing out through the broken window and seeing nothing but the tunnel's concrete wall whipping past, a grey blur. But he could still hear the wailing siren right behind him. Glancing back over his shoulder, he saw that the Mercedes was slowing down, though still advancing through the tunnel, another Gendarmerie squad car just in front of it, obviously intending to force it to stop when it came out of the tunnel. The first squad car, the one still right behind the Honda, was racing to catch up.

'Oh, shit!' Brolin exclaimed. 'That squad car's still right on our tail! Lose the fucker. *Go anywhere!*'

The Honda emerged from the tunnel and Jean-Pierre worked the steering wheel, making the vehicle go left and right, from one lane to the next and then back again, weaving through the dense traffic along the Avenue de New York, the floodlit Trocadero looming up on one side, the Eiffel Tower on the other, across the glittering Seine.

Cursing softly to himself, Brolin holstered his empty handgun and then glanced back over his shoulder, through the rear window.

'That Gendarmerie car's still coming,' he told Jean-Pierre. 'Lose the fucker, for Christ's sake.'

'I will,' Jean-Pierre promised.

Brolin hardly knew where they were anymore. He knew that they were still travelling alongside the Seine, one *quai* after the other, in what appeared to be an endless stream of racing cars, interweaving dangerously, overtaking each other on both the left and the right – and he certainly recognized the Maison Radio France when they passed it and, beyond it, the bourgeois splendour of the sixteenth *arrondissement*, the lights of its apartment blocks illuminating the night – but after that he was lost.

Somewhere beyond the sixteenth, in an area that Brolin didn't know, with the Gendarmerie squad car still trying to catch them, its siren wailing relentlessly, Jean-Pierre bawled 'Hold on!' and then made an abrupt right turn. The tyres squealed in a near-skid, taking them away from the river and along a narrow street that had a sign forbidding cars to enter.

Brolin knew why when they entered it. The street was so narrow that the sides of the Honda scraped along its walls, grinding away the brick and cement, creating showers of sparks and a hellish drumming sound that, combined with the dramatic shuddering of the car, made Brolin's head tighten. First the wing mirrors went, snapping off and flying away, followed by a door handle, then Brolin heard the dreadful metallic shrieking of the rear door on his side and saw that it was being torn from its hinges, though it managed to stay in place. Nevertheless, when he glanced back through the rear window, he saw that the Gendarmerie car was still there, also creating clouds of boiling dust and spectacular fountains of sparks.

'Fuck!' he said. 'They're determined.'

'So am I,' Jean-Pierre replied.

As if to prove that he meant what he'd said, when the Honda escaped from the narrow street Jean-Pierre put it into another abrupt, dangerous, tyre-shrieking turn and then raced along a dark road hemmed in by warehouses and industrial sites. The Gendarmerie squad car was still behind him, now catching up fast on the straight stretch, its siren still wailing. But Jean-Pierre braked abruptly again, going into a screeching spin, and came to a shuddering halt, positioned broadside across the road. The police car, racing onward, veered suddenly to the left, avoiding a crash with the Honda but bouncing onto the pavement, practically leaping off the ground. Then it smashed into a warehouse wall in a clamour of breaking glass and shrieking, rattling metal.

Even as the police car was still being mangled – windshield and windows exploding, one door swinging open and dangling from bent hinges, the front bumper buckling in clouds of dust created by smashed brick and pulverized cement – Jean-Pierre was swinging the Honda into a U-turn and putting his foot down again to race away from the scene of devastation. The road he was on took him deeper into what appeared to be a neglected industrial zone, an unsightly mess of derelict warehouses, empty parking lots, high wire fences and moonlit alleyways that narrowed away into ominous pitch darkness.

'Where the fuck are we?' Brolin asked.

'On the outskirts of Paris,' Jean-Pierre replied. 'We're approaching one of the worst *banlieues* of the city and that's where we're going to dump the car. It's a dangerous area and we'll have to watch out for ourselves until we can get to the RER. We're coming into it right now.'

Glancing out the remaining side window, which was rattling noisily, as was the battered, loose door, Brolin saw that the industrial zone had given way to rows of run-down shops, bars, cafés, pool halls and grim apartment blocks. It was an ethnic area, mostly African, and gangs of unemployed youths and their girlfriends were crowding the pavements, some drinking from bottles, most of them smoking, and yet others openly selling what could only be drugs.

The *banlieues* had once been more racially mixed, harmoniously so. But in the past few years, with the gap between rich and poor increasing and with unemployment rising rapidly, the different races – native French and immigrant Algerians, Africans and Turkish – had gradually come into conflict, fighting each other for territory, with the winners invariably forcing the losers off their turf and the separate ethnic groups eventually becoming ghettoized. These new *banlieues*, effectively ghettos, were ruled mostly by criminal elements: the police, more indifferent than frightened, rarely ventured into them.

This area, as Brolin could clearly see, was just such a ghetto, which meant that it was dangerous to outsiders. Jean-Pierre, however, seemed to be familiar with it, drove confidently through it, and eventually braked to a halt in a dark and derelict side street. He turned the ignition off and applied the handbrake, then twisted sideways in his seat to address Brolin.

'We'll leave the car here,' he said. 'Wrecked though it is, it'll be stolen in no time and taken to pieces in some backstreet garage. Those separate pieces will then be widely distributed and used for the repair of other cars. Certainly *this* car is going to disappear and never be seen again, so you've nothing to fear on that score.'

'Good,' Brolin said. 'Are we near an RER?'

'Pretty close,' Jean-Pierre replied as he opened his door, preparing to clamber out. 'Come on, let's go.'

When Brolin opened *his* door, it practically fell off its hinges. 'Christ,' he said, 'what a ride!'

Jean-Pierre grinned but did not reply, merely pointing towards the end of the derelict street and then starting off in that direction. Brolin hurried to catch up with him and then fell in beside him. This particular street was dark and empty because the houses were boarded up, the walls of some still black from the fires that had once raged in them, probably during some bloody riot.

Brolin and Jean-Pierre had just reached the end of the street when four Africans, all wearing blue denims and bomber jackets, stepped out in front of them, one raising his right hand to forbid them advancing any farther.

'Where the fuck do you think you're going?' he said in French.

'To the RER,' Jean-Pierre replied, distracting the men long enough to let Brolin reach across his own body and rest his hand over the butt of his hidden, empty handgun.

'What the fuck are you two white shites doing walking

around here?' the same man asked, still speaking in French.

'Car broke down,' Jean-Pierre explained, 'and we're heading for the RER.'

'You ain't fucking heading anywhere, man, until you hand over your wallets and empty your pockets.'

'And then?' Jean-Pierre asked.

'Then we might or might not let you go. Depends on how my three friends feel.'

'Go to hell,' Jean-Pierre said. He started to step around the group, but two of them pulled switchblades from their jacket pockets and released the blades that made sharp clicking sounds as they popped out, glittering thinly and viciously in the moonlight.

'The only way you're going to get out of here,' the first man said, slurring slightly, possibly drugged, 'is when they *carry* you out.'

As Jean-Pierre took a step backward, his gazed fixed on the two glittering, threatening switchblades, Brolin spread his legs, rapidly withdrew his empty handgun, held it in the two-handed firing position, and aimed it at the four men, repeatedly moving the barrel back and forth, from one man to the next.

'One move from any of you,' he said, 'and I'll blow your fucking brains out. Now drop those knives, you two.'

'Fuck you,' the first man said.

Brolin released the safety catch, which also made a distinct clicking sound. 'Drop the knives,' he said, silently praying that both men would do so, since the Browning was empty.

'Oh, fuck, man,' one of the knifemen said. Then he raised his right hand and opened his fingers to let Brolin see his switchblade falling to the pavement.

'You, too,' Brolin said to the other knifer, keeping his gun moving to and fro, to cover all four muggers. 'Drop that fucking switchblade.'

'Right on, man,' the second knifer said. 'You got it, man. No way am I gonna fuck with no fucking gun.' Then he, too, raised his hand and opened his fingers to let his switchblade fall to the ground.

'*Voilà!*' Brolin exclaimed softly, keeping the handgun aimed at the four Africans. 'Now step out onto the road and start walking. Don't stop until you reach the end of the street and turn the corner. I'll be watching you every inch of the way. OK, fuckers, get going.'

The four men did as they were told, mesmerized by the barrel of Brolin's pistol as they moved sideways into the middle of the road, clearing the pavement. Then they hurried away in the direction that Brolin and Jean-Pierre had just come from, glancing frequently over their shoulders to confirm that Brolin was still aiming the pistol at them. When they had turned the corner at the end of the street and disappeared from view, Brolin put the safety catch back on, securing an empty magazine, then placed the handgun back in its holster, hidden under his jacket.

'Well, damn it, it worked,' he said.

'The bluff of the year,' Jean-Pierre responded. 'You should get an award.'

'OK, hotshot, let's go.'

Jean-Pierre needed no prompting. Nodding, he led Brolin out of the dark, derelict street into a busier, brighter main road filled with bars and cafés and shops of all kinds, though the shops were mostly closed and the pavements were not exactly crowded with people. However, those folk that Brolin and Jean-Pierre passed gave them startled looks: they rarely saw white people out here and didn't want to see them.

'Where the fuck's the RER?' Brolin asked.

'Don't worry,' Jean-Pierre replied. 'We're practically there.'

Which was true enough. They reached the RER station a couple of minutes later and descended hurriedly, gratefully, to the platform, which was empty except for a few pitiful derelicts taking comfort from bottles of cheap wine or cans of strong beer. Ten minutes later, the two unsuccessful assassins were both slumped in a carriage of the train that would take them back to central Paris.

'What a fuck-up!' Brolin exclaimed despairingly as the train moved off.

'You're in trouble,' Jean-Pierre said.

CHAPTER FOURTEEN

Jean-Pierre had been right. Brolin *was* in trouble. As he stood at the exact same spot where he had stood only a few weeks before, in the Outer Circle of Regent's Park, equidistant between Hanover Lodge and the Mosque, he accepted this bitter truth. He was not looking forward to his forthcoming meeting with Sir Archibald Wainwright. Though he had been 'rendered invisible' by those who had hired him – in other words, once he accepted the job he was supposed to have no further contact with them – his failure to neutralize Bannerman, combined with the knowledge that Bannerman was now back in London, had compelled him to break that imposed silence and get in touch with Wainwright.

Naturally, he had not phoned Wainwright at the Ministry of Foreign Affairs in Whitehall. Instead, he had sent an e-mail message to the recently opened Whitehall website. This website was ostensibly a public relations exercise: it was supposed to be a way for disgruntled members of the public to instantly air their views on any subject to do with government, with 'official' replies always guaranteed. It was, of course, a website used mainly by the deranged. The guaranteed replies, which were supposed to come from 'highly placed' government officials and were also posted by e-mail, were actually composed by lowly government-paid copywriters.

In a briefing before he'd left for Paris, Brolin had been told what he should do if things went seriously wrong during his mission. So on his return to London he had sent an e-mail from one 'John Bright', complaining about rising taxation. He gave a return e-mail address that was actually a disguised indicator for a government intelligence agency that monitored the Whitehall website and that would, upon seeing the sender's name and e-mail address, know that the coded message was intended for Wainwright and pass it on to him. This was exactly what happened and, approximately twenty-four hours later, Brolin accessed the Whitehall website to find an 'official' response to his complaint: a formal apology for the rise in taxation and an explanation, couched in suitably obscure, convincingly official jargon, for why it had to be so. Knowing from this that his message had been received, Brolin had then made a point of not leaving his apartment in Camden Town for the next twenty-four hours. Sure enough, he soon received the phone call he had been expecting. When he picked the phone up, he simply said, 'Yes?' and did not give his name.

'Is that John Bright?' an unfamiliar male voice asked.

'Yes, this is John Bright.'

'Can you meet at the same place in Regent's Park at two p.m. tomorrow?'

'I can.'

'Good,' the voice said flatly. Then the line went dead.

Now, standing where he had found Sir Archibald Wainwright waiting for him the last time, Brolin was feeling nervous and slightly unreal, hardly able to believe that he was back in London. Nor that he was hiding out from his old friends and that he couldn't sleep at nights, not even in his familiar flat in Camden Town, because he couldn't forget what had happened in Paris.

His couple of weeks in that city now seemed like a lifetime and he felt that his whole being, his whole *existence*, was saturated with Bannerman, Feydal and Jean-Pierre, but, most of all, absolutely, with the still almost palpable presence of Marie-Francoise Lebon. He hadn't seen her since the day before the botched assassination attempt and had left Paris the morning after that awful evening without speaking to her. This had been because Jean-Pierre had advised him not to, saying, 'Just get out, my friend, and let the dust settle. Get out and go back to your masters and hear what they have to say. You've committed to them and they won't let you out of that, so you have to discuss it.' Jean-Pierre had also reminded him that Feydal and Bannerman would be wondering who had attempted to kill them and, indeed, just which one of them had been the intended target. 'They're not fools and they'll look into this carefully,' Jean-Pierre had added, 'so it's best you get out of Paris for now without speaking to anyone.' Brolin had done just that, taking a Eurostar train early the next morning. And now here he was, back in London, waiting to speak with Sir Archibald Wainwright about unpleasant matters.

When he saw the familiar Rolls-Royce come into view

around the bend in the road, he automatically stiffened, took a deep breath, then tried to relax.

You're not a schoolboy waiting for the cane, he thought. *Get a grip on yourself.*

Nevertheless, as he watched the Rolls-Royce pull up to the kerb a good way along the road, and when he saw Wainwright emerge from it and start to walk in his direction, he felt distinctly uneasy. He had failed and he felt like a failure and the feeling was not good.

Even from this distance, Wainwright looked as distinguished as ever – the very picture of an English gentleman – but Brolin knew that this particular English gentleman could, even with his impeccable manners, be utterly ruthless. It was no surprise, therefore, that when Wainwright eventually reached Brolin, his lean face, under his thick thatch of silvery-white hair, revealed nothing of what he was thinking. He did not offer his hand. Instead, he merely nodded in the direction of Baker Street and began walking in that direction, compelling Brolin to fall in beside him.

'So,' Wainwright said after an uncomfortable silence, 'you wanted a meeting and now you've got it. I must assume that you're here to discuss your failure to neutralize Bannerman.'

Brolin was surprised to hear that. 'How did you know I failed?'

'We have friends in the Gendarmerie and they informed us about a failed assassination attempt against Feydal Hussein. They told us that Bannerman was in the vehicle at the same time, so we assumed that the gunman was you. It *was* you, I take it?'

'Yes,' Brolin confessed.

'It was supposed to look like an *accident*,' Wainwright responded tartly. 'That was part of our agreement. So how did you end up trying to shoot him – and Feydal Hussein as well?'

'I gave up on the idea of organizing a traffic accident when I realized that it couldn't be done without causing a real accident that could easily have included a lot of civilian casualties. The traffic in Paris is too dense and there was certainly no sign of Bannerman travelling outside the city during his stay there.'

'So you decided to try a double-tap.'

'Yes.'

'Without our permission.'

'Yes. I didn't think there was a choice.' Brolin recalled what Jean-Pierre had told him. 'Also, I thought that if Feydal Hussein was killed at the same time, it would be assumed that it was a gangland killing with Feydal as the main target and Bannerman an incidental casualty.'

Wainwright nodded. 'So what went wrong?' he asked.

'Frankly, I'm not sure. A combination of factors. First, at the last minute, just before we got our vehicle into a firing position, at a right-hand turn-off, when Feydal's vehicle would have been stationary, another car pulled in between us and forced me to change my plans. Instead of opening fire when Feydal's Mercedes was stationary, I had to do it when the car was speeding down into the Alma tunnel. Naturally, that wasn't as easy. Particularly since by that time the occupants of the Mercedes were aware of what I was up to.'

'They saw your face?'

'I would think so.'

'That may not mean too much. You're not a celebrity,

after all, so knowing what you look like won't necessarily help them to track you down.'

'I'm relieved,' Brolin said.

'So what happened next?'

'Well, my first shots certainly made a mess of the windows of the Mercedes, but just before I fired, Bannerman and Feydal dropped low, out of sight, either stretched out on the seat or on the floor. They did so because they knew something that I didn't know: that the Mercedes was armour-plated. So when I fired my second burst, aiming low, trying to hit Bannerman and Feydal where they were hiding, the bullets just ricocheted off the Mercedes's bodywork. Then, when I'd emptied my handgun completely, all thirteen rounds, their bodyguard straightened up again and returned my fire. At which point a couple of Gendarmerie squad cars raced down into the tunnel, one obviously intending either to stop – or to protect – Feydal's Mercedes, the other in pursuit of my Honda. So I got the hell out of there.'

'You lost the police car?'

'Yes.'

'Did you dispose of the Honda?'

'Yes. I left it in one of the worst *banlieues* of the city; one that the French police rarely enter. It's bound to be stolen, stripped down and sold off in pieces. In other words, it'll disappear.'

'That, at least, was sensible.'

'Thanks,' Brolin rejoindered with scarcely concealed sarcasm.

They had reached Clarence Terrace and Wainwright, ignoring Brolin's sarcasm, stopped to gaze silently, thoughtfully, along the road to where the Foreign Secretary, Clive Sinclair-Lewis, had been assassinated a few weeks back, almost certainly at the behest of Bannerman. Still not speaking, Wainwright started forward again, leading Brolin across the road, weaving through the backed-up traffic to reach Cornwall Terrace and continue on around the Outer Circle. When Brolin glanced back over his shoulder, he saw that Wainwright's Rolls-Royce was following behind them, though keeping a discreet distance away as usual. Brolin looked to the front again.

'So what now?' he asked.

Wainwright sighed audibly. 'Clearly you have to go back to Paris,' he said, 'and finish the job.'

'Bannerman's back here in London,' Brolin retorted. 'I can do the job right here.'

'No, you can't,' Wainwright told him, sounding adamant. 'I repeat: he cannot be killed on British soil and, wherever he *is* killed, I insist that it must look like an accident.'

'What am I supposed to do? Poison him?'

This time, Wainwright took note of Brolin's sarcasm and acknowledged it with a thin smile. 'Why not?' he said. 'From what I've heard, our Police Commissioner enjoys his food and eats an awful lot of it. A little poison might go a long way, so why not consider it?'

'It's not my style,' Brolin said. 'Neither are traffic accidents. I still say that I have to use a weapon, some way or the other.'

'And I still maintain that, if you *do* use a weapon, there's a real risk that it won't seem like an accident.'

'That shooting in Paris,' Brolin said, 'like I told you before, if it had succeeded it would have seemed like an accidental killing of Bannerman.'

'I'd be grateful if you'd tell me why you think that would have been so.'

'A French friend was going to phone the press, pretending to be a member of a criminal gang in Marseille taking credit on behalf of his mob for the killing of Feydal. He was going to state that the execution had been ordered because Feydal was stepping on too many toes in the Marseille underworld. Given Feydal's reputation, such a statement would have seemed perfectly credible and the death of Bannerman would have seemed like an accident – just the wrong man in the wrong place at the wrong time. So, if I try for Bannerman again, using a weapon, or weapons, *with* your permission, I'll try to do it when he's with Feydal or someone like him – someone with genuine underworld enemies – who'll be widely viewed as the *intended* victim.'

Wainwright was silent, deep in thought, for some time. Then he nodded cautiously and said, 'It might work. It just *might* work. But it would still have to be done outside this country . . . Perhaps the next time Bannerman visits Feydal.'

'When will that be?' Brolin asked impatiently. 'We've no way of knowing.'

Wainwright ignored Brolin's rhetorical question. 'According to our copy of the Gendarmerie report on the attempted assassination at the Place de l'Alma, the shots were fired from the *rear* of the Honda.'

'Correct,' Brolin said, knowing what was coming and not wanting to hear it.

'Which suggests that you had someone driving it.'

'Also correct,' Brolin said.

'Can you tell me who it was?'

'No, sir, I can't.'

'Understood,' Wainwright said pragmatically. 'But can

you confirm that he doesn't belong to any official body in Paris?'

'I can confirm that,' Brolin said.

'Did he help you in any other way?'

'Quite a lot, actually. I couldn't have done it without him. He introduced me to Feydal's mistress, who's also Bannerman's whore when he's in Paris, and it was she who kept me informed of their movements. He also obtained the Honda for me – from a Gendarmerie wrecking yard and with a false registration plate – and it was he who suggested leaving it to be broken up and stolen in that particular crime-ridden *banlieue*.'

Wainwright stopped walking. They had reached a row of elegant Nash houses, located in the Cambridge Terrace and Gate area. The afternoon was grey and a light, chilly breeze was blowing Wainwright's silvery-white hair. His gaze was cold and perceptive. 'This woman is Feydal's mistress and is passed over to Bannerman as his whore when he goes to Paris?'

Brolin sighed. 'Yes.'

'Sounds rather unsavoury to me.'

'Do you mean the situation or the woman?'

'Both,' Wainwright said. 'Can such a woman be trusted?'

'Yes,' Brolin said. 'There's no question about it. Apart from the fact that my French friend, whose integrity can be trusted absolutely, strongly recommended her, she feels betrayed by Feydal, absolutely loathes Bannerman, and desperately wants to break free from them – so she certainly wasn't averse to helping me out.'

'Did she know you intended to try killing them?' Wainwright asked.

'Yes, she did.'

'And she still went ahead and helped you?'

'Yes,' Brolin said.

Wainwright nodded. 'Then, indeed, she must be trustworthy and we can use her again.'

'Again?' Brolin asked, startled, wondering nervously what Wainwright had in mind.

'Why not?' Wainwright said. He started walking again in a leisurely manner, as if just out for a gentle stroll, and Brolin fell in beside him. 'Bannerman goes to Paris quite often,' Wainwright continued, 'for pleasure as well as work, and certainly, if he's made a deal with Feydal, he'll have to see him again. He can only do so in Paris, so you have to go back there.'

'I'm not sure . . .'

'If the woman helped you before,' Wainwright interjected, preventing Brolin from expressing his doubts, 'she'll do so again. So you have to return to Paris and renew your – ah – acquaintance with her.'

'*Why?*' Brolin asked desperately.

'With Bannerman now back in London, the woman will have reverted to being Feydal's mistress – God, what an arrangement; only a Frenchman would think it normal! – and she can spy for you just as she did before. Except that this time her task will be to tell you the instant she learns from Feydal that Bannerman is returning to Paris. When he returns, you can then dispatch him by any means at your disposal, so long as it looks as though his death was an accident – caused only by his unfortunate proximity to Feydal during an unexpected gangland execution.'

Wainwright seemed to have adopted effortlessly Brolin's and Jean-Pierre's strategy as his own.

Brolin didn't want to return to Paris. He didn't want to see Marie-Francoise again. He thought of her night and day, was unhealthily obsessed with her, and now wanted to get her out of his system. She had not, after all, returned his feelings for her and had, indeed, slyly, repeatedly mocked them. So his humiliation, each time he thought about her, grew even more complete. Nevertheless, despite her attitude towards him, he had other, less selfish reasons for not wanting to return to Paris and involve her again.

'I'm not sure that we should do that,' he said to Wainwright as they walked on around the Outer Circle, followed at a discreet distance by the Rolls-Royce with tinted glass windows. 'What that woman was doing for me was extremely dangerous for her and could be even more so now that Feydal knows that someone is out to kill either him, Bannerman or both of them. I don't want Feydal to start wondering how his potential assassins seem to know so much about his movements. I don't want him to suspect the woman. She'd be dead if he did.'

'Clearly that's a chance she's willing to take,' Wainwright said. 'The price she's willing to pay for her freedom. She wants rid of Bannerman and she also wants revenge on Feydal for the way he's abused her by practically *giving* her to Bannerman. She'll take her chances, I'm sure.'

'I'm not sure that I *want* her to take her chances. I'm not sure that I'd want her death on my conscience if anything goes wrong.'

'Why should it be on your conscience?' Wainwright said, his pragmatism now infuriating Brolin. 'The woman has her own reasons for volunteering and she's clearly aware of the risk she's taking. So you'd have no reason to have her on your conscience, no matter what happened to her.'

'I just don't feel right about it,' Brolin said stubbornly

while trying not to lose his temper or show his disgust. 'I mean, using a woman this way . . . It just doesn't . . .'

'Nonsense,' Wainwright interjected again, this time showing his own brand of finely controlled impatience. 'We're not using the woman. It's *Feydal* who's doing that in giving her to Bannerman each time the brute turns up in Paris. We're simply giving her the opportunity to break free and that's what she wants.'

'I suppose so,' Brolin said without conviction since, in fact, he deeply resented Wainwright's callous exploitation of Marie-Francoise's predicament.

'So you *will* go back to Paris?' Wainwright asked him.

'Do I have a choice?' Brolin replied.

'Not really,' Wainwright said. 'You have to finish the job you started and that's all there is to it.'

'So when do I go back?'

'More or less immediately. You can take a day or two off, if you require it, but make sure you're back in Gay Paree by the end of this week.'

'Right,' Brolin said.

Wainwright stopped walking, glanced over his shoulder to ascertain that the Rolls-Royce had also stopped, then turned back to face Brolin. 'This French friend of yours,' he said. 'Not the woman. I mean the man who introduced you to her and also obtained the Honda for you.'

'Yes?' Brolin said. 'What about him?'

'Can I take it that this is the same man who was going to make that phone call to the media, taking credit for Feydal's death – had it occurred, of course – in the name of a criminal gang in Marseille?'

'Yes, it's the same man.'

'This man is a friend of the mistress of a notorious

criminal, namely Feydal Hussein. He's able to obtain untraceable cars from Gendarmerie wrecking yards. He's willing and able to drive that car during an attempted assassination. He knows exactly where to dump the car to ensure that it's stolen, stripped down, sold off in pieces and eventually, to all intents and purposes, disappears off the face of the earth. He's sufficiently acquainted with the media to be able to suggest the kind of phone call you mentioned and also experienced enough to personally make the phone call for you. I'd say, then, that such a man is one who's had to have considerable experience in the overlapping areas of crime, military-styled executions and the spreading of disinformation. Is that true or not?'

'Yes, it's true,' Brolin said.

'Can you therefore confirm – and I mean confirm *absolutely* – that this man is not at the present time formally involved with any kind of group in any of those areas?'

'I can confirm that absolutely. I've already told you that he's not part of any official organization in Paris,' Brolin said.

Wainwright stared steadily at him for a moment, then nodded and said, 'All right, Mr Brolin, I'll accept that. This man is obviously valuable to you, so continue to use him. But do so, I beg you, with great care, no matter how much you presently trust him. It's not a question of trust, anyway. It's what might happen if Feydal or Bannerman eventually find a trail that leads back to him – perhaps through the woman, if at some point they suspect her, correctly, of being the leak and force her to talk. Do you understand what I'm saying?'

'Yes,' Brolin said.

'Good. Now, do you have any last-minute queries before you go back to Paris?'

'I don't have a query,' Brolin said, 'but I *do* have a concern that has some bearing on my original reluctance to return to Paris.'

'Spit it out,' Wainwright said.

'I'm worried about those two Gendarmerie squad cars – the ones that seemed to appear out of nowhere as we headed down into the Alma tunnel. I'd like to know if they were on our tail all the time. Because if they were, it would strongly suggest that Feydal was – and is – receiving Gendarmerie protection. If that's the case, I'll have problems.'

Wainwright actually smiled, though he radiated little humour. Then he shook his head gently from side to side. 'It's *not* the case,' he said. 'We've already checked with the Gendarmerie, following up on their initial report on the incident. In fact, those two squad cars just happened to be parked in the Place de l'Alma, right by the tunnel entrance, near the memorial to Princess Diana, when you fired your first shots. The crews of the two squad cars heard the gunshots, saw the windows of the Mercedes exploding, heard more gunshots, then naturally took off in pursuit. One of them followed the Mercedes out of the tunnel, then went in front of it and forced it to stop; the other, as you know, followed your Honda and subsequently lost you – through crashing, I believe.'

'Correct,' Brolin said.

Wainwright nodded. 'There the story ends. The Gendarmerie were not – and *are* not – protecting Feydal, so you have no need to worry on that count.'

'Fine,' Brolin said.

'Anything else?'

'I don't think so.'

Wainwright actually held out his hand and Brolin found himself shaking it. The older man had a strong, confident grip.

'Enjoy Paris,' Wainwright said. He turned away to go back to his Rolls-Royce, which had stopped when he stopped walking and was now parked at the other side of the road. But abruptly, as if on an afterthought, he turned back to Brolin.

'Feydal's mistress,' he said. 'Bannerman's whore. Since, clearly, she's no secret in Paris, will you tell me her name?'

'Marie-Francoise Lebon,' Brolin said, aware that indeed she would be no secret in Paris and that Wainwright could have easily found her name from another source.

Wainwright looked thoughtful, then shook his head from side to side, as if disappointed. 'No,' he said, 'I don't know her. I just wondered, that's all. Thank you. *Au revoir.*' He waved his right hand in the air in languid farewell, then returned to his waiting Rolls-Royce.

Brolin waited until Wainwright had entered the Rolls-Royce and been driven away, then he walked on to Camden Town to get drunk, methodically, quietly, alone, thinking painfully of Marie-Francoise throughout most of the evening.

The next day, without having seen a single London friend, he took the train back to Paris.

CHAPTER FIFTEEN

'It's all a matter of control, isn't it?' Marie-Francoise said as she stared at Brolin with her green feline eyes slightly unfocused because of the smack she had started taking at Feydal's behest. 'Men *like* to control. I've known that for as long as I can remember, way back to my childhood. I knew it every time my father came up the stairs, practically on tiptoes, breathing heavily, unnaturally, and my flesh crawled before he even entered my bedroom to take control of me. That's what it really meant to him. Domination. Control. He needed that to get hard. I'm pretty sure he was mostly soft with my mother and that's what always sent him up to me. Of course, she knew what was going on and she didn't like it, but she liked sharing his bed even less, so he got away with it. I was his to command.'

'I don't think I want to hear this,' Brolin said.

'Yes, you do,' Marie-Francoise said. 'You may not like yourself for being curious, but of course you *are* curious.

You want to learn all about me, to know me, in order to take control of me, so now I'm going to tell you. I feel the need to talk these days.'

'It's the smack,' Brolin said.

'Let me talk,' Marie-Francoise said.

Brolin let her talk. She'd been doing a lot of that recently. The first day she had come to see him, nearly a fortnight ago, shortly after his return to Paris, he had sensed something different in her, a new kind of intensity allied to a growing distraction in her once-steady gaze. Gradually, over the course of the next few days, as they had continued to meet, either in his apartment or in hers, though always during the day, he had come to realize that she was on drugs. When, finally, he had summoned up the courage to ask her about it, she had given him a smile like that of a Cheshire cat and nodded affirmatively.

'Yes,' she had said. 'Smack. It's Feydal's new thing. He's heavily into it himself and he wants me to share the experience with him. It must be true love, *oui*?'

The sarcasm covered pain, the lasting hurt of her growing years, and the smack seemed to be opening all the doors that she had closed in her wake, compelling her to pass through them again and wander along forgotten, tortuously winding, shadowed pathways. Yes, the smack had loosened her tongue and set her free to roam dangerous grounds, emotional minefields. So, when she had met Brolin during the past two weeks, she was always under the influence of heroin, drank white wine on top of it, chain-smoked cigarettes and talked quietly, constantly. She spread her life out before him.

'Control,' she now said to Brolin. 'Isn't that what it's all about? My father controlled me because I was too young to argue and my mother would pretend it wasn't happening because it kept him away from her. She was guilty, of course. She drank a lot to kill her shame. Yes, she knew what was going on in that room and she had to drink to forget it. Can you imagine it, Brolin? The fear and helplessness I felt? A mere child, lying alone there in the darkness of my bedroom, waiting for the creaking of the stairs, the soft pad of his footsteps, coming up the stairs without his shoes, always breathing too heavily. He felt guilty as well, you see. But not enough to make him stop. He was breathing heavily because his heart was racing with lust and shame intertwined. But he never stopped. He was too weak and too hard for that. He would come in and sit on the side of the bed and begin by patting me on the head and asking if his little girl loved her papa. And of course I said yes. And, in a way, I suppose I meant it. All little girls *need* to love their papas and be loved in return. Little girls want to please. So, naturally, I tried to please him. Touch me here, he would say, and of course I would do it. Trying to smile, though terrified. Knowing full well that this was just the beginning and that the worst was yet to come. "Papa won't hurt you," he always promised, but of course he did just that.' Here she nodded affirmatively, grimly, in pained recollection. 'Yes, Brolin, I went to my bed every night as if going to hell, though I finally learned to live with it. But later, when I was older, just turned fifteen, when my mother had left home, not even leaving a farewell note, when my father had begun to treat me as if I was a full-grown woman, the kind he secretly despised and needed to dominate, he suddenly stopped calling me his little girl and started to beat me. After a few months of that, black and blue, inside and out, having learnt that my mother had committed suicide, I realized that I had to get out of there before I went mad. So just as my mother had done before me, I secretly packed my bag and fled ... and I never returned.'

They were in Marie-Francoise's apartment with its great view of the Ile Saint-Louis and the broad sweep of the Seine, both bathed in that golden afternoon light peculiar to Paris. Brolin was sitting on the sofa, drinking a beer. Marie-Francoise was lounging on a cushion on the floor, smoking and drinking white wine. She was wearing blue jeans and a loose white sweater, but no shoes. She had delicate white feet and thin ankles. Her toenails were painted red.

'Can you imagine what it's like for a fifteen-year-old girl in the streets of one of Paris's most notorious *banlieues*? Luckily, I wasn't alone. There were plenty of others just like me, and some of them travelled in packs, forming their own all-girl gangs to make it easier to protect themselves from the male gangs who were surviving, more or less, the same way. Those girls were like wild animals, sleeping rough in abandoned buildings, living for smack or other drugs, mugging drunks and old people for money, putting out if that failed. A gang like that took me in, a gang of girls about my own age, and soon I too was mugging drunks and old people, though always in a group, joining the others when we beat our victims insensible with half-size baseball bats. We hunted and robbed and took drugs in packs, but when we had no other choice, when we put out for money – to be blunt, when we whored – we always did it individually, alone. And I was grateful for that – yes, God knows, I was – because no matter how much I tried to rationalize my behaviour, I was always ashamed of it.'

She wasn't looking out of the window, at the wonderful

view across the Seine, but was holding her head back, staring up at the ceiling, exhaling streams of cigarette smoke through her nostrils. She seemed very far away.

'Yes,' she said, 'ashamed. Because the tasks that we all performed in the darkness of those back alleys, invariably standing upright, surrounded by rubbish, the stench of urine in the air, were not tasks designed to make us feel romantic about life's possibilities. Imagine the men who preyed on us, the only kind who would want us, those so low in the social scale that they had to feel superior to *someone* and we helped them to do that. They deliberately came to find us because they knew we were young and desperate, in no position to mock them, to despise their pathetic needs, and many of them, the alcoholics and drug addicts, were psychotically dangerous. Oh, yes, some of us suffered. Some didn't survive it. Friends would go out some night to pick up a trick and when they didn't return by the next morning, we'd know it was bad news. They were always found quickly, in some back alley or other, battered black and blue, bloody, throats cut, maybe stabbed or strangled. Then the Gendarmerie would come in and take notes and mop up and swop cynical, sexist jokes, but that was *all* they ever did. The next evening, we'd be back on the game, mugging or whoring, doing to others what was being done to us, then returning to our sleeping bags on the floors of ruined buildings to kill our pain and self-disgust with drugs. You live like that, at that age, fatherless, motherless, day in and day out, and eventually you learn to look at life with a hard, unblinking gaze. During the three years I was with a girl gang I developed that gaze. Then, with my emotions packed in ice, I struck out on my own.'

'I don't think I want to hear this,' Brolin repeated.

'I think you do,' Marie-Francoise said. 'I think you want to know me. I think you want me, but you don't know how to read me, so I'm helping you out. Don't you think that's kind of me?'

'No,' Brolin said. 'I think it's the opposite.'

Marie-Francoise smiled as she stubbed her cigarette out, lit another immediately, inhaled and blew out a thin stream of smoke. Brolin thought she was sighing.

'I was eighteen by then and considered to be a beauty, despite the fact that my clothes were like rags and I hardly ever washed properly. I was still sleeping with the all-girl gang, usually in abandoned buildings, and my whoring in back alleys, though invariably performed upright – no dignity whatsoever, often degraded, frequently beaten – had, nevertheless, taken on a veneer of professionalism that, combined with my good looks, eventually brought me to the attention of what might be termed a better-class clientele. Once learning that my reputation was spreading beyond the dregs of the *banlieue*, to the kind of men who came to find me in fancy cars instead of on foot, who wore decent clothes and invited me to their rooms, sometimes in apartments *outside* the *banlieue*, driving me there and back again and paying me a lot more money, I started spending less time with the other girls and more time at my whoring. Not that it was much improved. Those clients also had strange tastes. I certainly needed a hard, unblinking gaze and it served me in good stead. But at least those men were reasonably safe – they weren't back-alley psychotics – and a lot of them became regular customers and looked after me well. So I saved my money, spending as little as possible, and eventually I was able to give up mugging, leave the all-girl gang, and rent my own room in one of the better areas of the *banlieue* – better only in the sense that it was marginally safer than other areas, though the room itself was a fleapit in a horrible building. Nevertheless, that room was my home and I felt independent. Of course, it didn't last long.'

Marie-Francoise sighed. It was definitely a sigh this time. She shook her head wearily from side to side, sighed again, then inhaled on her cigarette, pursed her lips, and blew a few languid smoke rings towards the ceiling. She waited until they had dispersed before continuing her sorry tale.

'Everyone wants to control you and that's what happened to me. Once I moved out of the back alleys to serve a better class of customer, I came to the attention of the local pimps. They kept coming to me, one after the other, all insisting that I work for them, that they'd give me protection, and I realized, of course, that if I kept on refusing, I would end up needing protecting from *them*. Finally, one of them did indeed become aggressive, threatening to cut me with his flick knife – to make me *not* fit to whore, as he put it – if I refused to let him be my pimp. They all wanted to *control* me – as most men do; as my father did – and so just as I'd run from my father, I ran from that pimp. One evening, I took a train out of the *banlieue* and I never returned. I became a free girl in Paris.'

She lowered her eyelids, inhaled on her cigarette again, blew a thin cloud of smoke towards the ceiling, then opened her eyes. She looked directly at Brolin, her gaze steady but distracted, and he knew that she was not really seeing him, but was, instead, focused inward. He was oddly hurt by that knowledge, as if he was being rejected by her, though this was, he knew, an illusion because he had never been accepted by her in the first place. She had kept a safe, slightly chilly distance between them and that had hurt even more. Now, as she continued her monologue, he writhed with longing and loss.

'I gained my freedom in Paris. At least temporarily. I was under no one's control – not my father's, not a pimp's – and I'd saved enough money from my whoring in the *banlieue* to rent a cheap room in a street just off the Bastille. It was an area good for tourists and I worked it throughout the summer, taking my tricks back to my room, only a few minutes' walk from the Bastille itself, which was where I nearly always picked them up. Being tourists, mostly English-speaking – and I had, at least, learned decent English in my *lycée* in the *banlieue* – they were, by my standards, relatively well off. So, by the end of the summer, being careful with my money, I had saved enough francs to buy myself decent clothes and had also learnt a lot by watching and listening. What I learnt, most of all, was how to dress better, how to behave in bars and restaurants and, of course, how to talk better English – I was always obsessed with that. I knew, you see, just what I wanted to do. So once I'd gained enough confidence and had the money to dress properly and operate in more sophisticated areas, I moved away from the Bastille, into a *chambre de bonne* – a former maid's room – in what is otherwise an expensive *bourgeois* area: Ranelagh, in the sixteenth. In other words, though I still had no private bathroom or toilet, I had a prestigious address and phone number, which was what I had wanted.'

She stopped talking momentarily and glanced about her apartment, this expensive pad in the Marais, and Brolin sensed that she was thinking of just how far she had come and wondering at the price she had paid to get here. Eventually, she let her gaze roam to the window, to the radiant blue sky above the Seine, casting its golden autumnal light on the grand buildings of the Ile Saint-Louis, but her eyes were still distracted, focused inward, not seeing the beauty out there. Brolin wondered how much smack she was taking on a day-to-day basis; how much it was already affecting her, maybe warping her senses. He wanted to kill Feydal for introducing her to it, but he was, in fact, here to kill Bannerman and he had to keep this in mind. Marie-Francoise had gone back to spying on Feydal for him, doing so even as she was taking Feydal's drugs, and Brolin knew that he should be grateful for this, despite everything else. Nevertheless, when Marie-Francoise continued talking, Brolin felt an inexorably building rage that made his insides burn.

'From that point on,' Marie-Francoise continued, speaking softly, in a monotone, as if in a trance, 'I made a point of only working in the better areas of the city – those areas where commerce and tourism meet. Eventually I concentrated on the Champs Elysées, Madeleine, L'Opera, the *grands boulevards* and, of course, the Rue du Faubourg Saint-Honoré. Naturally, in such areas I didn't walk the streets, but instead let myself be picked up in good bars and hotel lobbies where, with my new, superficial sophistication, I looked as if I belonged. Now, however, when I picked up a trick, I always insisted that he took me to his own place – his apartment or hotel room – and always, when we were finished, I would give him some of my business cards with that address and phone number in the sixteenth. Impressed by this, the client would often pass my cards to his friends and so my pool of wealthy, well-placed friends grew ever wider. Even better than this was that the clients I was finding were way beyond what I had known – Parisian businessmen and wealthy tourists staying in luxury hotels – and I certainly benefited from getting to know those hotels. Apart from that, however, those men really weren't much different from the others I'd had, having the usual broad range of sexual proclivities and the need to either control or be controlled. They did, nonetheless, offer me a doorway to the world I was after – the world of the wealthy – and they taught me everything I needed to know before I walked through it: what I should wear and where to buy it; how to order good food and choose the wine to go with it; how to make intelligent conversation with well-educated, powerful and wealthy men; how to walk and dance, how to gamble in casinos, and how to satisfy their every whim, no matter how perverse, in order to screw small fortunes out of them. Literally. Thus, within two years, I had moved out of the *chambre de bonne* and into my own apartment in the Avenue Emile Zola. A couple of years after that, I could afford to move again – this time into the Marais. I had finally made it and was still independent . . . but that didn't last either.'

'Feydal,' Brolin said, speaking at last.

'Yes,' she said, 'Feydal.'

She stubbed her cigarette out, grinding it into the ashtray with violent twists of her wrist, her lips pursed, her cheeks flushed. Then she had another sip of her white wine, which seemed to calm her down, and immediately lit another cigarette. She inhaled like someone taking her last breath (the sheer *luxury* of it), then continued speaking through an exhalation of smoke that obscured her face, briefly making her ghostlike.

'At first I avoided the Place Vendôme, being worried

about the police outside the Ministry of Justice, not to mention the eagle-eyed security men of the Hôtel Ritz. As for the Ritz itself, well, despite all that I'd undergone in the past few years, I still had my working-class inhibitions and was frightened to walk through the front doors in case someone stopped me. Eventually, however, I was introduced to a new client in a brasserie in the Rue de la Paix – he was a wealthy computer manufacturer from Silicon Valley in the US – and he took me straight to the Ritz, where he was staying. Before going to his room, we had drinks and dinner in the Ritz-Espadon restaurant – and then I visited him in the hotel most evenings for the rest of his stay there. He was there for a fortnight. In that time, we managed to sample most of the amenities, including the bars, the restaurants, the swimming pool, and by the time he left I'd become a familiar face to those who worked there and so felt at my ease in those surroundings. After that, I had no hang-ups about walking through the front doors to work the lobby and bars: eventually I felt like a permanent fixture. To the staff, I was just another wealthy lady, wining or dining on my own, blending in with the scenery. They didn't know I was working there.'

'Jean-Pierre knew you were working there,' Brolin reminded her.

She nodded assent. '*Oui*, he did. But only because he was doing hotel security for the Gendarmerie and, later, for that special branch that protects VIPs – I forget the name of it. The hotel staff didn't know what I was up to and nobody asked.'

'Why bother a beautiful lady who's just spending good money or encouraging wealthy customers to spend theirs?'

'*Exactement*,' Marie-Francoise said. 'So I was having the time of my life ... Then, of course, I met Feydal.'

'And your independence ended,' Brolin said.

'Yes,' Marie-Francoise agreed sadly. 'It all ended with Feydal.' She had been gazing out the window again, as if trying to recall her freedom. But then she blinked a few times, as if being jerked out of a reverie, and turned her head to gaze directly at Brolin, her green gaze perfectly steady and, for the first time in many days, seemingly clear and concentrated, not distracted at all. She was looking at him, as he had often seen her look before, with a kind of benevolent mockery. 'Ah, *oui*,' she said in a soft, lilting tone, as if she were singing. 'Feydal!'

'What does that mean?' Brolin asked.

'Why is it that every time we talk about Feydal, I have the feeling that you deeply resent him? Perhaps, dare I say it, even more than you resent William Bannerman, the man you've come here to kill? Tell me, Brolin, why *is* that?'

It was a simple, direct question, but Brolin almost recoiled from it, understanding, by its very nature, that she had sensed just how desperately he wanted her and was, perhaps, trying to make him admit it. He wouldn't do so, however, because he did not trust her that way, having been mocked too often by her and, indeed, having been put in his place when he'd nearly admitted that he wanted her. So now he just drank his beer, wiped his wet lips with the back of his hand, smiled as if this was all a big joke, and then said, 'I'm here to get Bannerman – and Feydal, as you know, is my point of reference. If I sound like I resent him, it must be because I can't get to Bannerman without Feydal's unwitting help. So every time you mention Feydal, I think immediately of

Bannerman and feel frustrated because I know I can't touch him until he comes back to Paris – to see Feydal, of course. If you think my resentment is due to anything more than that, you're badly mistaken.'

Marie-Francoise smiled. 'Am I?'

'Yes,' Brolin said, 'you are.'

'I don't think so, my friend – my reticent English friend. What I think is that you can't stand the thought of me in bed with Feydal.'

'You share Bannerman's bed as well,' Brolin said brutally, 'so why should I resent only Feydal?'

He had deliberately said it to hurt her – just as she had hurt him – but she simply nodded, as if agreeing with him, then offered him an even broader smile. That smile, which should have warmed his heart, chilled him to the bone.

'The reason you resent Feydal more than Bannerman,' she said, sounding as if she was caressing him but actually quietly flaying him to the bone, 'is because Feydal had me first, he's the one who *controls* me, and every time Bannerman goes back to London, I return to Feydal's bed. It's that thought, more than Bannerman's occasional use of me, that you really can't stand.'

'Bullshit,' Brolin said, shocked by the sound of his own voice. 'That's absolute fucking nonsense.'

'You think so?'

'Yes, I think so.'

'What *I* think,' Marie-Francoise said, still speaking quietly, seductively, even though she was still mocking him, 'is that *you* want to have me, which means you want to *control* me, and though you are, in a way, already doing that—'

'How?'

'You have me spying on Feydal and reporting everything back to you—'

'Oh, great,' Brolin said sarcastically, but without much
conviction.

'And though you are, in a way, already controlling me,'
Marie-Francoise repeated, 'you imagine that once you've
put Feydal and Bannerman in their graves – through
the Feydal connection, of course – you can somehow
worm your way into my affections. Now isn't that true,
Monsieur Brolin?'

'Go fuck yourself,' Brolin said.

Marie-Francoise straightened her spine, still sitting
cross-legged on the big cushion, and looked at him with
histrionically widened eyes. 'Is that an answer to my
question?' she said. 'It sounds more like a statement.'

'It's anything you want it to be. Take it as you
want, lady.'

'*Lady*? I'm a *lady* at last? This must truly be love!'

'I'm getting out of here,' Brolin said. He finished
off his beer, put the bottle on the glass-topped table
that separated him from Marie-Francoise and stood up,
determined to take his leave. Then he succumbed to the
irresistible impulse to look down upon her. When he did,
he practically fell apart again and had to fight to contain
himself. 'Listen,' he said, trying to pull himself together.
'I've come here to do a job and you're part of that job
and if you don't want to do the fucking job then just beg
off and get out. Other than that, kindly treat me with
respect and stop feeding me all this sexist bullshit. I find
you attractive, yes – I'd be a liar to say otherwise – and
if I could get into your pants, as so many others have
done, I'd be more than delighted to do so. But I'm not
here for that. My personal feelings for you won't impinge

upon the job, so let's keep this whole thing on a working basis and we'll both be OK. You understand?'

'*Oui.*'

'OK. I'm going.' Brolin turned away from her and headed for the front door, but her voice, still soft, still seductive, still slightly mocking, pulled him back like a magnet.

'You want to know about Feydal, don't you? You want to know about him and me – and about me and Bannerman? Isn't that what you want?'

Brolin turned back to face her. 'Yes,' he confessed, despising himself. 'That's what I want.'

Marie-Francoise nodded towards the glass-topped table that had separated her from Brolin and upon which were resting her unfinished bottle of wine and some still, unopened beers.

'Sit down, Brolin' she said. 'Open another bottle of beer. You want to hear about me and Feydal and Bannerman? Well, all right, I'll tell you. Of course, it all starts with Feydal.'

Brolin opened another bottle of beer and sank back onto the sofa. Marie-Francoise, drinking white wine, smoking constantly, smiling secretly, told him everything that he had wanted to hear – and that he would certainly never want to hear again as long as he lived.

CHAPTER SIXTEEN

Feydal Hussein was different. He was out on his own there. Though born and bred on Earth – in Beaucheray, Algiers – of perfectly respectable wealthy Muslim parents, he was like someone who had come from outer space, blessed with unearthly, debased gifts.

Feydal had charm from the day he sprang to light. A beautiful baby, he smiled all the time and won the hearts of everyone who saw that smile. His parents had servants and the servants worshipped Feydal also; so by the time he went to school he already had the confidence of someone who had never been criticized and who had no idea of what it was like not to get what he wanted. Feydal *always* got what he wanted and, when he thought that he might not, he had the confidence to try anything that he thought would do the trick. Invariably, it worked. He rarely lacked for anything. And for that very reason, what he had was never enough: he always wanted more. Wanting more –

wanting the whole world in his hands – was as natural to him as breathing.

Thus, by the time he went to school he went in the belief that it was there solely for his benefit. When he learnt that it wasn't, that other pupils had equal claims, he took it upon himself to rectify that situation and place himself at the centre of this new world. In order to do so, he was willing to do absolutely anything that furthered his aim.

There were various ways of going about it, charm taking first place. Feydal could charm the birds off the trees: he knew it and used his power, concentrating on his teachers, having learnt quickly that his popularity with adults was the very thing that made him enemies among children his own age. He was good at school, of course, having the confidence of the spoilt. But when he sensed the resentment of the other pupils he understood, for the first time, that something more than charm might be required when loving adults were not there to protect him. Thus, believing absolutely that the world was his oyster, his confidence supreme, he went all out to win over the pupils who most deeply resented him.

He did so, in most cases, by playing on their vanity, giving them gifts, slyly corrupting them and, when that didn't succeed, by bullying them, instinctively under-standing that fear was easily induced and, once induced, hard to overcome. Indeed, he learnt at an early age, being gifted with animal cunning, that what most people feared unconsciously and therefore most deeply was the *thought* of fear itself: they would, if frightened enough, agree to anything to be rid of the fear and regain their dignity.

Thus, early on, the course of Feydal's life was set: he successfully charmed, cajoled, bribed, bullied and blackmailed his way through his schooldays, gathering other pupils around him, quietly pitting them against the pupils who still resented him, so learning to divide and rule, and making sure that he was always in control of anyone who remained within, or came into, his orbit. Those who wilfully stayed outside his sphere of influence were treated as enemies.

Though naturally bright, Feydal's brilliant academic record came about because he had the best pupils in his school (and, later, at the *lycée* and university) helping him, either willingly or reluctantly. Such was his charm that on many an occasion he was able to persuade certain teachers to take a lenient view of poor work and give him a higher grade than he deserved. When he failed to accomplish this, he cajoled or bribed fellow students into helping him with his homework or sneaking him answers to difficult questions during examinations. Few people, he learnt quickly, could refuse a decent bribe and for such purposes he often used money stolen from his own parents.

Blackmail was, however, even more efficient than bribery as it offered continuance without further cost (those blackmailed could be blackmailed again and again) and Feydal soon became particularly adept at it.

He had already begun blackmailing his fellow pupils at his *lycée* by encouraging them to steal purely 'for fun' from fellow pupils or local traders. Then, when they had done so, he would threaten to expose them if they tried to wriggle out of doing what he demanded of them. Later, at university, when he learnt all he needed to know about the singular power of sex (its unique ability to render the sane temporarily senseless and make the timid bold, the cowardly courageous), he blackmailed students, tutors and clerks alike (fellow Muslims beset by the temptations of modern times: the amoral post-Millennium age) into meeting his demands by first discovering, then threatening to expose to the still-rigorous religious authorities their sexual proclivities or clandestine affairs.

Feydal learnt about sex early, first starting in the *lycée* while not yet an adolescent, experimenting with girls in his class. Possessed of an unblinking, pragmatic curiosity, he lost his virginity when only thirteen and was, by fifteen, more sexually experienced than many adults. He used that experience, his sexual skills, not only for sensual pleasure but also as another tool of blackmail, first seducing, then threatening to expose the Muslim girls concerned when they displayed reluctance to accede to his more outrageous demands.

He was uncommonly astute, blessed with the instincts of the born predator, and this enabled him to look deep into the hearts of friends and enemies, young and old alike, then twist what it was they most desired until it suited his purposes. He was, in short, a born manipulator – and ruthless with it.

Shortly after turning sixteen, Feydal, then still at the University of Algiers, started spending most of his spare time in the various *quais* of the Bassin du Vieux Port and saw there great opportunities for making money. Gradually, over the months, he got to know a lot of the local youths, most of whom were ill-educated and unemployed, pulled a dozen of them together to form his own gang, then used them to mug unwary, often drunken, sailors and to buy or sell drugs.

Feydal loved the excitement of it and was thrilled to be in charge, giving orders and being obeyed. Even when caught by the police, which he was quite a few times, he could not give up his criminal activities. Eventually, however, he was arrested once too often, expelled from the university and eventually thrown out of his home by his deeply religious – and therefore shocked and humiliated – father. Feydal, who had little admiration for the piety of his parents, felt that he was making his escape, rather than being cast out.

Without fear or hesitation, he moved into a small house in the Kasbah, a rabbit warren of narrow, winding streets packed with traders of all kinds, dominated by its fortress and overlooking the gleaming white city, the mosques surrounded by southern European-style office buildings, and the ageless, unchanging blue sweep of the Mediterranean. Once there, Feydal proceeded to diversify and expand as a criminal entrepreneur, rapidly moving into the territory of the other criminal gangs by demanding protection money from local traders, taking a fat cut from the profits of the exporters of wine, vegetables, oranges, iron ore and phosphates, and eventually tightening his grip on the whole of the Bassin du Vieux Port (which he gazed down upon every day) by increasing his drug dealing and introducing organized prostitution, as distinct from the informal kind, to the rough, almost totally masculine, *quais*.

Violence came naturally to Feydal. While superficially witty and urbane, generally even-tempered, pragmatic rather than emotional – *disassociated*, as it were – he was fascinated by how thoroughly fear could change people and intrigued by how much the average person would endure in order to stay alive, despite the quality of the life they were living or *would* be living after Feydal, or his hard men, had finished with them.

From the day he had personally mugged a drunken

sailor, Feydal had known that violence could get results. From that point on, while still remaining dispassionate in his business dealings, he had used violence when he thought it necessary, though he usually let others do his dirty work. His personal high did not come from the violence, but from his dangerous lifestyle: from living with the knowledge that he could be captured or killed by the police ... any day ... any minute.

Feydal realized, then, that he only felt truly alive when he was risking something ... his life or his freedom. Danger gave him a charge.

Sex gave him a charge, too. Feydal had a low boredom threshold that made him restless in all areas of his life, including his sex life. Sexually experienced from a young age, he'd had a wide variety of women and was jaded beyond belief by the time he was twenty-five. By then, he had left Algiers for good, fleeing to Marseille when the Algerian police closed in on his criminal operations in the Kasbah and the dock area. In Marseille, when not busy creating the same kind of criminal business that he'd run in Algiers, he was experimenting sexually with a wide variety of women. Some of them were 'respectable' girls who were seduced by his wealth and charm; others were professional whores to whom he would, to their astonishment, teach tricks that even *they* hadn't imagined.

Indeed, Feydal's low boredom threshold, combined with his insatiable curiosity about the extent to which so-called 'normal' people would go for pleasure or survival, pushed him to the very limits of sexual experimentation (always heterosexual, apart from his fondness for voyeuristic sessions with lesbian couples) and, gradually, into erotic experiences heightened by marijuana, cocaine, speed and crack. While the professional whores were either already on such drugs or politely declined them, most of Feydal's more 'respectable' partners were new to them, often became addicted to them, and frequently ended up so desperate for them that they agreed to whore professionally for Feydal in return for a constant, guaranteed supply.

When Feydal saw what such women would do, or endure, for their drugs, his belief that human beings had no limits to their capacity for self-abasement was confirmed absolutely.

Murder also came naturally to Feydal. He had killed his first victim accidentally – by kicking him to death, instead of just insensible, during a midnight mugging in Algiers – but his first *deliberate* murder was the punishment shooting of one of his own men.

Feydal was then still only nineteen years old, operating out of the Kasbah and increasingly successful, but he found himself with a potential rebellion on his hands when his second-in-command, a bold but dim-witted seventeen-year old, decided that he wanted a bigger cut from the gang's criminal profits. When Feydal refused, the boy tried to turn the gang against him by filling their heads with greedy thoughts and in general making them discontent. Feydal solved the problem by calling a meeting in the abandoned cellar that they had been using for gang meetings. There he informed them that they had a 'traitor' in their midst before rapidly pulling a handgun out from under his shirt and blowing the young mutineer's brains out.

The look on the faces of the other youths in that cellar gave Feydal a real thrill and taught him, once and for all, just what real power was like. From that point on, he never relinquished or even shared his authority and never hesitated to kill when he felt that it was necessary. Power became everything to him; his sole reason for being.

After six years in Marseille, living in a mansion high in the hills above the bay, Feydal had to move on again, bribing his way out of a lengthy prison sentence even as the local police were rounding up his men and throwing them into cells to await trial. With the help of an influential friend, Feydal ended up in Alexandria, Egypt, ostensibly as an exporter of Egyptian furniture and importer of office supplies but actually using those businesses as fronts for his new, more lucrative interest in illegal arms dealing with weapons purchased in Libya and sold in Tunisia.

He soon had to move again: not because his arms dealing had got him into trouble, but because his social habits, including widely reported drug-fuelled 'orgies' in his large house in Khalid Pasha Street in Victoria, one of the most exclusive residential areas of Alexandria, outraged his wealthy, bourgeois neighbours and eventually led to scandalous stories in the press.

Most of the stories were true.

Wealthy by now even beyond his earlier wildest imaginings, his grubbier days of petty crime behind him and living almost entirely off the proceeds of his worldwide arms deals, Feydal moved to Paris. Here he purchased a mansion house in the rarefied Bois de Boulogne area, filled it with more beautiful women and drugs, and invited influential people, including politicians, to whom he gave a good time out of sight of the public eye. Then he asked them for favours that would help him with his business and threatened to make their activities public if they refused him. As few of them refused, Feydal was soon receiving more political support and being investigated less than any other arms dealer in France. His wealth grew proportionally.

Feydal tried the same thing in London but failed because of the closed nature of the British class system and, more crucially, because of that country's extraordinary laws of libel, which by and large protected the ruling classes. After moving into an apartment in Park Lane, where only the exceptionally wealthy could afford to live, he eased his way into the upper crust, with a particular emphasis on the politically well connected, and tried to repeat what he had done so successfully in Paris: inviting the powerful and influential to his hedonistic parties, where drugs were freely available, the meals and drink were served by naked waitresses (also available for other pleasures), and classy hookers, brought from Shepherd's Market and other 'high-class' pick-up areas, were seated as 'single' ladies between the male guests and were clearly there to tend to their every sexual whim. This time, however, whilst the powerful and influential initially attended Feydal's parties, when he then asked for favours and threatened to make their activities at his place public if they refused him, he was dropped like a hot brick. The media clammed up, and he suddenly found that the very same press, television and radio that he had hoped to use was accusing *him* of being responsible for the recent flood of illegal weapons into the most criminal areas of Britain. When Feydal then received visits from various members of MI5 and Scotland Yard, all asking awkward questions about his arms dealing, he swiftly sold his apartment in Park Lane and returned to Paris where, at least, he was reasonably well protected.

Eventually, however, in the year 2003, when even the

French were growing nervous about Feydal's increasing influence over their politicians, as well as being concerned about the number of prominent persons who had, reportedly, been assassinated on his orders, Feydal decided that it would be wise to move back to Marseille. Here his diversified range of criminal activities could be carried out with the minimum of official interference. Once there, living in a renovated villa overlooking the Mediterranean, he commuted regularly to Paris, staying always in a suite in the Hôtel Ritz, to hold meetings with the leaders of international terrorist groups, either to purchase weapons from them or to sell such items to them. When not thus engaged in the necessary conduct of his business, he would ever more desperately attempt to defeat his low boredom threshold by engaging in increasingly outrageous, even dangerous hedonistic activities.

By the year 2005, when Feydal was forty-five years old, though looking much younger despite his dissipation, the world of nation states had broken down into a chaotic shambles of ethnic, religious and tribal conflicts. Islamic fundamentalism had spread outward from the Near and Middle East to engulf Europe, the Mediterranean, the United States and virtually the whole of the developed world. The Middle East itself was still in turmoil, worse now than ever, and anti-Semitism was flourishing elsewhere. India had been torn apart by the increasingly frequent battles between Sikhs, Muslims and Hindus. African was fighting African, constantly, brutally, because of ethnic, tribal and linguistic differences. China was breaking down into social disorder, lawlessness, widespread political corruption and ever-growing organized crime. Bosnia, Serbia and Kosovo were still erupting in regular outbursts of bloody 'ethnic cleansing'. Russia, while being torn apart internally by a widespread, heavily armed *Mafiya*, was clandestinely backing the Serbs with smuggled military hardware for use in Kosovo in defiance of UN and NATO sanctions. Last, but by no means least, throughout the EU and the United States, extreme violence among every imaginable kind of self-styled 'minority' group, including Christian fundamentalists, Millennialists, doomsday cultists, radical blacks and even violent, often murderous feminists, homosexuals and animal liberationists, was on the rise. All of those countries, organizations and individuals needed the weapons that Feydal was all too willing to supply if the price was right. As desperation ensured that the price was always right, Feydal, when he first met Marie-Francoise, was already one of the richest men in the world.

He was also one of the most corrupt . . . and eternally bored.

By the time Feydal met Marie-Francoise, there was little that he hadn't experienced and could not have for the asking, so the only avenue left as an escape from his boredom was pushing his fellow humans as far as he could in order to find their breaking point. He did it with blackmail, with physical and mental torture, with engineering addiction to, followed by the withholding of, drugs; and, even more pleasurable than those manoeuvres, with the games that he could play with his many women, his attempts to *control* them, his need to humiliate them, to shame them, repeatedly, relentlessly, in order to see how much they could, or would, take before breaking. Invariably, when he found their breaking point (in other words, when they *manifestly broke*, succumbing to drug addiction, alcoholism, suicide) he lost interest instantly, falling back into his chronic boredom and indifference to life.

He was in such a mood, fighting his boredom with various drugs, when he first saw Marie-Francoise, dining outdoors, alone, in the splendid Ritz-Espadon restaurant during a fine summer's evening in Paris. Feydal couldn't resist her.

'You were so beautiful,' he told her later, 'so elegantly dressed, and so deliciously, irresistibly remote. What man *could* have resisted you?'

'A meek man,' she told him.

Feydal laughed. He had a genuine sense of humour, which was part of his charm, and he used it that first evening on Marie-Francoise, inviting her to join him at his table, saying that it wasn't proper for either of them to dine alone, particularly when sitting so close to each other. And, of course, she did join him, though she was not so charmed as he had imagined, soon informing him that she was on the game and expected considerable payment should they venture from the restaurant up to his suite. This knowledge amused Feydal, also, particularly because she was so beautiful, so truly *exceptionnelle*, and he gladly took her up to his suite and paid what she demanded. She was talented in bed, albeit still remote, and she gave him a great deal of satisfaction of the conventional kind. It was her remoteness, however, her air of distraction, a slight superiority, as if she was adrift in some sphere above that of mere mortals, that excited him even more than the sex, challenging him to break through somehow to her and destroy her defences. He wanted to break her down, make her dependent upon him, to control her, and he started hiring her on a regular basis for that very purpose.

'I'll hire you as long as I need to,' he had told her in his charmingly blunt way, 'and I'll keep you by paying you more per hour than all of your other clients put together. But some day you'll want me more than the money and that's the day I look forward to. Right now, you think you don't need *any* man, that you won't be controlled, but some day you're going to need me and *want* me to control you. I'll make sure of that, believe me. That's my challenge. That's what makes this so exciting. Every relationship has a winner and a loser and I don't like to lose.'

'Neither do I,' Marie-Francoise had responded. 'But as long as you pay me more than the others, I'll be willing to play your games. All men are boys at heart, aren't they?'

She had said it to sting him, make him angry, but again he was just amused and that became the bedrock of their relationship: his attempts to dominate her, both sexually and emotionally, even as she repeatedly mocked that aspiration. Marie-Francoise was convinced that she could beat him at his own game, retain her independence, avoid being *controlled*, but as Feydal knew – and as he bluntly informed her – women abused in childhood tended, despite themselves, to gravitate to abusive men. And women, like Marie-Francoise, who feared being controlled, often needed, deep down, to be controlled despite their fear of it.

For that reason, and despite Marie-Francoise's seeming self-containment, Feydal believed that once she had got used to him, when she had been reduced by him, seduced by his money, too much money to refuse, she would not be able to break free from him. When he told her so, she just chuckled sardonically . . . but she didn't deny it.

'He may be right,' she confessed softly to Brolin as they sat together in that expensive apartment overlooking the Seine, her drugged gaze unfocused. 'I think that's why he put me on to Bannerman: to see if I would swallow what revolted me if the price was right.'

'And, of course, you did,' Brolin said bitterly.

'Money talks,' Marie-Francoise said.

Then, because she knew that it would cause Brolin pain, she lit another cigarette and told him all about Bannerman.

CHAPTER SEVENTEEN

Feydal had charm, despite his ruthless, amoral nature. But Bannerman was darkness personified, a nightmare made flesh and bone. Massively proportioned, his chin sunk deep on his neck, broad, beefy shoulders seeming to frame his square block of a face (beetroot-red from good living, scarred by metallic splinters from a terrorist explosion, thick-lipped), humourless, his grey eyes as dead as stones beneath thinning, dark brown hair. He seemed more of an animal than a human being, inspiring fear just by breathing.

Bannerman had been in the Metropolitan Police for most of his life, starting by pounding the beat just like all the others, progressing to a squad car, making it to detective in the CID, then, just before the Millennium, transferring to the Special Branch. There he was tasked with forming a paramilitary police unit that would be used to combat the explosion of crime that was expected when the growing numbers of disenfranchised, many turning to religion for comfort and believing in the Second Coming, were forced to accept that the Messiah was not returning and, sorely disillusioned, would decide to take revenge on society.

This, in fact, was what happened. The possibility of a Second Coming in Millennium Year had been the hope of many of the deprived, offering the possibility of escape from their ever-growing poverty in a materialist world, from the hopelessness of their lives as social outcasts. Thus, when the year 2000 passed with no sign of a Second Coming, many of the disenfranchised, bitterly disillusioned and feeling more helpless than ever, turned in the opposite direction, from religion to crime – and this turned out to be a blessing for Bannerman.

Bannerman had joined the Metropolitan Police because he was moved by the impulse to exert control over others and the Force would enable him to do just that. The average man bowed to authority and Bannerman wanted to be feared, so entering the police force seemed a logical first step on the road that could lead him to a position of great authority. Also, Bannerman had seen from an early age that petty crime did not pay, by and large, and that the most successful criminals worked from the inside, from good positions in respectable professions: politics, commerce, banking and, of course, law enforcement. Indeed, as computerization took over most of society, including the financial institutions, the real crimes against society, the major scams, were computer thefts on a grand scale, insider stock-market dealing, money laundering, and an increasingly sophisticated international trade in drugs and armaments. 'Crude' crime, such as armed robbery, became the exclusive province of urban terrorists, warring ethnic 'tribes' and the growing numbers of the desperate terminally unemployed.

Bannerman had been born in Southwark, south London, and raised by hopelessly inadequate working-class parents, both of them heavily into drink, violent fighting, and so-called 'punishment' beatings of their only child. Bannerman's mother, Gladys, was the family's main support, working as a machine-stitcher in a nearby garment factory. She had to do this because her husband, Albert Bannerman, had been prematurely retired from London Transport on an inadequate disability pension after a traffic accident that had left him with pins in his smashed right hip, not to mention a great deal of bitterness that made him – and, as a consequence, his wife – drink even more. As a lot of their drinking was conducted in the worst of the local pubs, and as they frequently brought the denizens of those rough dens back to their terraced house for more drinking, Bannerman had mixed throughout his childhood and adolescence with a wide variety of petty criminals. Being physically handicapped and severely limited in what he could do, Albert Bannerman was inclined to romanticize his criminal friends. His son, William – called 'Bill' by all who knew him – was naturally inclined to view them the same way and did, indeed, have fantasies of becoming one of them when he grew up. In the event, during his early adolescence he let himself be used as a 'runner' by some of the gangs and once even took part in the robbery of a local Pakistani store. Eventually, however, it dawned on him that most of his father's friends were spending a lot of their time in prison and not living particularly well when outside, despite their burglaries, muggings and robbings of corner stores and post offices. Even worse, in his view, was that they were living that way, in that pitifully inadequate way, when the world was changing rapidly, when the *real* money was being made by men in 'respectable' vocations, including the police force. When the young Bannerman realized this, he saw the error of his ways and decided to get out while the going was good: before he was caught by the police and gained a criminal record. As a consequence, in 1980, when he was twenty-one, he joined the police force, determined to use it *not* for law and order but as a cover for *serious* illegal activities. It was a wise move on his part.

Bannerman had been abused so much by his alcoholic parents, had been so often exposed to criminals who viewed their activities as perfectly legitimate and repeatedly denounced the police as being more 'criminal' than they were, that he had nothing in his heart but contempt for the human race. He became obsessed with the need to do unto others what had been done to him. Many of the things that had been 'done' to him were, of course, imaginary, a compound of genuine recollections of parental abuse and fictitious abuses at the hands of their criminal friends. His view of the average human being was therefore jaundiced beyond cure and he was incapable of differentiating between a good human being and a bad one. Or, at least, if he recognized goodness in an individual, he viewed it as a weakness and only considered how it could be used to his advantage. He took that attitude with him into the police force and it stood him in good stead.

Over the next twenty years, as Bannerman advanced up the ladder, from the beat to the squad car, then CID and, finally, Special Branch, he moved adroitly between the criminal world and the police force, playing one against the other, making friends and enemies on both sides, bending the law when necessary, always using his growing authority to further his own ends and ruthlessly ruining the lives of any fellow policemen or detectives who tried to stand in his way. Bannerman did not, therefore, take to violence in any dramatic way, but rather drifted into it in the sense that violence was a natural part of his profession, used by criminals and police alike, with men dying on both sides in the line of business or duty. So it seemed natural to use that situation to get rid of those giving him trouble, whether they were criminals or fellow police officers. In fact, a lot of men died violently on Bannerman's instructions before he personally laid a hand on anyone.

'Once he started,' Feydal told Marie-Francoise during a lengthy conversation over a meal in his suite in the Ritz, 'he laid his hands on a lot of people and reportedly they all suffered dreadfully. Violence gave him a hard-on.'

Bannerman was a sexual animal produced by a brutal, claustrophobic upbringing in a two-up, two-down terraced house where his parents drank a lot, had violent fights, fucked each other in front of him and often administered vicious 'punishment' beatings to him, sometimes making him strip naked and then whipping him with soaked, knotted towels. The horror of all this convinced Bannerman that he had also been physically and, perhaps, even sexually abused by some of his parents' criminal friends, though certainly there was no evidence for either belief. Nevertheless, Bannerman saw his parents fucking, mixed it up with their violent fighting in his confused recollections, and eventually entered his adolescence with violence and sex fused in his mind.

He had his first fuck early, at fourteen years of age, in a dark alley with a girl the same age as himself. Though he didn't actually beat her up, he took her with some violence, clearly frightened her, and was excited even more by that knowledge than he was by the sex. From that moment on, he wanted sex all the time, was ruthless in pursuing it, had a lot of it, and was always most thrilled by it when he scared or humiliated his partner. He didn't beat up *all* of his women, but he bruised quite a few.

Bannerman didn't marry until he was twenty-eight, by which time his pride in his sexual prowess was enormous. He wanted a wife because, in the police force, unmarried men were sexually suspect in the eyes of their colleagues and, also, because he wanted an heir, preferably male, whom he could terrorize just as he, Bannerman, had been terrorized in childhood. The woman he chose to marry, Marion Kelly, was red-haired, voluptuous and sexually adventurous, but despite the hot, violent times they shared in bed for the next two years, they did not, to Bannerman's distress and humiliation, produce a child between them. Bannerman's humiliation was made all the more complete when he went for a medical check-up and learnt that it was he, not his wife, who was sterile. Thereafter, he could not have loathed her more.

Marion, on the other hand, being tough, cynical and self-sufficient, did little to regain his affections. Though far from being a prostitute, she had worked for years as a barmaid in a West End pub frequented by members of the Metropolitan Police, gradually drifted into their insular social world and had affairs with a good number of them. By the time she met Bannerman, she was looking to settle down and Bannerman, who was then with the Special Branch, seemed as good as she was likely to get. Thus, despite her reservations about his sexual proclivities, his need to dominate and humiliate, his reputation as a womanizer, Marion accepted his bluntly worded proposal.

'I need a wife and kids for appearance's sake,' he said, 'and you want a home and some security, so let's tie the knot.'

'Why not?' Marion responded. 'I'm sure I can handle you.'

She did, indeed, manage to handle him initially, enduring their loveless, uncomfortably rough sexual congress, tolerating the blows and slaps when he physically attacked her, closing her eyes to his contemptuously open affairs with other women, and keeping her mouth shut when he verbally humiliated her, particularly about their lack of a child after two years of marriage. Unfortunately for her, when it became clear that *he* was the one who was sterile, she could not resist getting her own back by reminding him of his 'failure as a man' at every available opportunity, both in private and, even worse, in front of mutual friends.

Eventually, after Bannerman had beaten her up once too often, Marion threatened him with divorce proceedings. Realizing that this could damage his chances for promotion within the Met, Bannerman actually contemplated having Marion murdered and making it seem like a road accident. Commonsense prevailed, however, and instead he suggested that they buy a much larger home in St John's Wood where they could lead separate lives while ostensibly still being married. On the additional promise of a greatly increased personal allowance, Marion agreed and soon they had moved into their new, much grander home. From that point on, Marion expertly played the role of good wife, always there by Bannerman's side when required, particularly at important social occasions, but quietly, ruthlessly leading her own life behind the scenes. She and Bannerman had separate holidays, separate love lives, separate finances, and neither criticized the other in public. They were two people using one another and they both did that well.

'I know a Special Branch detective who was fucking Marion,' Feydal informed Marie-Francoise while he was telling her various tales in his suite in the Ritz, 'and she told him all about her relationship with Bannerman. He said she told him that Bannerman could fuck anyone he wanted as long as he didn't fuck with her. Bannerman, of course, had the same attitude, so Marion stopped insulting him about the child they couldn't have. In return, Bannerman stopped beating her up and closed his eyes to her numerous affairs. Marion was, of course, expert at charming men who could be used and she certainly helped Bannerman socially, helping herself by pushing him up the ladder. It was a cold, pragmatic relationship and it worked well for both of them.'

The Millennium really made Bannerman. By the beginning of the year 2000, the gap between rich and poor had widened dramatically, unemployment was still rising with no hope of a cure, and the disenfranchised were turning more desperately for salvation to a wide variety of so-called 'millennialist' beliefs. Millennialist groups had therefore multiplied all over the country and their members were waiting breathlessly for salvation in the form of some great magical event: the Second Coming of Christ, Judgement Day, the return of the Mahdi, or extraterrestrial intervention in the affairs of mankind.

Thus, when Millennium Year passed without any such event, with no sign of a change, thousands of those millennialists, bitterly disappointed and now faced with the crude reality of their hopeless situation, turned to violent 'political' or criminal activities: urban terrorism, war between conflicting ethnic 'tribes', biological and chemical attacks; and, at a more down-to-earth level, armed robbery, mugging, burglary, kidnapping, ritualistic gang-rape and murder. In effect, the old moral laws of society started breaking down. Bannerman, as head of a heavily armed paramilitary police unit, was suddenly called upon to use it. He did so only to extend his own power base and strike terror into the hearts of all those who opposed him.

'I wanted the members of my paramilitary unit to be the most feared men in Britain,' he once told Feydal, who later recounted the story to Marie-Francoise, 'and the only way to make that happen was to ensure that no other paramilitary group could steal their thunder. The only unit that could possibly do that, back then, was 22 SAS. That's why I had to have that regiment disbanded, once and for all.'

Bannerman worked to that end for many a month, using bribery, blackmail and deceit against well-placed politicians and high-ranking military officers, many of whom had their own reasons for wanting the SAS disbanded. He also courted the media, informing them that because the SAS's overseas role was redundant in the modern world, the regiment was being used instead to combat urban crime, which it did not properly understand. It was, therefore, causing more ills than it cured and hampering the valiant efforts of the Metropolitan Police to deal properly with the situation. Eventually, losing the propaganda war created by Bannerman, 22 SAS was disbanded.

'That's one of the reasons I hate that bastard,' Brolin told Marie-Francoise as she smoked relentlessly and he drank beer in her apartment overlooking the Seine. 'I could kill him for that alone.'

'You're no better than he is,' Marie-Francoise replied. 'You're just the other side of the same coin. A reversed image, *oui*?'

'No,' Brolin said. 'I'm not like Feydal and I'm not like fucking Bannerman, so get off my case.'

'Your . . . *case*?'

'Never mind,' Brolin said.

'Let me tell you the rest of it,' Marie-Francoise softly insisted. 'Let me get to the end of it.'

'I can't stop you,' Brolin said.

With the SAS disbanded, Bannerman's paramilitary police unit was given a free rein and Bannerman used it to gallop to the finishing line and make himself unassailable. Within months of the disbandment of the SAS, Bannerman's paramilitary police unit had become the most notorious in Great Britain, not only for fighting urban terrorists and ethnic gangs but also for overtly smashing certain crime rings (those not making payments to Bannerman), covertly supporting other crime rings (those that were making payments to Bannerman), rounding up 'suspected insurgents' (Bannerman's most vocal critics) and (this was widely believed, though few would openly discuss it) assassinating powerful criminals, businessmen and politicians on behalf of those rivals who were willing pay for it. Thus, by the year 2005, Bannerman had become one of the most powerful and feared men in Great Britain.

'He is, of course, an animal,' Marie-Francoise informed Brolin, 'and that's why Feydal offered me to him when he first came to Paris. Feydal knew Bannerman – knew the pig for what he was – and he knew that *I* would loathe him. So this was his way of finding out just how much I would endure before refusing the money on offer. It was the kind of money you don't give up easily if you come from my background. I would have to swallow my own vomit to earn it and Feydal wanted to see if I would do that. Well, I did it. I had to. Because, apart from the money, by refusing to go with Bannerman as a professional whore I'd be revealing a weakness to Feydal and I didn't want to hand him that victory. So when Feydal said, "The sky is the limit with regard to the money," I said, "Give me the money." And so I came to know Bannerman.'

'I really *don't* want to hear this,' Brolin said.

'Yes, you do,' Marie-Francoise insisted. 'Now listen to this . . .'

Though the scandals of Feydal's private life had forced him to leave England, he had by that time made connections with influential people who were still willing to deal with him once he was safely back in Marseille or Paris. One of those was William Bannerman. While living in the apartment in Park Lane, Feydal had learnt of Bannerman's growing need for illegally purchased arms, particularly since he was, as strongly substantiated rumour had it, planning to solve his major crime problem in London by covertly linking up with the very people causing the problem, the Chinese Triads and the Russian *Mafiya*, and then becoming the link between them and those who could either help them or oppose them in England. In this way, Bannerman hoped to become *the* most powerful man in the country and one of the most feared men in the whole of the new heavily criminalized Europe. So Bannerman had talked to Feydal about purchasing arms and Feydal had invited him to Paris to discuss the matter further.

'This man coming to Paris,' Feydal had told Marie-Francoise, 'is something of an animal, but I really need to keep him feeling good. What will make him feel good is a woman who, no matter how seemingly sophisticated, will agree to his every sordid whim. For this I will pay you more than you can imagine. Are you willing to do it?'

'Just how bad is this animal?'

'A pig in a trough.'

'*Why* do you want me to do it?'

'Because to keep this pig happy, you'll have to swallow your own vomit and I want to see how long you'll do that before deciding that nothing is worth it.'

'You think I won't be able to take it, is that it?'

'Yes,' Feydal said, 'that's it.'

'I'll take your money, Feydal.'

Marie-Francoise met Bannerman. She heard him breathing before she saw him. He was breathing like a beast in its dark lair as he came through the door. It was the door of Feydal's suite, normally spacious and sunny. But when Bannerman walked in for the first time, the suite suddenly seemed like a stifling cave. Marie-Francoise would never forget it: the sheer size of the man, his brute features and massive frame, the stony gaze, the smile that cut like a whip, his shadow reaching out to envelop her, his head making an eclipse in the window to darken the light. She knew then, on the instant, just what Feydal had meant. She would have to swallow more than her own vomit to keep this brute happy. She would have to *endure*.

'I endured,' Marie Francoise said, still speaking to Brolin, still sitting cross-legged on the floor, oblivious to the beauties of the Seine as she exhaled cigarette smoke. 'I became his for the duration, lying beneath him – God, the weight! – sitting astride him – God, that sight! – and I soon learnt that offering the slightest smile was an invitation to trouble. The pig liked to play God, to have total autonomy, to hurt and humiliate and degrade without fear of redress. He didn't want to see a smile. What he wanted were tears. When I stopped smiling, but still offered no tears, he became more demanding. "Do it this way," he would say. "Take that," he would say. "If you weren't a natural whore," he would say, "you wouldn't be here right now." Of course, I never replied. I wouldn't give him that satisfaction. Instead, I would do whatever he demanded and make sure I did it well. That was my pride, you see. That I could *do* it without tears. And, ironically, the very fact that I could do it excited him even more. He hated women – that was certain – he thought *all* women were whores at heart – and because he couldn't live without his whores, he hated them even more. So I was his to be hated. I was his to humiliate. I was his to reduce to tears of despair, though he never got those from me. When he failed, when my compliance defeated him, he wanted me all the more.'

Feydal was part of it – he was paying her, after all – and when, with his animal instincts, his predator's intuition, he sensed that she was enduring and Bannerman's patience was wearing thin, her endurance his defeat, he would ease the pressure a little by coming between them, taking them on the town and royally entertaining

Bannerman with Marie-Francoise, not entertained at all, forced to tag along. There was rich food and good wine, there were casinos and discos, and always, given Bannerman's insatiable appetite for sex, the darker pits of the Parisian club circuit. Bannerman was a voyeur with esoteric tastes – the more degrading the act, the better he liked it – and Feydal knew this and guided him to the lower levels of hell, the dark rooms of the gay clubs and S&M parlours where they could look on as naked figures writhed together on steel-frame beds, dangled from leather thongs from bars fixed to the ceilings, were crucified on high crosses with chained wrists and ankles, to be penetrated front and rear, swallowed and gobbled, whipped and cut and burnt, their tormentors (their benefactors) wearing leather masks and chains, studded gloves and spiked boots, with the sobs and cries of pain, the unique bliss of the masochistic, drawing ecstatic sighs from some of the spectators and the discharge of come through frantic fingers.

Bannerman never sighed with ecstasy nor played with himself, but he enjoyed his voyeurism, especially since Marie-Francoise was with him, a prisoner at his side, an elegant lady in this den of filth, being boldly stared at by perverts, often groped by grubby hands, rubbed against (that heavy breathing in her ear), and subjected to many other gross indignities. Bannerman liked that most of all, the degradation of his high-class bitch, and when she still didn't break, when she refused to turn away, he made her take hold of the exposed penis of the gasping pervert by her side and bring him off as the couple they were watching also gasped to their climax. Marie-Francoise did it, betraying not a single emotion, just standing there in all her elegance, a living rebuke to the filth around her, methodically working on the swollen organ in her right hand until the pervert, startled and clearly disbelieving, gasped and shuddered and came, still standing upright. Job done, Marie-Francoise wiped her hand on a paper handkerchief and then threw it contemptuously on the ground at Bannerman's feet. Bannerman wanted to murder her.

'He *often* wanted to murder me,' Marie-Francoise told Brolin, 'but he never even hit me, not once, because part of the thrill for him, as it was and is for Feydal, was to see just how far he could push before I broke and refused. But I never refused. There was nothing I wouldn't do. And so Bannerman, though frustrated on the one hand, was, on the other, always kept on a high of excitement of the kind that he couldn't do without. I was his slave and his impossible dream simultaneously – and that kept him from killing me, though some day he might. Either him or Feydal, maybe both, because they are, though very different in their personalities, two sides of the same coin.'

'You think so?' Brolin asked, trying to keep his voice steady, not wanting to reveal just how shocked he felt.

'Oh, yes,' Marie-Francoise said, nodding vigorously, affirmatively, her eyes large and too bright. 'Feydal knew, when he looked at Bannerman, that he was seeing his reverse image, his dark reflection, and it wasn't something that he was ready to face. Deep down he knows that Bannerman is what he, Feydal Hussein, might become – and he can't bear the thought of that. In fact, he'd rather die, he told me, than end up as someone like Bannerman – someone that crude and animalistic. He'd rather die, he said, by the hands of that unknown assassin who had tried to kill either him or Bannerman, maybe both of them, when they were in their car at the approach to the Alma tunnel. "Better to die like that, cleanly and quickly," Feydal told me, "than to grow old and become like Bannerman."'

'I might oblige him,' Brolin said.

CHAPTER EIGHTEEN

Of course, Marie-Francoisc knew who the 'unknown' assassin at the Alma tunnel had been: Brolin, who was sitting directly in front of her right now, drinking beer from a can and trying to look calm, though in fact he was deeply shocked by what she had told him. Though hardly a puritan, Brolin had led a reasonably straightforward sexual life: losing his virginity at eighteen when drunk enough to have the courage; having the usual on-and-off relationships for a few years after that, none of them out of the ordinary; falling in love with and marrying a local girl, Jacquie Bradshaw; eventually being divorced by her, but only because of the strain caused by his SAS activities; and then becoming routinely promiscuous when once more a bachelor – all of it behaviour within the boundaries of 'normal' sexual conduct. He was shocked, therefore, not by Marie-Francoise's revelations of promiscuity (he had known from the beginning, after all, that she whored for a living) but by the sheer perversity of it, the sordid depths to which she had descended with Feydal and Bannerman. To Brolin, there was something masochistic about it, something dreadfully self-destructive, convincing him that she would come to a bad end if he did not somehow help her.

Yet how could he help her when he couldn't even reach her, when she held him at bay with mockery, playing slyly with his feelings, obviously aware of what he felt for her and merely amused by it? She viewed him as some kind of innocent child and he deeply resented it.

Nevertheless, he was not here to worry about Marie-Francoise, but to terminate Bannerman when he came back to Paris and to make sure that he did it right this time. Unfortunately, until Marie-Francoise told him that Bannerman was actually on his way back, there was little that Brolin could do except hope every day that the next of his daily meetings with her would produce that good news. So far, after two weeks, this had not happened and, until it did, he would continue to have these meetings with Marie-Francoise and feel deepening pain because of what she was telling him as the smack, which she now took daily with Feydal, gradually got to her. He was convinced that the smack was already an addiction that could turn Marie-Francoise inside out and do her permanent damage. His heart felt like it was breaking at the thought of it.

'So when did Feydal start taking smack?' Brolin asked, hoping to distract himself from thoughts of her and Bannerman, Beauty and the Beast, rooting about in a pit of mud.

'As long as I've known him,' Marie-Francoise replied. 'Though, of course, you'd never know to look at him. He's *very* controlled.'

'So why have *you* started to take it? Just because he asked you?'

'Because he said he'd pay me more if I took it. Because he wants to fuck when we're both under the influence.' She smiled. 'Does that thought make you jealous?'

'Maybe,' Brolin said, knowing damned well that it did, though it didn't hurt as much as the thought of her with that fat pig Bannerman. 'Except I think he's making you take that shit as a means of breaking down your resistance. Take enough and you *will* become dependent upon him – if you aren't already, of course.'

'You think I am, Brolin?'

'It sure sounds like it to me. There's not much that he demands that you don't do and now you're taking fucking smack at his request. You get addicted to that and he *will* be able to control you, simply by offering it or denying it, depending on what he wants from you. As you said, maybe that's what you really want – to be controlled – and taking the smack will make it easier for you. My stomach churns at the thought of it.'

Marie-Francoise smiled, pursed her lips, blew some smoke rings, then flicked the cigarette ash into an ashtray and stared out the window. The Ile Saint-Louis was bathed in a golden light that made it seem like a movie set. Marie-Francoise turned her gaze back on Brolin, smiling at him again.

'I think you're drunk, Brolin.'

'What if I am?'

'What's the difference between you being drunk and me taking smack?'

'Smack's a fucking drug – *that's* the difference – and it could do your head in.'

'And you hate the thought of me doing my head in? Is that why your stomach churns?'

'Right.'

'Wrong. Your stomach churns at the thought of me and Feydal fucking, with or without drugs.'

Brolin couldn't deny it, so he didn't bother trying. He just stared at her, drinking her in, forced to accept that he wanted her more desperately every day and was tormented by the thought of her in bed with Feydal *or* Bannerman. She was still sitting on a large cushion on the floor, wearing blue jeans and a loose white sweater, her ankles thin and graceful, her feet delicate, the toenails painted red. He wanted to kiss those feet and suck those toes, but he didn't dare move.

'Just how badly do you want me, Brolin?'

'A lot,' he admitted for the first time.

'Poor Brolin. How sad!' She uncoiled her legs, long and shapely in the skintight denims, then stubbed her cigarette out in the ashtray and stood upright. Raising her arms above her head, she stretched herself, rendering Brolin breathless, then she went to the window and looked out over the Ile Saint-Louis. Brolin twisted to the side to look up at her. She was framed by the window, silhouetted by the light, and every curve, every line of her body held him mesmerized.

'You're more like Feydal and Bannerman,' she said eventually, speaking over her shoulder, 'than you care to admit.'

'Am I?' Brolin responded rhetorically, not caring to hear this.

'Yes.'

'I don't think so.'

'*I* think so,' Marie-Francoise said. 'Didn't you once tell me that you drank too much in England and got into a lot of fist fights?'

'Yes,' Brolin admitted.

'And didn't you also have a violent fight with your last girlfriend just before you came to Paris?'

'Yes.' Brolin sighed. 'But I hardly think—'

'And you were in the SAS, weren't you?'

'I don't have to answer that.'

'All right, you *were* in the SAS. Isn't that regiment renowned for producing the best fighting men in the world?'

'I know what you're trying to imply, but—'

'Killing machines?' Marie-Francoise interjected.

'I think that description is pretty melodramatic.'

'Is it? So why are you here in Paris? You're here to assassinate William Bannerman – and if Feydal happens to be with Bannerman at the time, you'll kill him as well.'

'Correct,' Brolin said.

'So you *are* a killing machine.'

'I'm a former soldier doing a job.'

'And that job is killing human beings.' She turned back to face him and he saw that slight, dangerous smile in the middle of the striations of sunlight beaming in all around her. 'Wouldn't you say, Brolin, that despite your protestations to the contrary—'

'God, your English is so good,' he said sarcastically.

'That despite your protestations to the contrary,' she repeated, 'you're not much different from Feydal and Bannerman: you make your living from violence.'

'*Necessary* violence,' Brolin corrected her.

'A fine distinction,' Marie-Francoise said. 'The point is

that you make your living from killing, just like Feydal and Bannerman.'

'The point is that those bastards are into a lot of nasty shit, including drug dealing, organized prostitution, protection rackets and . . .'

'Paid assassinations?'

'Oh, fuck off,' Brolin said, annoyed and starting to rise to his feet until, with surprising speed, Marie-Francoise moved away from the window and pushed him back down onto the settee. '*Oui*,' she said, standing over him, looking down at him, 'paid assassinations. You may not deal in drugs or organized prostitution, but you're certainly here as a paid assassin. Now isn't that true?'

'*Oui*.' Brolin sighed again. 'Yes, that's true.'

'So wouldn't you say that you're not much different than they are?'

'No, I wouldn't say that. I'd say you're twisting things to suit your own ends. I'd say you're being fucking disingenuous to make a lousy comparison.'

'Wouldn't you agree that you're a violent man, just like they are? I mean, you joined the SAS and the only men who do that are men who like violence and danger. When you left the SAS and were deprived of all that, you started to get into fist fights. You also get into fights with your women—'

'Damn you,' Brolin spat back, feeling really angry now, 'I've never hit a woman in my life, so don't even suggest it.'

'But you get into fights with them, kicking doors and throwing things, which suggests that you're just suppressing the violence that you fully express elsewhere – through the SAS and so on.'

'That's psychological bullshit.'

'Is it, Brolin? Is that all it is?'

'Yes, that's all it is.'

Marie-Francoise smiled again, a slight, dangerous smile, still standing over him, looking down upon him, her breasts rising and falling. She spread her legs to prevent him rising from the couch and the blue jeans tightened on her crotch, across the flat belly, the broad hips. Looking at her, he hardened.

'I don't think so, Brolin. I think you're just like them. You're naturally violent and you make your living by killing and you lust after me. You *want* to kill them, don't you? It's not *just* a job now. You *want* to kill them because you're lusting after me but I'm shared between those two. That makes you burn, Brolin, makes your heart race, makes you sick, but there's not a damned thing you can do about it while those two are still alive. That's the truth of it, isn't it? They have me and you want me. You came here to kill Bannerman – it was just a job then – but now you hate them both because of me and you want them out of your way. Yes, you're just like them, Brolin – you'll kill for what you want – and nothing you say, nothing you do, will alter that fact. Even now, while you're looking at me, you want me – and I suspect you'd do anything to have me. You would, wouldn't you, Brolin?'

'No,' Brolin said, though it came out as a whisper, sounding as confused as he felt. In truth, he could hardly think. Her proximity was overwhelming. He was looking straight at her flat belly, the apex of her outspread legs, and when he tried to look away, raising his gaze, he saw her heaving breasts, her green gaze, the smile formed by her luscious lips. He was hard and he knew that she knew it and that only excited him more.

She placed her hand on his shoulder.

'I can see that you want me,' she said, 'and I can't let you suffer. Don't move, Brolin. Say nothing.'

She squeezed his shoulder, affectionately, like an old friend, then closed her legs and sank to her knees directly in front of him, now looking up at him. She smiled and then lowered her gaze to study his crotch.

'Yes,' she said, speaking softly, though not whispering, 'I can see that you want me. There's no denying it, Brolin.'

With a sigh, a slight smile, she reached out to his crotch, placed her hand over his hardness, pressed gently, then raised the hand and let her fingers curl down to unzip his fly. He watched her, mesmerized, scarcely believing that this was happening, and then felt the startling warmth of her fingers curling around him. Exposed, he was rigid, his senses draining down to there, and when she slid her lips over him, taking him into her mouth, he lost his senses completely and closed his eyes and groaned like a dying man. Her lips moved up and down, her tongue sliding along him, and he felt that he was sliding down her throat to her dark, secret centre. All his senses congealed there, became one, then one with her, as his own groaning reverberated through his head like the sounds of the dead come to haunt him.

Startled, even fearful, he opened his eyes again, glanced down and saw the back of her head, the black hair like a stain on his white flesh, her hands clasped on his belly. He placed his hand on her head, running his fingers through her hair, then pressed gently, wanting even more of her, and felt her responding. She sucked him up and devoured him.

'Ah, God!' he gasped, removing his hand from her head

in order to unbutton his shirt frantically and tug it off his body. Feeling his movement, she removed her lips from his cock, raised her eyes to glance up at him, smiled tightly, then lowered her eyes again. She unbuckled his belt, tugged his trousers down around his ankles, once more ran her tongue along his erection, then sank her teeth into his right thigh and sucked up the skin. He gasped and quivered, but otherwise did not move. Removing her lips, she unlaced his shoes, took off his shoes and socks, threw them carelessly over her right shoulder, then stood up in front of him. His breath sounded like the wind blowing through a canyon and his heart was a pounding hammer.

'What now?' she said.

As if stung by a whip, he jumped to his feet, stood naked before her, then pulled her, still fully dressed, into his arms and mashed his lips on hers. She opened her mouth to receive his tongue, letting his mouth have her tongue, and he felt his erection pushing between her legs as she rolled her belly against him. His hands were on her spine, on the soft wool of the loose jumper, but when she pressed her belly and bosom against him, he slid one hand under the jumper to massage her right breast. The breast was soft and warm. The nipple hardened against his palm. He squeezed and rubbed the breast and then pushed the jumper up to suck the hardened nipple into his mouth as he grabbed her rump with his free hand. He squeezed that as well, pressing her tighter to his belly, then moved his lips from one breast to the other, licking, sucking and groaning. She sighed, then groaned as well. They both groaned at the same time. His eyes were closed and he saw a light-flecked cosmos, the great spinning of galaxies. There was more moaning and groaning. His own harsh breathing was like a storm. He pushed her arms up and tugged the jumper over them and let the jumper fall to the floor. Her black hair was disarrayed, falling over her glazed green eyes, and she reached down to unbuckle her own belt and unzip her blue denims.

Brolin slapped her hands away. He unzipped the denims for her. Still breathing harshly, he dragged her denims down her legs as he dropped to his knees. Her bare feet were a wonder to him, the toenails painted red. She raised one foot, then the other, to let him pull the denims away and throw them over the cushion just behind her. He bent over to kiss her left foot, gripping her ankle to raise it, as he ran his free hand up the back of her leg and grasped the back of her knee. Straightening up, he pulled the knee towards him and gradually made the leg buckle. When she fell to her knees, directly in front of him, he kissed her belly and breasts, then placed his hands on her shoulders and pushed her back onto the large cushion, letting her spread her legs for him. They were both naked now, in primal hunger, and nothing could stop them.

As Brolin stretched out above her, about to lower himself onto her, she slid her right hand down between them and took hold of him to guide him inside her. He entered her with ease, slipping into heat and damp, and she raised her legs to let him penetrate more deeply, belly slapping on belly. She gasped. They both gasped. She curled her legs across his spine. Her fingernails dug into his shoulders as he rose and fell on her soft, warm body, his weight squeezing the breath out of her, releasing her, then coming back down upon her. There was heat and there was sweat, white skin slicked with sweat, and he saw that sweat glistening on her forehead, on her cheeks, on the pale, straining stem of her neck, trickling down to her breasts. He licked the sweat up, sucked the skin on her shoulders, moving in and out rhythmically, first taking his time about it, delaying his climax, then moving more urgently as he was overwhelmed by his own feelings, swept away by excitement. He lost himself at that point, melting down through his outer shell, dissolving into her and becoming one with her and knowing nothing except her. She cried out when she felt him coming, gripped him tighter with arms and legs, and he groaned and gasped incoherent words as the spasms whipped through him. He shuddered violently and came, feeling as if he was exploding, and she thrust upward, pressing tighter to him, as if to drain his life out of him. He came and came again, one spasm piled on the other, seeing spinning lights and darkness, the bottomless well of the self, feeling as if he had just lost himself and was fighting to get back to his own skin. He managed to do so, coming back down to Earth, collapsing upon the mattress of her soft, yielding body and gradually subsiding into stillness.

He lay there a long time, for what seemed like an eternity, letting his racing heart settle down, breathing normally once more. Eventually, when he felt that he could speak, he raised his cheek from her breast and whispered, 'Now I'm all yours.'

'God help me,' she said.

CHAPTER NINETEEN

The call came the following day. Brolin was lying flat on his back on his bed, fully dressed, hands clasped behind his head, just gazing at the ceiling and thinking relentlessly of what had happened between him and Marie-Francoise the previous day. In fact, when the telephone rang, it was Marie-Francoise calling. 'Meet me in half an hour at the Pont Louis-Philippe,' she said without preamble, sounding tense. 'At the bridge itself, directly across the road from the bar.'

'Can't I just come to your room?' Brolin asked without thinking, though he realized what he had been thinking, or hoping for, the instant the words popped out of his mouth.

'No,' Marie-Francoise responded abruptly, then she cut him off.

Slightly shocked at the businesslike tone of her voice, particularly after yesterday, but realizing that something important had obviously come up, Brolin switched off his cellular phone, rolled off the bed, put on his light windcheater jacket and left the apartment. Stepping out of the courtyard, into the narrow, bustling Rue des Rosiers, he checked his wristwatch and noted that it was 3.35 p.m. As he made his way from the Jewish quarter to the Rue Saint-Antoine, heading for the Seine, he thought, as he had been doing almost non-stop since yesterday, of what had occurred between him and Marie-Francoise, still not quite believing that it had actually happened at last. He had wanted her for so long, fantasized and dreamed about it; now, having actually experienced it and not found it wanting, he ached with the need to possess her again.

Not that 'possess' was quite the word for it, since Marie-Francoise had in fact instigated the lovemaking, controlled it every second (or so he recalled it), and then made it clear, when they had finished, that he, Brolin, still had no claims upon her. In fact, Brolin wasn't too sure if he *wanted* to stake a claim, wanted that kind of involvement; he only knew that he was thinking constantly about her, was sexually obsessed with her, but also had the kind of growing concern for her that suggested his true feelings ran deeper than mere sexual need. Brolin wasn't at all sure that a man his age could 'fall in love' but he certainly knew that what he felt for Marie-Francoise was more than routine lust. In fact, he felt that she had permeated his very flesh to become a part of him.

After crossing the traffic-laden Rue Saint-Antoine, he turned right and made his way along a packed pavement that led past patisseries, *boulangeries*, cafés and bistros, all with lengthy queues trailing out of them, reminding him in no uncertain terms of the Parisian's love of food and drink. Though it also reminded him that he had not eaten lunch, he did not feel remotely hungry, only excited and anxious, as he made his way along the Rue F. Miron. He was excited because the call from Marie-Francoise indicated that she must have heard something important; and he was anxious because of the terse, even unfriendly manner in which she had spoken to him on the phone.

Now, as he turned into the Rue Louis-Philippe, which led down to the Seine, Brolin found himself recalling Marie-Francoise's accusation that he was just the same as Bannerman and Feydal. She had, of course, been referring to his SAS activities, to the fact that he was here to neutralize Bannerman, and her comments, though offending him, had also compelled him to question the nature of the life he had led – and was, indeed, still living. 'Neutralization' was, in fact, a soft euphemism for assassination, for murder, and that was what Marie-Francoise had accused him of engaging in. She had made him think of himself, for the first time, as a professional killer; and though he was willing to accept the validity of the accusation, he was deeply upset that it had come from her lips. To be compared to Bannerman and Feydal was not easy to take.

As he came down to the Café Louis-Philippe, the sun broke through the clouds and cast its golden light on the seventeenth-century mansions of the Ile Saint-Louis that divided the broad sweep of the river. Marie-Francoise was standing at the far side of the road, by the bridge, directly facing the bar, looking casually elegant in blue denims, high-heeled boots, and an open-necked white blouse under a light grey jacket with wide lapels. Like many Parisian women, she had a long scarf knotted around her neck with one end trailing down her front and the other thrown back over her right shoulder. She was smoking a cigarette and patting down her windblown hair with her free hand.

When Brolin had crossed the road to join her, his impulse was to kiss her on both cheeks, but her grave demeanour soon put him off that idea. Instead, he just nodded and said, '*Bonjour*, Marie-Francoise.'

'Let's walk,' she responded curtly, throwing her smouldering cigarette to the ground and turning away from him. Brolin fell in beside her as she started across the bridge, heading for the tranquil river-island formerly favoured by Paris's affluent gentry, now a favourite with tourists.

'So what's up?' he asked, glancing down at the river as two packed *Bateaux-Mouches* passed each other, going in opposite directions, creating white, foaming wakes, as tourists waved from one boat to the other in the fading afternoon sunlight.

'Bannerman's coming back,' she told him.

'When?' Brolin asked, feeling a mixture of excitement and relief, wanting to put an end to it.

'The day after tomorrow.'

'Is he staying in the Ritz again?'

'Only for one night. He and Feydal are leaving for Marseille first thing the next morning.'

'Marseille? They're going to Feydal's place?'

'Yes. For a couple of weeks. They've come to some kind of arrangement with that arms dealer, Idris Khadduri, and he's back in Tripoli right now, making arrangements for the delivery.'

'The weapons will be shipped from Tripoli to Marseille?'

'*Oui*. Itemized as office supplies.'

'That doesn't sound like a good cover,' Brolin said.

'Khadduri always does it that way. He gets away with it because he has friends in all the right places in Tripoli: in the courts and in the police and in Customs. Feydal has similar friends in Marseille. So he and Bannerman are going to Marseille to receive the weapons. Once the weapons have arrived, Feydal and Bannerman between them will arrange for their illegal shipment to England. Then – and only then – will that fat pig Bannerman fly home.'

'That's a long time for Bannerman to be away from Scotland Yard,' Brolin noted.

'Bannerman *runs* Scotland Yard,' Marie-Francoise replied. 'At least, so he tells me. He can do what he wants there, he says, because they're terrified of him. As the politicians are also terrified of him, he receives few complaints.'

'That's true enough,' Brolin said.

Reaching the far side of the bridge, they turned left into the Quai de Bourbon and walked alongside the Seine, high above the river. Poplar trees soared up from the embankment below, their leafy branches spreading over the pavement. At the far side of the narrow *quai* were rows of grey and white stone houses with white-painted shutters and black-painted wrought-iron balconies. This was an elegant area.

'When are the weapons due to arrive in Marseille?' Brolin asked.

'About four weeks from now.'

'That's a long time for Bannerman to stay in Marseille. Why doesn't he stay in Paris, which he loves, and just go to Marseille a few days before the shipment arrives? Why's he leaving Paris so quickly?'

'He and Feydal are concerned about that recent assassination attempt. Your botched-up job.'

'Thanks a million,' Brolin said sarcastically.

Marie-Francoise smiled slightly. 'Sorry. Anyway, they're concerned that someone has tried to assassinate one of them, or both of them, here in Paris and might try to do so again, so they both agreed that it would be safer for them to spend the next few weeks in Feydal's heavily defended villa in Marseille.'

'Shit!' Brolin exclaimed softly. He and Marie-Francoise, still walking side by side, had crossed to the Quai d'Anjou and were passing the opulently ornamental façade of the Hôtel Lauzun, built in the 1650s and once frequented by the decadent poet Charles Baudelaire. Just beyond the hotel, at the Pont Sully, they turned along the Rue Saint-Louis-en-l'Ile, this time passing the Hôtel Lambert where Voltaire had once had a tempestuous affair with the Marquise du Châtelet. Even *thinking* about a passionate affair, *any* affair, made Brolin feel queasy, first recollecting his one afternoon of passion with Marie-Francoise, then masochistically imagining her having sex with William Bannerman, either under or astride his gross body. His stomach churned at the thought of it. 'What's their general feeling about the assassination?' he asked, trying desperately to fill his head with something other than those tormenting erotic images.

'They haven't a clue,' Marie-Francoise replied. 'They don't know if the person who fired at them intended to kill Feydal, Bannerman or both of them – and they don't know the motive. Feydal thinks it may be one of his rivals trying to put him out of business, though that would be more likely to happen in Marseille than in Paris

– or so he told Bannerman in my presence. On the other hand, Bannerman thinks it may be one of *his* rivals or enemies, of which he has many – but again, in his case, why Paris instead of London where he normally lives? So, not knowing who was behind that failed assassination or, indeed, which one of them the gunman was trying to kill, they've chosen Feydal's fortress-villa as the safer option.'

'So I'll have to go to Marseille,' Brolin said.

'Well, it certainly looks like it,' Marie-Francoise replied. 'And perhaps I can help you there as well.'

When Brolin stopped walking, briefly frozen by her statement, Marie-Francoise stopped walking as well and turned in to face him. They were halfway along the Rue Saint-Louis-en-l'Ile, being jostled by the many passers-by. This picturesque, narrow street, with its many boutiques, art galleries and restaurants, drew lots of tourists, all year round.

'You're going with them?' Brolin asked.

Marie-Francoise nodded. 'Yes.'

'Why?'

'Bannerman insisted upon it and Feydal agreed to it. So I have to go with them.'

'You *have* to?'

'*Oui.*' She shrugged, then pointed towards the Pont Saint-Louis at the far end of the street. 'Come, let's keep moving.' They walked in silence for a while, neither comfortable with the other, then eventually Marie-Francoise said, 'I have to go because Bannerman wants me there and Feydal wants me to keep Bannerman happy. I have to go because I can't refuse Feydal and that's the simple truth of it.'

'*Why* can't you refuse him? Because of the money?'

'*Oui.*'

'Is it just the money or is it Feydal himself? Can it be that you're dependent upon him? That despite your desire to control your own life, you now need to be under his control? Is that not the truth of it?'

'No,' Marie-Francoise responded. 'That's just your jealousy talking. It's because of the money. Because of that *and* because of what he did to me – or, more precisely, had done to me – the last time I attempted to defy him.'

'When he sent those two hoodlums to visit you.'

'Yes. So it's because of that as well – because of my fear of him. I don't want acid thrown in my face and I don't want to lose all I've gained so far. Feydal *has* me under his control, but not the way you're suggesting. I'm frightened of him but I also want his money and that's all there is to it.'

'I hope so,' Brolin said.

As they continued along the narrow street, feeling safe in the tide of other walkers, Brolin fell silent, lost in his thoughts, which were mostly focused on tormenting images of Marie-Francoise servicing William Bannerman. Those images were repugnant to him and he tried to cast them out, tried to concentrate on the job, tried to struggle with the question of how he could neutralize Bannerman when the pig was staying in Feydal's heavily defended villa in Marseille – and, worse, with Marie-Francoise sharing his bedroom. Clearly, if Marie-Francoise still feared Feydal and loathed Bannerman, she truly would, as she had stated, still be willing to help get rid of them and Brolin might indeed require her help. He would, therefore, despite his loathing of the very idea of Marie-Francoise being there with Bannerman, in the bloated pig's bed, try to make good use of her again. In order to do so, however, he would have to swallow his own bile and he wasn't sure that he could. A pimp's life would be easier.

'So how can you help me?' he asked.

'The same way I helped you here,' she replied. 'By feeding you information as often as possible.'

'That might not be as easy in Marseille as it has been here.'

'Why not?'

'You won't be in a hotel, coming and going in your spare time. You'll be in Feydal's villa which is, I believe, located outside the city. This suggests that your movements will be restricted. That could make things difficult.'

'Not necessarily,' she responded. 'I'm sure I'll be given a car and be allowed to come and go as I please. All I need to know is where you're staying. I can call you from a public phone and arrange to meet you somewhere. Just like we've been doing here, in fact. The only difference is that you won't be able to visit me in my apartment because I won't actually *have* an apartment. But certainly we can meet elsewhere. How does that sound?'

'Good and bad,' Brolin said.

'What does that mean?'

Having left the Rue Saint-Louis-en-l'Ile behind them and crossed the Pont Saint-Louis, they were walking towards Notre-Dame, that magnificent medieval cathedral with a soaring spire, majestic towers and breathtaking flying buttresses. Even from here it looked immense, dominating the nineteenth-century buildings around it, blocking out a low, cloudy sky, illuminated here and there with cobwebs of weak sunlight.

'Good because we'll still be meeting and I want to see you again,' Brolin said. 'Bad because we won't be meeting in the privacy of your apartment and I'm seriously going to miss that.'

The remarks did not change Marie-Francoise's grave composure; did not make her smile. 'Nothing's lost,' she said with quiet brutality. 'What happened yesterday would not have happened again, even if we were staying here in Paris. It was a one-off, Brolin. Nothing important. Just something that I did on an impulse, perhaps because I was curious. Don't get excited about it.'

Brolin felt that he'd been slapped in the face, but he tried not to show it.

'Curious about what?' he asked.

Marie-Francoise shrugged. 'About how much you wanted me,' she said. 'A woman, even a whore like me, always has that particular curiosity.'

'So how much did I seem to want you?' Brolin asked.

'A lot. Far too much. I don't want to be wanted that much. I don't want to be responsible for feelings of that intensity. That's why it wouldn't have happened again and why nothing will be lost in Marseille. From here on in, it's strictly business. Please keep that in mind.'

'I don't believe you,' Brolin said, speaking the truth as he saw it. 'I think it meant a lot more than that to you, but you just can't admit it. You've been whoring so long, you can't believe that any man could want you for yourself, rather than just wanting your expensive tits, cunt and ass. You don't believe that you have any personal worth or that someone who doesn't want to buy you could have feelings for you. Once a whore, always a whore, you think, but I don't agree with you. I think you have worth and I value you and want to have more than your tits, cunt and ass, which I refuse to pay for.'

'Why?'

'Because I believe that paying for it would degrade what it is I feel for you. So how does *that* grab you, *Madame*?'

They had reached the *parvis*, or square, in front of the great cathedral and kept walking until they were approximately halfway across it. There Marie-Francoise stopped and again turned in to face Brolin, though carefully keeping a distance between them. He noted this and felt hurt.

Marie-Francoise smiled. 'You have a crude tongue, *Monsieur* Brolin.'

'That isn't an answer.'

'Think what you want, Brolin. I don't have an answer for you. I am what I am and I'm not sure what that is, but what I *do* know is that I want my freedom back and you can help me in that regard. Beyond that, despite what you think of me, I have no plans for you. I repeat: from now on this is strictly business, strictly professional, so don't go to Marseille with any high expectations about anything other than getting to Bannerman. Don't turn romantic on me, Brolin, because that won't help a bit. I'll help *you* if you promise faithfully to keep your mind on your work.'

'OK, I promise.'

'*Merci*,' Marie-Francoise said. She glanced distractedly around the *parvis*, at the many tourists milling about the front of the great cathedral, queuing up for entrance, taking photos, buying souvenirs, drinking from cans and bottles, eating *baguettes*, *crêpes*, pizzas and ice cream cones. She wasn't actually seeing much at that moment;

her gaze was focused inward. Then she turned her lovely feline eyes back on Brolin. 'So when will you be going to Marseille?'

'I'll arrive two or three days after you,' Brolin said.

'In order to call you,' she responded, 'I need to know when you're going to be there. I also need to know where you'll be staying.'

'Do you have any recommendations?' Brolin asked, trying now to be strictly professional.

'No. I've never been to Marseille.'

'Can you call me tomorrow?'

'Yes. In the afternoon.'

'OK. Call me tomorrow afternoon. By then I'll have been to a travel agent and booked a hotel. As for my date of arrival, you can take it as read that I'll be there no later than next Thursday – five days from now.'

'*Parfait*,' Marie-Francoise said. 'Alas, I have to leave you now and return to the Ritz, where Mr Bannerman is waiting to be serviced.'

'You bitch,' Brolin said, knowing that she had made that remark just to hurt him and instantly failing, with his instinctive response, in his bid to be strictly professional.

Marie-Francoise just smiled again. A lovely, radiant, slightly mocking smile. 'See you in Marseille,' she said, waving her hand in farewell. Then she walked away from him to disappear into the crowd of noisy Germans gathered around a tourist bus at the far end of the *parvis*.

Letting his breath out in a sigh, aware that his heart was racing slightly, Brolin walked back the way he had come, not stopping until he had reached his apartment block in the Marais. Entering the apartment, he kicked off his shoes and, as he had done that morning, stretched out on the bed. Clasping his hands under his head, he stared blankly at the ceiling for a long time, thinking, just thinking. Then eventually, having thought enough, having decided what he must do, he rolled off the bed and picked up his cellular phone.

Brolin called a few friends.

CHAPTER TWENTY

They met in a sleazy bar in Pigalle because Brolin had promised his old SAS buddies Don Clayton and Pat Dogherty a real night out in the more traditional Gay Paree (as Dogherty had spelt it in his e-mail, received by a pseudonymous Brolin in an Internet café in Saint-Germain des Prés). The bar was in the Place Blanche, directly facing the Moulin Rouge, and the owner compensated for his rotten, overpriced wine with a string of strippers who performed, one after the other, under multicoloured spotlights on a postage-stamp stage. Clayton and Dogherty found this highly amusing, even exotic, though Jean-Pierre Duval, now included in Brolin's plans, was clearly bemused by this *anglais* fascination with pitifully downmarket eroticism.

'Those girls should be working in a flea market in the Porte de Clignancourt,' Jean-Pierre said, looking in disbelief at the latest girl to gyrate her bony hips in a flickering, fluorescent pink spotlight that was being used

– not effectively – to disguise her numerous physical blemishes. 'They shouldn't be exposing their pitiful lack of talent as aspirants to the Lido. Alas, they will never make it as far as the Champs Elysées, though they might well succeed in driving me from here to there in desperation. Brolin, what are we *doing* here?'

'We're here,' Brolin said, 'to discuss a job I have to do in Marseille. We're here because this bar is nearly always empty and it's a good place to talk. Finally, we're here because my two friends—' he nodded to indicate Clayton and Dogherty '—have a taste for the red-light areas of foreign cities. Does that explain it, you French git?'

'Oh, la, la!' Jean-Pierre exclaimed melodramatically, rolling his brown eyes.

'So what *is* the job?' Clayton asked, distractedly running his fingers through his curly jet-black hair while watching the girl stripping on the tiny stage at the far end of the bar to the sound of the Rolling Stones's 'Satisfaction'.

'Yeah, right,' Dogherty added. 'Don and me were intrigued by your e-mail, which was, of course, suitably ambiguous.' He put his hand into his jacket pocket, withdrew a piece of paper, obviously a printout from a computer, unfolded it and read from it. 'Hi, Pat. If you want something to do – something really challenging – come to Paris straightaway and we'll talk. Pass this message on to Clayton. I promise that if you come you won't be disappointed. E-mail details of your arrival to this address and I'll meet you wherever. Accommodation will be arranged. A good time will be had by all. Yours, Antonsas.' Pat looked up again, grinning broadly as he refolded the piece of paper and put it back into his jacket pocket. 'So,' he said, 'here we both are in Paris, staying at a very nice hotel – thanks, pal – and simply *dying* to know why we've been summoned.'

'Right,' Clayton said. 'So let's discuss it and then hit the bright lights for that good time you promised us.'

'The good time is the job,' Brolin said.

'I hope so,' Dogherty said. 'I'm more interested in the job than I am in hitting the bright lights of Paris. I was so fucking bored back in London, I thought I was losing my mind. This job comes as a blessing. So what is it, Tony?'

'A neutralization,' Brolin said.

'Oh?' Clayton murmured, unperturbed by the thought of an assassination. 'Who's the victim?'

'William Bannerman. The Commissioner for the Metropolitan Police.'

Clayton and Dogherty glanced at each other with raised eyebrows. Then Dogherty pursed his lips and gave a low whistle. 'That's some job,' he said.

'Fucking A,' Clayton added. 'It sounds more like a suicide mission. I mean, Bannerman's a really important man, widely feared and powerful. How the hell did you get involved with this one?'

Brolin explained the background to the situation, including the involvement of Sir Archibald Wainwright and the Prime Minister. When he had finished his lengthy discourse, Clayton and Dogherty were suitably impressed.

'Jesus,' Dogherty said, 'I didn't realize when you said you had a job that it was something *this* big. I mean, going for someone like Bannerman ... That's really hair-raising, Brolin.'

'Damned right,' Clayton said. 'I mean, I hate that fat bastard – we all do – for what he did to the Regiment; but the idea of *us* taking him out ... Well ... I don't know.'

'What don't you know?' Brolin asked.

'I don't know that it's something we should be doing, given who that bastard is and all. I mean, we're talking about our own Police Commissioner and that's not the same as toppling some foreign despot.'

'He may not be a foreigner but he's certainly a despot,' Brolin said. 'In fact, he's worse than a despot. More dangerous than one of those. Bannerman's taken police corruption to a whole new level and now he's one of the most feared men in England. The bastard has no morals whatsoever, no patriotism, no loyalty, and he's preparing to sell our country out to the Chinese Triads and British-based Russian *Mafiya* in return for his own throne of turds on top of the shit pile. Pretty soon, if he's not stopped, he's going to be heading one of the biggest and most vicious criminal empires in the world, so he has to be stopped.'

'I didn't know you were so righteous,' Clayton said sardonically. 'I mean, you're coming on there like Jesus Christ.'

Suitably chastened, Brolin grinned. 'OK, I get the message. Sorry for sermonizing. I'll admit I'm in this for the money and, I guess, the thrill; but what I'm saying is that if the task is to neutralize someone, then Bannerman, despite the fact that he's British, deserves what he has coming to him as much as anyone we've ever tackled. It may not be the same as toppling a foreign despot, but the cause is a just one. I've no guilt on that count.'

Clayton and Dogherty nodded agreement simultaneously, then Dogherty said, 'Right. Let's just keep reminding ourselves of who this bastard is and we'll all feel a hell of a lot better.'

'Hear, hear,' Clayton said. He glanced at the stripper,

who by now was down to a G-string and about to untie it teasingly. He waited until she had finished the job and was standing naked before them all, her arms raised in the air, breasts proudly upthrust, then he clapped his hands, thus encouraging the others to do the same, albeit self-consciously. When the girl, smiling with innocent pride, had taken her bow and rushed off the dance floor, Clayton returned his dark, steady gaze to Brolin. 'So you've already tried to neutralize Bannerman here in Paris, but it didn't come off.'

'Correct,' Brolin said.

'And Bannerman was, at the time, travelling in the car of this arms dealer, Feydal Hussein.'

'Correct again,' Brolin said.

'There was nothing about that in the British newspapers,' Clayton said.

'Nor in the French media,' Jean-Pierre informed him. 'The Gendarmarie, at Feydal Hussein's request, didn't report the incident. Feydal has powerful friends here.'

'And, of course,' Brolin added, 'Bannerman didn't report the incident either – for the obvious reasons. Anyway, in view of the failure of the assassination attempt here, I've decided that the only way to take Bannerman out is to launch an assault against Feydal's villa in Marseille when Bannerman is there as his guest. Which is why I need you guys – and, of course, Jean-Pierre here.'

Like Brolin, Clayton and Dogherty had worked with Jean-Pierre when they were on detachment from the SAS to the French GIGN. They knew how he worked and they respected him.

'Fine,' Dogherty said, brushing a lock of red hair from his green eyes as he nodded vigorously. 'But why the hell don't we just wait until Bannerman leaves the villa, which he's bound to do on occasion, and neutralize him while he's travelling in his car? Doing it *properly*, this time.'

'First,' Brolin said, ignoring the friendly jibe and glancing at the only other customer in the dimly lit bar, an old guy with a peaked cap and a crumpled suit who was leaning across his table, staring intently at the empty stage and repeatedly, lasciviously licking his lips. 'He'll be in one of Feydal's cars and those vehicles are all bullet-proof – as I learnt to my cost. Second, after the fiasco here in Paris, I've decided that an attempted kill in the streets leaves too much leeway for accidents. It also endangers the lives of innocent people – other drivers and pedestrians. So an assault on the villa strikes me as being the best way.'

'That could create a lot of noise,' Clayton said sardonically, 'and waken the neighbours.'

'The villa's in an isolated location,' Jean-Pierre said, 'well out of earshot of its nearest neighbours.'

'What if Feydal calls the cops for help as we're breaking in?'

'We'll cut the telephone wires *before* we go in.'

'Fine,' Dogherty said. 'We *always* do that. A small point, however. If we launch an attack on the villa, Bannerman's not the only one who's going to get hurt.'

'What does that mean?'

'I'm thinking of Feydal's bodyguards and, more importantly, Feydal himself. Almost certainly, we're going to have to put him down as well – if he doesn't get us first, of course.'

'No great loss,' Brolin said. 'As Feydal's the middleman between that Libyan gunrunner and Bannerman, I don't think his loss will cause the British government any heartbreak. In fact, I think that taking Feydal out as well would be a good thing.'

'He sounds like a tough nut to crack,' Dogherty said.

'He will be,' Brolin replied, 'but we've cracked those before.'

'Right,' Clayton said. 'I'm in.'

'Me as well,' Dogherty added.

'So what's the game plan?' Clayton asked.

'The game plan is to take the train to Marseille, hole up in a hotel, survey Feydal's villa, decide how best to get into it, then launch the assault.'

'Piece of cake, is it?' Dogherty asked ironically.

'I doubt it,' Brolin replied. 'Given Feydal's line of business, that villa will be heavily defended.'

'Apart from the fact that it's heavily defended,' Clayton asked, 'do we have any hard information on the place?'

'Practically nothing,' Jean-Pierre said. 'I've checked with Gendarmarie friends and there are no floor plans available. We only know that it's very large, that it's surrounded by high walls, that it's protected by high-tech surveillance systems and that it's located high in the hills above the Corniche John F. Kennedy, overlooking the Mediterranean Sea.'

'Very nice,' Clayton said, glancing at the tiny stage where one girl had been replaced by another. The new girl was lean and leggy, wearing a skintight miniskirt, a sequined halter that exposed her belly, and impossibly high stiletto-heel shoes. Her auburn hair was pinned up on her head, but she was taking the pins out one by one, letting her long hair down slowly and seductively, as she performed a fairly crude bump-and-grind to Sade's 'Smooth Operator'.

'Fucking hell,' Dogherty said with a mixture of lust and despair. 'I've got a hard-on and nowhere to put it. Coming here was a *bad* idea.' He returned his gaze to Brolin. 'So how come,' he said, 'if this Feydal's a well-known Marseille criminal, the police down there haven't run the bastard in?'

'He has the local police in his pocket,' Jean-Pierre said, 'which explains why they've never even surveyed his villa. Feydal extensively renovated and greatly expanded his already large nineteenth-century villa in 1998, then he built a solid, high wall all around it. Now only he and his cronies know what it's like inside.'

'I'm sure we can find out,' Brolin said.

'How?'

'The architect?' Clayton asked.

'What about him?'

'Presumably he lives in Marseille.'

'*Oui*,' Jean-Pierre said. 'Name of Julian Lombard. The local architect for the wealthy. He lives in a villa in Endoume, not far from Feydal. Naturally, since he's always looking for business, he's listed in the phone book.'

'So,' Brolin said, 'he's bound to have a copy of his original designs for Feydal's villa somewhere in his office. We break in some evening, nick the designs, then, if necessary, steal something more obvious – any money lying around or, perhaps, a computer – to make it look like a straightforward burglary. As Lombard has no reason to look for those designs, it could be years before he even knows they're missing.'

'The designs could be in a computer – not in an old-fashioned filing cabinet.'

'So we call up that file in the computer, print it out

on the same computer system, and walk out of there carrying our own copy. No problem at all.'

Clayton and Dogherty nodded simultaneously, indicating their agreement. Then, as if reading each other's minds, they glanced at the tiny stage where the latest stripper had removed the last pin from her long hair and was now shaking her head frantically to make her tresses whip around her gyrating body. Though she hadn't started to take off the few clothes she was wearing, she certainly *seemed* to be naked. Clayton and Dogherty, both new to Paris, sighed with longing and looked away.

'OK,' Dogherty said, speaking to Brolin. 'We steal the designs for the house. That lets us know the layout, but it's not going to help us get inside. For a start, we need to know their routine: when they're going to be there; when the guards are changed and so on.'

'That woman I told you about,' Brolin said, feeling pain just at the thought of Marie-Francoise. 'Bannerman's woman. She's going to keep me informed of their movements in Marseille just as she did here in Paris.'

'Bannerman's whore,' Clayton said, causing Brolin still more pain. 'That's really pretty neat. But how can she contact us when she doesn't even know where we'll be staying?'

'She *does* know where we'll be staying,' Brolin said. 'I've already booked our hotel and it's located in the main drag, La Cannebière, down near the Vieux Port.'

'The what?' Dogherty asked.

'The old port,' Jean-Pierre explained. 'It's still a colourful area, filled with bars, gangsters and whores—'

'Oh, yummee!' Clayton interjected.

'—and I happen to have friends there,' Jean-Pierre

continued. 'Or, more accurately, criminal acquaintances who'll be able to help us with various matters – weapons and so forth. So Brolin and I thought that would be a good place to stay.'

Dogherty grinned at Brolin. 'So you've already booked us into an hotel?' he asked.

'Yes,' Brolin said.

'You must have been pretty confident that we'd take the job.'

'How could you resist it?' Brolin said, smiling. 'It's just what you were looking for. So I booked the hotel in advance and our contact, Marie-Francoise, has been given the details. Yes, she knows where to find me.'

Clayton and Dogherty grinned at each other, glanced at the stripper as she gyrated her hips and prepared to take her few bits of clothing off, then turned back to Brolin and nodded their agreement.

'Right,' Clayton said. 'How could we resist it?'

'And we didn't,' Dogherty added.

'So,' Clayton said, steering them back on course while glancing again in the direction of the stripper who was now slowly, teasingly starting to remove the sequined halter from her siliconed breasts while the music played on. 'This Marie-Francoise broad already knows where we'll be staying. Is she bright enough to find out what kind of security they've got there?'

'She's bright enough,' Brolin said, 'and I've certainly asked her to do that. I'm pretty sure she'll be giving us that information once we get to Marseille.'

'What about weapons, explosives, communications, abseiling equipment and so forth? We're not in the SAS any more, so where do we get what we need?'

'From the people I've just mentioned,' Jean-Pierre said.

'My criminal acquaintances in the old port. They'll get us anything we need – if the price is right, of course.'

'The money's no problem,' Brolin assured him.

'What do you think we'll need?' Dogherty asked.

'We won't know that until Marie-Francoise gives us precise information about the villa's security, including the number and placement of armed guards and details of the high-tech surveillance equipment used there. Obviously, as we're talking about a major assault against a protected building, this will be something like a hostage-rescue operation of the kind we carried out with the Regiment. So we'll certainly be needing counter-terrorist clothing and assault aids, including abseiling equipment, communications and a variety of personal weapons. We won't know exactly what kind until we get to Marseille and check out the situation.'

Clayton tore his eyes away from the stripper on the stage to look directly at Jean-Pierre. 'And you can get us that kind of shit?'

'*Oui*,' Jean-Pierre said. 'That kind of equipment and weaponry is smuggled through Marseille all the time, either coming from or going to a wide variety of terrorist gangs. Ironically, Feydal's villa is our target and it's Feydal who controls most of the men doing the smuggling in the old port and at certain locations along the coast.'

'So in a sense,' Clayton said, 'we'll be attacking Feydal with his own illegal weapons and equipment.'

'*Exactement*,' Jean-Pierre said.

'Fucking great,' Dogherty said with a big, freckled grin. Then he turned his glance to the stage where the stripper was now shaking her bare breasts as well as her long hair.

'You,' Clayton said to Brolin, 'me, Dogherty and Jean-Pierre here. That makes us a four-man team, just like in the good old days.'

He was referring to the concept of the four-man team first devised by David Stirling, the creator of the SAS, during World War Two and always viewed by the Regiment, right up to its demise, as the most efficient and effective size for most kinds of operation. Less than four men in a team would have restricted how much firepower and supplies they could carry; it would also have left them less able to defend themselves if one of them was wounded or killed. The four-man team was also considered to be the best because fighting men tend instinctively to divide into pairs when tackling most tasks and troopers always find it easier to look after a single partner. Finally, more than four men would make a team that would be harder to conceal from the enemy and would also be less cohesive in action. The four-man team, then, being in effect composed of two pairs, was far and away the best for most SAS missions.

'Yes,' Brolin said. 'That was the idea. You, Pat,' he continued, turning to Dogherty, 'will be our demolition specialist, tasked with blowing up anything that stands in our way – or maybe you'll just have to create a diversion. You, Don,' he added, turning to Clayton, 'will be our transport man, tasked with driving us to the villa and getting us out of there. Jean-Pierre here, with his specialist GIGN training, will be our signals expert, tasked with destroying their communications and surveillance equipment.'

'And you?' Clayton asked with a mocking grin.

Brolin grinned back. 'I'm the PC,' he said, using the old SAS acronym for Patrol Commander. 'And as such I'll be coordinating the activities of you three and leading the assault when it starts.'

'Which means you travel lightly,' Clayton said.

'Lucky me,' Brolin said. He glanced at the stage and was gratified to see that the stripper had just removed her panties and was standing, stark naked, legs apart, with her hands above her head and her panties dangling from one of them. Her skin was pink and immaculate – an illusion – in the overhead lighting. Brolin sighed, thinking of Marie-Francoise, and turned back to his colleagues. 'Any questions, guys?'

'Yeah,' Dogherty said. 'When do we leave for Marseille?'

'One night seeing the bright lights,' Brolin said. 'Then we leave in the morning. Any complaints?'

There were no complaints, so the following morning, after a wild night on the town, the four-man team boarded the train for Marseille.

PART TWO

MARSEILLE

CHAPTER TWENTY-ONE

In the year 2005, Marseille was no longer the exotic seaport of legend, with its hillside honeycomb of narrow streets and colourful characters overlooking a lively waterfront area. Instead, it was a vastly expanded city of tall housing developments, elevated highways, vehicular tunnels, dense traffic, and citizens who appeared to be more northern than Mediterranean. Though it was certainly a bustling, noisy and modernized city, it had lost its former charm and seemed, at least to Brolin's jaded eye, to have sadly deteriorated.

The hotel into which Brolin and the others were booked was in a similar state, with faded flock wallpaper, tattered carpets, depressing period furniture, boring reproduction paintings of sailboats and steamships on the walls, dim lighting and a general atmosphere of gloom. Entering his own room to shower and change his clothes, having spent three hours on the new express train from Paris and now feeling distinctly grubby, Brolin studied the big double bed, thought instantly of Marie-Francoise, and realized that he was looking forward to seeing her again, though for reasons that were not all to do with the job at hand. He felt guilty about that. Having arranged to meet Jean-Pierre, Clayton and Dogherty in the hotel lobby in an hour, he glanced with distaste at the dirty lime-coloured curtains, the holes in the dark green carpet, the dark-varnished chest of drawers, equally depressing armchairs and even more dreary maritime paintings. Then he unpacked his travelling bag, had a shower, put on fresh clothing and went downstairs.

The other three were already waiting for him in the lobby, all wearing light clothing appropriate to the warmth of noon – even at this time of year – in the south of France.

'I'm starving,' Clayton said. 'Let's have lunch.'

'Yeah, right,' Dogherty said. 'And a couple of regenerating beers for my parched tongue and throat.'

Brolin turned to Jean-Pierre. 'This pair of fucking schoolboys never think of anything but their bellies. You're supposed to know this town, my French friend, so any suggestions regarding where we can satisfy them?'

'*Oui*,' Jean-Pierre replied. 'Let's go down to the Vieux Port. There are enough restaurants there to feed the bellies of the whole of Caesar's army, so our starving friends should be satisfied.'

'Always knew I could depend on you, Jean-Pierre,' Clayton said. '"F" for food and "F" for French, right? You bastards *live* for food, *oui*?'

'"F" for "fuck off",' Jean-Pierre retorted with a grin.

Clearly unperturbed by Clayton's bullshit, which he understood from past experience, he led them out of the hotel and into the dazzling sunshine of La Cannebière, the most famous avenue in the city, broad, traffic-jammed, filled with cafés, cinemas, department stores and a variety of eighteenth- and nineteenth-century commercial buildings. La Cannebière led to the Vieux Port where Jean-Pierre found them an empty table at one of the many restaurants lining the *quai*, overlooking the forest of masts and brightly-coloured sails of the pleasure boats in the calm, turquoise-green water. From where they were sitting, they could gaze directly across the water, beyond the many boats, to another bar-filled *quai* located at the base of limestone hills that were covered with high-rise apartment blocks and dominated by the steeple of Notre-Dame de la Garde, which soared 150 feet above the hillside and was surmounted by a thirty-foot gilded statue of the Virgin Mary.

Sitting at their table, wearing sunglasses against the dazzling light that even this late in the year made the many greystone buildings on the hillside look white-washed, Brolin and the others sipped cold beers and enjoyed plates of delicious *bouillabaisse* – a fish stew strongly flavoured with garlic and saffron – while listening to the cries of fishmongers farther along the port. They watched the Marseillaises – Frenchmen, Corsicans, Africans, North Africans, expatriate former colonials – pass by. Most of all, however, they watched the girls of darkly striking Mediterranean beauty and were sorely frustrated.

'Oh, my God,' Dogherty said. 'The best years of my life spent in fucking England and now here I am, faced with what I've missed for most of my life. Are these women for *real*?'

'They're for real, but they're not for us,' Clayton said.

'To them we'd be just a bunch of working-class wankers. These women like men with style.'

'Which leaves me out in the cold,' Dogherty said before raising his glass of beer to his lips and slugging it down.

'That,' Jean-Pierre said, pointing to the *quai* at the far side of the boat-jammed port, 'is the Quai de la Rive Neuve. Those bars and cafés you see are a lot less respectable than the ones on this side.'

'It looks innocent enough,' Dogherty said.

'It isn't. Back in the late 1990s that *quai* and the area behind it, the Quartier de l'Arsenal, was one of the most colourful places in the city – a bit like London's Soho – but it's changed dramatically in the past five years. Now, though it's still colourful, it's where gangsters, whores, drug addicts and the more stupid or bold tourists hang out at night. It's also where we'll find my gun-running friends when we know what weapons and equipment we require.'

'You buy what we need,' Clayton joked, 'while I sample the whores.'

'Not recommended,' Jean-Pierre replied. 'Those whores aren't the prettiest girls in town and a lot of them have AIDS.'

'Life's a bitch,' Clayton said, disappointed.

'So where would Feydal's villa be?' Brolin asked, studying the limestone hillside that had once been a honeycomb of streets with small houses and was now covered with high-rise apartment blocks.

'The other side of those hills,' Jean-Pierre replied, noting the direction of Brolin's gaze. 'Then due south-east. No distance at all. By car, we can get there in about fifteen minutes.'

'Where can we rent a car?'

'I've already done it,' Jean-Pierre said with a smile. 'I booked it from Paris and it should be parked outside the hotel when we get back. The keys'll be with the desk clerk in the hotel. If you want, when we finish lunch, we can go back for the car and drive straight out there to eyeball Feydal's villa. I've already checked with a local friend and he circled the villa on my map, so we won't have any trouble finding it.'

'What a bright boy you are,' Brolin said.

'For a Frog,' Dogherty added.

'Don't try your SAS bullshit on me,' Jean-Pierre replied without rancour. 'I've heard enough of it to last me a lifetime. Now it rolls off me like water from a duck's back.'

'For a Frog you're pretty good with the English,' Clayton said, still shovelling his bullshit.

'*Parlez-vous français?*' Jean-Pierre asked.

'*Oui*,' Clayton retorted. 'My French begins and ends there, pal.'

In fact, he was lying. Like Dogherty and Brolin, when in the SAS he had been taught French – and Spanish – at the army's Hereford School of Languages and, of course, he knew that Jean-Pierre knew this, since they had once worked together in the GIGN. During that time Clayton had been compelled to speak French every day and Jean-Pierre knew this as well. The bullshit, therefore, was just for fun, indicating their mutual restlessness. Aware of this, Brolin said, 'Hurry up and finish your beers, guys, while I generously foot this huge bill. It's time to start work.'

'Christ, I'm just settling in here,' Dogherty complained. 'Cooling my palate with this beer and heating my loins by watching these gorgeous French, African and Algerian babes pass by. Just one more hour, boss.'

'Not one more minute,' Brolin replied. 'Finish your beers and let's go.'

'Life really *is* a bitch,' Clayton said with a big, lazy grin.

The bill was already resting beneath the ashtray on the table and Brolin checked it, then put the money on the table, also under the ashtray to prevent it from being blown away in the wind. Without waiting for the waiter to come and collect it, he pushed his chair back and stood up, preparing to leave. Taking this for the broad hint that it was, Clayton, Dogherty and Jean-Pierre hurriedly finished their beers and did likewise. Then they all walked away from the table, automatically grouping into two pairs, Brolin with Jean-Pierre and Clayton with Dogherty, as they made their way out of the old port and back along the sunlit, crowded La Cannebière.

Ten minutes later they were back at the hotel. Brolin, Clayton and Dogherty waited outside, taking in the local colour, while Jean-Pierre went inside to collect the car keys from the desk clerk. When he emerged again, they all went together to look for the car, a sky-blue Peugeot 306, and found it parked by the pavement about twenty yards along from the hotel. They slipped in one at a time, with Brolin sitting up front beside Jean-Pierre, who was in the driver's seat. Jean-Pierre took a map from the glove compartment, spread it out on the steering wheel, studied it for a moment, then refolded it and put it back where he had found it.

'Right,' he said, 'I know where the villa is. We'll be there in no time.'

Switching on the ignition and putting the car into gear,

he drove back down La Cannebière in the direction of the old port, turned left just before reaching it, headed along the Quai de la Rive Neuve – lots of bars on one side, docked boats on the other – then along the Boulevard Charles Livon, passing the Tunnel St Laurent, where, across the port, they saw the ancient Fort St Jean, silhouetted against the white sheet of the sky. Shortly after passing the green lawns of the Parc du Pharo, which marked the promontory dominating the entrance to the old port, Jean-Pierre turned south-east, onto the Corniche Président John F. Kennedy, which ran for nearly five kilometres along the sea front.

Jean-Pierre kept driving along the Corniche, giving the others a scenic journey. Soon they passed above the Vallon des Auffes, a picturesque fishing port with many cafés and *cabanons* that was also crammed with pleasure boats. The Mediterranean, turquoise-green and glittering, swept out to the Pomègues and Ratonneau islands, the legendary Château d'If and, in the distance, the Massif de Marseilleveyre, all hazed in shimmering heat waves and eerily beautiful. To their left, climbing up from the Corniche, were the hills of Endoume, honeycombed with narrow streets, dotted here and there with sun-bleached pine trees.

When they had crossed the spectacular viaduct and continued on along the Corniche, approaching the Port du Prophete, the densely packed houses of Endoume gave way to the larger villas of the old colonials and the *nouveaux riches*, widely scattered over the hills of Roucas Blanc, so called because it featured white rock that flared with phosphorescent brilliance, reflecting the sunlight. Though some of the villas had been built in the first half of the nineteenth century and were constantly being renovated, albeit managing to retain their former appearance, many, like Feydal's, were relatively new and modern. However, Feydal's villa, when eventually they reached it, proved to be something special.

As viewed from the Corniche, it was perched over a sheer drop to the lower slopes directly above the road, about twenty metres up, and surrounded by a featureless whitewashed wall about ten metres high, which was higher than normal. The tips of a couple of Moorish-style towers, obviously rising up from opposite ends of the main structure, could be seen above and behind that wall, but nothing else of the villa could be seen from the road. The building was obviously set in a large area of levelled ground – the couple of acres mentioned previously by Jean-Pierre – and the rest of the hill soared dramatically above it.

'We can't scale that wall without being seen,' Brolin said. 'Not even at night. As for the rest of the hill, rising up behind the villa, it falls away too obliquely to give us a decent view. So presumably, even if we can get around to the back of the property, we'll see nothing other than those two towers rising above the back wall.'

'We'll find out soon enough,' Jean-Pierre said as he continued driving along the Corniche, high above the glittering Mediterranean. 'We take the next exit for the road that should lead up to the villa's entrance. And, indeed, there it is.'

With the enviable skill of a true Parisian driver, he swept off the slip road, took the northern exit, and drove up the narrow, winding road that led into the hills above the Corniche. A few minutes later, he turned left again, this time heading west, speeding along another narrow tarmac track that eventually brought them to a bend with a left-hand slip exit. This slip road, also tarmacked, extended for about a hundred metres to a set of high black wrought-iron gates in what was clearly the eastern wall of Feydal Hussein's spacious property.

As he didn't plan to drive along that slip road, not wishing his car's details to be recorded by Feydal's surveillance cameras, Jean-Pierre simply slowed to a crawl when he approached it. His intention was to follow the gentle bend in the road where it curved around the northern side of the property; he had therefore slowed down only to give himself and the others time to study the entrance. When they passed the slip road and got a direct view of the gates, Brolin saw that they were closed and that a surveillance camera had been placed at one side of them. It was moving constantly to and fro, covering the approach road and the grounds on either side of it. The driveway on the far side of the gate ran as straight as an arrow to the eastern side of the big white house, which was located a good half-mile away. Brolin caught a glimpse of the white-painted side of one of the gable-end towers and ornate stone-walled balconies front and rear, then the building was lost to view as the car moved into the bend in the road and continued on around it until it was at the rear, the northern side, of the property. The road ran parallel to the featureless white wall, which was, as Brolin had guessed when he had viewed it from the Corniche, about ten metres high, certainly long enough to encompass an area of two acres, and set back a good fifteen metres from the road's edge.

'That's some fucking property,' Dogherty said admiringly from where he was sitting beside Clayton in the rear of the car.

'Xanadu,' Clayton mused, being a movie buff and an

Orson Welles fan. 'Our Feydal is as secluded as Citizen Kane. I think it's time he had company.'

'The bastard will soon have plenty of *that*,' Dogherty said.

'This is a public road?' Brolin asked, glancing north to see more steep hills covered with pine trees and dotted with what seemed like whitewashed villas, though the whiteness was, of course, an illusion caused by the sunlight. The other villas were, however, widely scattered and a good distance away. Certainly their inhabitants would be out of earshot of the calamitous din that would result from any assault on Feydal's place.

'*Oui*,' Jean-Pierre replied.

'Where does it go?'

'It cuts through Roucas Blanc and heads back in the general direction of Marseille, leading eventually to the Bassin de Carénage in the old port, almost directly facing the Tunnel St Laurent.'

'Used much?'

'Yes. As you can see, there are many side roads running off it, leading to those other properties.'

'So we have to get into those grounds under cover of darkness and do so without making too much noise.'

'I would say so, my friend.'

When the car reached the end of the northern wall of Feydal's property, Brolin glanced left and saw that the western wall was also white and featureless. He glanced back over his shoulder to double-check as the car sped on. Then he turned his head to the front again.

'No entrance that side, either,' he said to Jean-Pierre as the road unfurled in front of the car. To his left, the parched, barren earth fell steeply to the Corniche and, beyond it, to the glittering blue-green sweep of the

Mediterranean. To his right were the various side roads, some no more than dusty tracks, that snaked steeply upwards into the soaring hillside and led eventually to one or other of the villas widely scattered around Roucas Blanc. The vast sky was a silvery sheet. 'So the only entrance is through those high gates in the eastern wall of the property.'

'Correct,' Jean-Pierre said.

'*Not* correct,' Clayton said. 'The only *legal* entrance is through those gates, but we're not going to give the bastard notice. We could blow the gates open.'

'Or scale the walls,' Dogherty added.

'We could do a lot of things,' Brolin said, speaking over his shoulder while squinting into the still-dazzling sunlight over the road straight ahead. 'But not until we have a pretty good idea of the layout of the property. With someone like Feydal, the grounds of his own property could be landmined, never mind what he has inside the villa by way of protection. So before we go in, we need to know exactly what's behind those high walls.'

'Well,' Clayton responded, 'we're going to find that out when we get our hands on the architect's designs. So when do we do that?'

'This evening,' Jean-Pierre said. 'Lombard's office is an annexe of his villa, in the heart of Endoume.'

'I thought Endoume was for your average man,' Brolin said. 'Not a place for a wealthy architect to be living.'

'It's *because* he's an architect that he's living there,' Jean-Pierre replied. 'Lombard was clever. He saw where the cheap properties were and he bought something modest for an equally modest price. Then, using his own skills and his underpaid workers, he converted it into a luxury home. An increasing number of monied people are moving into Endoume, so the area's changing fast. Anyway, I'm going there right now to let us all eyeball the place. We'll be there in a minute.'

Looking around him, Brolin saw that they were now in a hilly area more densely populated than the one they had just left, with roads leading off in all directions to the recently built houses covering the hills that fell to the Corniche. Eventually, Jean-Pierre turned off along a tarmac road that led past a row of detached greystone houses with wrought-iron balconies and red-tile roofs to an empty stretch that had, at its far end, a large, recently renovated villa situated in spacious gardens planted with pine trees and surrounded by a low whitewashed wall. There was a garage to the side of the house; and the annexe used by Lombard as his office thrust out from the rear.

Jean-Pierre stopped to let them have a good look.

'Given the height of that wall,' Clayton said, 'Lombard's obviously not too concerned about being burgled.'

'That's true enough,' Jean-Pierre said. 'There isn't much crime this far out of town, but almost certainly he'll have a burglar-alarm system.'

'We can put that out of action,' Brolin said, 'so it isn't a problem. If we come back under cover of darkness – pretty late, when Lombard's in bed – I think we'll be OK.'

'All four of us?' Dogherty asked.

'No,' Brolin said. 'Only two. One man to keep watch from the car, prepared to drive off, while the other breaks in and steals the drawings.'

'Do we toss for it?' Clayton asked.

'No, we don't,' Brolin said. 'Jean-Pierre drives and I do the job. Meanwhile, you two will stay in the hotel – in the bar, if you want – but certainly remaining inside the building.' Clayton and Dogherty moaned melodramatically. 'I don't want you going out,' Brolin continued, 'and getting drunk and talking to people. Just stay in that hotel bar and drink as much as you want, but then go to your separate lonely beds. In other words, you pair of potential fuck-rats, I want you to remain silent and invisible. You got that?'

'Yes, boss!' Clayton and Dogherty sang in unison while rolling their eyes.

Brolin nodded at Jean-Pierre. 'OK, my friend, let's go back to the hotel for a siesta. Then we'll have a meal and leave for Lombard's place just before midnight.'

'*Parfait*,' Jean-Pierre said.

They drove back to the hotel.

CHAPTER TWENTY-TWO

Back in the hotel, Brolin had his brief siesta and awakened two hours later, just after 1900 hours, feeling refreshed. After a shower and a shave, he felt even better and was ready to join the others for a leisurely meal in the restaurant. However, while Clayton and Dogherty were able to drink as much as they wanted, Brolin and Jean-Pierre were obliged to stick with Perrier water to ensure that they were fully alert when they broke into Lombard's place.

Though taking his time, Brolin could not stretch the meal out to much later than 2100 hours, so he went back to his room and lay down once more on the bed, this time fully dressed, then closed his eyes to let his thoughts drift. They drifted, naturally enough, to images of Marie-Francoise, who right now was in Feydal's villa, doing God knew what with the foul and despicable William Clive Bannerman. The very thought of it was an anguish, depriving Brolin of true rest, and his state of agitation was made all the more acute by the fact that Marie-Francoise still hadn't made contact with him. As he refused to believe that she had betrayed him, he could only assume that she was in trouble and this possibility too disturbed him. He did not have a good rest.

Eventually, at 2300 hours, he rolled off the bed, splashed cold water on his face, dried himself, combed his hair, then put on his light windcheater jacket. Removing a small electronic blocking device and a set of all-purpose keys from his travelling bag, he put each item into a separate pocket of his jacket, clipped a torch to his belt, hidden under the jacket, then left his room and went downstairs to join Jean-Pierre in the lobby.

'Where's Clayton and Dogherty?' he asked.

Jean-Pierre nodded in the direction of the bar just off the lobby. 'In there, still drinking. You believe they'll stay there?'

'They wouldn't be here if they weren't disciplined,' Brolin said with total confidence. 'So, yes, I'm sure they'll stay there and take themselves off to beddy-byze when they've had enough. Are you ready to leave?'

'*Oui.*'

'Then let's go.'

Brolin and Jean-Pierre drove back to the renovated villa in Endoume, arriving there twenty minutes later, and parked at the end of the road, tucking the car in between two other vehicles. The road was in darkness, except for a few well-scattered lights. Walking along to the home of Julian Lombard, they saw that the lights in the annexe were turned off, but lights were still on in the front room and the room directly above it, obviously a bedroom. Brolin looked at Jean-Pierre and together, without saying a word, they returned to their parked car.

They sat in the Peugeot for another hour. While they waited, both bored shitless, a few other cars came into the street and parked either at the kerb or in the driveways of the houses. The people in the cars got out and entered their homes – just as, almost certainly, they did most days of their lives – and nothing unusual occurred.

At 0025, both men left their vehicle and returned to the front of Lombard's house. All the lights were now out. Brolin nodded at Jean-Pierre who turned away and walked back to the parked car. Meanwhile, Brolin crossed the road and crept through the front gardens and along the side of Lombard's house, until he had reached the annexe at the back. He waited there, hugging the wall, until the Peugeot 306 came along the street, made a sharp, quiet U-turn, and parked at the opposite side of the road, positioned for a quick getaway if necessary.

There wasn't a soul in the street.

Satisfied, Brolin inched along the wall of the annexe until he had reached its only door. The grey steel box of a burglar-alarm system was fixed to the wall above the door frame. Brolin removed the electronic blocking device from his jacket pocket, stood on tiptoe, attached the magnetized blocking device to the alarm box and then turned it on by pressing a green button. He waited for a few seconds until a red light on the blocking device started winking repeatedly. When he saw that, he knew that the burglar alarm would be deactivated for as long as the blocking device remained fixed to it.

Satisfied again, he withdrew the set of all-purpose keys from his other pocket. These keys were cut as near as possible to most of the standard patterns and it was just a matter of trying them one after the other until he found the one that slotted in most easily. When he found that key, he simply had to manipulate it patiently, slipping it in and out, turning it this way and that, until its standard edges found the required grooves and the lock clicked open. When it did, he opened the door, slipped inside the building, then closed the door quietly behind him.

He found himself in a large open-plan room, presently unlit but helpfully illuminated by the moonlight beaming in through the large plate-glass windows. Brolin saw the architect's drawing table with angle lights fitted to its sloping sides, another desk holding a Macintosh computer with a twenty-seven inch monitor, ink-jet printer, scanner and piles of software, a third desk obviously used for paperwork and presently almost bare, and a couple of good old-fashioned filing cabinets. Though aware that the plans for Feydal's villa might now be stored on the hard disk of the computer, Brolin reasoned that the architect would almost certainly have kept all of his original drawings for posterity and that they would be in one of the filing cabinets. Thus convinced, he unclipped his torch, switched it on and made his way to the filing cabinets.

He was in luck. Both the filing cabinets had labels on them, one indicating 'A-K', the other 'L-Z'. Holding the torch in one hand, Brolin opened the first filing cabinet with his other, then awkwardly flipped through the 'H' section until he came to 'Hussein, F.' He removed that file from the cabinet, went to the writing desk, sat in the chair, opened the file and found a set of architectural drawings inside. Partially unfolding the drawings and spreading them out on the desk, he was able to examine them by torchlight and confirm that they were, indeed, the drawings for Feydal's immense villa. Pleased, he refolded the drawings, which were bulky, tucked them down behind his belt, then replaced the file in its original place. He closed the filing cabinet, switched off his torch and left the building, carefully closing the door behind him and locking it with his all-purpose key. He then switched off the electronic blocking device, detached it from the burglar alarm and placed it back in his pocket. Removing the drawings from behind his belt, he held them firmly in his right hand and made his way back to the Peugeot that was still parked at the other side of the road. When he slipped in beside Jean-Pierre and gave him a nod, Jean-Pierre turned on the ignition, shifted into first gear and moved off along the street as quietly as possible. He only speeded up when they had turned the corner at the far end and were heading back to the city.

'How did it go?' he then asked.

'I got the drawings,' Brolin said.

'Then we're all set to run.'

'Not until we hear from Marie-Francoise.'

'Let us pray,' Jean-Pierre said.

Their prayers went unanswered.

CHAPTER TWENTY-THREE

Five days later, which was two days after the original deadline given by Brolin, Marie-Francoise still hadn't called. At first deeply depressed, then feeling betrayed, and finally growing anxious, wondering if something bad had happened to her, Brolin decided that he could not wait any longer and would have to launch his assault on Feydal's house.

In fact, during that time, while waiting vainly for the expected message from Marie-Francoise, Brolin had been working on plans for the assault by studying the architectural drawings stolen from Julian Lombard's study and making the other three men do the same, until each of them had its details etched firmly in his mind. Clearly, as the drawings showed, Feydal's villa had not been constructed simply as an expansive home but as a thinly disguised fortress. The towers at the gable ends of the large rectangular two-storey structure had been designed as watchtowers with enough floor space to hold comfortably three or four men at a time, viewing windows devoid of glass, and four-foot-high concrete walls that had long, narrow openings for the barrels of personal weapons or even machine-guns to poke through. All the windows in the villa had been made with bulletproof glass and covered with black wrought-iron bars.

'I can blow those bars off if necessary,' Dogherty said during a final strategy discussion in Brolin's hotel room, with the architect's drawings spread out between them. 'They're no problem at all.'

'You're worth your weight in gold,' Brolin responded. 'And presumably you can do the same to the main gates and the front door of the villa?'

'I sure can,' Dogherty said.

'OK, let's see what we've got to deal with once we're inside the building.'

The drawings showed that the upstairs floor of the villa had sixteen guest rooms, all with en suite bathrooms, on both sides of a central corridor that ran the whole length of the building, from one tower to the other. The towers could be accessed either via the doors at each end of that upstairs corridor or by doors at ground level, both facing the southern lawn, which was dominated by a swimming pool about three-quarters the length of the building, overlooking the Corniche John F. Kennedy and the Mediterranean. All the bedrooms overlooked the grounds north and south of the villa, with the southern rooms overlooking the swimming pool and giving panoramic views of the Mediterranean. Apart from clothes closets located between various of the guest rooms, there was nothing else of importance upstairs.

'No surprises here,' Brolin said, 'though there are

bound to be bodyguards in some of those bedrooms, sleeping in shifts. Please note, however, that if we can't take out the machine-gun crews in the watchtowers from the grounds outside, we can gain entrance through those doors in that central corridor. My suggestion, therefore, is that if we get into the main building without first knocking out the men in the watchtowers, two of us will concentrate on clearing the downstairs area while the other two advance up the stairs, methodically clear the bedrooms, working in opposite directions, from the central staircase to the doors at the ends of the corridor, then enter the watchtowers through those doors and dispatch the machine-gun crews at close range.'

'A-one,' Clayton said.

'Best remember, though' Dogherty said, 'when we're clearing the building, that if Bannerman, Feydal, or anyone else for that matter is upstairs when we enter the building, they could make their escape down the stairs of those two towers and out onto the southern lawns.'

'Good point,' Brolin said. 'So let's adjust our plan accordingly. Jean-Pierre, I'm going to place you in charge of an L4 light machine-gun. While the rest of us are entering the building, you'll take up a firing position equidistant between the two gable-end towers, at the southern side of the swimming pool, and cover both exits with the L4. We don't want to kill Marie-Francoise or members of the domestic staff by accident, so be careful who you fire at. As a general rule of thumb, I'd say don't fire at anyone who isn't firing at you unless you clearly recognize Feydal or Bannerman, in which case waste the bastards.'

'Right,' Jean-Pierre said.

'While you're taking up that firing position,' Brolin

continued, 'the rest of us will enter the building and attempt to clear the ground floor. As soon as the ground floor, if not entirely cleared, seems manageable, Clayton and Dogherty will advance up the stairs to clear the top floor. I'll follow them up when the ground floor is secured.'

'So what's downstairs?' Clayton asked.

The ground floor of the villa was more elaborate than upstairs. It included two large living rooms, one with a well-stocked library, a modern kitchen with an extending galley-shaped dining room and a laundry room out back, a study, a pool room and a 'security' office, all of which were accessed from a large reception area on the southern side, where the front door was actually located at the end of the driveway that circled around the front of the building from the east-side main gates.

'We'll be going in late at night,' Brolin said, 'so the domestic staff will either have gone home or, if they live there, they'll be asleep upstairs. The only people we're likely to run into, therefore, are Feydal's security men. Some will be in that security room, probably surveying the grounds and property with CCTV surveillance systems; others may be on shift duty at various points on the ground floor.'

'We just don't know where,' Jean-Pierre said.

'No,' Clayton said, 'because your precious Marie-Francoise failed to deliver.'

'Probably being fucked senseless by Feydal or Bannerman. Or both,' Dogherty said, unaware of Brolin's feelings for the lady and inadvertently making him wince. 'We should have known better.'

'So forget her,' Brolin said, wishing that *he* could do

so. 'We're now in the dark about their surveillance, so we have to go in without that knowledge.'

'That's fucking dodgy,' Clayton said.

'I agree,' Jean-Pierre said, 'but I don't think we necessarily have to do it. If I can get my hands on some advanced MEMS – and I think I can – we can at least find out where their outside surveillance cameras are located. Again, using MEMS, we could short-circuit their electricity, which would include their surveillance systems, before we go in.'

'Beautiful,' Dogherty asked. 'I'd forgotten all about those fucking fire ants.'

He was referring to the Micro Electro-Mechanical Systems (MEMS) that Jean-Pierre and the others had practised with just before the SAS was disbanded. The particular MEMS that Jean-Pierre was referring to was actually a Micro-UAV, or Unmanned Aerial Vehicle, not much larger than a beetle, powered by a tiny pulse jet, remote-controlled and capable of a wide variety of activities, whether in flight, on the ground or while advancing on miniature legs. For this reason it was fondly known as a 'fire ant'.

'The fire ants I'm thinking of,' Jean-Pierre said, 'are considerably more advanced than the ones you practised with and by using two different kinds we should be able, silently and invisibly, to survey the grounds of the villa, then incapacitate the guards before we launch the assault.'

'How come?' Clayton asked.

'One type of fire ant,' Jean-Pierre explained, 'is a surveillance device that can be flown over the grounds of the villa to relay back to the Visual Display Units in our computerized helmets the position of the guards picked out by its infra-red and sonic sensors. Once we know where the guards are, we can then send the required number of chemical-warfare fire ants over the gate to seek out the individual guards and land silently, practically invisibly, beside them. By which I mean that even if a guard saw a fire ant descending in the darkness, he'd probably mistake it for some kind of bug. Then, when the fire ant is on the ground, we can make it explode by remote control, releasing a gas that'll render the guards unconscious for at least six hours. Which leaves us free to launch the assault on the villa.'

'What about the surveillance systems?' Dogherty asked.

'A third kind of fire ant is a miniature flying EOCS, or Electrical-Optical Countermeasures System, that uses a laser beam of the particular megawatt range that works against electronic and optical sensors. So if we attack the outside surveillance cameras of Feydal's villa with flying EOCS devices, the whole system, including the cameras inside, will be knocked out. The same goes for the other electrical systems, including telephones.'

Dogherty gave a low whistle of admiration.

'This is fucking *Star Wars*,' Clayton said. 'It's not like real soldiering.'

'It's technologically advanced soldiering,' Jean-Pierre corrected him, 'and we should be grateful for it.'

'I'm on my fucking knees with gratitude,' Clayton said. 'You just didn't notice, is all.'

'OK,' Brolin said. 'Jean-Pierre's proved his worth again. I've tasked him with destroying Feydal's surreillance and communications systems and it looks like he's found a way to do it. So we render the guards unconscious without having to go anywhere near them, we knock out the surveillance systems and telephones while still being outside the premises, then Dogherty here blows the main gates open to let us enter the grounds and penetrate the house.'

'Sounds cool,' Dogherty said.

'What then?' Clayton asked. 'I mean, we're using all this technology to break in, so what do we use once we're inside?'

'Conventional weapons,' Brolin said without pause. 'MP5 sub-machine guns, Browning High Power handguns—'

'The good old Nine Milly,' Clayton interjected using the SAS nickname for that much-loved weapon.

'—flash-bangs and CRW clothing,' Brolin continued, referring to stun grenades and the standard black Counter-Revolutionary Warfare assault suits. 'And, so that we can use Jean-Pierre's MEMS, computerized helmets with Head-Up Display and night-vision optics.'

'You can get all that from your friends in the old port?' Clayton asked disbelievingly of Jean-Pierre who had been jotting Brolin's requirements down in a notebook. 'Even that way-out *Star Wars* shit?'

'*Oui.*' Jean-Pierre nodded emphatically. 'The past five years or so have seen a dramatic increase in the demand for such weapons and equipment from religious and political terrorist groups and urban criminals. As quickly as the army or the police update their technology, the terrorists and criminals do the same, so the market for high-tech weaponry is wide open and *growing*. We'll have no trouble buying *anything*. You can take that as read.'

'Great fucking world we live in,' Dogherty said in disgust. 'Once it was only the soldiers who were fighting; now *everyone's* doing it. I'm starting to feel kind of redundant.'

'You'll survive,' Brolin said.

'What's that?' Clayton asked, jabbing his index finger down on the architect's drawing, indicating a set of parallel lines composed of dots that were joined by other lines, rather like a railway track, drawn in pale blue ink, beginning in the reception area and running off the end of the page.

'Very observant of you,' Brolin said.

'I'm a bright boy,' Clayton retorted. 'So what the fuck is it?'

'We can't be too sure, but Jean-Pierre and I believe it's a flight of stairs leading down from the southern side of that reception area to a basement that covers approximately the same area as the ground floor. The basement contains an underground car park with ramps leading back up to the driveway on the eastern lawns. Even more interesting,' he continued, flipping the top drawing over to reveal another beneath, this one showing the basement and, beside it, a sketch of the area between Feydal's property and the seafront, with the Corniche John F. Kennedy in between, 'is this uncompleted sketch indicating an underground tunnel with steps. It appears to lead all the way from the basement, down the side of the hill and under the Corniche. Please note that about halfway across the Corniche the lines indicating the tunnel terminate.'

'Which means?' Clayton asked.

'Obviously,' Brolin replied, 'this was intended to be an escape tunnel. Given the way those dotted lines end abruptly, either the plan to have such a tunnel was dropped entirely, the tunnel was dug out to as far as halfway under the Corniche but not completed – or Feydal didn't want even the architect to know where the tunnel emerged.'

'Right,' Jean-Pierre said. 'If in fact it was completed, it's not likely that they planned to emerge from a manhole in the middle of the main road. More likely is that it continued on to the coastline at the far side of the Corniche, probably emerging in a small bay where Feydal could keep a motor launch for escape in an emergency.'

'But we've no way of knowing where that bay is.'

'Alas, no,' Jean-Pierre said.

'So we change our plan again,' Brolin said. 'If that tunnel *does* exist and leads to the sea, then almost certainly, if Feydal and Bannerman try to make their escape, they'll use that instead of emerging from the base of the watchtowers onto the southern lawn. It's therefore vital that we three—' he pointed to himself, then to Clayton and Dogherty '—secure the ground floor completely; then, when it's secured, you two will clear the upstairs floor and watchtowers while I go down to the basement and check out that tunnel. When you've secured the upstairs floor and watchtowers, you'll contact Jean-Pierre, still covering the exit doors to the watchtowers, and give him the all-clear to enter the building. The three of you will then take charge of anyone who surrenders, preferably locking them up in one of the bedrooms. You'll stay there, guarding the prisoners, until I return from the basement. If I don't return in fifteen minutes, you're to get the hell out of the building, dump the weapons and kit in the sea, then get out of Marseille and go your separate ways.'

'We don't come and look for you?' Dogherty asked, looking concerned.

'No, you don't,' Brolin said. 'Even though Feydal's villa is isolated from other dwellings and his telephone lines will have been cut, we can't complete that kind of assault without someone, perhaps passing motorists, seeing or hearing something and reporting it. That means we have to get in and out of the building as quickly as possible. So, if I don't come out of the tunnel in fifteen minutes, you're to assume that either I'm dead or I've reached the sea at the other end of the tunnel, in which case I'll look after myself, thanks.'

Clayton shrugged. 'If you say so.'

'I do say so,' Brolin retorted firmly. 'Fifteen minutes after the villa is secured, you all get the hell out of there.'

'What about the prisoners?' Dogherty asked.

'They'll either be bodyguards or domestic staff, of no interest to us. So just keep them locked in a bedroom, as I suggested, then leave the building and go back to the car.'

'And what about the woman, Marie-Francoise?' Clayton asked.

Still deeply pained at even the thought of Marie-Francoise, wondering what had happened to her, Brolin tried to keep his face composed when he replied, 'She's to be treated just like any other prisoner and locked up with the others.'

'So what happens to them when we light out of there?'

'As we know from our eyeball recces of the place over the past five days, certainly some of the domestic staff live at home, coming and going every morning and evening. One of them will find the prisoners the next morning, let them out of the locked room and then, presumably, call the local Gendarmerie. By which time, if we're all still in one piece, we'll be on our way back to Paris.'

In fact, though it would not have been possible to watch the main and only gates of Feydal's property from the approach road without being seen by the surveillance cameras fixed above them, Brolin had managed to place the gates under constant eyeball surveillance despite this, with himself and the other three taking round-the-clock four-hour shifts. In order to avoid the cameras, they did not park the rented Peugeot anywhere near the property. Instead, the man on watch duty had taken up an observation position hidden in an olive grove behind some high, shrub-covered ground by the side of the track that led up from the Corniche John F. Kennedy, halfway around the bend in the road where it led to the turn-off to Feydal's property. From there, though hidden from passers-by, the man in the watch position could see the main gates of the property. Each man coming on shift drove himself from the hotel in Marseille to a location approximately a quarter-mile short of the observation point. After parking the car there, he walked the rest of the way. The man he was replacing then walked the quarter-mile back to the car and drove himself back down to Marseille. Thus, the car was never parked for long in the vicinity and, even when parked briefly well away from the the watch position, it could not be seen by Feydal's surveillance cameras.

During those eyeball recces, they had seen the domestic staff come and go. More importantly, they had seen Feydal and Bannerman come and go in Feydal's armour-plated, bullet-proof limousines, though Marie-Francoise was never seen to emerge. After five days had passed with still no sign of her, Brolin was convinced that something had gone wrong: either she was being held prisoner in Feydal's villa or she had never come to

Marseille in the first place. Either way, Brolin was sure that Marie-Francoise had not changed her mind about helping him but was simply no longer able to do so. It was this thought that tormented him the most, convincing him that Feydal and Bannerman had somehow connected Marie-Francoise to his attempted assassination of them in Paris. Or, if they had not quite connected her to it, they had perhaps deduced that only she could have provided the information required by the would-be assassin. If this were true, Feydal and Bannerman would certainly want to punish Marie-Francoise in some way. Brolin didn't even want to think about that, let alone try to imagine how they might do it.

Was Marie-Francoise in the villa or not?

That was his major concern.

'I think we should launch the attack as soon as possible,' he said, trying to stick to the business at hand and addressing Jean-Pierre, 'Now we know exactly what we're going to do and what we're going to need. How soon can you fix us up?'

'Almost immediately,' Jean-Pierre replied. 'I've already connected up with my contact in the old port and he can deliver anything I want within twenty-four hours.'

'Deliver it *where*?' Brolin asked impatiently.

'A garage I've already rented,' Jean-Pierre said with a triumphant grin, 'located out in an old industrial zone near L'Estaque. It's in an area that's dead at night, so the weapons and equipment will be delivered to the garage in a van. That van will be followed by a car driven by a second man. Our Peugeot won't hold all the weapons and equipment, so the van containing them will be left in that garage – locked up, of course – and the driver will then be taken back to where he came from by the man in the car behind. L'Estaque is only about fifteen minutes' drive from here, so when we decide to launch the assault, we simply go out there in our Peugeot, park it in the garage, then drive to Feydal's place in the van. We change into our CRW suits and distribute the weapons and other equipment while still inside the van, then make our way to Feydal's villa by foot. Any problems, my friend?'

'Only the question of timing,' Brolin said. 'You said twenty-four hours, so can you guarantee delivery by tomorrow evening, to enable us to launch the assault the following evening?'

'*Oui*,' Jean-Pierre said with confidence. 'I can guarantee that.'

'Then let's do the job,' Brolin said.

CHAPTER TWENTY-FOUR

Though unable to sleep, Brolin lay on his bed in the hotel in La Cannebière, resting his eyes by keeping them closed, thinking of what was to come. He was not bothered by the thought of the assault itself but he was seriously concerned at the troublesome matter of Marie-Francoise's silence and, even more, by her virtual disappearance: she had not once been seen either leaving or entering Feydal's villa during the past five days. More than ever, Brolin was convinced that Feydal and Bannerman had either definitely learned of Marie-Francoise's part in the attempted assassination in Paris or had realized that she had certainly been in a position to report their movements to the would-be assassin. On the other hand, he reasoned, Feydal's or Bannerman's bodyguards could also have supplied that information, so they, too, would have come under suspicion. Therefore, if Marie-Francoise was indeed still with Feydal and Bannerman, she was surely being kept a virtual prisoner in the villa. Either that or she had not come to Marseille in the first place, which strongly suggested that she might have been murdered as punishment for betraying Feydal and Bannerman. Understandably, this possibility, more than any other, sorely tormented Brolin.

As he lay there, resting his eyes but inwardly agitated, he realized that although he had initially embarked on this mission to eliminate Bannerman, with Feydal being merely a side issue, disposable if necessary though not specifically targeted, he was now putting Feydal first in his thoughts, as if *he* had become the main target and Bannerman only a secondary problem. This was a dangerous and unexpected turn of events and Brolin had to face the fact that it had come about because of his personal interest in Marie-Francoise. In truth, if being 'in love' was possible at his age, he was in love with Marie-Francoise – or at least obsessed with her – and this was making him think stupidly, dangerously, of Feydal Hussein as his rival. Indeed, while he still tormented himself with thoughts of Marie-Francoise sweating and heaving either under or upon the gross William Bannerman, it was her relationship with Feydal that he most feared because it was that, more than her whoring with Bannerman, that dominated her life. The masochistic element of the relationship both baffled and haunted Brolin, whose own sexual life had been relatively straightforward, and he now felt that he had to destroy Feydal to set Marie-Francoise free.

If she was still alive.

Yes, the possibility that Marie-Francoise had been killed in Paris by Feydal or Bannerman rarely left Brolin's thoughts now and the thought was even more difficult to endure because if Marie-Francoise had indeed been punished with death then he, Brolin, was responsible for it. On the other hand, she could still be alive, perhaps a prisoner in the villa. This other possibility had strengthened Brolin's conviction that he and his men should launch an assault on the villa rather than trying to attack Feydal and Bannerman while they were on a public road in one of the arms dealer's bulletproof limousines. Yet as this decision had been made for what were not, in truth, purely tactical reasons, Brolin felt that he was betraying all his training and, perhaps, his own men. He was confused and disturbed by this.

Opening his eyes, he squinted against the overhead light, then checked his wristwatch and noted that it was 2330 hours: time to meet the others at the rented car parked farther along La Cannebière. They had decided to meet there, rather than in the lobby, so that they could all leave the hotel separately and would not be seen by the desk clerk going out as a group this late in the evening.

Sighing, but keen to get going, Brolin rolled off the bed, slipped into the rubber-soled lace-up Danner boots that he would wear for the assault, then put on his windcheater jacket and left the room, closing and locking the door behind him. He was only on the first floor, so he took the stairs down and crossed the lobby without handing in his key to the desk clerk, who did not even look up and notice his departure. Once outside the building, Brolin turned left and walked up La Cannebière, bright in lamplight and moonlight, still lively at this late hour, for approximately fifty metres until he had reached the rented Peugeot 306. Jean-Pierre was already behind the steering wheel and Clayton was in the rear seat. Dogherty had not yet arrived. Checking his wristwatch again, Brolin saw that it was now 2343 hours. As they had arranged to meet at 2345 hours, Dogherty still wasn't late. Satisfied, convinced that Dogherty would turn up in time, Brolin slipped into the seat beside Jean-Pierre.

'*Bon soir,*' he said.

'*Bon soir,*' Jean-Pierre replied.

'Looks like we got a nice evening for it,' Clayton said. 'Dry and reasonably warm and moonlit.'

'*Parfait,*' Jean-Pierre said.

'You checked everything?' Brolin asked him.

'*Oui,*' Jean-Pierre replied. 'The van was loaded in a warehouse in the La Jolette docks and I ticked off every single item as it went in. I stayed with the van, beside the driver, throughout the journey from the docks to the garage in that industrial zone in L'Estaque. I personally locked the doors of the garage before travelling back to the docks in a car that had followed us out there, specifically to take me and the driver back. So the locked van is in that locked garage and everything I ordered is in the van. My criminal friends kept their word.'

'You can always trust a crook,' Clayton said, 'to be honest in business.'

'*Exactement,*' Jean-Pierre said. 'They're not politicians, after all.'

'Nor police,' Brolin said, thinking bitterly of William Clive Bannerman.

'Too fucking true,' Clayton added.

Dogherty came along the pavement and reached the car at what was, according to Brolin's precisely set watch, 2345 hours on the dot. Dogherty rarely arrived early anywhere, but he was never late either. Grinning, he slipped into the rear of the car beside Clayton.

'How's my boyos?' he said.

'We're all fine,' Brolin said. 'I hope you guys took it easy in the hotel and didn't rest in the bar.'

'We were in our respective bedrooms just like you two,' Clayton replied, 'so we're both fresh as daisies.'

'OK,' Brolin said, 'Let's go.'

Jean-Pierre switched on the ignition and headlamps, then pulled away from the pavement, heading north along La Cannebière which was, at this late hour, still filled with traffic. He turned left onto the Rue d'Aix Cours Belsunce, stayed on it for a few more minutes, then picked up the autoroute heading west. When, approximately fifteen minutes later, he turned off the autoroute and entered L'Estaque, the traffic had thinned out considerably and when he actually reached the old, virtually abandoned industrial zone, where the traffic lights were few and moonlit darkness prevailed, there was not another vehicle in sight.

Relieved, Jean-Pierre drove through the industrial zone, past rusting Portakabins, old showrooms with broken windows and derelict warehouses, eventually braking to a halt in front of a large locked garage constructed from unpainted breeze blocks but with a red-painted corrugated-iron roof. Leaving the engine running, he handed Brolin a set of keys.

'For the locks,' he said simply. 'One for the garage and the other for the doors of the van inside.'

Nodding, Brolin slipped out of the Peugeot and walked through the moonlit darkness to the garage. He unlocked the doors, pushed them apart and saw a dark blue van parked inside. It was a large garage with room for three or four vehicles, but the van was the only vehicle there. After pushing the two doors back against the walls, one after the other, Brolin stepped aside and waved

Jean-Pierre on. When the Peugeot was inside the garage, Brolin closed the doors again.

Jean-Pierre switched off the Peugeot's ignition and headlamps. Then, while the others were clambering out of the car, he unlocked and opened the rear doors of the van. The back of the van contained a good number of wooden crates and cardboard boxes. A small crowbar, to be used for opening the wooden crates, was lying on top of one of them. Pleased to see that Jean-Pierre's criminal friends had been thoughtful enough to leave that, Brolin nodded at Clayton and Dogherty, then jabbed his finger towards the rear of the van, indicating that they should clamber in. When they were in, sitting at opposite sides and staring at each other over the heaped wooden crates and cardboard boxes, Brolin closed the doors.

'OK, Jean-Pierre, let's move it.'

While the Frenchman was clambering into the driver's seat of the van, Brolin again opened the two doors of the garage. Jean-Pierre started the van, then reversed out. When the van was parked outside, Brolin closed and locked the garage doors, then climbed up to take the seat beside Jean-Pierre. He gave the keys to the Frenchman.

'If I go down into that tunnel and don't come back, you're going to need these,' he said. Jean-Pierre nodded and pocketed the keys. 'Hit the road, Jack,' Brolin said.

Jean-Pierre drove away from the garage, out of the industrial zone, and then turned east, heading back to Marseille and, eventually, to Feydal's house high in the hills of Roucas Blanc. Approximately twenty minutes later, they had passed through Marseille and were turning once more onto the Corniche Président John F. Kennedy.

As the van sped through the night, Brolin glanced to

his right and saw the glittering Mediterranean far below. Glancing upwards to his left, he saw the soaring hills and scattered pine trees silhouetted against the moonlit, star-drenched sky. Nevertheless, he barely registered what he was looking at, being too concerned with what was to come and with his growing macabre fascination with Feydal Hussein, whom he now viewed as the Svengali who had a perverse magical grip on Marie-Francoise and was either keeping her prisoner or had, God forbid, already killed her. Now Brolin was itching to get into Feydal's villa, not only to complete his task by neutralizing that bastard Bannerman but also to find out what had happened to Marie-Francoise. Knowing this, aware that he wasn't being strictly professional, he felt a twinge of contempt for himself. But he had to live with it.

After travelling along the Corniche for about ten minutes, Jean-Pierre turned off, heading north, and took the steep, winding road that snaked up the hillside and led to the southern wall of Feydal's villa, high above. Just before the slip road that led to the main gates, he pulled into the relative shelter of the grove of olive trees that they had been using as an observation post for the past five days. He drove into the trees as far as he could manage, then doused his headlights and killed the engine.

'This is as good as it gets,' he said.

'All out,' Brolin responded.

While he and Jean-Pierre dropped down from their respective sides of the driver's cabin, Clayton pushed the rear doors open and slipped out that way. Dogherty remained in the van, preparing to push out the wooden crates and cardboard boxes. The van was now turned sideways to the narrow road that ran up from the

Corniche and curved around Feydal's property, but Jean-Pierre stood watch by the lip of the road, preparing to signal any time he saw the lights of another vehicle. Right now there was nothing, so he used a hand signal to indicate that the others could start unloading.

They did so immediately, with Dogherty pushing out the crates and boxes while Brolin and Clayton took turns at grabbing them and carrying them through the trees to a small clearing at the other side. The clearing was angled in line with the sheer slope that ran all the way down from the southern wall of Feydal's villa to the Corniche far below. Brolin, however, was not concerned as he knew that they could not be seen in the darkness from this high up.

It only took a few minutes to unload everything, during which time no other vehicles came along the road. When the last box had been deposited on the dusty earth of the dark slope at the other side of the olive grove, Dogherty emerged from the van, Jean-Pierre locked the doors, then both men joined Brolin and Clayton. These two were already opening the wooden crates and boxes, Brolin breaking the crates open with his crowbar, Clayton cutting the wide tape around the cardboard boxes with a penknife. When every crate and box had been opened, they prepared for the assault.

First, they stripped off their own clothes and put on the all-black CRW suits that had been delivered in the cardboard boxes. These were, in fact, old GD Specialist Supplies suits formerly used by the SAS and obviously sold on the black market by disgruntled veterans after the Regiment was disbanded. The suits were made of Nomex, which gave a high level of protection, and pads had been inserted in both knees and elbows for extra protection.

An Armourshield GPV (General Purpose Vest), utilizing 'soft' Kevlar armour with a trauma shield and giving wraparound protection against high-velocity rounds, was put on over the CRW suit. Footwear being so important, each man was already wearing his old broken-in Danner boots, made out of full-grain leather and cordura nylon, with a Gore-Tex lining. Jean-Pierre had the French equivalent, retained from his days with the GIGN.

In the old days, the CRW suit would have incorporated an integral respirator, anti-flash hood and ballistic helmet. But time had moved on and now, courtesy of Jean-Pierre's technologically advanced criminal friends, each man was given a lightweight, ballistic-resistant plastic helmet with night-vision optics and a so-called 'Head-Up Display' that rested on the forehead and could be pulled down over the eyes to allow him to see in all conditions. It also showed, on a miniature screen, his location, the location of the enemy and the locations of the others in the patrol. The Head-Up Display in the helmet was activated by a slimline computer strapped to each man's back and controlled by the buttons on a miniature keyboard strapped to his forearm. The Head-Up Display, keyboard and computer were all wired together and powered by disposable batteries that had a life of approximately eight hours. These batteries also charged the CT100L body-worn microphones that were connected to the helmet and enabled the men in the team to speak to each other despite any high-pressure sound from grenades and gunfire.

Now fully dressed and with communications operational, the men removed the weapons from the opened wooden crates and passed them around until each man had what he required. The single L4 7.62mm light machine-gun, along with a canvas bag filled with thirty-round box magazines, went to Jean-Pierre, for the covering of the exit doors of the watchtowers. Each of the men, Jean-Pierre included, picked up a small metal case containing a collection of MEMS and slipped it into one of the big pockets in the side of his suit. Each of them also picked up a Heckler & Koch MP5 sub-machine gun fitted with infra-red sights and taking thirty-round box magazines. This was a favoured weapon with all of them because it was exceptionally accurate, rarely jammed and offered a choice of single-shot, full-automatic or three-round-burst fire. Each man also strapped on a holstered Mark 3 Browning Double-Action 9mm High Power handgun, known affectionately as the 'Nine Milly', and clipped thirteen-round box magazines for it to his webbed belt. Also included with their weapons were explosive door cutters (charges wrapped in flexible foam, enabling them to be bent and shaped according to demand), MX8 stun grenades, or 'flash-bangs', CS gas grenades and miniature wire-cutters.

Lastly, since they had decided not to blow open the main gates because the noise would give warning to those inside the villa, each two-man team – Brolin with Jean-Pierre and Clayton with Dogherty – removed the separate pieces of sectional lightweight aluminium assault ladders from their wooden crates and prepared to carry them up the dark hill, hugging the tree line, until they could see the main gates whilst still being hidden by the trees from the ever-shifting infra-red surveillance cameras.

'Call in your names,' Brolin said into the mouthpiece of his helmet, which was wired to the microphone on his chest and to the earpiece now in his ear.

'Jean-Pierre!'

'Clayton!'

'Dogherty!'

'All present and correct,' Brolin said, satisfied that their communications were in order. 'OK, follow me.'

They advanced up the dark hill.

CHAPTER TWENTY-FIVE

Brolin advanced up the hill at the half-crouch with the men doing the same in single file behind him, each burdened with his weapons, ammunition and other equipment. Once they were in sight of the white walls of Feydal's property, viewing the main gates from a forty-five degree angle in the pale light of the moon, with the wind from the Mediterranean sweeping across them, moaning, they knelt on the ground and quietly put the two sectional ladders together. When the ladders were ready for use, Brolin removed the small steel case from his side pocket and held it up in the air, indicating that the other men should do the same. As they were doing so, Brolin spoke into his mouthpiece.

'I'll concentrate on this wall and the main gates. Jean-Pierre covers the southern wall. Clayton covers the western wall and Dogherty covers the north wall. Attack with chemical-warfare fire ants, the green ones, all guards you see. Then, when the guards are down, locate and neutralize all surveillance cameras with the laser fire ants, the red ones. OK, commence.'

As the others did the same, Brolin opened the small steel case to reveal a line of what looked like flying beetles, some green and some red. These were the MEMS. Brolin removed six green fire ants from the case and laid them in neat formation on the ground beside him. He then pulled a thin lead from the side of his computerized helmet and plugged it into the miniature keyboard strapped to his forearm. On his helmet VDU (Visual Display Unit) he brought up the walls of the villa, lit by the eerily unreal light of night-vision optics. A green light blinking on the keyboard indicated that all was ready.

Pressing the red button on the keyboard, he activated all six of his fire ants. Powered by tiny whisper jets, humming almost inaudibly, they hopped simultaneously into the air, rising to about four feet, then hovered there, bobbing indecisively. They were able to hover, Brolin knew from his training with the early models, because of the minute sensors and actuators spread across tissue-thin wings that maximized lift from every square millimetre of surface while making them seem to ripple like live muscles.

By pressing another button and increasing or decreasing pressure upon it, Brolin was able to make his fire ants rise to slightly higher than the top of the wall around Feydal's property. They hovered there for a moment, as did the fire ants of the other men. Then, at the pressing of another button on the miniature keyboards on each man's forearms, all twenty-four fire ants flew over the wall, spreading out in different directions, and soon disappeared in the moonlit darkness beyond.

Knowing that the other men were controlling their

individual fire ants, Brolin looked into the eyepiece of his VDU and saw the grounds of Feydal's property from a height of about thirty feet, again lit in the eerie green-and-white glow of night-vision optics. Using the various buttons on his keyboard, he was able to switch from one fire ant to the other and see the images that they were relaying to his VDU.

Concentrating on the grounds between the eastern wall and the villa, making his fire ants glide along the wall on both sides of the main gates, Brolin soon saw the ghostly images of armed guards positioned along the perimeter of the grounds, close to the wall. Each time he saw a guard, he pressed another button and caused a fire ant to fall silently to the ground, close to its victim. When the fire ant was on the ground, Brolin, by pushing down on another button, was able to make it crawl forward on its minute legs until it was as close to the guard as he wanted it. Once it was in position, he left it there and switched to another fire ant, repeating the procedure until four of his fire ants were lying silently on the ground near to a guard.

In fact, he only found four guards: two manning the main gates, one on each side of them, and the other two patrolling the inside of the eastern wall.

With four of his fire ants in position and the other two still hovering over the middle of the east lawns, Brolin glanced at the three men lying belly down around him and received the thumbs-up signal from them, one after the other.

'Jean-Pierre?' Brolin asked, whispering into his mouthpiece.

'Ready.'

'Clayton?'

'Ready.'

'Dogherty?'

'Ready.'

'Fire!' Brolin whispered.

Knowing that the others were doing the same, he pressed a button to make his first fire ant explode and release its incapacitating gas. Brolin saw the ghostly image of one of the guards in his eyepiece and the small silent explosion on the dark ground near the man's feet in the extreme foreground of the display. Instantly, the image of the guard blinked out, confirming that the fire bug had indeed exploded, releasing its poison gas over the guard while destroying itself and no longer relaying back to him. Immediately, he switched to the next fire ant and repeated the procedure, then repeated it twice more until all four of his fire ants had been exploded and none were relaying images back to him.

When he had exploded the last chemical-warfare fire ant, he activated his remaining two and sent them flying from one of his selected targets to the other and in each case he either saw the guard lying unconscious or staggering drunkenly before falling to the ground. Within a few minutes, every guard found by the fire ants around the perimeter had been rendered unconscious and would remain so for at least four hours.

Satisfied that his own guards had been knocked out, Brolin spoke into his mouthpiece, asking each of the other men in turn what their situation was.

'Jean-Pierre?'

'My guards, including those manning the front door of the house, on the southern side, are all unconscious,' Jean-Pierre reported. 'Four guards in all. The south lawn is now clear.'

'Clayton?'

'Mine, too,' Clayton said. 'Only one guard, patrolling the whole length of the western wall. There was no one else there. The west lawn is clear.'

'Dogherty?'

'Two guards patrolling the whole length of the north wall,' Dogherty side, 'each covering one half of it because of its length. Both guards down. The north lawn is now clear.'

'We're dumb cunts,' Brolin said.

'Pardon?' Jean-Pierre responded.

'What?' Dogherty said.

Clayton, always patient, just listened in.

'We don't have to worry about the machine-gun crews in the watchtowers,' Brolin said. 'I've got two chemical-warfare fire ants left and you guys must have pretty much the same.'

'Two left,' Jean-Pierre said.

'Five,' Clayton said.

'Four,' Dogherty said.

'Good,' Brolin said. 'You, Jean-Pierre, and you, Clayton, send your total of seven fire ants up into the western watchtower and knock out the men manning its machine-gun. You, Dogherty, send your four fire ants up into the eastern machine-gun tower and I'll do the same with my two. The seven in the western tower and the six in the eastern tower should be enough to knock out both machine-gun crews.'

'*Parfait!*' Jean-Pierre exclaimed in a whisper.

'Then let's do it,' Brolin said.

Controlling his remaining two chemical-warfare fire ants with his miniature keyboard and switching constantly from one to the other, Brolin felt truly unreal as, through the images relayed back to the eyepiece of his VDU, he glided up through that eerie green-and-white light to the eastern watchtower. He saw the ghostly images of three men grouped around a tripod-mounted machine-gun under a conical roof supported on four concrete posts, with no windows to impede the progress of the MEMS. Through the eyes of the MEMS Brolin glided down between two of the concrete posts, hovered just behind the machine-gun crew, then settled both his fire ants onto the floor beside their feet. Sitting there – or, at least, convinced that he was sitting there, metamorphosed into a bug – Brolin saw four other insect-like forms settling down around him. When they had all settled on the floor and were motionless, Brolin spoke into his mouthpiece.

'Fire,' he said as he pressed a button on his own keyboard.

Instantly, the images being relayed back from the watchtower blinked out in his eyepiece.

The fire ants had exploded silently in the watchtower, destroying themselves to release their poison gas.

'Dogherty?' Brolin asked.

'I can't get an image back,' Dogherty said, 'so I assume my fire ants have exploded.'

'Jean-Pierre?' Brolin asked.

'I think mine have exploded.'

'Mine, too,' Clayton said.

'Good,' Brolin said, knowing that his voice could be heard by all of them. 'Let's check that both machine-gun crews are out of action. Then, if that's confirmed, we'll seek out and destroy the surveillance cameras. That should knock out the whole electricity system as well as the telephones. Deploy your red fire ants.'

Knowing that the others would be doing the same, Brolin removed his six red fire ants, the laser MEMS, from the small steel case, placed them on the ground beside him, then punched a button on his miniature keyboard to send them flying over the high white wall. Controlling them with his keyboard, he made them circle the whole villa and scan both of the watchtowers. In both cases he saw the men of the machine-gun crews, ghostlike in infra-red, either sprawled over their weapon or stretched out, unconscious, on the floor.

Satisfied, Brolin used his fire ants to scan the whole length of the eastern wall of the villa and found a surveillance camera at each end of it. The cameras were scanning all around, covering the whole of the eastern lawn, including the driveway leading to the main gates. Again, feeling that he had metamorphosed into a flying insect, Brolin sent a red fire ant to each of the cameras, remote-controlled each device to hover over them, then asked the others what they had found.

'Two surveillance cameras over the front door,' Jean-Pierre reported, 'one on each side of it, moving to and fro to scan both sides of the driveway. Also, one at each end of the south wall, covering the whole of the south lawn. I've got red fire ants hovering over all of them.'

'Clayton?'

'Two surveillance cameras, one at each end of the west wall, covering the whole west lawn between them. I've placed my fire ants near both of them.'

'Dogherty?'

'The same,' Dogherty said. 'Two surveillance cameras, one at each end of the north wall, covering the whole north lawn between them. I've placed my fire ants near both of them.'

Brolin checked his wristwatch. It was 0033 hours. 'Activate your fire ants at 0035 hours,' he said. They all came back with 'Check!'

Brolin raised his Head-Up Display and looked around him. He was feeling very strange. He had spent the last thirty minutes hovering out there in virtual space, feeling as if he was no more than a set of eyes and ears, a metamorphosed flying insect, communicating with ghostly voices, the voices of those who once were his friends. Now, with a shock, using his own eyes again, he realized that those friends hadn't moved and were in fact still lying belly down around him, mere inches away, albeit in the darkness. Each of them had taken a different side of the building and each, he suspected, must now be feeling as unreal as he felt.

Rubbing his eyes, he looked up at the vast, starry sky, then down at the glittering Mediterranean, and sighed with something approaching real longing, lowering his Head-Up Display again. He stared into the eyepiece and saw one of the surveillance cameras, an eerie shape in the infra-red, then switched to the other fire ant and saw the other camera. Resting his hand on the miniature keyboard, he touched one of the buttons.

'Fire!' he said into his mouthpiece, pressing the button.

In this case, since the fire ants had not been detonated but instead had sent minute laser beams shooting into the surveillance cameras, the images did not wink out and Brolin saw the cameras, which had been scanning constantly, coming to an abrupt halt. Instantly, he used the keyboard to make his fire ants descend past the gable end until they reached the first window.

The lights inside the villa had gone out.

'Jean-Pierre?'

'*Oui?*'

'Have the lights inside the villa gone out on your side?'

'Yes.'

'Clayton?'

'Lights out.'

'Dogherty?'

'Lights out.'

'Good,' Brolin said.

Knowing by this that the electrical supply in the villa had been short-circuited and that the telephone lines would also be down, Brolin raised his Head-Up Display, which he no longer needed, then removed his helmet completely. When he looked around him, at the other three men, he saw them doing the same.

'Attack!' Brolin barked.

CHAPTER TWENTY-SIX

Instantly, each man grabbed one end of a sectional ladder and helped his partner – Brolin with Jean-Pierre and Clayton with Dogherty – carry it up the remaining few yards of the sheer slope to the level ground of the east wall, left of the main gates. The two ladders were angled against the walls, then extended rapidly until they reached the top.

With his MP5 slung over his right shoulder, Brolin went up one ladder, followed by Jean-Pierre who had his MP5 *and* the L4 strapped to his back. Clayton went up the other ladder, followed by Dogherty. Reaching the top of the wall, Brolin unslung a hooked abseiling rope, harness and descendeur from his left shoulder, hooked the rope to the top of the wall, then rapidly abseiled down the other side. He had barely slipped out of the harness when Jean-Pierre and Clayton started their descent, followed almost immediately by Dogherty. Leaving the abseiling ropes to dangle from the wall, they advanced rapidly at the half-crouch across the moonlit east lawn until they reached the swimming pool on the south lawn.

At that moment, the lights inside the villa came back on, obviously powered by an emergency generator, and beamed out over the south lawn and the swimming pool.

Two of the unconscious bodyguards were lying beside a table by the swimming pool; two others were lying by the front door.

'Keep advancing!' Brolin snapped. Then he bolted towards the south wall of the house, actually the front of the building, with Clayton and Dogherty close behind, even as Jean-Pierre, fully exposed in the light, ran around to the south side of the pool, which had a four-foot-high white-painted wall, unslinging his light machine-gun while on the move.

Reaching the wall of the house, Brolin and the others pressed against it. Then Brolin inched along until he came to the first window. He peered around the window frame and saw a well-furnished but otherwise empty lounge. He heard men shouting somewhere else inside, so dropped below the windowsill and raced up to the front door, stepping over the two unconscious guards, with Clayton and Dogherty close behind him. Clayton took one side, Dogherty the other and Brolin aimed his MP5 at the lock of the door, preparing to blow it to hell.

Suddenly, glass smashed noisily above and rained down upon them. Then someone started firing a pistol from the broken window, obviously aiming at Jean-Pierre, who had just placed his light machine-gun on its tripod and was shielded by the four-foot-high wall of the swimming pool. Jean-Pierre instantly swung the barrel of his LMG upwards, aiming at the window, then fired a short burst, the weapon making a fierce roaring sound. Bullets ricocheted off the wall around the window and lumps of plaster rained down.

Brolin fired his MP5, blowing the front-door lock to pieces. Then Clayton swung around, kicked the door open and burst into the villa, dropping low as he went in to enable Brolin to give him covering fire. Brolin did so, firing a short burst in a broad arc, peppering as much of the lobby as he could see, then stopping to let Dogherty, also dropping low, rush in. After firing another short burst, Brolin himself entered, crouching low and preparing to fire his weapon.

He saw two men wearing short-sleeved grey shirts and grey trousers and with empty holsters on their hips coming out of what he knew to be the security room, already raising their pistols to fire. Clayton and Dogherty fired first, simultaneously, their sub-machine guns roaring savagely, and both men were punched backwards as plaster and wood exploded from the wall behind them, showering them with debris even as they collapsed.

Instantly, Dogherty ran forward, jumped over the two dead men, threw a flash-bang into the security room, pressed himself to the wall outside as it exploded, then rushed into the smoke. His sub-machine gun roared again as he blew the security equipment to hell, by which time Clayton was throwing a flash-bang into the library.

Jean-Pierre's machine-gun roared out on the south lawn, clearly raking the front wall of the villa, concentrating on upstairs, which was where most of the bawling was coming from. Brolin heard pistol shots from up there, followed by bursts from a sub-machine gun, as he went to one of the two living rooms, kicked the door open, threw in a flash-bang, and then jumped to the side and pressed his shoulder to the wall until the grenade had exploded. He heard another explosion – Clayton's flash-bang going off – then, when the silvery flare of his own grenade had faded, as black smoke billowed out, he spun on the balls of his feet and rushed into the room, crouched low and moving the barrel of his MP5 from left to right.

The room was empty.

Rushing out again, Brolin saw a bulky man in a grey suit coming down the stairs, aiming a pistol two-handed at Clayton as he emerged from the smoke of the library. Brolin fired a sustained burst and the man shuddered convulsively, dropped his pistol, then fell forward and rolled down the stairs, bouncing brutally from one stair to the next and finally landing on the tiled floor of the lobby.

A second bodyguard, who had just appeared on the landing halfway up the stairwell, fired wildly at Brolin, then disappeared around a corner as Brolin fired a burst at him, the bullets ricocheting off the bannister, chips of wood flying in all directions.

As Brolin raced across the lobby to enter the kitchen and dining room, Dogherty was throwing a flash-bang into the second living room and Clayton was taking up a position at the bottom of the stairs, preparing to give covering fire until the downstairs floor had been cleared.

Brolin heard the roar of Dogherty's exploding flash-bang as he reached the doorway to the kitchen, caught a glimpse of movement, saw a man's head and shoulders, then heard bullets whipping past his head, mere inches away, to ricochet off the wall to his right. Brolin fired a short burst from his MP5, heard a yelp of pain, then transferred his MP5 to his left hand to unclip and hurl a flash-bang with his right. The light flared up, died and was followed by billowing smoke. Brolin advanced at the half-crouch, holding his MP5 at the ready.

Entering the kitchen, he saw a man in a blue tracksuit, clasping his bloody right arm, his hand still holding a pistol, and coughing violently as he staggered blindly about. He must have seen Brolin because he raised his damaged arm, trying to aim the pistol. But Brolin put another burst into him, making him spin backwards and crash into a low table, which collapsed beneath him as he fell.

Brolin advanced farther into the kitchen, still at the half-crouch and moving the barrel of his MP5 left and right. He heard movement in the adjoining room, obviously the dining room, so he threw himself against the wall at the side of that doorway, hurled a flash-bang, blinked when it exploded, then charged into the room, firing a sustained burst as he did so.

A rendered wall ahead exploded into flying debris and dust, the bullets whining as they ricocheted. A man wearing a roll-neck pullover rose up from behind the long table, as if inviting death, though he was actually aiming a pistol, and received Brolin's burst in his chest. He was virtually picked off the floor and punched backwards, arms flailing, to crash into the wall that was now peppered with bullet holes. He slid down the wall, leaving a trail of blood behind him, and seemed to sigh as he sat on the floor, legs splayed, until he bent from the waist and his head fell forward, as if he was taking a bizarre bow.

Brolin rushed up to him, checked that he was dead, then walked around him until he came to the doorway leading into the laundry room. He threw a flash-bang in, waited for it to explode, then entered and found that the room, though blackened by the grenade, was empty. Satisfied, he turned around and made his way back through the dining room and kitchen, then out into the lobby.

Clayton was still standing at the bottom of the stairs, aiming his MP5 upwards but not firing, as Dogherty was running to join him. The latter stuck his thumb up in the air, indicating that the ground floor had been cleared. Brolin nodded, then used his CT100L microphone to make contact with Jean-Pierre, still outside and, judging by the roaring of his LMG, still raking the upstairs of the building.

'Brolin here. Come in, Jean-Pierre.'

The roaring of the machine-gun ceased instantly.

'Jean-Pierre here.'

'What's happening out there?'

'A few men still upstairs with handguns and a couple more dead. Some tried to get out by the downstairs door of the watchtowers, coming out firing, but none of them got more than a couple of feet. Those not killed retreated back inside and right now they're firing from the upstairs windows, obviously desperate.'

'Only a few?'

'No more than four or five, so Clayton and Dogherty should be able to take care of them.'

'Can you stay out there until that top floor is cleared?'

'No problem,' Jean-Pierre said. 'I'm hidden behind the four-foot-high wall of the swimming pool and the only thing they can see is the smoke from the barrel of my machine-gun. So I'll stay here until I'm called upstairs.'

'Good man,' Brolin said. 'Over and out.'

He was convinced that neither Feydal nor Bannerman, who would have been upstairs in their bedrooms when the attack was launched, would have had the time to make their way downstairs and enter the basement. And, since he was also obsessed by the question of where Marie-Francoise was, Brolin decided to help Clayton and Dogherty clear the upper floor instead of descending to the basement. He indicated this to them by pointing to the stairs with his free hand, then racing ahead of them to the first stair.

He advanced slowly, quietly up the first flight to the landing, hugging the wall opposite where the stairwell turned away from him, his finger on the trigger of his MP5, preparing to fire. Clayton and Dogherty, coming up behind him, were being equally careful.

Brolin froze just before reaching the landing. Clayton and Dogherty did the same. He heard the crack of a pistol from somewhere upstairs, the answering roar of Jean-Pierre's machine-gun, then abrupt silence. A floorboard squeaked around the blind side of the stairwell, then the pistol cracked again upstairs, obviously firing in one of the guest rooms. Jean-Pierre's LMG roared in reply.

Moving as little as possible, Brolin unclipped a flash-bang from his belt, released the pin, leaned forward and threw the grenade towards the blind turn of the landing. The instant the grenade left his hand, he threw himself to the other side of the stairwell to give himself protection and closed his eyes just before the grenade exploded. Even with eyes closed, he saw the silvery flare. He also felt a wave of heat and heard a scream and then he was bounding around the corner of the landing, his MP5 roaring as he fired on the move.

A man materialized in front of him, rubbing his closed

eyes with his free hand, dropping his pistol from the numbed fingers of the other, then going into violent convulsions as the bullets from Brolin's MP5 smashed into his chest. He staggered back, then fell forward. Brolin pushed him to the side, glimpsed him sliding down the wall, then continued advancing up the stairs with Clayton and Dogherty still bringing up the rear, their weapons at the ready.

Another guard was up there. Brolin fired, the man collapsed, and then the long central corridor of the upstairs floor lay stretched out to each side of him.

Clayton came up on Brolin's left, Dogherty on his right, and the three of them studied the long corridor with the sixteen guest rooms, eight to each side of the staircase. Handguns were firing from both sides, but it was impossible to tell from which rooms the shots were coming so they would all have to be cleared methodically, one after the other.

'You take that side,' Brolin said to Clayton, indicating the corridor to his right, 'and I'll take this one. You, Dogherty, stay here to give us covering fire and to prevent anyone from trying to leave a room and making their escape down the stairs of either of the watchtowers.'

'Right, boss,' Dogherty said.

While Dogherty remained there, Brolin and Clayton moved off in opposite directions along the central corridor. Reaching the first door on his right, Brolin turned the handle, threw the door open, pressed himself to the wall by the door frame, then unclipped and hurled a flash-bang, all in one swift movement. When the flash-bang exploded, he raced into the room, dropping low and moving the barrel of his MP5 left and right even as the light was still flaring and the room was filling up with smoke. Finding no one in the first room, he went to the opposite room and repeated the procedure, but that too was empty.

As he emerged from the second room, however, the door of a room farther along opened and a man holding a handgun leaned out and fired a wild shot down the corridor. Brolin fired back, his burst taking in a broad arc, tearing the wall and door frame to shreds and making the man duck back inside.

Brolin ran along the corridor, unclipping a flash-bang while on the move, then kicked the door wide open as it was closing and threw in the flash-bang. When it exploded, he rushed in, crouching low and preparing to fire, and saw three people huddled up fearfully in a far corner: two elderly women and a middle-aged balding man, the women wearing nightdresses, the man in pyjamas – obviously the domestic staff. Then he saw another man dropping down behind the double bed to fire a wild shot.

The bullet whipped past Brolin's head and ricocheted off the door frame. Then Brolin fired at the bed, under it, swinging the barrel left and right, and the man let out a cry that was instantly drowned out by the terrified screaming of the women huddled up on the floor. The man behind the bed fell, rolled onto his back, legs twitching, as Brolin glanced around the smoke-filled room to confirm that no other gunmen were in it. Satisfied that it was clear, he bawled to the three huddled up on the floor, 'Don't move! Stay here!' Then he rushed out of the room and back into the corridor in time to see Jean-Pierre bounding up the stairs.

'Take that side!' Brolin bawled, indicating that Jean-Pierre should check the remaining three rooms at the opposite side of the corridor. Ignoring the still-smoking room, Jean-Pierre went to the next room, kicked the door open, hurled in a flash-bang and then rushed inside even before the flash had subsided. Brolin glanced along the other side of the corridor, where Clayton was at work, and heard the savage roar of his MP5 from inside a smoke-filled room.

Satisfied, Brolin was about to enter the next room on his side of the corridor when a man rushed out of the last room, wildly firing a pistol in his direction as he headed for the door that led into the watchtower. Instantly, Dogherty opened fire with his MP5, first peppering the door with ricocheting bullets, then finding the man and cutting him down. The man danced like a puppet on a string, dropped his handgun, slammed into the exploding wall near the door, then collapsed to the floor.

Brolin kicked the door of the next room open, hurled in a flash-bang, waited for the explosion and then went in, dropping low. He saw a bulky man in a tracksuit frantically trying to open a window with one hand while holding a pistol in the other. Brolin fired a burst at him. The man screamed and was punched forward, smashing through the window-pane, then flopped head first over the wooden frame and remained that way, his feet still on the floor and his backside turned up, the white wall on both sides of him splashed with blood. There was no one else in the room, so Brolin hurried back out.

Looking to the other side of the central corridor, he saw two men in shirts and slacks walking towards Dogherty with their hands in the air. Clayton was close behind them, keeping them covered with his MP5.

'All clear!' Clayton bawled when he saw Brolin. 'All clear this side! Where do we put them?'

Brolin indicated the room where he had found the three members of the domestic staff. 'In there!' he bawled. 'Lock the door and then guard the room. You come with me, Dogherty.'

'Right,' Dogherty said.

Another flash-bang exploded behind Brolin and he turned around to see Jean-Pierre rushing into the last of the rooms on his side of the corridor. Without waiting to see if Jean-Pierre had found anyone, Brolin went to the third room along and found the door locked. Dogherty came up behind him. Brolin listened at the door and heard someone moving inside, the squeaking of hinges, possibly someone whispering, though he could have imagined that.

Using a hand signal, he indicated that Dogherty should move to the other side of the door. Dogherty did so. Brolin stepped away from the door, spread his legs wide and aimed his MP5 at the door handle. Dogherty pressed his back to the wall, then slid a little way down it with his weapon angled across his chest, preparing to spin around and enter. When he nodded to Brolin, indicating that he was ready, Brolin fired a short burst at the door handle, tearing the wood around it to shreds and then blowing the metal lock through to the other side. Dogherty spun around and kicked the smashed door open. Then the floor beneath him exploded, picking him up and hurling him violently backwards into the corridor in spewing splinters of wood, geysering yellow flames and boiling black smoke. His clothes were on fire and his legs blown to bits.

'Booby trap!' Brolin bawled.

What was left of Dogherty, black and blistered, still burning, struck the floor with a sickening thud. Even as

Jean-Pierre emerged from the opposite room and rushed to put out the flames, Brolin, enraged, plunged into the smoke of the room that he had to clear, going in low, almost doubled over, swinging the barrel of his MP5 left and right, preparing to fire at any male he found in there.

Someone was in there.

But Brolin didn't fire.

As he entered, crouched low, he heard the clatter of footsteps to his right ... footsteps that sounded as if they were descending stairs. He looked in that direction, preparing to fire, and saw an open door in the wall, revealing what looked like a dark walk-in closet. The back of a tall, broad man – a man as big as William Bannerman – filled the doorway and disappeared, obviously going down a flight of stairs that gave off a dull, metallic ringing.

But still standing in the doorway in the wall, looking directly at Brolin and wearing a black windcheater, open-necked shirt and blue denims, his hands raised as if in surrender and a smile on his face, was Feydal Hussein.

It was the smile that stopped Brolin from firing.

'So where's Marie-Francoise?' Feydal said mockingly.

Then he disappeared.

CHAPTER TWENTY-SEVEN

Brolin blinked, shocked, wondering if he had hallucinated. Then he realized as he straightened up and Jean-Pierre rushed into the smoke-filled room that Feydal had simply stepped back into that dark closet and slammed the door shut.

'Was that Feydal I glimpsed?' Jean-Pierre asked.

'Yes,' Brolin replied. 'Dogherty's dead?'

'*Oui*. So let's get those two bastards.'

Jean-Pierre rushed to the closet door, reaching out to open it. But Brolin grabbed him by the shoulder and jerked him back. 'No!' he snapped. 'That door might be booby-trapped as well. The stairs behind it must go down to the basement, so let's take the door down in the lobby and try cutting them off.'

'You go down that way,' Jean-Pierre said as he removed a flexible frame charge from a pouch on his webbed belt. 'Meanwhile, I'll blow this door off, setting off their booby trap, if there is one, then follow them down those stairs.

Between us, we might be able to box them in.'

'Right,' Brolin said, turning away instantly and hurrying out of the room, stepping over the scattered pieces of Dogherty's mutilated legs and feet, even as Jean-Pierre was attaching the frame charge to the handle of the closet door. When he stepped out into the corridor, he froze automatically at the sight of Dogherty's still smouldering, black and blistered, unrecognizable remains. Brolin had seen a lot in his time, but he was still immeasurably shocked by that sight. As his heart raced with a potent mixture of rage and revulsion, he looked away quickly and saw that Clayton, as instructed, was standing guard outside the locked room containing the captured bodyguards and the three shocked members of Feydal's domestic staff.

'Stay there,' Brolin said as he hurried past Clayton, heading for the top of the stairs.

'Get those bastards for Dogherty,' Clayton said emotionally, frustrated to have the shit job of guarding the room and looking like he wanted to murder someone for what had been done to his friend. 'Waste both of the fucks.'

'Don't worry, I will.'

Brolin hurried down the stairs, smelling the acrid stench of cordite and smoke, thinking of the exceptionally broad back that he had seen disappearing into the walk-in closet before Feydal had made his taunting remark and then closed the door. Brolin was convinced that the broad back belonged to Bannerman and that the corrupt police chief and Feydal intended making their escape either by car from the garage or by the tunnel that had been only partially drawn on the plans by the architect and so might or might not exist.

Believing this, however, did not help Brolin when he recollected Feydal's taunting remark about Marie-Francoise. He found himself wondering, in confusion and dread, just what Feydal had meant by it. Certainly, the remark suggested that he knew about Brolin's feelings for Marie-Francoise and only Marie-Francoise could have told him that.

Why would she have done so? More important: when? Had she simply confessed to her spying? Or had Feydal or, perhaps, Bannerman forced the truth out of her? And if so, had it been back in Paris, before Feydal and Bannerman came to Marseille, either with or without her? Finally, if Marie-Francoise wasn't here with Feydal and Bannerman, was she, wherever she might be, alive or dead?

That question now haunted Brolin and made him more determined than ever to complete his task.

Reaching the bottom of the stairs, he could still smell the cordite and he saw smoke still drifting out of all the rooms cleared by him and the others. Knowing that no one was left on this floor, he felt safe enough as he crossed the lobby and then entered the narrow hallway that ran along one side of the library where, according to the architect's drawing, there was a flight of stairs leading down to the basement and, perhaps, to the beginning of a tunnel that led under the Corniche John F. Kennedy and on to the sea. Indeed, at the end of the hallway, exactly where the map had shown the stairs to start, Brolin found a closed door.

At that moment, he heard the distant though distinctive roaring of an MP5, followed instantly by the return fire of handguns and some other type of sub-machine gun. Realizing that those weapons were firing in the basement, indicating that Jean-Pierre had engaged in a firefight with *someone*, Brolin was desperate to get down there. But he did not dare to kick the door in for fear that it might be booby-trapped. Instead, he withdrew an explosive door cutter from a pouch on his webbed belt. In less than a minute, he had bent the charge around the door handle and inserted a 'det' cord and a time fuse with a non-electric firing cap, set to detonate in sixty seconds. Then he ran back along the short hallway, turned the corner at the end and waited for the explosion. When it came, it was followed instantly by another, even louder explosion, confirming that the door had, indeed, been booby-trapped.

Without waiting for the smoke to clear, Brolin ran back along the hallway, dropped low at the door, which was now scattered in scorched, smouldering pieces around the small landing at the top of a stairwell, and found himself looking down into a basement as large as the ground floor of the villa. In fact, it looked like a public car park, with lots of parking bays framed by concrete pillars, enough bays for twenty cars, and a ramp leading up to the driveway in the east lawns.

Bannerman and Feydal were down there.

Marie-Francoise was not.

In fact, Bannerman and Feydal were surrounded by bodyguards, most of whom were wearing casual clothing – windcheater jackets, open-necked shirts and trousers – obviously thrown on in a hurry when the assault against the villa had started. All of them were armed, some with handguns, others with Kalashnikov AK-47 assault rifles, and they were firing at Jean-Pierre who, hidden behind a pillar located near the bottom of the flight of stairs leading down from the guest room where Dogherty had died, was trying to keep them pinned down with steady bursts from his MP5. Two of the bodyguards had already been killed or wounded – they were lying on the ground, one frozen in death, the other twitching – and even as Brolin looked down, another was caught in a burst from Jean-Pierre's weapon and went slamming backwards into the side of a parked Mercedes-Benz. The windows of the vehicle then exploded as bullets smashed through them.

Shocked to note that Marie-Francoise was not with them, suddenly overwhelmed with the dread that Feydal or Bannerman had killed her back in Paris, Brolin had to force himself to focus on completing his task.

Looking down from the top of the steps in the gloomy basement, he noted that Feydal, Bannerman and their bodyguards had obviously made their way from the other flight of stairs at the far side of the basement to the first parking bays, perhaps intending to escape in one or two of the cars. However, before they had managed to actually get to a car, Jean-Pierre had kept them pinned down with repeated fire from his MP5. Now, as Jean-Pierre continued firing at them, creating a hellish, reverberating din – the roaring of the weapons; the constantly ricocheting bullets and shattering concrete – they were returning his fire while inching painfully backwards, moving from one protective pillar to another towards a bay in which a black limousine with tinted windows was parked.

Convinced more than ever that Feydal and Bannerman were hoping to make their escape by car, Brolin, still out of their line of vision, made his way down the stairs and along the high wall until he was behind a pillar placed just in front of the ramp leading out of the basement.

His intention was to open fire with his MP5 from here, creating a crossfire, but that wouldn't stop the two criminals if the limousine they appeared to be heading for was bulletproof – which it almost certainly was.

Wanting a way to block the exit entirely, Brolin looked about him and saw that drums of oil were stacked up against the wall just behind him, almost parallel to the foot of the ramp leading up to the closed doors of the basement. Slinging his MP5 over one shoulder, he went to the stacked drums and pulled down the one on the top, which brought others tumbling to the concrete floor, creating a hollow, metallic clamour that drew the attention of Feydal's men.

Instantly, a couple of them turned in Brolin's direction and started firing at him, but their bullets just ricocheted off the pillar behind which he was hidden, showering him with pieces of concrete and white powder. Ignoring the bullets and the flying debris, Brolin pushed the first oil drum as hard as he could and it rolled across the level floor in front of the ramp, eventually coming to a halt mere inches from the opposite wall. As more bullets ricocheted off the pillar on one side of him and the wall on the other, Brolin pushed another oil drum across the level floor in front of the ramp and this one fell just short of the first.

Jean-Pierre's MP5 roared. Feydal's men were firing back and also firing at Brolin with a combination of Kalashnikov AK-47s and handguns. The noise was appalling, but Brolin was unperturbed. Relatively safe behind the pillar, he rolled one drum after another across the flat floor until they formed a barricade across the ramp leading up to the exit doors of the basement. When the drums were all in place, Brolin unslung his MP5 from his shoulder, spread his legs wide and fired a sustained burst from the hip, peppering all the oil drums with bullets.

Hot though the bullets were, they did not ignite the oil, though it was gushing out from the many holes and spreading rapidly. Observing this, Brolin unclipped a white phosphorous incendiary grenade from his belt, released the pin and threw it into the middle of the line of oil drums. The grenade struck the ground, causing oil to splash upwards. Then it exploded, igniting the oil, and a jagged sheet of vivid white and yellow flame, reaching up to the ceiling and giving off a foul black smoke, shot across the level floor at the foot of the ramp and effectively created a wall of fire.

'Get through that, you bastards,' Brolin muttered as he temporarily hid himself behind the nearest pillar to avoid the fierce heat.

Glancing around the pillar, he saw that one of Feydal's bodyguards, enraged, was running towards him, cursing loudly and firing an AK-47 from the hip. The bullets ricocheted noisily off the pillar behind which Brolin was hiding, showering him with falling concrete and dust. But Brolin stepped out quickly enough to fire his own burst, which caught the running man full in the chest, smashing it all to hell and soaking his clothes with blood. He flung his arms up, releasing his weapon, which clattered loudly to the floor, then staggered backwards, legs buckling, arms twitching, and finally keeled over like a falling tree.

Surprisingly, given that the wall of fire now covered the whole width of the ramp and was nearly as high as the ceiling, its flames actually curling back down with black smoke boiling out of them, Feydal, Bannerman and their remaining couple of bodyguards were still working their way around the second bay to get into the third where the limousine with tinted windows was parked. Assuming that they were boxed in, with nowhere else to go, Brolin used a hand signal to indicate to Jean-Pierre, still firing from behind a concrete pillar at the other side of the basement, that he should advance. Then Brolin too began to advance, darting from one pillar to the next, always running at the half-crouch and weaving repeatedly to avoid the bullets still being fired at him.

Resting behind a pillar about halfway to the parking bay he wanted to reach, Brolin leaned out for a quick eyeball recce and saw Feydal and Bannerman clearly, the former's handsome, almost delicate features framed between the shoulders of two of his burly bodyguards, the latter towering above even the bodyguards and looking every inch the animal that he truly was. There was, indeed, something Neanderthal about Bannerman, something primitive and brutish, whereas Feydal seemed the very soul of sophistication, more of a wicked schoolboy than a major criminal with a reputation for ruthlessness. Cruelty showed in every line of Bannerman's face whereas Feydal's showed only sardonic wit and a trace of good-humoured cynicism. It was hard to imagine Feydal as evil, which Bannerman certainly was.

Brolin studied them at length, trying to work up hatred for them, trying to justify what he was doing. But though he certainly felt contempt for Bannerman, his only feeling about Feydal was one of intense curiosity. This was, after all, the man who had virtually owned Marie-Francoise, first charming her, then terrifying her, but who had seemed to have the kind of control over her that could not be explained by fear alone. This was, indeed, the man who knew more about Marie-Francoise than Brolin could ever hope to know.

This man was Brolin's true rival.

Now, being reminded that Marie-Francoise wasn't here, that her fate was a mystery and, more importantly, that one way or the other he had almost certainly lost her, Brolin determined to try to take Feydal or Bannerman alive and make them talk. He had considered putting an end to this by hurling an incendiary grenade, taking the whole group – Feydal, Bannerman and the bodyguards – out at once, but the thought of killing those two men and never learning about the fate of Marie-Francoise was too much to handle. Instead, despite the risk to Jean-Pierre and himself, he would do it the hard way: continuing this firefight until the bodyguards were neutralized, then concentrating solely on Feydal and Bannerman, taking at least one of them alive and making him talk.

This was not a sensible way of completing this task, but Brolin just couldn't help himself.

Looking straight ahead, he saw that Feydal, Bannerman and their remaining four bodyguards were at the last protective pillar before they would have to make the run to the parking bay containing the limousine with the tinted windows. They were glancing left and right, first at Jean-Pierre, then at Brolin, preparing to make the run. But since the wall of fire had made escape by car impossible, there seemed little sense in what they were doing and they were surely only doing it because they had no other choice. With Jean-Pierre advancing from one side, Brolin advancing from the other, and the wall of fire blocking the exit, their only other choice would have been to run straight across to the stairs that Brolin had just come down; that, however, would have left them exposed to the crossfire repeatedly being laid down by Jean-Pierre and Brolin.

It seemed, therefore, that their retreat to that parking bay was based solely on the impulse to survive. They were going backwards only because that was the one direction left to them. That they would eventually find their backs to the wall might not have entered their heads at all. The hope of survival always rested on buying time and this was what they were doing.

Or so Brolin assumed.

Glancing straight ahead, he saw that the men he was after were preparing to make their final run to the parking bay. Glancing left, he saw that Jean-Pierre, now halfway across the vast, dimly lit basement, was peering out repeatedly from behind his pillar, waiting for them to make that final run and preparing to fire at them. Concerned that Jean-Pierre might kill Feydal or Bannerman before he could talk to them, Brolin could only pray that they would be protected by the bodyguards until they were in the parking bay, at which point he, Brolin, would be able to move in on them personally before Jean-Pierre got to them.

The bodyguards were either fanatically dedicated to – or terrified of – their boss because when they emerged from behind the last protective pillar, they had formed a semicircle around Feydal and Bannerman, a human shield, and they came out moving sideways with all guns blazing, two of which were roaring AK-47s.

Jean-Pierre opened fire immediately, raking the whole group. But Brolin was shocked to find himself holding off, not wanting the guards to be killed too soon – at least, not until Feydal or Bannerman, or both, reached the shelter of their chosen parking bay. Jean-Pierre, however, apart

from being an excellent shot, was also firing in a wide
arc. Almost instantly, two of the bodyguards were cut
down, their weapons clattering noisily to the floor, their
legs buckling and their arms flailing as they shuddered
violently, staggered drunkenly and then collapsed.

Instantly, Feydal and Bannerman broke away from
the remaining two bodyguards and started running,
Feydal firing his handgun at Brolin while on the move,
Bannerman shooting at Jean-Pierre. The bodyguards ran
as well, both spraying bullets wildly with their AK-47s as
Brolin and Jean-Pierre added to the general bedlam with
bursts from their MP5s.

Feydal and Bannerman made it safely into the parking
bay just as one of the remaining two bodyguards was
caught in the crossfire and went into violent convulsions,
jerking this way and that, doubling over as if punched
in the stomach, then bending backwards and twisting
sideways and finally falling to strike the concrete floor
with a sickening thud, his AK-47 making a noisy rattling
as it rolled away from him.

The other bodyguard made it, hurling himself the
last few metres to slam into the front of the limousine,
jackknife across the bonnet, then slide off and scramble
back to his feet. He joined Feydal and Bannerman where
they were standing at the rear of the vehicle, between it
and the wall.

Jean-Pierre burst out from the shelter of his pillar and
ran towards the parking bay.

Brolin did the same. He was holding his weapon at
the ready, preparing to kill the bodyguard, still hoping
to spare either Feydal or Bannerman. But then he saw
Feydal, still behind the limousine, swinging his right
arm and releasing something from his hand. He did

not throw it hard – he threw it languidly, as if playing – and Brolin saw something shaped like a small metal pineapple falling, as if in slow motion, onto the gleaming black bonnet of the limousine.

'HAND GRENADE!' Brolin bawled as he threw himself to the side, still holding his MP5 in one hand, slapping the ground with the other to break his fall, then pushing hard to make himself roll over two or three times, as far away from the blast as time permitted. He heard the explosion, but it wasn't very loud and he didn't feel the pressure of the blast.

Surprised, he raised his head and saw that the parking bay had filled up with billowing black smoke so dense that it had almost obscured the black limousine. Glancing to the side, he saw that Jean-Pierre had heeded his warning and thrown himself to the ground but was already rising to his feet. Brolin did the same and then advanced on the parking bay, crouched low and weaving left and right, preparing to fire. He heard movement behind the limousine, someone shouting, something slamming, between the limousine and the wall, but when he advanced to the bonnet of the car, he choked in the smoke and was almost blinded, his eyes wet and stinging.

Jean-Pierre came up beside him.

Realising that the hand grenade had only been a smoke bomb and that Feydal had deliberately thrown it gently so that it would fall close and fill the parking bay with smoke, Brolin put on his respirator, which had been resting on his chest, then dropped onto his belly. Jean-Pierre did the same. With a silent hand signal, Brolin indicated that Jean-Pierre should take the other side of the car. The Frenchman duly did so, crawling around the front of the vehicle on his belly and, as Brolin could see by looking under the vehicle, starting to crawl along to the back of the parking bay.

Brolin did the same on his side, crawling forward on his belly while painfully holding his MP5 with the barrel pointed upwards, prepared to fire if he saw any kind of movement.

When he and Jean-Pierre reached the end of the parking bay, they saw only an empty space between the rear of the limousine and a solid wall.

Then they saw a trapdoor.

CHAPTER TWENTY-EIGHT

The smoke was already clearing when Brolin and Jean-Pierre saw the tunnel through which Feydal, Bannerman and their bodyguard had undoubtedly escaped. This, Brolin realized, was the tunnel that he had seen on the architect's drawings for the villa, though the drawing hadn't shown where the tunnel ended. Nevertheless, Feydal and Bannerman, as well as their bodyguard, were somewhere down there and Brolin was determined to find them.

Again, though his instinct was to raise the trapdoor, he didn't do it. Instead, as he had done with the door to the basement, he fixed a frame charge to it and blew it to hell. The explosion triggered off another, even noisier explosion, indicating that this door too had indeed been booby-trapped.

'Smart bastard,' Brolin said as he inched carefully into the smoke that was swirling above the jagged hole where the trapdoor had been. Laying his MP5 on the ground beside him, taking care to make no noise, he removed his Browning High Power from its holster, cocked it, held it at the ready, then bellied forward the last few inches to the jagged, charred lip of the hole. Looking down, he saw a square-shaped concrete landing with concrete steps running at a steep angle into a deepening gloom and, eventually, a darkness fractionally illuminated by what appeared to be dim overhead lamps that, Brolin assumed, were powered by the emergency generator.

Definitely a clever bastard, Brolin thought. *He worked everything out.*

There was no one in sight, though Brolin thought he could hear the sound of footsteps receding hurriedly a good distance down the tunnel. Assured that the bodyguard was not in the immediate vicinity, ready to ambush him, Brolin sat upright, holstered his handgun, picked up his MP5, nodded at Jean-Pierre, indicating that he should follow, then lowered himself down onto the first step. He had to duck slightly to get his head below floor level, but after making his way down a few more steps, he was able to straighten up again and walk normally.

Jean-Pierre followed him into the hole and then kept about ten feet behind him to minimize the risk of both of them being hit at once if they were ambushed.

As Brolin went down the steps, moving as quietly as humanly possible, scanning left and right and letting the barrel of the MP5 follow his gaze, he saw that the tunnel had plain concrete walls covered in damp and cobwebs, was something over six feet in height, and went down as far as he could see, eventually disappearing into a darkness that was fractionally illuminated by what were, indeed, dim electric lights in protective metal cages fixed to the ceiling. It was clear to him, from the angle and apparent length of the tunnel, that it was indeed running down the side of the steep hill upon which Feydal's villa was perched. Since it curved quite a bit, often making sharp bends, he assumed that during its construction the builders had often had to detour around layers of immovable rock. For Brolin, those bends were dangerous, presenting him with blind turns, and despite his urgent desire to move on as quickly as possible, he approached them slowly and carefully, virtually inching around them, always expecting to find a weapon pointing at him. So far, though, after descending for twenty minutes, he had not seen a thing.

He did, however, hear things: the scuffling of rats and mice, the steady drip of water, the normally imperceptible squeaking of the rubber soles of his and Jean-Pierre's boots: then faint rumbling sounds above, accompanied by a vibration that could be felt underfoot as the steps came to an end at a point where the tunnel levelled out and ran as straight as an arrow above a fissure in the earth, a virtual bridge with black-painted iron handrails, before disappearing once more into lamplit gloom.

Listening to that rumbling sound, which came from directly above, Brolin realized that he was hearing the sound of traffic racing along the Corniche John F. Kennedy. He also realized, because of the nature of the vibration (the wheels of the vehicles shaking the earth beneath the road), that the tunnel was not very deep. Indeed, the steady vibration was causing dust to rain steadily from the low concrete ceiling.

Glancing back over his shoulder, Brolin saw that Jean-Pierre was still behind him but had also stopped advancing in order to keep the same distance between them, still mindful of being caught in an ambush. Reassured, Brolin indicated with a silent hand signal that he was going to cross the bridge over that dizzying underground fissure. Realizing that there he would be dangerously exposed, he took a deep breath, held his weapon at the ready, then started walking.

Jean-Pierre, still about ten feet behind him, did exactly the same.

Stepping onto the bridge, which was made of concrete like the steps, the walkway built solidly on the damp rocky outcroppings on either side, Brolin glanced down and saw a dizzying drop through the pitch-black darkness of the deep, narrow chasm. Looking down there, he felt drawn to its deadly depths; looking up, he felt the mass of the earth pressing heavily upon him. The feeling in both cases was odd, divorcing him from himself, making him feel unreal, so he moved faster when he reached the halfway mark, wanting to get across quickly.

He was three-quarters of the way across the bridge when a single shot rang out.

The bullet whipped past Brolin's head and he threw himself belly down on the walkway, swinging his MP5 around in front of his head and firing a wild, blind burst straight ahead, into that square of dimly lit darkness where, he assumed, the steps began again. His bullets ricocheted off the concrete that formed the mouth of this second tunnel and went whistling off in all directions. Then another, more accurate burst sent the bullets flying straight into the tunnel. Nevertheless, the instant Brolin stopped firing, another single shot rang out.

Jean-Pierre screamed behind Brolin.

Rolling over slightly to glance back over his shoulder,

Brolin saw that Jean-Pierre was also stretched out on the walkway, but at a peculiar angle, his left leg obviously smashed by one shot from the man in the tunnel and his right arm shattered by the other. Shocked, Brolin also wondered why the unseen assailant had shot at Jean-Pierre instead of at the lead man: himself.

He soon found out when a third shot rang out and Jean-Pierre jerked violently and screamed again, his right leg now pouring blood and twitching spasmodically, its white bone gleaming through torn flesh. It became clear to Brolin in that instant that the man firing the pistol was aiming quite deliberately at Jean-Pierre, purposely missing Brolin. It was also clear that his intention was to torture Jean-Pierre before actually killing him.

They're keeping me until the end, Brolin realized, *and forcing me to watch Jean-Pierre die. Those fuckers are sadists.*

Another shot rang out and Jean-Pierre screamed again, this time a long, drawn-out shriek that reverberated between the rocks on either side of the walkway and cut like a knife through Brolin's heart. Glancing back over his shoulder, Brolin saw that the latest bullet had punched Jean-Pierre, who was still screaming and shuddering in agony, towards the edge of the walkway – either that or Jean-Pierre was deliberately wriggling in that direction, intending to put himself out of his misery by joining the Exit Club – committing suicide – by throwing himself over the edge.

Shocked and horrified, Brolin was about to jump to his feet and race to Jean-Pierre's side when another two shots rang out: Jean-Pierre's body jerked twice and was punched further sideways by the bullets. He screamed again as his left arm and leg fell over the edge, dangling briefly in open air, twitching violently, dripping blood. Then the dead weight of his limbs pulled the rest of him over and he slid off the walkway and plunged, yelling dementedly, down into the inky-black fissure, the first portal of hell. His screaming was cut off abruptly when he struck the bottom after what seemed like an eternity.

Abruptly losing control, almost out of his mind with grief and rage, Brolin jumped to his feet and ran straight for the other side of the bridge, at the half-crouch and weaving, firing his MP5 from the hip in a sustained burst that either had to keep the gunman pinned down or make him retreat. In fact, he retreated. As Brolin rushed into the tunnel at the other side, expecting to see the bodyguard, he was stunned to see Feydal's face rising up out of darkness, his mocking grin clearly visible. Then a hand swung through the uncertain light in a farewell wave and Feydal disappeared. Brolin threw himself to the ground again, raising his MP5 to fire, and heard Feydal's footsteps receding, then someone else laughing. The laughter was deep-throated, a kind of animal rumbling, and Brolin knew it was Bannerman.

The footsteps of more than one man receded, descending the steps that went farther downhill.

Brolin jumped up and followed them.

Now he felt nothing but a blinding, murderous rage that was aimed more at Feydal than at anyone else. It was Feydal, he realized, who had decided to toy with him by torturing Jean-Pierre before killing him and Feydal who was still playing his sick game by deliberately luring him on. Brolin went for the bait, unable to stop himself, no longer thinking of his own safety, a foolish soldier for the first time, and in his foolishness he was jumping three or four steps at a time. Then he hurried around a bend in the tunnel and tripped over something.

He went down spinning, hitting the sharp edge of a step with his right shoulder, sliding down a couple more even as he rolled onto his back, saw the trip cord vibrating like the string on a bow, and instinctively raised his MP5 as someone rushed towards him.

It was the last bodyguard, a big man, all meat and muscle, bald as an eggshell, and he was raising his handgun as he raced back up the stairs with Bannerman clearly visible behind him. He was still bringing his handgun up to the firing position when Brolin fired a sustained burst, taking no chances and swinging the barrel of his gun from left to right, covering a wide arc. The hail of bullets punched into the running man, sprayed the wall behind him, the low roof above him, found him again to turn him into a crude imitation of an epileptic having a fit. Blood burst through his tattered shirt, splashed on the step beside Brolin and into Brolin's face. Then the man fell to the side, slid slowly down the wall, tumbled backwards and went bouncing back down the steps, his weapon clattering after him, as Brolin jumped to his feet and started forward again.

He saw Bannerman's back farther down and fired a burst at it. The bullets ricocheted off the concrete around Bannerman's feet, off the walls and ceiling, but Bannerman, untouched, turned another bend and disappeared from view.

'Fuck!' Brolin exploded as he continued down the steps, this time taking them one at a time, though he was certainly moving as fast as he could. Reaching another bend in the tunnel, where it seemed to be levelling out again, he took it slowly, carefully, inching around with his shoulder grazing the inner wall. Then he flung himself round the corner, preparing to fire his MP5.

He was in time to see the back of Feydal disappearing around another bend and Bannerman, like a great ape, lumbering after him. Brolin fired at Bannerman just before the police chief made the bend. The bullets ricocheted noisily off the left-hand wall, causing lumps of concrete to fly away in all directions and clouds of dust to billow. Bannerman let out a shocked, anguished scream as his left leg buckled. Then he sank to his hands and knees and crawled, like a gross, four-legged beast, around the same bend that Feydal had taken.

Brolin rushed forward to follow him. Reaching the bend, he dropped to one knee, holding his MP5 across his chest, then carefully inched around the straight edge of the corner wall. Looking ahead, about twenty metres farther on, he saw a rectangle framing bright stars and silhouetting an outcropping of rocks. That was the end of the tunnel: the rocks were just inside it and Bannerman, more beastlike than ever, was crawling awkwardly towards them.

'Help me!' he bawled.

A tall, slim figure appeared in the rectangular exit, silhouetted against the stars and holding a pistol in his right hand.

'Help me!' Bannerman bawled again as he continued crawling towards the rock outcropping. 'Damn it, Feydal, help me!'

Brolin wanted Bannerman alive, so he fired a burst at the silhouetted Feydal. His bullets ricocheted off the rock outcropping just in front of Feydal, who jumped to the side and out of sight.

'No can do!' Feydal shouted mockingly. 'It's too late,

Bannerman. Your wonderful SAS man, a great warrior, your nemesis, is coming implacably for justice. It's either you or me, Bannerman, and, alas, it can't be me, so he's all yours my friend. Life is lived on a wing and a prayer, so say your prayers and take wing. If he gets past you, *then* he'll come for me and he'll surely deserve me. *Au revoir* and good luck.'

'Fuck you!' Bannerman wailed.

Brolin heard Feydal laughing, then the sound of receding footsteps. He fired at Bannerman and sent a stream of nine-millimetre bullets shooting towards the police chief as the gross figure started crawling behind the rock outcropping until only his lower legs and feet were exposed. The bullet-stream smashed into Bannerman's thick ankles, shattering the bone, and he screamed like a stuck pig as he dragged himself all the way behind the rocks.

Brolin took that golden opportunity to run forward again.

He advanced at the half-crouch, weaving left to right, and was approximately fifteen metres from his goal when Bannerman's head and shoulders appeared over the rocks. His hand came into view too, holding a pistol. Brolin threw himself to the ground, rolling behind other rocks jutting up from the floor of the tunnel as Bannerman's pistol cracked and the bullets whistled past his head to ricochet off the wall above him. Brolin fired a short burst from his MP5, but received no response.

Brolin waited, catching his breath and thinking, still wanting either Bannerman or Feydal alive in order to find out what had happened to Marie-Francoise. He still didn't know where the end of the tunnel (that frustratingly short distance away) opened out onto but Feydal had certainly emerged from it and was doubtless making his getaway right now. Therefore, having lost Feydal, Brolin felt that he had to take Bannerman alive and grill him about Marie-Francoise.

Unfortunately, there was that fifteen metres of exposed terrain between himself and Bannerman with nowhere to hide in between. If Bannerman wasn't too weak to fire his weapon, Brolin was trapped here. He decided to find out.

'Bannerman!' he called out. There was no reply, so Brolin tried again. 'I know your ankles are smashed up, Bannerman, and you can't get away, so why not throw your weapon over those rocks and let me come and fetch you?' Still there was no reply. 'Feydal's deserted you, Bannerman. Your friend ran away and left you. He treated you as some kind of joke, so why die while he gets away? Throw your gun over those rocks and let me come for you and I'll take you back in one piece. Can you hear me, Bannerman?'

Again, there was no reply, so Brolin stood up cautiously, holding his weapon at the ready.

Bannerman's hand appeared over the rocks again, still holding the pistol, and a single shot rang out. Bannerman had fired blindly, but the bullet whistled past Brolin's head, mere inches away, and Brolin dropped low again.

'Bannerman!' he called out.

This time he was answered with an anguished groaning from behind the rocks. 'Ah, Jesus!' Bannerman groaned. 'Christ Almighty, the pain! You fucking bastard, you shitehole.'

'I can help you, Bannerman! I've got morphine in my first-aid kit. Let me come over there, Bannerman, and I'll put you out of your misery.'

Bannerman laughed hoarsely, contemptuously. 'With a bullet in the head,' he shouted back. 'That's what you came here to do, you lump of SAS shit, and you're going to do it.'

'I'll take you back alive,' Brolin said, suddenly wondering just what he *would* do if he captured Bannerman. Could he shoot him down in cold blood at close range? Brolin seriously doubted it. 'It's true I was sent to kill you, but I failed, so I'll take you back alive now.'

'Who sent you?' Bannerman asked.

'I can't tell you that,' Brolin replied.

'Only someone highly placed would have sent you and that has to mean someone in the government. You came here on a covert mission for the British government, so don't tell me you'll take me back. They don't *want* you to bring me back. They want me to disappear and that's what you were tasked with. If I let you come over here, Brolin, you're going to have to complete your task – and the only way you can do that is to put a fucking bullet in my head . . . Ah, Jesus, the pain.'

Bannerman groaned again and then fell silent. Brolin listened intently, trying to hear Bannerman's breathing, knowing that he would be bleeding badly from the dreadful wounds to his legs and ankles. Brolin hoped that Bannerman might weaken to the point where he would become unconscious.

'How did you know my name?' Brolin shouted.

Bannerman took a long time to reply. But eventually he did, sounding even more hoarse and weak. 'From that whore you were using as a spy. The whore you fucked, Brolin. *My* whore. Feydal's whore. She told us who you were, what you were here for, you SAS shit. Did you think we'd be so dumb that we wouldn't question everyone in a position to know of our movements? Well, we did and we narrowed it down to that bitch and she sang like a bird.'

'Where is she now?' Brolin asked, deeply pained by Bannerman's description of Marie-Francoise.

Bannerman laughed, but then the laughter broke down into painful coughing before he managed to speak again. 'Wouldn't *you* like to know? Sweat on it, you cunt.'

'I'm going to kill you, Bannerman,' Brolin said, now filled with blind fury and inserting another thirty-round box magazine into his weapon.

'Not if I kill you first,' Bannerman retorted. 'And I can still fire this pistol.'

'Fuck you,' Brolin said. Then he jumped up and started running, weaving left and right, firing a sustained burst from his MP5 while still on the move. The bullets ricocheted off the rocks, creating a curtain of dust and flying splinters, but Bannerman fired another wild shot from his handgun and Brolin had to throw himself belly down on the ground.

Brolin was now less than two metres from the rocks and knew that Bannerman would have to reveal himself before he could fire down upon him.

Brolin started crawling forward, his MP5 held out in front of him, preparing to roll to the side and open fire if Bannerman managed to sit up high enough to aim at him. Bannerman failed to do so. Instead, he swore aloud – 'Fuck!' – and then Brolin heard the heavy slithering of his body on the ground as he desperately tried to crawl away from the rocks to the star-filled rectangular opening at the very end of the tunnel. Brolin jumped back to his feet and advanced to the rock outcropping, then ran around it and saw Bannerman on his belly, trying to haul his great bulk forward with one hand, his pistol still in the other.

'Stop!' Brolin bawled, spreading his legs and taking aim with his MP5 at Bannerman's broad back.

Bannerman froze. 'Fuck!' he growled again. He was about three metres away from that rectangle of stars, the gateway to freedom, but he sighed like a great beast expiring and then rolled onto his back.

Suddenly, he raised the pistol in his right hand, aiming at Brolin.

Brolin's MP5 roared and Bannerman went into convulsions, his massive bulk shuddering and twisting as the bullets tore through him, soaking his clothing with blood and exposing white bone. When Brolin stopped firing, Bannerman gasped and then groaned. The pistol fell from his numbed fingers. He stopped shuddering and his head fell to the side, but his eyes remained open.

Brolin walked up to him and stood over him. He studied him for a moment, then leaned down and slipped his free hand under his cheek. He rolled Bannerman's head around until the dying man was looking up at him with eyes losing their lustre.

'Where's Marie-Francoise?' Brolin asked.

Bannerman stared dully at Brolin for a moment, obviously losing consciousness, but eventually he managed a weak, sneering smile. 'The smack-addicted whore is where she belongs,' he said hoarsely, 'and whether that's in heaven or in hell, she's no longer your concern. Go fuck yourself, Brolin.'

Then Bannerman choked and died.

Brolin stood there for some time, looking down at the dead man, realizing that he had completed his mission but that this wasn't the end of it. Eventually, taking a deep breath letting it out with a sigh, he walked to the end of the tunnel and stepped out to see the vast sweep of the Mediterranean under a starry, moonlit sky.

He was in a small horseshoe–shaped bay with rocky outcroppings and a small, white sandy beach.

There was no sign of Feydal.

CHAPTER TWENTY-NINE

Brolin remained standing at the mouth of the tunnel, studying the quiet moonlit bay located below the Corniche John F. Kennedy. The rock face encircling the bay was too high and sheer to climb quickly, so Feydal could not have escaped that way. Straight ahead, however, about ten metres away, a wooden jetty thrust out into the sea. A couple of rowboats were tied to the jetty and beyond them, perhaps a quarter-mile out, was a large silhouetted motor boat. Since the only way out of the bay was by sea, Feydal had to be on that boat. Assuming that he was, he could have made his escape by now. That he hadn't bothered to do so meant that he was waiting for Brolin.

Why?

With this question writ large in his thoughts, Brolin slung his MP5 over his shoulder, walked to the jetty, clambered into the first of the rowboats and cast off. There was very little wind and the boat bobbed only a little as Brolin, who had trained with the Special Boat

Squadron (SBS), rowed expertly towards the large craft anchored out to sea.

He was, of course, fully exposed in the rowboat to anyone on the other craft who saw him coming, but he was convinced that he wasn't in danger – at least, not until he had reached his destination. Either Feydal was waiting there for some final confrontation or he would mock Brolin again by suddenly racing away in the motor boat just as Brolin reached it. There was no way of knowing.

As he drew steadily closer, Brolin saw that Feydal's boat wasn't as big as he had imagined and could probably hold only three or four people in its centrally located cabin. It was, however, a luxurious craft and obviously powerful. There were lights on in the cabin, indicating that *someone* was on board.

While continuing to row, surrounded by the soft murmuring of the light breeze on the sea and the splashing of waves, seeing the moonlight reflected off the water, Brolin kept his gaze fixed on the motor boat, but there appeared to be no one on deck. When he was about two hundred metres away, coming within the firing range of sub-machine guns or pistols, he stopped rowing, unslung his MP5, laid it on the bottom of the boat, then removed his Browning 9mm High Power handgun from its holster and rested it on the flat wooden strut than ran across his outstretched legs. Then he started rowing again.

He approached the motor boat from its stern, keeping himself out of the striations of light that were beaming down into the sea from the cabin. This was his most nerve-racking moment, because he knew that if Feydal suddenly turned on the engine of the motor boat, the turbulence would overturn the rowboat. In the event, nothing happened. There was a rope ladder dangling down the side of the motor boat, from the gate in the railing to the sea, about midway between the stern and the central cabin area, so Brolin rowed to that position, tied the gently bobbing rowboat to a steel ring fixed to the hull, put his handgun back into its holster, then stood up, rocking precariously, and reached out for the rope ladder. Trying to make as little noise as possible, he put his left foot on the first rung and hauled himself up. When his head was level with the gateway in the railing, he peered over the edge of the deck, looking left and right, but he saw not a soul. Listening intently for the sounds of conversation or movement in the cabin below decks, he heard nothing, though he was convinced that Feydal was down there. Eventually, satisfied that he was safe for now, he made his way up the last few rungs of the rope ladder, grabbed the railing on both sides of the gateway and pulled himself up onto the deck.

He looked left and right, but there was still no one in sight. Removing his handgun from its holster, he went along the starboard side to glance through the window of the cabin, but he could only see the stairs leading down into the living accommodations, which were out of sight. Frustrated, he moved on in order to check out the prow of the boat, but he saw no-one there either. Moving around the front of the cabin, silent in his rubber-soled boots, he went along the port side of the cabin, looked in through the window, but again saw only the stairs leading down to the unseen living accommodations. Now knowing that the deck was clear, he crept around the front of the cabin . . . and found Feydal Hussein waiting for him.

Feydal was leaning against the railing of the stern and had his hands in the air. He was smiling at Brolin.

'I surrender,' he said.

Brolin studied him carefully, ascertaining that he had no weapon, intrigued by the smile on his face that was genuinely good-humoured, albeit slightly mocking. Feydal was framed by the starry sky, his features softened by moonlight. He seemed almost brotherly. Brolin was aiming his handgun at Feydal and the barrel was steady.

'Where did you come from?' he asked.

'From the cabin, of course,' Feydal replied. 'I saw you coming – rowing expertly, I might add – and then I heard you padding about the deck. It's very quiet out here, Brolin.'

'Why didn't you try shooting me while I was still in the rowboat? I must have made a pretty tempting target.'

'Because I wanted to see your face,' Feydal said. 'And I wanted to have these few words with you. Can I lower my hands now?'

'Not yet. Turn around and face the stern.'

Feydal did so. Brolin checked that there was no weapon tucked into the belt at his back, then he stepped forward, still aiming the handgun at him, and frisked him with his free hand. Satisfied that Feydal was not carrying a concealed weapon, Brolin stepped back again.

'Turn and face me,' he said. Feydal did so. 'OK,' Brolin said. 'You can lower your hands now.'

'Thanks,' Feydal said.

He grinned and nodded, then leaned back, languidly crossed his legs and placed his hands, turned backwards, upon the railing, his fingers curling around it.

'So,' Brolin said, 'here I am. You can see my face now. What do you see?'

'You intrigued me,' Feydal said. 'Marie-Francoise told

me all about you. She didn't exactly volunteer the information, but she talked in the end.'

'You fucks tortured her,' Brolin said.

'No, my friend, we didn't. Marie-Francoise was already a tortured soul and I simply used her torments to make her talk. The smack helped, of course. Marie-Francoise was addicted to it. She was addicted because I encouraged her to become so and in the end it enslaved her. She became dependent upon it and that, of course, made her dependent upon me, her single source of supply. So when I decided that it was Marie-Francoise who had reported my movements – my movements with Bannerman – I simply locked her in her room without her daily supply of smack, sat back and waited for her to break down.'

'Very nice,' Brolin said sarcastically.

Feydal merely smiled and shrugged, then continued: 'When she broke down and begged me for smack, we came to an agreement. She would get her drugs in return for the truth. So, naturally, she talked. She named you as the person who tried to assassinate us in Paris and she confessed that you'd fucked her at least once – and for free, no less! And since that, to the best of my knowledge, was a first for Marie-Francoise, I asked her to explain why she'd done it – given you a free fuck.'

'So what did she say?' Brolin felt his stomach tightening as he waited for the answer and he knew, in that instant, precisely why he had come all this way. He had loved her and he needed to know if she had loved him, at least for that brief time. He had not come here for Feydal or Bannerman; he had come for Marie-Francoise. 'Just tell me, you bastard.'

Feydal smiled again, clearly amused by Brolin's passion. 'She said that she thought she might have been in love with you. Of course, since she'd never admitted to such a feeling before, I became more than a little intrigued by you.'

'What the fuck does that mean?'

'It explains why, as I said, I had to see your face; why I had to have this little talk. I wanted to know what kind of man could make Marie-Francoise – a woman sexually abused from childhood and not knowing what love is, having shelved her emotions and viewing men purely as sexual animals – suddenly feel that she had found love with him. I wanted to know what kind of man that man was: the kind of man who would come all this way in the hope of saving the life of a pitiful, drug-addicted whore, albeit a real beauty. Now, when I look at your face, I can see all there is to know.'

'So what the fuck *do* you see?'

'I see myself,' Feydal said. His eyes were radiant with amusement. 'She told me that you were very much like me: the other side of the same coin. Adventurous – as I am. Strong-willed – as I am. A man easily bored – as I am – and always in need of excitement. A violent man, also – as I am – but, unlike me, a man who tried to channel his violence into fields less morally squalid than my own. Yes, Brolin, when I look at your face I virtually see my reflection.'

'How can you?' Brolin said, intrigued despite himself. 'I don't operate in your "morally squalid fields" and that sets us apart.'

'Does it? I don't think so. I'm just less hypocritical than you. I don't pretend that the violence I commit has a moral imperative. You're a mercenary, Brolin. You kill for money and excitement. When you were in the SAS, you killed, ho, ho, for Queen and Country, but also for wages and for the thrill of the adventure. Now, though you're no longer in the army, you kill for the same reasons. Queen and Country used to disguise the fact that you were killing for money and the excitement you can't live without. You're a murderer, just like I am, Brolin. You just can't admit it.'

'That's bullshit,' Brolin said, though he was feeling distinctly uncomfortable, forced to accept that there was considerable truth in what Feydal was saying.

'No, it's not,' Feydal said. 'You've killed a lot in your time. You didn't consider it to be murder because you did it for Queen and Country, as a member of the SAS, but anyone who kills for wages is a murderer and that's all there is to it. As for Bannerman and me, well, you went to Paris to kill us – at least, to kill Bannerman – and now you've come all the way to Marseille to make good on your failure. You tried to assassinate Bannerman. That's cold-blooded murder. Now you're here, or so you think, to kill me and that, too, would be murder. Yes, Brolin, you and I are the same, which is why Marie-Francoise, so dependent upon me, started feeling the same way about you. Take my picture and reverse the negative and you'll come up with my face. That's what Marie-Francoise saw in you.'

'She saw more than that in me.'

'No, she didn't, Brolin. Marie-Francoise is a woman who fears being controlled by men, yet can't shake off the influence of her abusive, controlling father, and now she needs the very thing she fears: dependence on men with strong will. Men like you and me. You have a strong will, Brolin, and you live close to the edge. Marie-Francoise, who feared me and needed me at the same time, briefly imagined that she loved you when, in fact, she was just growing dependent upon you and hoped to find escape from her misery through you. Oh, she *may* have loved you, Brolin, in her own, perverted way, but love is something that she simply can't accept; something that she can't, in the end, believe in without feeling fear. So she returned to me, Brolin, back to fear and dependence, and if any hope ever existed for you, the smack put an end to it. Marie-Francoise is now a drug addict, Brolin, and that's why she needs me. In the end, she betrayed you for drugs and she would do so again if necessary. You can take this as gospel.'

'You smart bastard,' Brolin said.

'You didn't come here for Bannerman. You didn't even come here for me. You came here for Marie-Francoise, a whore and a drug addict, and that was a foolish thing to do. Now you're standing here and I know you *want* to kill me. But the question, Brolin – the hard, unavoidable question – is this: just how much like me are you?'

'I'm not remotely like you.'

'No? If it was me in your position, I'd certainly pull the trigger, but I believe that because you're the other side of the coin, my reverse negative, as it were, your one weakness is that although you're a professional killer – yes, Brolin, that's what you are – you won't be able to kill me in cold blood and, more crucially, at close range. Will you pull the trigger, Brolin?'

'You have a silver tongue,' Brolin said, finally accepting the brutal truth of Feydal's words and, though feeling shocked by what he had learnt about himself, now angry enough to go the whole limit. 'And you think that in the end I won't do it. But you left one thing out.'

'And what's that, my friend?'

'I came here to find out what happened to Marie-Francoise and I'm going to make sure you tell me. I didn't come here for you. I came to get Bannerman – and, also, to learn about Marie-Francoise – so if you tell me what's happened to her, if you at least let me know if she's still alive or dead, I promise to let you go.'

'You won't kill me at close range. That's your one weakness, Brolin. It's the kind of weakness that gets a man killed, but I know you won't pull that trigger. Not even if I refuse to tell you what it is you so desperately want to know. My lips are sealed, Brolin.'

Brolin raised his handgun higher and aimed the barrel right between Feydal's eyes.

'Believe me, I'll do it,' Brolin said and this time he meant it. 'I'll count to five and then I'll squeeze the trigger. You'd better start talking, Feydal.'

'You're really going to do it?' Feydal asked.

'One,' Brolin said.

Feydal shook his head from side to side. 'You won't do it. I know you won't.'

'Two.'

'My God, I think you just might.'

'Three.'

'This will be cold-blooded murder, Brolin.'

'Four.'

'If you want to know about Marie-Francoise,' Feydal said, 'why not ask her yourself?'

'Where is she?' Brolin asked.

'Right here,' Marie-Francoise said. Then Brolin felt the cold steel of a pistol barrel resting lightly against the back of his head. 'Drop that handgun, Brolin.'

Brolin didn't move. His blood turned to ice and fire. He was swept with hot flushes, then turned cold and then burned up again. Still he didn't move. He kept his handgun aimed at Feydal. He felt the barrel of Marie-Francoise's pistol moving away from his head as she took a step back, then another. 'Drop the handgun, Brolin,' she repeated, 'or I'll blow your head off. Believe me, I'll do it.'

'And she will,' Feydal said with a wide smile, uncrossing his legs and removing his hands from the railing behind him. 'Believe *me*, Brolin, this fine lady, this whore and drug addict, will do anything for another fix of smack and you don't have that to give her. Better drop the handgun.'

'If I do, then *you'll* kill me,' Brolin said. 'It's one or the other.'

Feydal shrugged and spread his hands in the night air as if releasing a trapped bird. 'Given your love for this lady – misplaced though it is – perhaps the question is: whose hand do you want to die by? It's one thing to die, my friend, at the hands of an enemy – an honourable tradition, in fact – but it's quite another to be killed by a woman you love and once trusted. Spare yourself that particular indignity and drop the handgun.'

As Feydal was speaking, Marie-Francoise had been shuffling sideways in a semicircle, moving around Brolin, and now she was standing on Brolin's right-hand side, though slightly to the front where he could see her, still aiming at him with a Glock-18 handgun.

Brolin was shocked by the sight of her. She had lost weight and was deathly pale. Her green eyes, which had formerly been bright, were now glazed and unfocused; but the handgun, he noticed, was steady and that wasn't good news. Brolin was still aiming his pistol at Feydal and his grip was steady as well.

'Would you really kill me?' he asked.

'Don't make me do it, Brolin.'

'What is it with you,' Brolin asked, 'that you'll do this for that bastard?'

'I'll do it,' she confirmed.

'She certainly will,' Feydal said. 'She'll do it because she can't live without me, despite her fear of me. She'll also do it because of the smack and that makes her mine, Brolin.'

'Is that true?' Brolin asked.

'Yes,' Marie-Francoise said. 'You better believe it, Brolin. You can't accept that a woman of my intelligence can be so dependent. But that's my disease and curse, what motivates me and destroys me, and a man like you, no matter how much you might otherwise care for me, could never learn to live with it. Feydal can live with it. My weakness is his strength. I stay with him because I can't live without him despite my fear of him. That's dependency of a suicidal kind but it's all I've got now. So, yes, Brolin, if I see you squeeze that trigger, I'll fire at the same time.'

'I'm sorry,' Brolin said, 'but I don't believe you. I just can't accept that. You won't squeeze that trigger.'

Tears ran down Marie-Francoise's cheeks even as she raised her handgun slightly higher and squinted along the sights. 'Damn you, Brolin,' she said, 'I'll do it. I'll *have* to do it. But if you love me, if you truly love me, you'll save me the anguish of this by dropping your handgun. Don't force me, of all people, to kill you, Brolin. Please, God, free me from this.'

Brolin glanced at her, saw the tears on her cheeks, the wild and demented gleaming of her eyes, and he realized that despite her feelings for him, her fear and need for

Feydal might indeed make her do it. He loved her too much to take that chance, so he lowered his handgun to his side and let it fall to the deck. It made a harsh ringing sound.

Marie-Francoise sighed with relief. Then, still keeping the handgun aimed at Brolin, she walked over to Feydal and started to hand the weapon to him.

'You damned fool!' Feydal hissed as the barrel of the pistol turned briefly away from Brolin.

Seeing his opportunity, Brolin threw himself to the deck, grabbed his fallen handgun, then rolled over twice and came to rest on his belly while raising the weapon to take aim.

Take aim at whom?

Feydal? Or Marie-Francoise, who still had the handgun?

Brolin's finger froze on the trigger as Marie-Francoise automatically turned towards him to take aim again. Brolin couldn't shoot her. Instead, he aimed at Feydal. He heard a shot ring out and thought that Marie-Francoise had fired. But then he saw Marie-Francoise stagger backwards, arms flailing, and heard her handgun clattering to the deck even before she crashed back into the wall of the cabin and then slowly slid down it, leaving a trail of blood behind her.

'No!' Brolin shouted.

Shocked, realizing that the gunshot had come from behind him, he glanced over his shoulder and saw Clayton clambering over the railing of the port side, still aiming with the handgun he had just fired. Realizing that Clayton had obviously left his prisoners in the locked room of the villa, then followed the others down through the tunnel and taken the second rowboat out to Feydal's motor boat,

Brolin was about to look to the front again when another shot rang out and Clayton, still perched precariously on the railing, almost jackknifed, dropped his handgun, then coughed blood, shuddered violently and fell back the way he had come, splashing into the sea below.

Brolin turned back to the front and squeezed the trigger repeatedly without looking, moving the barrel from left to right, firing in a broad arc even before he saw Feydal aiming the Glock-18 handgun at him. His bullets found Feydal who let out a short, sharp scream as his left leg bent at a peculiar angle and then buckled beneath him. He dropped the handgun as he fell to the floor with part of his shin bone protruding from his bloody, torn leg and more blood squirting from a wound in his left arm. After rolling onto his back, he wriggled and pushed his way up into a sitting position, resting his back against the cabin wall. Marie-Francoise was stretched out beside him in another spreading pool of blood. Feydal gazed at her with detached curiosity. Then he looked up at Brolin.

'Nice friends you have,' he said mockingly. 'Just look at the state of her.'

Without replying, though boiling with grief and rage, Brolin walked over to Marie-Francoise, then knelt beside her to check her condition. Though drenched in her own blood, Marie-Francoise was still alive. She was as white as a sheet, her breathing was harsh, her feline eyes were rapidly losing their lustre, but she managed a weak smile. Her right hand came off the deck, very slowly, visibly trembling, and she lightly stroked Brolin's cheek with frail, bloody fingers.

'Ah, God, Brolin,' she said. 'Where's the sense? Where's the meaning? Perhaps it really *was* love with us. Forgive me, Brolin. Pray for me. Ah, God, Brolin, I . . .'

Her words were cut short when she coughed blood, closed her eyes, shuddered, and then exhaled her last breath.

Marie-Francoise was dead.

Straightening up again, his rage now like ice within him, Brolin took a few steps sideways, then spread his legs and adopted the two-handed firing position, aiming at Feydal.

'You bastard,' he said.

Bloody but unbowed, Feydal offered his charming smile. 'Would she have killed you or not?' he asked. 'Alas, now you'll never know. And that question, my friend, is going to haunt you for the rest of your life.'

'At least I'll still have a life,' Brolin said, 'which is more than *you'll* have.'

'I repeat,' Feydal said, unperturbed. 'You won't be able to kill me in cold blood and at close range. Marie-Francoise might well have shot you – she was a drug addict, after all, courtesy of me, of course – but you're a man still under the control of his civilized values and for that reason – and that reason alone – you won't pull the trigger.'

'Want to bet?' Brolin said.

He waited until he saw the dawn of recognition in Feydal's eyes – the recognition of himself in another man – which was when the fear came. When Brolin saw the fear in Feydal's eyes, the Algerian's first and final fear, he fired his handgun twice, a double tap, and Feydal, looking surprised, fell sideways, dead.

'We all make mistakes,' Brolin said.

CHAPTER THIRTY

Five days later, Brolin was standing in the Outer Circle of Regent's Park, equidistant between Hanover Lodge and the Mosque, watching thoughtfully as Sir Archibald Wainwright emerged from the Rolls-Royce with tinted windows, which the chauffeur had parked a reasonable distance away, and started walking towards him. Wainwright looked as distinguished as always, but Brolin was no longer intimidated by him, having learnt so much so quickly and not forgetting the lessons. Reaching him, Wainwright simply nodded, not smiling, and said, 'Let's walk.'

They proceeded to walk. As they did so, the Rolls-Royce behind them, at the other side of the road, kept up with them, travelling at a snail's pace. But Brolin knew that if anything untoward happened, the car would swiftly accelerate.

'A good job well done,' Wainwright said. 'Did you see the newspapers?'

'No,' Brolin said. 'The story had dropped out of the papers by the time I got back.'

'Too bad. Nevertheless, dear boy, you did an excellent job and, as you'd anticipated, the general view is that the attack on Feydal Hussein's villa was launched by other gangsters in Marseille where, of course, Feydal had many enemies. Naturally, given that Bannerman was already notorious in this country as a bent copper, albeit highly placed, when his body was found at the exit to the escape tunnel of Feydal's villa, we leaked the news that he was involved in an illegal arms deal with Feydal and died during the attack simply because he happened to be in the wrong place at the wrong time. So no one has even remotely connected us, the British government, with what went on there. Rather good, don't you think?'

'Rather good,' Brolin echoed, though he didn't feel good at all and did not trust this knighted gentleman one inch. Distracting himself from the disturbing thoughts running through his head, he glanced across the road to the green sweep of the gardens under a low sky in which dark clouds were gathering. Not comforted by that sight, he returned his gaze to the front.

'According to our intelligence reports,' Wainwright continued as they walked side by side along the Outer Circle, 'one of those found dead in Feydal's villa was a British citizen, so badly burnt and dismembered by a grenade explosion that he could not be identified, though he'd clearly been wearing CRW clothing. A friend of yours, was he?'

'Yes,' Brolin said, recalling Pat Dogherty being blown up and scorched by the booby-trapped doorway in Feydal's villa and still horrified by the recollection.

'Can I ask who he was?'

'No.'

Wainwright smiled. 'Very good. I admire a man who protects his friends. And it hardly matters now, after all. Any mention of that particular British citizen was helpfully dropped, at our request, from the Gendarmerie records. So what about the others?'

'What about them?' Brolin asked, deeply pained to even have to think about them and despising Wainwright's urbane pragmatism.

'The Gendarmerie found no trace of them when they examined the villa and the grounds around it. Does that mean they're still alive?'

'Why do you ask?'

'Because I'm concerned about potential witnesses who would be, in this case, also participants. So I need to know if they're still alive or not.'

'No, they're not,' Brolin said.

They had reached the end of Hanover Terrace and Wainwright glanced, with what seemed like deep appreciation, at the bright blue pediments and statuary silhouetted against the cloudy, late-autumnal sky.

'Is that the truth?' he asked bluntly. 'Please don't lie to me, Brolin. You have no need to protect them. I don't want to know their names, after all. I just need to know if they're alive or dead. So please answer the question.'

'They're dead,' Brolin said, knowing that even if they were still alive he would not have told Wainwright and gradually realizing why this was so.

'The Gendarmerie found no trace of them,' Wainwright said, 'so where are the bodies?'

'You're one cold bastard,' Brolin said before he could stop himself.

Wainwright just smiled again. 'I'm a man doing his job,' he said. 'No more and no less. I repeat: so where are the bodies?'

Recalling Jean-Pierre plunging, screaming, to his death into that deep, dark fissure and Clayton falling over the side of the boat, riddled with bullets, Brolin felt so distraught that he could barely contain himself.

'One fell to his death in an underground chasm where he'll never be found. The other, after being shot dead, fell off the side of Feydal's boat. Presumably, since his body hasn't been washed up, he was swept out to sea.'

'Excellent,' Wainwright said.

They were now at Clarence Terrace and Wainwright stopped for a moment to point to the centre of the road, at the traffic turn-off to Baker Street, where the Foreign Secretary, Clive Sinclair-Lewis, had been assassinated a couple of months ago.

'That's where all of this began for you, Brolin.'

'Yes, I know,' Brolin said.

'You don't sound too pleased,' Wainwright said.

'It was a job and I did it.'

'Quite so. Let's keep walking.'

They crossed the road together, dodging through the traffic, to reach Cornwall Terrace and continue on around the Outer Circle. Brolin glanced back over his shoulder and saw that the Rolls-Royce was still following them, keeping its distance. He had no doubt that there were armed men in that vehicle, ready to kill him or anyone else who threatened Wainwright. He kept that thought in mind.

'The boat,' Wainwright said. 'Feydal's boat. It was found at the bottom of the Mediterranean, near the shore, and witnesses reported seeing it exploding and then catching fire. The boat burned so completely that there was practically nothing left of it. A few pieces of drifting wood and a lot of ash – that's all the Marseille Coast Guard could find when the smoke led them to it. Were you responsible for that as well?'

'Yes,' Brolin said truthfully, recalling how, with more anguish than he had ever experienced before, he had opened a drum of kerosene, drenched the bodies of Feydal and Marie-Francoise with some of it, then poured the rest of it over the deck of the motor launch. That task completed, he had left a small Semtex bomb on board, timed to detonate in ten minutes, then taken one of the two rowboats, the other of which had been used by Clayton, and rowed himself back to the bay. En route he had stripped off his CRW clothing, under which he had been wearing a T-shirt and blue denims – appropriate wear for Marseille even in autumn – then dropped the CRW clothing and his weapons and explosives into the sea. He had just reached the bay when the Semtex bomb exploded, destroying part of Feydal's motor launch and turning the rest of it into a ball of fire that illuminated the night while incinerating Feydal and Marie-Francoise. Finally, using the skills he had learned in the Mountain Group of the SAS, Brolin had climbed up the sheer face of limestone surrounding the small bay, made his way back to the Corniche John F. Kennedy, and walked from there back to the hotel in La Cannebière. There he had spent an anguished, sleepless night, tossing and turning on his bed, tormented by thoughts of his best friends and of Marie-Francoise in particular. The next morning, still badly shaken by what had happened, he had taken the train back to Paris.

Now, as he glanced across the Outer Circle at Regent's College and the circular Queen Mary's Gardens, it all seemed like a bad dream ... or, more accurately, a nightmare.

Fuck you, Sir Archibald Wainwright, he thought. *Fuck you* and *your Establishment. It all ends today.*

'Can I assume,' Wainwright asked, as pragmatic as ever, 'that Feydal Hussein died on the boat?'

'Yes,' Brolin said. 'I shot him. He was dead before I set fire to the boat.'

'Parfait,' Wainwright said. 'So Bannerman is dead and we got Feydal as a bonus and no one you used remains alive.'

'That's right,' Brolin said, inflamed, quietly burning. 'No one that I used remains alive. I trust that makes you feel better.'

'Is that sarcasm, dear boy?'

'It just slipped out,' Brolin said.

'You're too emotional to be doing what you do, though I must say you do it well.'

'Thanks,' Brolin said.

Wainwright kept walking with Brolin beside him, then he stopped and coughed into his fist. Brolin stopped as well and turned to face him. They were standing in front of a row of elegant Nash houses, directly opposite Cambridge Terrace and Gate, and the wind here seemed colder. Dark clouds were drifting in from the east, threatening rain. Wainwright looked directly at Brolin, his gaze steady and thoughtful.

'I sense a certain antagonism in you,' he said.

'Don't worry about it,' Brolin replied. 'Just give me my money.'

'I already have, Mr Brolin. It was sent by electronic transfer into your account. With a bonus included.'

'Thanks,' Brolin said.

'Can I call if I ever need you again?'

'No,' Brolin said.

Wainwright smiled. 'Very wise.'

Brolin glanced along the road and saw that the Rolls-Royce had stopped, waiting for him and Wainwright to move on. Wainwright held out his hand and Brolin shook it, not knowing what else to do.

'I'm sorry about your friends,' Wainwright said while still clasping Brolin's hand in his own. 'But, in truth, it's always best when there are no witnesses.' He shrugged and smiled bleakly. 'Another one of life's little cruelties.'

Brolin tugged his hand out of Wainwright's grasp. '*I'm* a witness,' he said.

'Ah, yes,' Wainwright said, smiling brightly, 'but you, at least, can be trusted. Goodbye, Mr Brolin.'

'Goodbye,' Brolin said.

He turned away and continued walking north, heading for Gloucester Gate. When he had walked a good distance, he glanced back over his shoulder and saw Wainwright clambering into the Rolls-Royce. When Wainwright had closed the door behind him, the vehicle moved off again, making a U-turn and heading south, almost certainly taking Wainwright back to Whitehall.

'Thank God for that,' Brolin said.

He walked back to his apartment in Camden Town, opened a bottle of whisky and drank steadily while packing a travelling bag. After darkness had fallen, with the rain coming down heavily outside, he gathered together his most important documents, including his passport, and slipped them into his jacket pocket. When he went to bed at midnight, deliberately not undressing, but simply stretching out on top of the quilt, still wearing his rubber-soled shoes, he was comforted by the feeling of something familiar and hard beneath his pillow.

He did not sleep well. Instead, he tossed and turned for a few hours, falling in and out of shallow sleep, tormented by visions of a boat burning in the Mediterranean, by thoughts of Marie-Francoise and the love that she might or might not have felt for him, and, most of all, by recollections of what Sir Archibald Wainwright had said about the lack of witnesses to what had happened in France. He no longer trusted that pragmatic knighted gentleman and his suspicions were soon confirmed.

At some ungodly hour of the morning, Brolin heard the sound that he had, in fact, been expecting. It was the gentle clicking of an all-purpose key in the lock of his front door.

Instantly, Brolin slid off the bed, withdrew his Browning 9mm High Power handgun from beneath his pillow, then padded quietly into his dark living room. Pressing his back to the wall beside the open door that led into the hallway, he listened for the sound of the front door opening.

He heard the slight squeaking of the hinges as the door was pushed open.

Brolin waited. Someone entered the hallway. Brolin waited some more until he heard footsteps coming along the hallway, very quiet, almost on tip-toe. Then he switched the living-room light on, flooding the hallway with light, and stepped around into the doorway to brace his legs and raise his old SAS Nine Milly in the traditional two-handed firing position.

The man in the hallway had a stocking stretched over his head and the stocking had two eyepieces cut into it. He too was holding a Browning 9mm High Power handgun in his right hand. Though dazzled by the light, his eyes blinking frantically in the eyepieces, he managed to raise his handgun to the firing position before Brolin shot him.

Brolin shot him with a double tap. The man was punched backwards into the end of the hallway and hit the floor with an audible thud. He dropped his handgun. His arms and legs twitched for a moment. Then he coughed blood and died.

Instantly, Brolin bent over him, ripped the stocking from his head, and recognized him as Laurence Seabrooks, an MI5 agent who had instructed the Quick Reaction Force in various covert skills mere months before the SAS was disbanded.

He was one of Wainwright's men.

Brolin didn't stick around. Realizing that he was a marked man – a witness – and would be so for the rest of his life, he put on his jacket, grabbed his travelling bag, and left the apartment before anyone who had heard the noise could come down and see him. Then, having made prior arrangements with an old SAS friend, another marked man, he walked to a terraced house in Kentish Town and rang the doorbell. The door opened to reveal his old friend, looking sleepy and wearing a shabby dressing gown over his pyjamas.

'I need to go undercover,' Brolin said.

'Say no more. Step inside.'

Brolin stepped into his old friend's house to gain a new identity. He emerged two days later, with forged documents, as an invisible man.

Brolin disappeared.